BORDERS®
CLASSICS

VOLTAIRE

Candide

and

The Maid of Orléans

BORDERS.
CLASSICS

Please direct sales or editorial inquiries to:
BordersTradeBookInventoryQuestions@bordersgroupinc.com

This edition is published by
Borders Classics, an imprint of Borders Group, Inc.,
by special arrangement with
Ann Arbor Media Group, LLC
2500 South State Street, Ann Arbor, MI 48104

Printed and bound in the United States of America
by Edwards Brothers, Inc.

Quality Paperback ISBN 13: 978-1-58726-482-5
ISBN 10: 1-58726-482-X

11   10   09   08   07   10 9 8 7 6 5 4 3 2 1

CONTENTS

CANDIDE

or Optimism

Translated from the German of Doctor Ralph
with the additions found in the Doctor's pocket
upon his death in Minden in the
Year of Our Lord 1759

English translation by Richard Aldington (1928)

1

How Candide was brought up in a noble castle,
and how he was expelled from the same

In the castle of Baron Thunder-Ten-Tronckh in Westphalia there lived a youth, endowed by Nature with the most gentle character. His face was the expression of his soul. His judgment was quite honest and he was extremely simple-minded; and this was the reason, I think, that he was named Candide. Old servants in the house suspected that he was the son of the Baron's sister and a decent honest gentleman of the neighbourhood, whom this young lady would never marry because he could only prove seventy-two quarterings, and the rest of his genealogical tree was lost, owing to the injuries of time.

The Baron was one of the most powerful lords in Westphalia, for his castle possessed a door and windows. His Great Hall was even decorated with a piece of tapestry. The dogs in his stable-yards formed a pack of hounds when necessary; his grooms were his huntsmen; the village curate was his Grand Almoner. They all called him "My Lord," and laughed heartily at his stories.

The Baroness weighed about three hundred and fifty pounds, was therefore greatly respected, and did the honours of the house with a dignity which rendered her still more respectable. Her daughter Cunégonde, aged seventeen, was rosy-cheeked, fresh, plump and tempting. The Baron's son appeared in every respect worthy of his father. The tutor Pangloss was the oracle of the house, and little Candide followed his lessons with all the candour of his age and character.

Pangloss taught metaphysico-theologo-cosmolo-nigology. He proved admirably that there is no effect without a cause and that, in this best of all possible worlds, My Lord the Baron's castle was the best of castles and his wife the best of all possible Baronesses.

"'Tis demonstrated," said he, "that things cannot be otherwise; for, since everything is made for an end, everything is necessarily for the best end. Observe that noses were made to wear spectacles; and so we have spectacles. Legs were visibly instituted to be breeched, and we have breeches. Stones were formed to be quarried and to build castles; and My Lord has a very noble castle; the greatest Baron in the province should have the best house; and as pigs were made to be eaten, we eat pork all the year round; consequently, those who have asserted that all is well, talk nonsense; they ought to have said that all is for the best."

Candide listened attentively and believed innocently; for he thought Miss Cunégonde extremely beautiful, although he was never bold enough to tell her so. He decided that after the happiness of being born Baron of Thunder-Ten-Tronckh, the second degree of happiness was to be Miss Cunégonde; the third, to see her every day; and the fourth to listen to Dr. Pangloss, the greatest philosopher of the province and therefore of the whole world.

One day when Cunégonde was walking near the castle, in a little wood which was called The Park, she observed Dr. Pangloss in the bushes, giving a lesson in experimental physics to her mother's waiting-maid, a very pretty and docile brunette. Miss Cunégonde had a great inclination for science and watched breathlessly the reiterated experiments she witnessed; she observed clearly the Doctor's sufficient reason, the effects and the causes, and returned home very much excited, pensive, filled with the desire of learning, reflecting that she might be the sufficient reason of young Candide and that he might be hers.

On her way back to the castle she met Candide and blushed; Candide also blushed. She bade him good-morning in a hesitating voice; Candide replied without knowing what he was saying. Next day, when they left the table after dinner, Cunégonde and Candide found themselves behind a screen; Cunégonde dropped her handkerchief, Candide picked it up; she innocently held his hand; the young man innocently kissed the young lady's hand with remarkable vivacity, tenderness and grace; their lips met, their eyes sparkled, their knees trembled, their hands wandered. Baron Thunder-Ten-Tronckh passed near the screen, and, observing this cause and effect, expelled Candide from the castle by kicking him in the backside frequently and hard. Cunégonde swooned; when she recovered her senses, the Baroness slapped her in the face; and all was in consternation in the noblest and most agreeable of all possible castles.

2

What happened to Candide among the Bulgarians

Candide, expelled from the earthly paradise, wandered for a long time without knowing where he was going, turning up his eyes to Heaven, gazing back frequently at the noblest of castles which held the most beautiful of young Baronesses; he lay down to sleep supperless between two furrows in the open fields; it snowed heavily in large flakes. The next morning the shivering Candide, penniless, dying of cold and exhaustion, dragged himself towards the neighbouring town, which was called Waldberghoff-trarbk-dikdorff. He halted sadly at the door of an inn. Two men dressed in blue noticed him.

"Comrade," said one, "there's a well-built young man of the right height."

They went up to Candide and very civilly invited him to dinner.

"Gentlemen," said Candide with charming modesty, "you do me a great honour, but I have no money to pay my share."

"Ah, sir," said one of the men in blue, "persons of your figure and merit never pay anything; are you not five feet five tall?"

"Yes, gentlemen," said he, bowing, "that is my height."

"Ah, sir, come to table; we will not only pay your expenses, we will never allow a man like you to be short of money; men were only made to help each other."

"You are in the right," said Candide, "that is what Dr. Pangloss was always telling me, and I see that everything is for the best."

They begged him to accept a few crowns, he took them and wished to give them an I.O.U.; they refused to take it and all sat down to table.

"Do you not love tenderly . . . ?"

"Oh, yes," said he. "I love Miss Cunégonde tenderly."

"No," said one of the gentlemen. "We were asking if you do not tenderly love the King of the Bulgarians."

"Not a bit," said he, "for I have never seen him."

"What! He is the most charming of kings, and you must drink his health."

"Oh, gladly, gentlemen."

And he drank.

"That is sufficient," he was told. "You are now the support, the aid, the defender, the hero of the Bulgarians; your fortune is made and your glory assured."

They immediately put irons on his legs and took him to a regiment. He was made to turn to the right and left, to raise the ramrod and return the ramrod, to take aim, to fire, to double up, and he was given thirty strokes with a stick; the next day he drilled not quite so badly, and received only twenty strokes; the day after, he only had ten and was looked on as a prodigy by his comrades.

Candide was completely mystified and could not make out how he was a hero. One fine spring day he thought he would take a walk, going straight ahead, in the belief that to use his legs as he pleased was a privilege of the human species as well as of animals. He had not gone two leagues when four other heroes, each six feet tall, fell upon him, bound him and dragged him back to a cell. He was asked by his judges whether he would rather be thrashed thirty-six times by the whole regiment or receive a dozen lead bullets at once in his brain. Although he protested that men's wills are free and that he wanted neither one nor the other, he had to make a choice; by virtue of that gift of God which is called *liberty*, he determined to run the gauntlet thirty-six times and actually did so twice. There were two thousand men in the regiment. That made four thousand strokes which laid bare the muscles and nerves from his neck to his backside. As they were about to proceed to a third turn, Candide, utterly exhausted, begged as a favour that they would be so kind as to smash his head; he obtained this favour; they bound his eyes and he was made to kneel down. At that moment the King of the Bulgarians came by and inquired the victim's crime; and as this King was possessed of a vast genius, he perceived from what he learned about Candide that he was a young metaphysician very igornant in worldly matters, and therefore pardoned him with a clemency which will be praised in all newspapers and all ages. An honest surgeon healed Candide in three weeks with the ointments recommended by Dioscorides. He had already regained a little skin and could walk when the King of the Bulgarians went to war with the King of the Abares.

3

How Candide escaped from the Bulgarians
and what became of him

Nothing could be smarter, more splendid, more brilliant, better drawn up than the two armies. Trumpets, fifes, hautboys, drums, cannons formed a harmony such as has never been heard even in hell. The cannons first of all laid flat about six thousand men on each side; then the musketry removed from the best of worlds some nine or ten thousand blackguards who infested its surface. The bayonet also was the sufficient reason for the death of some thousands of men. The whole might amount to thirty thousand souls. Candide, who trembled like a philosopher, hid himself as well as he could during this heroic butchery.

At last, while the two kings each commanded a *Te Deum* in his camp, Candide decided to go elsewhere to reason about effects and causes. He clambered over heaps of dead and dying men and reached a neighbouring village, which was in ashes; it was an Abare village which the Bulgarians had burned in accordance with international law. Here, old men dazed with blows watched the dying agonies of their murdered wives who clutched their children to their bleeding breasts; there, disembowelled girls who had been made to satisfy the natural appetites of heroes gasped their last sighs; others, half-burned, begged to be put to death. Brains were scattered on the ground among dismembered arms and legs.

Candide fled to another village as fast as he could; it belonged to the Bulgarians, and Abarian heroes had treated it in the same way. Candide, stumbling over quivering limbs or across ruins, at last escaped from the theatre of war, carrying a little food in his knapsack, and never forgetting Miss Cunégonde. His provisions were all gone when he reached Holland; but, having heard that everyone in that country was rich and a Christian, he had no doubt at all but that he would be as well treated as he had been in the Baron's castle before he had been expelled on account of Miss Cunégonde's pretty eyes.

He asked an alms of several grave persons, who all replied that if he continued in that way he would be shut up in a house of correction to teach him how to live.

He then addressed himself to a man who had been discoursing on charity in a large assembly for an hour on end. This orator, glancing at him askance, said:

"What are you doing here? Are you for the good cause?"

"There is no effect without a cause," said Candide modestly. "Everything is necessarily linked up and arranged for the best. It was necessary that I should be expelled from the company of Miss Cunégonde, that I ran the gauntlet, and that I beg my bread until I can earn it; all this could not have happened differently."

"My friend," said the orator, "do you believe that the Pope is Anti-Christ?"

"I had never heard so before," said Candide, "but whether he is or isn't, I am starving."

"You don't deserve to eat," said the other. "Hence, rascal; hence, you wretch; and never come near me again."

The orator's wife thrust her head out of the window, and, seeing a man who did not believe that the Pope was Anti-Christ, she poured on his head a full . . . O Heavens! To what excess religious zeal is carried by ladies!

A man who had not been baptised, an honest Anabaptist named Jacques, saw the cruel and ignominious treatment of one of his brothers, a featherless two-legged creature with a soul; he took him home, cleaned him up, gave him bread and beer, presented him with two florins, and even offered to teach him to work at the manufacture of Persian stuffs which are made in Holland. Candide threw himself at the man's feet, exclaiming:

"Dr. Pangloss was right in telling me that all is for the best in this world, for I am vastly more touched by your extreme generosity than by the harshness of the gentleman in the black cloak and his good lady."

The next day when he walked out he met a beggar covered with sores, dull-eyed, with the end of his nose fallen away, his mouth awry, his teeth black, who talked huskily, was tormented with a violent cough and spat out a tooth at every cough.

4

How Candide met his old master in philosophy,
Doctor Pangloss, and what happened

Candide, moved even more by compassion than by horror, gave this horrible beggar the two crowns he had received from the honest Anabaptist, Jacques. The phantom gazed fixedly at him, shed tears and threw its arms round his neck. Candide recoiled in terror.

"Alas!" said the wretch to the other wretch, "don't you recognise your dear Pangloss?"

"What do I hear? You, my dear master! You, in this horrible state! What misfortune has happened to you? Why are you no longer in the noblest of castles? What has become of Miss Cunégonde, the pearl of young ladies, the masterpiece of Nature?"

"I am exhausted," said Pangloss. Candide immediately took him to the Anabaptist's stable, where he gave him a little bread to eat; and when Pangloss had recovered:

"Well!" said he, "Cunégonde?"

"Dead," replied the other.

At this word Candide swooned; his friend restored him to his senses with a little bad vinegar which happened to be in the stable. Candide opened his eyes.

"Cunégonde dead! Ah! best of worlds, where are you? But what illness did she die of? Was it because she saw me kicked out of her father's noble castle?"

"No," said Pangloss. "She was disembowelled by Bulgarian soldiers, after having been raped to the limit of possibility; they broke the Baron's head when he tried to defend her; the Baroness was cut to pieces; my poor pupil was treated exactly like his sister; and as to the castle, there is not one stone standing on another, not a barn, not a sheep, not a duck, not a tree; but we were well avenged, for the Abares did exactly the same to a neighbouring barony which belonged to a Bulgarian Lord."

At this, Candide swooned again; but, having recovered and having said all that he ought to say, he inquired the cause and effect, the sufficient reason which had reduced Pangloss to so piteous a state.

"Alas!" said Pangloss, "'tis love; love, the consoler of the human race, the preserver of the universe, the soul of all tender creatures, gentle love."

"Alas!" said Candide, "I am acquainted with this love, this sovereign of hearts, this soul of our soul; it has never brought me anything but one kiss and twenty kicks in the backside. How could this beautiful cause produce in you so abominable an effect?"

Pangloss replied as follows:

"My dear Candide! You remember Paquette, the maid-servant of our august Baroness; in her arms I enjoyed the delights of Paradise which have produced the tortures of Hell by which you see I am devoured; she was infected and perhaps is dead. Paquette received this present from a most learned monk, who had it from the source; for he received it from an old countess, who had it from a cavalry captain, who owed it to a marchioness, who derived it from a page, who had received it from a Jesuit, who, when a novice, had it in a direct line from one of the companions of Christopher Columbus. For my part, I shall not give it to anyone, for I am dying."

"O Pangloss!" exclaimed Candide, "this is a strange genealogy! Wasn't the devil at the root of it?"

"Not at all," replied that great man. "It was something indispensable in this best of worlds, a necessary ingredient; for, if Columbus in an island of America had not caught this disease, which poisons the source of generation, and often indeed prevents generation, we should not have chocolate and cochineal; it must also be noticed that hitherto in our continent this disease is peculiar to us, like theological disputes. The Turks, the Indians, the Persians, the Chinese, the Siamese and the Japanese are not yet familiar with it; but there is a sufficient reason why they in their turn should become familiar with it in a few centuries. Meanwhile, it has made marvellous progress among us, and especially in those large armies composed of honest, well-bred stipendiaries who decide the destiny of States; it may be asserted that when thirty thousand men fight a pitched battle against an equal number of troops, there are about twenty thousand with the pox on either side."

"Admirable!" said Candide. "But you must get cured."

"How can I?" said Pangloss. "I haven't a sou, my friend, and in the whole extent of this globe, you cannot be bled or receive an enema without paying or without someone paying for you."

This last speech determined Candide; he went and threw himself at the feet of his charitable Anabaptist, Jacques, and drew so touching a picture of the state to which his friend was reduced that the good easy man did not hesitate to succour Pangloss; he had him cured at his own expense. In this cure Pangloss only lost one eye and one ear. He could write well and knew arithmetic perfectly. The Anabaptist made him his bookkeeper. At the end of two months he was compelled to go to Lisbon on business and took his two philosophers on the boat with him. Pangloss explained to him how everything was for the best. Jacques was not of this opinion.

"Men," said he, "must have corrupted nature a little, for they were not born wolves, and they have become wolves. God did not give them twenty-four-pounder cannons or bayonets, and they have made bayonets and cannons to destroy each other. I might bring bankruptcies into the account and Justice which seizes the goods of bankrupts in order to deprive the creditors of them."

"It was all indispensable," replied the one-eyed doctor, "and private misfortunes make the public good, so that the more private misfortunes there are, the more everything is well."

While he was reasoning, the air grew dark, the winds blew from the four quarters of the globe and the ship was attacked by the most horrible tempest in sight of the port of Lisbon.

5

Storm, shipwreck, earthquake, and what happened to
Dr. Pangloss, to Candide and the Anabaptist Jacques

Half the enfeebled passengers, suffering from that inconceivable anguish which the rolling of a ship causes in the nerves and in all the humours of bodies shaken in contrary directions, did not retain strength enough even to trouble about the danger. The other half screamed and prayed; the sails were torn, the masts broken, the vessel was leaking. Those worked who could, no one co-operated, no one commanded. The Anabaptist tried to help the crew a little; he was on the main-deck; a furious sailor struck him violently and stretched him on the deck; but the blow he delivered gave him so violent a shock that he fell head-first out of the ship. He remained hanging and clinging to part of the broken mast. The good Jacques ran to his aid, helped him to climb back, and from the effort he made was flung into the sea in full view of the sailor, who allowed him to drown without condescending even to look at him. Candide came up, saw his benefactor reappear for a moment and then be engulfed forever. He tried to throw himself after him into the sea; he was prevented by the philosopher Pangloss, who proved to him that the Lisbon roads had been expressly created for the Anabaptist to be drowned in them. While he was proving this *a priori*, the vessel sank, and everyone perished except Pangloss, Candide and the brutal sailor who had drowned the virtuous Anabaptist; the blackguard swam successfully to the shore and Pangloss and Candide were carried there on a plank.

When they had recovered a little, they walked toward Lisbon; they had a little money by the help of which they hoped to be saved from hunger after having escaped the storm.

Weeping the death of their benefactor, they had scarcely set foot in the town when they felt the earth tremble under their feet; the sea rose in foaming masses in the port and smashed the ships which rode at anchor. Whirlwinds of flame and ashes covered the streets and squares; the houses collapsed, the roofs were thrown upon the foundations, and the foundations were scattered; thirty thousand inhabitants of every age and both sexes were crushed under the ruins. Whistling and swearing, the sailor said:

"There'll be something to pick up here."

"What can be the sufficient reason for this phenomenon?" said Pangloss.

"It is the last day!" cried Candide.

The sailor immediately ran among the debris, dared death to find money, found it, seized it, got drunk, and having slept off his wine, purchased the favours of the first woman of good-will he met on the ruins of the houses and among the dead and dying. Pangloss, however, pulled him by the sleeve.

"My friend," said he, "this is not well, you are disregarding universal reason, you choose the wrong time."

"Blood and 'ounds!" he retorted, "I am a sailor and I was born in Batavia; four times have I stamped on the crucifix during four voyages to Japan; you have found the right man for your universal reason!"

Candide had been hurt by some falling stones; he lay in the street covered with debris. He said to Pangloss:

"Alas! Get me a little wine and oil; I am dying."

"This earthquake is not a new thing," replied Pangloss. "The town of Lima felt the same shocks in America last year; similar causes produce similar effects; there must certainly be a train of sulphur underground from Lima to Lisbon."

"Nothing is more probable," replied Candide; "but, for God's sake, a little oil and wine."

"What do you mean, probable?" replied the philosopher; "I maintain that it is proved."

Candide lost consciousness, and Pangloss brought him a little water from a neighbouring fountain.

Next day they found a little food as they wandered among the ruins and regained a little strength. Afterwards they worked like others to help the inhabitants who had escaped death. Some citizens they had assisted gave them as good a dinner as could be expected in such a disaster; true, it was a dreary meal; the hosts watered their bread with their tears, but Pangloss consoled them by assuring them that things could not be otherwise.

"For," said he, "all this is for the best; for, if there is a volcano at Lisbon, it cannot be anywhere else; for it is impossible that things should not be where they are; for all is well."

A little, dark man, a familiar of the Inquisition, who sat beside him, politely took up the conversation, and said:

"Apparently you do not believe in original sin; for, if everything is for the best, there was neither fall nor punishment."

"I most humbly beg your excellency's pardon," replied Pangloss still more politely, "for the fall of man and the curse necessarily entered into the best of all possible worlds."

"Then you do not believe in free-will?" said the familiar.

"Your excellency will pardon me," said Pangloss; "free-will can exist with absolute necessity; for it was necessary that we should be free; for in short, limited will . . ."

Pangloss was in the middle of his phrase when the familiar nodded to his armed attendant who was pouring out port, or Oporto, wine for him.

6

*How a splendid auto-da-fé was held to prevent
earthquakes, and how Candide was flogged*

After the earthquake which destroyed three-quarters of Lisbon, the
wise men of that country could discover no more efficacious way of
preventing a total ruin than by giving the people a splendid *auto-da-fé*.
It was decided by the University of Coimbra that the sight of several
persons being slowly burned in great ceremony is an infallible secret
for preventing earthquakes.

Consequently they had arrested a Biscayan convicted of having
married his fellow-godmother, and two Portuguese who, when eating
a chicken had thrown away the bacon; after dinner they came and
bound Dr. Pangloss and his disciple Candide, one because he had
spoken and the other because he had listened with an air of approba-
tion; they were both carried separately to extremely cool apartments,
where there was never any discomfort from the sun; a week afterwards
each was dressed in a *san-benito* and their heads were ornamented with
paper mitres; Candide's mitre and *san-benito* were painted with flames
upside down and with devils who had neither tails nor claws; but
Pangloss's devils had claws and tails, and his flames were upright.

Dressed in this manner they marched in procession and listened
to a most pathetic sermon, followed by lovely plain-song music. Candide
was flogged in time to the music, while the singing went on; the
Biscayan and the two men who had not wanted to eat bacon were
burned, and Pangloss was hanged, although this is not the custom.
The very same day, the earth shook again with a terrible clamour.

Candide, terrified, dumbfounded, bewildered, covered with blood,
quivering from head to foot, said to himself:

"If this is the best of all possible worlds, what are the others? Let it
pass that I was flogged, for I was flogged by the Bulgarians, but, O my
dear Pangloss! The greatest of philosophers! Must I see you hanged
without knowing why! O my dear Anabaptist! The best of men! Was it

necessary that you should be drowned in port! O Miss Cunégonde! The pearl of women! Was it necessary that your belly should be slit!"

He was returning, scarcely able to support himself, preached at, flogged, absolved and blessed, when an old woman accosted him and said:

"Courage, my son, follow me."

7

*How an old woman took care of Candide and
how he regained that which he loved*

Candide did not take courage, but he followed the old woman to a
hovel; she gave him a pot of ointment to rub on, and left him food
and drink; she pointed out a fairly clean bed; near the bed there was a
suit of clothes.

"Eat, drink, sleep," said she, "and may our Lady of Atocha, my
Lord Saint Anthony of Padua and my Lord Saint James of Compostella
take care of you; I shall come back tomorrow."

Candide, still amazed by all he had seen, by all he had suffered,
and still more by the old woman's charity, tried to kiss her hand.

"'Tis not my hand you should kiss," said the old woman, "I shall
come back tomorrow. Rub on the ointment, eat and sleep."

In spite of all his misfortune, Candide ate and went to sleep. Next
day the old woman brought him breakfast, examined his back and
smeared him with another ointment; later she brought him dinner,
and returned in the evening with supper. The next day she went
through the same ceremony.

"Who are you?" Candide kept asking her. "Who has inspired you
with so much kindness? How can I thank you?"

The good woman never made any reply; she returned in the evening
without any supper.

"Come with me," said she, "and do not speak a word."

She took him by the arm and walked into the country with him for
about a quarter of a mile; they came to an isolated house, surrounded
with gardens and canals. The old woman knocked at a little door. It
was opened; she led Candide up a back stairway into a gilded apartment, left him on a brocaded sofa, shut the door and went away.
Candide thought he was dreaming, and felt that his whole life was a
bad dream and the present moment an agreeable dream.

The old woman soon reappeared; she was supporting with some

difficulty a trembling woman of majestic stature, glittering with precious stones and covered with a veil.

"Remove the veil," said the old woman to Candide. The young man advanced and lifted the veil with a timid hand. What a moment! What a surprise! He thought he saw Miss Cunégonde, in fact he was looking at her, it was she herself. His strength failed him, he could not utter a word and fell at her feet. Cunégonde fell on the sofa. The old woman dosed them with distilled waters; they recovered their senses and began to speak: at first they uttered only broken words, questions and answers at cross purposes, sighs, tears, exclamations. The old woman advised them to make less noise and left them alone.

"What! Is it you?" said Candide. "You are alive, and I find you here in Portugal! Then you were not raped? Your belly was not slit, as the philosopher Pangloss assured me?"

"Yes, indeed," said the fair Cunégonde; "but those two accidents are not always fatal."

"But your father and mother were killed?"

"'Tis only too true," said Cunégonde, weeping.

"And your brother?"

"My brother was killed too."

"And why are you in Portugal? And how did you know I was here? And by what strange adventure have you brought me to this house?"

"I will tell you everything," replied the lady, "but first of all you must tell me everything that has happened to you since the innocent kiss you gave me and the kicks you received."

Candide obeyed with profound respect; and, although he was bewildered, although his voice was weak and trembling, although his back was still a little painful, he related in the most natural manner all he had endured since the moment of their separation. Cunégonde raised her eyes to heaven; she shed tears at the death of the good Anabaptist and Pangloss, after which she spoke as follows to Candide, who did not miss a word and devoured her with his eyes.

Cunégonde's Story

"I was fast asleep in bed when it pleased Heaven to send the Bulgarians to our noble castle of Thunder-Ten-Tronckh; they murdered my father and brother and cut my mother to pieces. A large Bulgarian six feet tall, seeing that I had swooned at the spectacle, began to rape me; this brought me to, I recovered my senses, I screamed, I struggled, I bit, I scratched, I tried to tear out the big Bulgarian's eyes, not knowing that what was happening in my father's castle was a matter of custom; the brute stabbed me with a knife in the left side where I still have the scar."

"Alas! I hope I shall see it," said the naïf Candide.

"You shall see it," said Cunégonde, "but let me go on."

"Go on," said Candide.

She took up the thread of her story as follows:

"A Bulgarian captain came in, saw me covered with blood, and the soldier did not disturb himself. The captain was angry at the brute's lack of respect to him, and killed him on my body. Afterwards, he had me bandaged and took me to his billet as a prisoner of war. I washed the few shirts he had and did the cooking; I must admit he thought me very pretty; and I will not deny that he was very well built and that his skin was white and soft; otherwise he had little wit and little philosophy; it was plain that he had not been brought up by Dr. Pangloss. At the end of three months he lost all his money and got tired of me; he sold me to a Jew named Don Issachar, who traded in Holland and Portugal and had a passion for women. This Jew devoted himself to my person but he could not triumph over it; I resisted him better than the Bulgarian soldier; a lady of honour may be raped once, but it strengthens her virtue. In order to subdue me, the Jew brought me to this country house. Up till then I believed that there was nothing on earth so splendid as the castle of Thunder-Ten-Tronckh; I was undeceived."

"One day the Grand Inquisitor noticed me at Mass; he ogled me continually and sent a message that he wished to speak to me on secret affairs. I was taken to his palace; I informed him of my birth; he pointed out how much it was beneath my rank to belong to an Israelite. A proposition was made on his behalf to Don Issachar to give me up to His Lordship. Don Issachar, who is the court banker and a man of influence, would not agree. The Inquisitor threatened him with an *auto-da-fé*. At last the Jew was frightened and made a bargain whereby the house and I belong to both in common. The Jew has Mondays, Wednesdays and the Sabbath day, and the Inquisitor has the other days of the week. This arrangement has lasted for six months. It has not been without quarrels; for it has often been debated whether the night between Saturday and Sunday belonged to the old law or the new. For my part, I have hitherto resisted them both; and I think that is the reason why they still love me.

"At last My Lord the Inquisitor was pleased to arrange an *auto-da-fé* to remove the scourge of earthquakes and to intimidate Don Issachar. He honoured me with an invitation. I had an excellent seat; and refreshments were served to the ladies between the Mass and the execution. I was indeed horror-stricken when I saw the burning of the two Jews and the honest Biscayan who had married his fellow-godmother; but what was my surprise, my terror, my anguish, when I saw in a *sanbenito* and under a mitre a face which resembled Pangloss's! I rubbed my eyes, I looked carefully, I saw him hanged; and I fainted. I had scarcely recovered my senses when I saw you stripped naked; that was the height of horror, of consternation, of grief and despair. I will frankly tell you that your skin is even whiter and of a more perfect tint than that of my Bulgarian captain. This spectacle redoubled all the feelings which crushed and devoured me. I exclaimed, I tried to say: 'Stop, barbarians!' but my voice failed and my cries would have been useless. When you had been well flogged, I said to myself; 'How does it happen that the charming Candide and the wise Pangloss are in Lisbon, the one to receive a hundred lashes, and the other to be hanged, by order of My Lord the Inquisitor, whose darling I am? Pangloss deceived me cruelly when he said that all is for the best in the world.'

"I was agitated, distracted, sometimes beside myself and sometimes ready to die of faintness, and my head was filled with the massacre of my father, of my mother, of my brother, the insolence of my horrid Bulgarian soldier, the gash he gave me, my slavery, my life as a kitchen-wench, my Bulgarian captain, my horrid Don Issachar, my abominable Inquisitor, the hanging of Dr. Pangloss, that long plain-song *miséréré*

during which you were flogged, and above all the kiss I gave you behind the screen that day when I saw you for the last time. I praised
God for bringing you back to me through so many trials, I ordered my
old woman to take care of you and to bring you here as soon as she
could. She has carried out my commission very well; I have enjoyed
the inexpressible pleasure of seeing you again, of listening to you, and
of speaking to you. You must be very hungry; I have a good appetite;
let us begin by having supper."

Both sat down to supper; and after supper they returned to the
handsome sofa we have already mentioned; they were still there when
Signor Don Issachar, one of the masters of the house, arrived. It was
the day of the Sabbath. He came to enjoy his rights and to express his
tender love.

9

*What happened to Cunégonde, to Candide, to
the Grand Inquisitor and to a Jew*

This Issachar was the most choleric Hebrew who had been seen in
Israel since the Babylonian captivity.

"What!" said he. "Bitch of a Galilean, isn't it enough to have the
Inquisitor? Must this scoundrel share with me too?"

So saying, he drew a long dagger which he always carried and, thinking this his adversary was unarmed, threw himself upon Candide; but
our good Westphalian had received an excellent sword from the old
woman along with his suit of clothes. He drew his sword, and although
he had a most gentle character, laid the Israelite stone-dead on the
floor at the feet of the fair Cunégonde.

"Holy Virgin!" she exclaimed, "what will become of us? A man
killed in my house! If the police come we are lost."

"If Pangloss had not been hanged," said Candide, "he would have
given us good advice in this extremity, for he was a great philosopher.
In default of him, let us consult the old woman."

She was extremely prudent and was beginning to give her advice
when another little door opened. It was an hour after midnight and
Sunday was beginning.

This day belonged to My Lord the Inquisitor. He came in and saw
the flogged Candide, sword in hand, a corpse lying on the ground,
Cunégonde in terror, and the old woman giving advice.

At this moment, here is what happened in Candide's soul and the
manner of his reasoning:

"If this holy man calls for help, he will infallibly have me burned;
he might do as much to Cunégonde; he had me pitilessly lashed; he is
my rival; I am in the mood to kill, there is no room for hesitation."

His reasoning was clear and swift; and, without giving the Inquisitor time to recover from his surprise, he pierced him through and
through and cast him beside the Jew.

"Here's another," said Cunégonde, "there is no chance of mercy;

we are excommunicated, our last hour has come. How does it happen that you, who were born so mild, should kill a Jew and a prelate in two minutes?"

"My dear young lady," replied Candide, "when a man is in love, jealous, and has been flogged by the Inquisition, he is beside himself."

The old woman then spoke up and said:

"In the stable are three Andalusian horses, with their saddles and bridles; let the brave Candide prepare them; madam has moidores and diamonds; let us mount quickly, although I can only sit on one buttock, and go to Cadiz; the weather is beautifully fine, and it is most pleasant to travel in the coolness of the night."

Candide immediately saddled the three horses. Cunégonde, the old woman and he rode thirty miles without stopping.

While they were riding away, the Holy Hermandad arrived at the house; My Lord was buried in a splendid church and Issachar was thrown into a sewer.

Candide, Cunégonde and the old woman had already reached the little town of Avacena in the midst of the mountains of the Sierra Morena; and they talked in their inn as follows.

10

*How Candide, Cunégonde and the old woman arrived at Cadiz
in great distress, and how they embarked*

"Who can have stolen my pistoles and my diamonds?" said Cunégonde,
weeping. "How shall we live? What shall we do? Where shall we find
Inquisitors and Jews to give me others?"

"Alas!" said the old woman, "I strongly suspect a reverend Franciscan
father who slept in the same inn at Badajoz with us; Heaven forbid
that I should judge rashly! But he twice came into our room and left
long before we did."

"Alas!" said Candide, "the good Pangloss often proved to me that
this world's goods are common to all men and that everyone has an
equal right to them. According to these principles the monk should
have left us enough to continue our journey. Have you nothing left
then, my fair Cunégonde?"

"Not a maravedi," said she.

"What are we to do?" said Candide.

"Sell one of the horses," said the old woman. "I will ride postillion
behind Miss Cunégonde, although I can only sit on one buttock, and
we will get to Cadiz."

In the same hotel there was a Benedictine friar. He bought the
horse very cheap. Candide, Cunégonde and the old woman passed
through Lucena, Chillas, Lebrixa, and at last reached Cadiz. A fleet
was there being equipped and troops were being raised to bring to
reason the reverend Jesuit fathers of Paraguay, who were accused of
causing the revolt of one of their tribes against the kings of Spain and
Portugal near the town of Sacramento. Candide, having served with
the Bulgarians, went through the Bulgarian drill before the general of
the little army with so much grace, celerity, skill, pride and agility, that
he was given the command of an infantry company. He was now a
captain; he embarked with Miss Cunégonde, the old woman, two servants, and the two Andalusian horses which had belonged to the Grand
Inquisitor of Portugal.

During the voyage they had many discussions about the philoso-phy of poor Pangloss.

"We are going to a new world," said Candide, "and no doubt it is there that everything is for the best; for it must be admitted that one might lament a little over the physical and moral happenings in our own world."

"I love you with all my heart," said Cunégonde, "but my soul is still shocked by what I have seen and undergone."

"All will be well," replied Candide; "the sea in this new world al-ready is better than the seas of our Europe; it is calmer and the winds are more constant. It is certainly the new world which is the best of all possible worlds."

"God grant it!" said Cunégonde, "but I have been so horribly un-happy in mine that my heart is nearly closed to hope."

"You complain," said the old woman to them. "Alas! you have not endured such misfortunes as mine."

Cunégonde almost laughed and thought it most amusing of the old woman to assert that she was more unfortunate.

"Alas! my dear," said she, "unless you have been raped by two Bul-garians, stabbed twice in the belly, have had two castles destroyed, two fathers and mothers murdered before your eyes, and have seen two of your lovers flogged in an *auto-da-fé*, I do not see how you can surpass me; moreover, I was born a Baroness with seventy-two quarterings and I have been a kitchen-wench."

"You do not know my birth," said the old woman, "and if I showed you my backside you would not talk as you do and you would suspend your judgment."

This speech aroused intense curiosity in the minds of Cunégonde and Candide. And the old woman spoke as follows.

11

The old woman's story

"My eyes were not always bloodshot and red-rimmed; my nose did not always touch my chin and I was not always a servant. I am the daughter of Pope Urban X and the Princess of Palestrina. Until I was fourteen I was brought up in a palace to which all the castles of your German Barons would not have served as stables; and one of my dresses cost more than all the magnificence of Westphalia. I increased in beauty, in grace, in talents, among pleasures, respect and hopes; already I inspired love, my breasts were forming; and what breasts! White, firm, carved like those of the Venus de Medici. And what eyes! What eyelids! What black eyebrows! What fire shone from my two eyeballs, and dimmed the glitter of the stars, as the local poets pointed out to me. The women who dressed and undressed me fell into ecstasy when they beheld me in front and behind; and all the men would have liked to be in their place.

"I was betrothed to a ruling prince of Massa-Carrara. What a prince! As beautiful as I was, formed of gentleness and charms, brilliantly witty and burning with love; I loved him with a first love, idolatrously and extravagantly. The marriage ceremonies were arranged with unheard-of pomp and magnificence; there were continual fêtes, revels and comic operas; all Italy wrote sonnets for me, and not a good one among them.

"I touched the moment of my happiness when an old marchioness who had been my prince's mistress invited him to take chocolate with her; less than two hours afterwards he died in horrible convulsions; but that is only a trifle. My mother was in despair, though less distressed than I, and wished to absent herself for a time from a place so disastrous. She had a most beautiful estate near Gaeta; we embarked on a galley, gilded like the altar of St. Peter's at Rome. A Salle pirate swooped down and boarded us; our soldiers defended us like soldiers of the Pope; they threw down their arms, fell on their knees and asked the pirates for absolution *in articulo mortis*.

"They were immediately stripped as naked as monkeys and my mother, our ladies of honour and myself as well. The diligence with which these gentlemen strip people is truly admirable; but I was still more surprised by their inserting a finger in a place belonging to all of us where we women usually only allow the end of a syringe. This appeared to me a very strange ceremony; but that is how we judge everything when we leave our own country. I soon learned that it was to find out if we had hidden any diamonds there; 'tis a custom established from time immemorial among the civilised nations who roam the seas. I have learned that the religious Knights of Malta never fail in it when they capture Turks and Turkish women; this is an international law which has never been broken.

"I will not tell you how hard it is for a young princess to be taken with her mother as a slave to Morocco; you will also guess all we had to endure in the pirates' ship. My mother was still very beautiful; our ladies of honour, even our waiting-maids possessed more charms than could be found in all Africa; and I was ravishing, I was beauty, grace itself, and I was a virgin; I did not remain so long; the flower which had been reserved for the handsome prince of Massa-Carrara was ravished from me by a pirate captain; he was an abominable negro who thought he was doing me a great honour. The Princess of Palestrina and I must indeed have been strong to bear up against all we endured before our arrival in Morocco! But let that pass; these things are so common that they are not worth mentioning.

"Morocco was swimming in blood when we arrived. The fifty sons of the Emperor Muley Ismael had each a faction; and this produced fifty civil wars, of blacks against blacks, browns against browns, mulattoes against mulattoes. There was continual carnage throughout the whole extent of the empire.

"Scarcely had we landed when the blacks of a party hostile to that of my pirate arrived with the purpose of depriving him of his booty. After the diamonds and the gold, we were the most valuable possessions. I witnessed a fight such as is never seen in your European climates. The blood of the northern peoples is not sufficiently ardent; their madness for women does not reach the point which is common in Africa. The Europeans seem to have milk in their veins; but vitriol and fire flow in the veins of the inhabitants of Mount Atlas and the neighbouring countries. They fought with the fury of the lions, tigers and serpents of the country to determine who should have us. A Moor grasped my mother by the right arm, my captain's lieutenant held her by the left arm; a Moorish soldier held one leg and one of our pirates seized the other. In a moment nearly all our women were seized in the same way by four soldiers. My captain kept me hidden behind him; he had a scimitar in his hand and killed everybody who opposed his fury. I saw my mother and all our Italian women torn in pieces, gashed, massacred by the monsters who disputed them. The prisoners, my companions, those who had captured them, soldiers, sailors, blacks, browns, whites, mulattoes and finally my captain were all killed and I remained expiring on a heap of corpses. As everyone knows, such scenes go on in an area of more than three hundred square leagues and yet no one ever fails to recite the five daily prayers ordered by Mohammad.

"With great difficulty I extricated myself from the bloody heaps of corpses and dragged myself to the foot of a large orange-tree on the bank of a stream; there I fell down with terror, weariness, horror, despair and hunger. Soon afterwards, my exhausted senses fell into a sleep which was more like a swoon than repose. I was in this state of weakness and insensibility between life and death when I felt myself oppressed by something which moved on my body. I opened my eyes and saw a white man of good appearance who was sighing and muttering between his teeth: O *che sciagura d'essere senza coglioni!*"

12

"Amazed and delighted to hear my native language, and not less surprised at the words spoken by this man, I replied that there were greater misfortunes than that of which he complained. In a few words I informed him of the horrors I had undergone and then swooned again. He carried me to a neighbouring house, had me put to bed, gave me food, waited on me, consoled me, flattered me, told me he had never seen anyone so beautiful as I, and that he had never so much regretted that which no one could give back to him.

"'I was born at Naples,' he said, 'and every year they make two or three thousand children there into capons; some die of it, others acquire voices more beautiful than women's, and others become the governors of States. This operation was performed upon me with very great success and I was a musician in the chapel of the Princess of Palestrina.'

"'Of my mother,' I exclaimed.

"'Of your mother!' cried he, weeping. 'What! Are you that young princess I brought up to the age of six and who even then gave promise of being as beautiful as you are?'

"'I am! my mother is four hundred yards from here, cut into quarters under a heap of corpses. . . .'

"I related all that had happened to me; he also told me his adventures and informed me how he had been sent to the King of Morocco by a Christian power to make a treaty with that monarch whereby he was supplied with powder, cannons and ships to help to exterminate the commerce of other Christians.

"'My mission is accomplished,' said this honest eunuch, 'I am about to embark at Ceuta and I will take you back to Italy *Ma che sciagura d'essere senza coglioni!*'

"I thanked him with tears of gratitude; and instead of taking me back to Italy he conducted me to Algiers and sold me to the Dey. I had scarcely been sold when the plague which had gone through Africa,

Asia and Europe broke out furiously in Algiers. You have seen earthquakes; but have you ever seen the plague?"

"Never," replied the Baroness.

"If you had," replied the old woman, "you would admit that it is much worse than an earthquake. It is very common in Africa; I caught it. Imagine the situation of a Pope's daughter aged fifteen, who in three months had undergone poverty and slavery, had been raped nearly every day, had seen her mother cut into four pieces, had undergone hunger and war, and was now dying of the plague in Algiers. However, I did not die; but my eunuch and the Dey and almost all the seraglio of Algiers perished.

"When the first ravages of this frightful plague were over, the Dey's slaves were sold. A merchant bought me and carried me to Tunis; he sold me to another merchant who re-sold me at Tripoli; from Tripoli I was re-sold to Alexandria, from Alexandria re-sold to Smyrna, from Smyrna to Constantinople. I was finally bought by an Aga of the Janizaries, who was soon ordered to defend Azov against the Russians who were besieging it.

"The Aga, who was a man of great gallantry, took his whole seraglio with him, and lodged us in a little fort on the islands of Palus-Maeotis, guarded by two black eunuchs and twenty soldiers. He killed a prodigious number of Russians, but they returned the compliment as well. Azov was given up to fire and blood, neither sex nor age was pardoned; only our little fort remained; and the enemy tried to reduce it by starving us. The twenty Janizaries had sworn never to surrender us. The extremities of hunger to which they were reduced forced them to eat our two eunuchs for fear of breaking their oath. Some days later they resolved to eat the women.

"We had with us a most pious and compassionate Imam who delivered a fine sermon to them by which he persuaded them not to kill us altogether.

"'Cut,' said he, 'only one buttock from each of these ladies and you will make very good cheer; if you have to return, there will still be as much left in a few days; Heaven will be pleased at so charitable an action and you will be saved.'

"He was very eloquent and persuaded them. This horrible operation was performed upon us; the Imam anointed us with the same balm that is used for children who have just been circumcised; we were all at the point of death."

"Scarcely had the Janizaries finished the meal we had supplied when the Russians arrived in flat-bottomed boats; not a Janizary escaped. The Russians paid no attention to the state we were in. There are French doctors everywhere; one of them who was very skilful, took care of us; he healed us, and I shall remember all my life that, when my wounds were cured, he made propositions to me. For the rest, he told us all to cheer up; he told us that the same thing had happened in several sieges and that it was a law of war.

"As soon as my companions could walk they were sent to Moscow. I fell to the lot of a Boyar who made me his gardener and gave me twenty lashes a day. But at the end of two years this lord was broken on the wheel with thirty other Boyars owing to some court disturbance, and I profited by this adventure; I fled; I crossed all Russia; for a long time I was servant in an inn at Riga, then at Rostock, at Wismar, at Leipzig, at Cassel, at Utrecht, at Leyden, at the Hague, at Rotterdam; I have grown old in misery and in shame, with only half a backside, always remembeing that I was the daughter of a Pope; a hundred times I wanted to kill myself, but I still loved life. This ridiculous weakness is perhaps the most disastrous of our inclinations; for is there anything sillier than to desire to bear continually a burden one always wishes to throw on the ground; to look upon oneself with horror and yet to cling to oneself; in short, to caress the serpent which devours us until he has eaten our heart?

"In the countries it has been my fate to traverse and in the inns where I have served I have seen a prodigious number of people who hated their lives; but I have only seen twelve who voluntarily put an end to their misery; three negroes, four Englishmen, four Genevans and a German professor named Robeck. I ended up as servant to the Jew, Don Issachar; he placed me in your service, my fair young lady; I attached myself to your fate and have been more occupied with your adventures than with my own. I should never even have spoken of my misfortunes, if you had not piqued me a little and if it had not been the custom on board ship to tell stories to pass the time. In short, Miss, I have had experience, I know the world; provide yourself with an entertainment, make each passenger tell you his story; and if there is one who has not often cursed his life, who has not often said to himself that he was the most unfortunate of men, throw me head-first into the sea."

13

*How Candide was obliged to separate from
the fair Cunégonde and the old woman*

The fair Cunégonde, having heard the old woman's story, treated her
with all the politeness due to a person of her rank and merit. She
accepted the proposition and persuaded all the passengers one after
the other to tell her their adventures. She and Candide admitted that
the old woman was right.

"It was most unfortunate," said Candide, "that the wise Pangloss
was hanged contrary to custom at an *auto-da-fé*; he would have said
admirable things about the physical and moral evils which cover the
earth and the sea, and I should feel myself strong enough to urge a few
objections with all due respect."

While each of the passengers was telling his story the ship proceeded on its way. They arrived at Buenos Ayres. Cunégonde, Captain Candide and the old woman went to call on the governor, Don
Fernando d'Ibaraa y Figueora y Mascarenes y Lampourdos y Souza.
This gentleman had the pride befitting a man who owned so many
names. He talked to men with a most noble disdain, turning his nose
up so far, raising his voice so pitilessly, assuming so imposing a tone,
affecting so lofty a carriage, that all who addressed him were tempted
to give him a thrashing. He had a furious passion for women.
Cunégonde seemed to him the most beautiful woman he had ever
seen. The first thing he did was to ask if she were the Captain's wife.
The air with which he asked this question alarmed Candide; he did
not dare say that she was his wife, because as a matter of fact she was
not; he dared not say she was his sister, because she was not that either; and although this official lie was formerly extremely fashionable
among the ancients, and might be useful to the moderns, his soul was
too pure to depart from truth.

"Miss Cunégonde," said he, "is about to do me the honour of
marrying me, and we beg your excellency to be present at the wed-
ding."

Don Fernando d'Ibaraa y Figueora y Mascarenes y Lampourdos y Souza twisted his moustache, smiled bitterly and ordered Captain Candide to go and inspect his company. Candide obeyed; the governor remained with Miss Cunégonde. He declared his passion, vowed that the next day he would marry her publicly, or otherwise, as it might please her charms. Cunégonde asked for a quarter of an hour to collect herself, to consult the old woman and to make up her mind.

The old woman said to Cunégonde:

"You have seventy-two quarterings and you haven't a shilling; it is in your power to be the wife of the greatest Lord in South America, who has an exceedingly fine moustache; is it for you to pride yourself on a rigid fidelity? You have been raped by Bulgarians; a Jew and an Inquisitor have enjoyed your good graces; misfortunes confer certain rights. If I were in your place, I confess I should not have the least scruple in marrying the governor and making Captain Candide's fortune."

While the old woman was speaking with all that prudence which comes from age and experience, they saw a small ship come into the harbour; an Alcayde and some Alguazils were on board, and this is what had happened:

The old woman had guessed correctly that it was a long-sleeved monk who stole Cunégonde's money and jewels at Badajoz, when she was flying in all haste with Candide. The monk tried to sell some of the gems to a jeweller. The merchant recognised them as the property of the Grand Inquisitor. Before the monk was hanged he confessed that he had stolen them; he described the persons and the direction they were taking. The flight of Cunégonde and Candide was already known. They were followed to Cadiz; without any waste of time a vessel was sent in pursuit of them. The vessel was already in the harbour at Buenos Ayres. The rumour spread that an Alcayde was about to land and that he was in pursuit of the murderers of His Lordship the Grand Inquisitor. The prudent old woman saw in a moment what was to be done.

"You cannot escape," she said to Cunégonde, "and you have nothing to fear; you did not kill His Lordship; moreover, the governor is in love with you and will not allow you to be maltreated; stay here."

She ran to Candide at once.

"Fly," said she, "or in an hour's time you will be burned."

There was not a moment to lose; but how could he leave Cunégonde and where could he take refuge?

14

How Candide and Cacambo were received
by the Jesuits in Paraguay

Candide had brought from Cadiz a valet of a sort which is very common on the coasts of Spain and in the colonies. He was one-quarter Spanish, the child of a half-breed in Tucuman; he had been a choirboy, a sacristan, a sailor, a monk, a postman, a soldier and a lackey. His name was Cacambo and he loved his master because his master was a very good man. He saddled the two Andalusian horses with all speed.

"Come, master, we must follow the old woman's advice; let us be off and ride without looking behind us."

Candide shed tears.

"O my dear Cunégonde! Must I abandon you just when the governor was about to marry us! Cunégonde, brought here from such a distant land, what will become of you?"

"She will become what she can," said Cacambo. "Women never trouble about themselves; God will see to her; let us be off."

"Where are you taking me? Where are we going? What shall we do without Cunégonde?" said Candide.

"By St. James of Compostella," said Cacambo, "you were going to fight the Jesuits; let us go and fight for them; I know the roads, I will take you to their kingdom, they will be charmed to have a Captain who can drill in the Bulgarian fashion; you will make a prodigious fortune; when a man fails in one world, he succeeds in another. 'Tis a very great pleasure to see and do new things."

"Then you have been in Paraguay?" said Candide.

"Yes, indeed," said Cacambo. "I was servitor in the College of the Assumption, and I know the government of *Los Padres* as well as I know the streets of Cadiz. Their government is a most admirable thing. The kingdom is already more than three hundred leagues in diameter and is divided into thirty provinces. *Los Padres* have everything and the people have nothing; 'tis the masterpiece of reason and justice.

For my part, I know nothing so divine as *Los Padres* who here make war on the Kings of Spain and Portugal and in Europe act as their confessors; who here kill Spaniards and at Madrid send them to Heaven; all this delights me; come on; you will be the happiest of men. What a pleasure it will be to *Los Padres* when they know there is coming to them a captain who can drill in the Bulgarian manner!"

As soon as they reached the first barrier, Cacambo told the picket that a captain wished to speak to the Commandant. This information was carried to the main guard. A Paraguayan officer ran to the feet of the Commandant to tell him the news. Candide and Cacambo were disarmed and their two Andalusian horses were taken from them. The two strangers were brought in between two ranks of soldiers; the Commandant was at the end, with a three-cornered hat on his head, his gown tucked up, a sword at his side and a spontoon in his hand. He made a sign and immediately the two new-comers were surrounded by twenty-four soldiers. A sergeant told them that they must wait, that the Commandant could not speak to them, that the reverend provincial father did not allow any Spaniard to open his mouth in his presence or to remain more than three hours in the country.

"And where is the reverend provincial father?" said Cacambo.

"He is on parade after having said Mass, and you will have to wait three hours before you will be allowed to kiss his spurs."

"But," said Cacambo, "the captain, who is dying of hunger just as I am, is not a Spaniard but a German; can we not break our fast while we are waiting for his reverence?"

The sergeant went at once to inform the Commandant of this.

"Blessed be God!" said that lord. "Since he is a German I can speak to him; bring him to my arbour."

Candide was immediately taken to a leafy summer-house decorated with a very pretty colonnade of green marble and gold, and lattices enclosing parrots, humming-birds, colibris, guinea-hens and many other rare birds. An excellent breakfast stood ready in gold dishes; and while the Paraguayans were eating maize from wooden bowls, out of doors and in the heat of the sun, the reverend father Commandant entered the arbour.

He was a very handsome young man, with a full face, a fairly white skin, red cheeks, arched eyebrows, keen eyes, red ears, vermilion lips, a haughty air, but a haughtiness which was neither that of a Spaniard nor of a Jesuit. Candide and Cacambo were given back the arms which had been taken from them and their two Andalusian horses; Cacambo fed them with oats near the arbour, and kept his eye on them for fear of a surprise.

Candide first kissed the hem of the Commandant's gown and then they sat down to table.

"So you are a German?" said the Jesuit in that language.

"Yes, reverend father," said Candide.

As they spoke these words they gazed at each other with extreme surprise and an emotion they could not control.

"And what part of Germany do you come from?" said the Jesuit.

"From the filthy province of Westphalia," said Candide; "I was born in the castle of Thunder-Ten-Tronckh."

"Heavens! Is it possible!" cried the Commandant.

"What a miracle!" cried Candide.

"Can it be you?" said the Commandant.

"'Tis impossible!" said Candide.

They both fell over backwards, embraced and shed rivers of tears.

"What! Can it be you, reverend father? You, the fair Cunégonde's brother! You, who were killed by the Bulgarians! You, the son of My Lord the Baron! You, a Jesuit in Paraguay! The world is indeed a strange place! O Pangloss! Pangloss! How happy you would have been if you had not been hanged!"

The Commandant sent away the negro slaves and the Paraguayans who were serving wine in goblets of rock-crystal. A thousand times did he thank God and St. Ignatius; he clasped Candide in his arms; their faces were wet with tears.

"You would be still more surprised, more touched, more beside yourself," said Candide, "if I were to tell you that Miss Cunégonde, your sister, whom you thought disembowelled, is in the best of health."

"Where?"

"In your neighbourhood, with the governor of Buenos Ayres; and I came to make war on you."

Every word they spoke in this long conversation piled marvel on marvel. Their whole souls flew from their tongues, listened in their ears and sparkled in their eyes. As they were Germans, they sat at table for a long time, waiting for the reverend provincial father; and the Commandant spoke as follows to his dear Candide.

15

How Candide killed his dear Cunégonde's brother

"I shall remember all my life the horrible day when I saw my father and mother killed and my sister raped. When the Bulgarians had gone, my adorable sister could not be found, and my mother, my father and I, two maid-servants and three little murdered boys were placed in a cart to be buried in a Jesuit chapel two leagues from the castle of my fathers. A Jesuit sprinkled us with holy water; it was horribly salt; a few drops fell in my eyes; the father noticed that my eyelid trembled, he put his hand on my heart and felt that it was still beating; I was attended to and at the end of three weeks was as well as if nothing had happened. You know, my dear Candide, that I was a very pretty youth, and I became still prettier; and so the Reverend Father Croust, the Superior of the house, was inspired with a most tender friendship for me; he gave me the dress of a novice and some time afterwards I was sent to Rome. The Father General wished to recruit some young German Jesuits. The sovereigns of Paraguay take as few Spanish Jesuits as they can; they prefer foreigners, whom they think they can control better. The Reverend Father General thought me apt to labour in his vineyard. I set off with a Pole and a Tyrolese. When I arrived I was honoured with a subdeaconship and a lieutenancy; I am now colonel and priest. We shall give the King of Spain's troops a warm reception; I guarantee they will be excommunicated and beaten. Providence has sent you here to help us. But is it really true that my dear sister Cunégonde is in the neighbourhood with the governor of Buenos Ayres?"

Candide assured him on oath that nothing could be truer. Their tears began to flow once more.

The Baron seemed never to grow tired of embracing Candide; he called him his brother, his saviour.

"Ah! My dear Candide," said he, "perhaps we shall enter the town together as conquerers and regain my sister Cunégonde."

"I desire it above all things," said Candide, "for I meant to marry her and I still hope to do so."

"You, insolent wretch!" replied the Baron. "Would you have the impudence to marry my sister who has seventy-two quarterings! I consider you extremely impudent to dare to speak to me of such a foolhardy intention!"

Candide, petrified at this speech, replied:

"Reverend Father, all the quarterings in the world are of no importance; I rescued your sister from the arms of a Jew and an Inquisitor; she is under considerable obligation to me and wishes to marry me. Dr. Pangloss always said that men are equal and I shall certainly marry her."

"We shall see about that, scoundrel!" said the Jesuit Baron of Thunder-Ten-Tronckh, at the same time hitting him violently in the face with the flat of his sword. Candide promptly drew his own and stuck it up to the hilt in the Jesuit Baron's belly, but, as he drew it forth smoking, he began to weep.

"Alas! My God," said he, "I have killed my old master, my friend, my brother-in-law; I am the mildest man in the world and I have already killed three men, two of them priests."

Cacambo, who was acting as sentry at the door of the arbour, ran in.

"There is nothing left for us but to sell our lives dearly," said his master. "Somebody will certainly come into the arbour and we must die weapon in hand."

Cacambo, who had seen this sort of thing before, did not lose his head; he took off the Baron's Jesuit gown, put it on Candide, gave him the dead man's square bonnet, and made him mount a horse. All this was done in the twinkling of an eye.

"Let us gallop, master; everyone will take you for a Jesuit carrying orders and we shall have passed the frontiers before they can pursue us."

As he spoke these words he started off at full speed and shouted in Spanish:

"Way, way for the Reverend Father Colonel. . . ."

16

What happened to the two travellers with two girls,
two monkeys, and the savages called Oreillons

Candide and his valet were past the barriers before anybody in the camp knew of the death of the German Jesuit. The vigilant Cacambo had taken care to fill his saddle-bag with bread, chocolate, ham, fruit, and several bottles of wine. On their Andalusian horses they plunged into an unknown country where they found no road.

At last a beautiful plain traversed by streams met their eyes. Our two travellers put their horses to grass. Cacambo suggested to his master that they should eat and set the example.

"How can you expect me to eat ham," said Candide, "when I have killed the son of My Lord the Baron and find myself condemned never to see the fair Cunégonde again in my life? What is the use of prolonging my miserable days since I must drag them out far from her in remorse and despair? And what will the Journal de Trévoux say?"

Speaking thus, he began to eat. The sun was setting. The two wanderers heard faint cries which seemed to be uttered by women. They could not tell whether these were cries of pain or of joy; but they rose hastily with that alarm and uneasiness caused by everything in an unknown country.

These cries came from two completely naked girls who were running gently along the edge of the plain, while two monkeys pursued them and bit their buttocks. Candide was moved to pity; he had learned to shoot among the Bulgarians and could have brought down a nut from a tree without touching the leaves. He raised his double-barrelled Spanish gun, fired, and killed the two monkeys.

"God be praised my Cacambo, I have delivered these two poor creatures a great danger; if I committed a sin by killing an Inquisitor and a Jesuit, I have atoned for it by saving the lives of these two girls. Perhaps they are young of quality and this adventure may be of great advantage to us in this country."

He was going on, but his tongue clove to the roof of his mouth when he saw two girls tenderly kissing the two monkeys, shedding tears on their bodies and filling the air with the most piteous cries.

"I did not expect so much human kindliness," he said at last to Cacambo, who replied:

"You have performed a wonderful masterpiece; you have killed the two lovers of these young ladies."

"Their lovers! Can it be possible? You are jesting at me, Cacambo; how can I believe you?"

"My dear master," replied Cacambo, "you are always surprised by everything; why should you think it so strange that in some countries there should be monkeys who obtain ladies' favors? They are quarter men, as I am a quarter Spaniard."

"Alas!" replied Candide, "I remember to have heard Dr. Pangloss say that similar accidents occurred in the past and that these mixtures produce Aigypans, fauns and satyrs; that several eminent persons of antiquity have seen them but I thought they were fables."

"You ought now to be convinced that it is true," said Cacambo, "and you see how people behave when they have not received a proper education; the only thing I fear is that ladies may get us into difficulty."

These wise reflections persuaded Candide to leave the plain and to plunge into the woods. He ate supper there with Cacambo and, after having cursed the Inquisitor of Portugal, the governor of Buenos Ayres and the Baron, they went to sleep on the moss. When they woke up they found they could not move; the reason was that during the night the Oreillons, the inhabitants of the country, to whom they had been denounced by the two ladies, had bound them with ropes made of bark. They were surrounded by fifty naked Oreillons, armed with arrows, clubs and stone hatchets. Some were boiling a large cauldron, others were preparing spits and they were all shouting:

"Here's a Jesuit, here's a Jesuit! We shall be revenged and have a good dinner; let us eat the Jesuit, let us eat the Jesuit!"

"I told you so, my dear master," said Cacambo sadly. "I knew those two girls would play us a dirty trick."

Candide perceived the cauldron and the spits and exclaimed:

"We are certainly going to be roasted or boiled. Ah! What would Dr. Pangloss say if he saw what the pure state of nature is? All is well, granted; but I confess it is very cruel to have lost Miss Cunégonde and to be spitted by the Oreillons."

Cacambo never lost his head.

"Do not despair," he said to the wretched Candide. "I understand a little of their dialect and I will speak to them."

"Do not fail," said Candide, "to point out to them the dreadful inhumanity of cooking men and how very unchristian it is."

"Gentlemen," said Cacambo, "you mean to eat a Jesuit today? 'Tis a good deed; nothing could be more just than to treat one's enemies in this fashion. Indeed the law of nature teaches us to kill our neighbour and this is how people behave all over the world. If we do not exert the right of eating our neighbour, it is because we have other means of making good cheer; but you have not the same resources as we, and it is certainly better to eat our enemies than to abandon the fruits of victory to ravens and crows. But, gentlemen, you would not wish to eat your friends. You believe you are about to place a Jesuit on the spit, and 'tis your defender, the enemy of your enemies, you are about to roast. I was born in your country; the gentleman you see here is my master and, far from being a Jesuit, he has just killed a Jesuit and is wearing his clothes; which is the cause of your mistake. To verify what I say, take his gown, carry it to the first barrier of the kingdom of *Los Padres* and inquire whether my master has not killed a Jesuit officer. It will take you long and you will have plenty of time to eat us if you find I have lied. But if I have told the truth, you are too well acquainted with the principles of public law, good morals and discipline not to pardon us."

The Oreillons thought this a very reasonable speech; they deputed two of their notables to go with all diligence and find out the truth. The two deputies acquitted themselves of their task like intelligent men and soon returned with the good news.

The Oreillons unbounded their two prisoners, overwhelmed them with civilities, offered them girls, gave them refreshment and accompanied them to the frontiers of their dominions, shouting joyfully:

"He is not a Jesuit, he is not a Jesuit!"

Candide could not cease from wondering at the cause of his deliverance.

"What a nation," said he. "What men! What manners! If I had not been so lucky as to stick my sword through the body of Miss Cunégonde's brother I should infallibly have been eaten. But, after all, there is something good in the pure state of nature, since these people, instead of eating me, offered me a thousand civilities as soon as they knew I was not a Jesuit."

17

Arrival of Candide and his valet in the country
of Eldorado and what they saw there

When they reached the frontiers of the Oreillons, Cacambo said to Candide:

"You see this hemisphere is no better than the other; take my advice, let us go back to Europe by the shortest road."

"How can we go back," said Candide, "and where can we go? If I go to my own country, the Bulgarians and the Abares are murdering everybody; if I return to Portugal I shall be burned; if we stay here, we run the risk of being spitted at any moment. But how can I make up my mind to leave that part of the world where Miss Cunégonde is living?"

"Let us go to Cayenne," said Cacambo, "we shall find Frenchmen there, for they go all over the world; they might help us. Perhaps God will have pity on us."

It was not easy to go to Cayenne. They knew roughly the direction to take, but mountains, rivers, precipices, brigands and savages were everywhere terrible obstacles. Their horses died of fatigue; their provisions were exhausted; for a whole month they lived on wild fruits and at last found themselves near a little river fringed with cocoanut-trees which supported their lives and their hopes.

Cacambo, who always gave advice as prudent as the old woman's, said to Candide:

"We can go no farther, we have walked far enough; I can see an empty canoe in the bank, let us fill it with cocoanuts, get into the little boat and drift with the current; a river always leads to some inhabited place. If we do not find anything pleasant, we shall at least find something new."

"Come on then," said Candide, "and let us trust to Providence."

They drifted for some leagues between banks which were sometimes flowery, sometimes bare, sometimes flat, sometimes steep. The river continually became wider; finally it disappeared under an arch of frightful rocks which towered up to the very sky. The two travellers were bold enough to trust themselves to the current under this arch. The stream, narrowed between walls, carried them with horrible rapidity and noise. After twenty-four hours they saw daylight again; but their canoe was wrecked on reefs; they had to crawl from rock to rock for a whole league, and at last they discovered an immense horizon, bordered by inaccessible mountains. The country was cultivated for pleasure as well as for necessity; everywhere the useful was agreeable. The roads were covered or rather ornamented with carriages of brilliant material and shape, carrying men and women of singular beauty, who were rapidly drawn along by large red sheep whose swiftness surpassed that of the finest horses of Andalusia, Tetuan and Mequinez.

"This country," said Candide, "is better than Westphalia."

He landed with Cacambo near the first village he came to. Several children of the village, dressed in torn gold brocade, were playing quoits outside the village. Our two men from the other world amused themselves by looking on; their quoits were large round pieces, yellow, red and green, which shone with peculiar lustre. The travellers were curious enough to pick up some of them; they were of gold, emeralds and rubies, the least of which would have been the greatest ornament in the Mogul's throne.

"No doubt," said Cacambo, "these children are the sons of the King of this country playing at quoits."

At that moment the village schoolmaster appeared to call them into school.

"This," said Candide, "is the tutor of the Royal Family."

The little beggars immediately left their game, abandoning their quoits and everything with which they had been playing. Candide picked them up, ran to the tutor, and presented them to him humbly, giving him to understand by signs that their Royal Highnesses had forgotten their gold and their precious stones. The village schoolmaster smiled, threw them on the ground, gazed for a moment at Candide's face with much surprise and continued on his way.

The travellers did not fail to pick up the gold, the rubies and the emeralds.

"Where are we?" cried Candide. "The children of the King must be well brought up, since they are taught to despise gold and precious stones."

Cacambo was as much surprised as Candide. At last they reached the first house in the village, which was built like a European palace. There were crowds of people round the door and still more inside;

very pleasant music could be heard and there was a delicious smell of cooking. Cacambo went up to the door and heard them speaking Peruvian; it was his maternal tongue, for everyone knows that Cacambo was born in a village of Tucuman where nothing else is spoken.

"I will act as your interpreter," he said to Candide; "this is an inn, let us enter."

Immediately two boys and two girls of the inn, dressed in cloth of gold, whose hair was bound up with ribbons, invited them to sit down to the table d'hôte. They served four soups each garnished with two parrots, a boiled condor which weighed two hundred pounds, two roast monkeys of excellent flavour, three hundred colibris in one dish and six hundred humming-birds in another, exquisite ragouts and delicious pastries, all in dishes of a sort of rock-crystal. The boys and girls brought several sorts of drinks made of sugar-cane.

Most of the guests were merchants and coachmen, all extremely polite, who asked Cacambo a few questions with the most delicate discretion and answered his in a satisfactory manner.

When the meal was over, Cacambo, like Candide, thought he could pay the reckoning by throwing on the table two of the large pieces of gold he had picked up; the host and hostess laughed until they had to hold their sides. At last they recovered themselves.

"Gentlemen," said the host, "we perceive you are strangers; we are not accustomed to seeing them. Forgive us if we began to laugh when you offered us in payment the stones from our highways. No doubt you have none of the money of this country, but you do not need any to dine here. All the hotels established for the utility of commerce are paid for by the government. You have been ill entertained here because this is a poor village; but everywhere else you will be received as you deserve to be."

Cacambo explained to Candide all that the host had said, and Candide listened in the same admiration and disorder with which his friend Cacambo interpreted.

"What can this country be," they said to each other, "which is unknown to the rest of the world and where all nature is so different from ours? Probably it is the country where everything is for the best; for there must be one country of that sort. And, in spite of what Dr. Pangloss said, I often noticed that everything went very ill in Westphalia."

18

What they saw in the land of Eldorado

Cacambo informed the host of his curiosity, and the host said:

"I am a very ignorant man and am all the better for it; but we have here an old man who has retired from the court and who is the most learned and most communicative man in the kingdom."

And he at once took Cacambo to the old man. Candide now played only the second part and accompanied his valet.

They entered a very simple house, for the door was only of silver and the panelling of the apartments in gold, but so tastefully carved that the richest decorations did not surpass it. The antechamber indeed was only encrusted with rubies and emeralds; but the order with which everything was arranged atoned for this extreme simplicity.

The old man received the two strangers on a sofa padded with colibri feathers, and presented them with drinks in diamond cups; after which he satisfied their curiosity in these words:

"I am a hundred and seventy-two years old and I heard from my late father, the King's equerry, the astonishing revolutions of Peru of which he had been an eye-witness. The kingdom where we now are is the ancient country of the Incas, who most imprudently left it to conquer part of the world and were at last destroyed by the Spaniards.

"The princess of their family who remained in their native country had more wisdom; with the consent of the nation, they ordered that no inhabitants should ever leave our little kingdom, and this it is that has preserved our innocence and our felicity. The Spaniards had some vague knowledge of this country, which they called Eldorado, and about a hundred years ago an Englishman named Raleigh came very near to it; but, since we are surrounded by inaccessible rocks and precipices, we have hitherto been exempt from the rapacity of the nations of Europe, who have an inconceivable lust for the pebbles and mud of our land and would kill us to the last man to get possession of them."

The conversation was long; it touched upon the form of the government, manners, women, public spectacles and the arts. Finally

Candide, who was always interested in metaphysics, asked through Cacambo whether the country had a religion. The old man blushed a little.

"How can you doubt it?" said he. "Do you think we are ingrates?"

Cacambo humbly asked what was the religion of Eldorado. The old man blushed again.

"Can there be two religions?" said he. "We have, I think, the religion of everyone else; we adore God from evening until morning."

"Do you adore only one God?" said Cacambo, who continued to act as the interpreter of Candide's doubts.

"Manifestly," said the old man, "there are not two or three or four. I must confess that the people of your world ask very extraordinary questions."

Candide continued to press the old man with questions; he wished to know how they prayed to God in Eldorado.

"We do not pray," said the good and respectable sage, "we have nothing to ask from him; he has given us everything necessary and we continually give him thanks."

Candide was curious to see the priests; and asked where they were. The good old man smiled.

"My friends," said he, "we are all priests; the King and all the heads of families solemnly sing praises every morning, accompanied by five or six thousand musicians."

"What! Have you no monks to teach, to dispute, to govern, to intrigue and to burn people who do not agree with them?"

"For that, we should have to become fools," said the old man; "here we are all of the same opinion and do not understand what you mean with your monks."

At all this Candide was in an ecstasy and said to himself:

"This is very different from Westphalia and the castle of His Lordship the Baron; if our friend Pangloss had seen Eldorado, he would not have said that the castle of Thunder-Ten-Tronckh was the best of all that exists on the earth; certainly a man should travel."

After this long conversation the good old man ordered a carriage to be harnessed with six sheep, and gave the two travellers twelve of his servants to take them to court.

"You will excuse me," he said, "if my age deprives me of the honour of accompanying you. The King will receive you in a manner which will not displease you and doubtless you will pardon the customs of the country if any of them disconcert you."

Candide and Cacambo entered the carriage; the six sheep galloped off and in less than four hours they reached the King's palace, which was situated at one end of the capital. The portal was two hundred and twenty feet high and a hundred feet wide; it is impossible to describe its material. Anyone can see the prodigious superiority it must have over the pebbles and sand we call *gold* and *gems*.

Twenty beautiful maidens of the guard received Candide and Cacambo as they alighted from the carriage, conducted them to the baths and dressed them in robes woven from the down of colibris; after which the principal male and female officers of the Crown led them to his Majesty's apartment through two files of a thousand musicians each, according to the usual custom. As they approached the throne-room, Cacambo asked one of the chief officers how they should behave in his Majesty's presence; whether they should fall on their knees or flat on their faces, whether they should put their hands on their heads or on their backsides; whether they should lick the dust of the throne-room; in a word, what was the ceremony?

"The custom," said the chief officer, "is to embrace the King and to kiss him on either cheek."

Candide and Cacambo threw their arms round his Majesty's neck; he received them with all imaginable favour and politely asked them to supper.

Meanwhile they were carried to see the town, the public buildings rising to the very skies, the marketplaces ornamented with thousands of columns, the fountains of rose-water and of liquors distilled from sugar-cane, which played continually in the public squares paved with precious stones which emitted a perfume like that of cloves and cinnamon.

Candide asked to see the law-courts; he was told there were none, and that nobody ever went to law. He asked if there were prisons and was told there were none. He was still more surprised and pleased by the palace of sciences, where he saw a gallery two thousand feet long, filled with instruments of mathematics and physics.

After they had explored all the afternoon about a thousandth part of the town, they were taken back to the King. Candide sat down to table with his Majesty, his valet Cacambo and several ladies. Never was better cheer, and never was anyone wittier at supper than his Majesty. Cacambo explained the King's witty remarks to Candide, and even when translated they still appeared witty. Among all the things which amazed Candide, this did not amaze him the least.

They enjoyed this hospitality for a month. Candide repeatedly said to Cacambo:

"Once again, my friend, it is quite true that the castle where I was born cannot be compared with this country; but then Miss Cunégonde is not here and you probably have a mistress in Europe. If we remain here, we shall only be like everyone else; but if we return to our own world with only twelve sheep laden with Eldorado pebbles, we shall be richer than all the kings put together; we shall have no more Inquisitors to fear and we can easily regain Miss Cunégonde."

Cacambo agreed with this; it is so pleasant to be on the move, to show off before friends, to make a parade of the things seen on one's travels, that these two happy men resolved to be so no longer and to ask his Majesty's permission to depart.

"You are doing a very silly thing," said the King. "I know my country is small; but when we are comfortable anywhere we should stay there; I certainly have not the right to detain foreigners, that is a tyranny which does not exist either in our manners or our laws; all men are free, leave when you please, but the way out is very difficult. It is impossible to ascend the rapid river by which you miraculously came here and which flows under arches of rock. The mountains which surround the whole of my kingdom are ten thousand feet high and as perpendicular as rocks; they are more than ten leagues broad, and you can only get down from them by way of precipices. However, since you must go, I will give orders to the directors of machinery to make a machine which will carry you comfortably. When you have been taken to the other side of the mountains, nobody can proceed any farther with you; for my subjects have sworn never to pass this boundary and they are too wise to break their oath. Ask anything else of me you wish."

"We ask nothing of your Majesty," said Cacambo, "except a few sheep laden with provisions, pebbles and the mud of this country."

The King laughed.

"I cannot understand," said he, "the taste you people of Europe have for our yellow mud; but take as much as you wish, and much good may it do you."

He immediately ordered his engineers to make a machine to hoist these two extraordinary men out of his kingdom.

Three thousand learned scientists worked at it; it was ready in a fortnight and only cost about twenty million pounds sterling in the money of that country. Candide and Cacambo were placed on the machine; there were two large red sheep saddled and bridled for them to ride on when they had passed the mountains, twenty sumpter sheep laden with provisions, thirty carrying presents of the most curious productions of the country and fifty laden with gold, precious stones and diamonds. The King embraced the two vagabonds tenderly.

Their departure was a splendid sight, and so was the ingenious manner in which they and their sheep were hoisted on to the top of the mountains.

The scientists took leave of them after having landed them safely, and Candide's only desire and object was to go and present Miss Cunégonde with his sheep.

"We have sufficient to pay the governor of Buenos Ayres," said he, "if Miss Cunégonde can be bought. Let us go to Cayenne, and take ship, and then we will see what kingdom we will buy."

19

What happened to them at Surinam and how
Candide made the acquaintance of Martin

Our two travellers' first day was quite pleasant. They were encouraged by the idea of possessing more treasures than all Asia, Europe and Africa could collect. Candide in transport carved the name of Cunégonde on the trees.

On the second day two of the sheep stuck in a marsh and were swallowed up with their loads; two other sheep died of fatigue a few days later; then seven or eight died of hunger in a desert; several days afterwards others fell off precipices. Finally, after they had travelled for a hundred days, they had only two sheep left. Candide said to Cacambo:

"My friend, you see how perishable are the riches of this world; nothing is steadfast but virtue and the happiness of seeing Miss Cunégonde again."

"I admit it," said Cacambo, "but we still have two sheep with more treasures than ever the King of Spain will have, and in the distance I see a town I suspect is Surinam, which belongs to the Dutch. We are at the end of our troubles and the beginning of our happiness."

As they drew near the town they met a negro lying on the ground wearing only half his clothes, that is to say, a pair of blue cotton drawers; this poor man had no left leg and no right hand.

"Good Heavens!" said Candide to him in Dutch, "what are you doing there, my friend, in this horrible state?"

"I am waiting for my master, the famous merchant Mr. Vanderdendur."

"Was it Mr. Vanderdendur," said Candide, "who treated you in this way?"

"Yes, sir," said the negro, "it is the custom. We are given a pair of cotton drawers twice a year as clothing. When we work in the sugar-mills and the grind-stone catches our fingers, they cut off the hand; when we try to run away, they cut off a leg. Both these things happened to me. This is the price paid for the sugar you eat in Europe. But when my mother sold me for ten patagons on the coast of Guinea, she said to me: 'My dear child, give thanks to our fetishes, always worship them, and they will make you happy; you have the honour to be a slave of our lords the white men and thereby you have made the fortune of your father and mother.' Alas! I do not know whether I made their fortune, but they certainly did not make mine. Dogs, monkeys and parrots are a thousand times less miserable than we are; the Dutch fetishes who converted me tell me that we are all of us, whites and blacks, the children of Adam. I am not a genealogist, but if these preachers tell the truth, we are all second cousins. Now, you will admit that no one could treat his relatives in a more horrible way."

"O Pangloss!" cried Candide. "This is an abomination you had not guessed; this is too much, in the end I shall have to renounce optimism."

"What is optimism?" said Cacambo.

"Alas!" said Candide, "it is the mania of maintaining that everything is well when we are wretched."

And he shed tears as he looked at his negro; and he entered Surinam weeping.

The first thing they inquired was whether there was any ship in the port which could be sent to Buenos Ayres. The person they addressed happened to be a Spanish captain, who offered to strike an honest bargain with them. He arranged to meet them at an inn. Candide and the faithful Cacambo went and waited for him with their two sheep.

Candide, who blurted everything out, told the Spaniard all his adventures and confessed that he wanted to elope with Miss Cunégonde.

"I shall certainly not take you to Buenos Ayres," said the captain. "I should be hanged, and you would too. The fair Cunégonde is his Lordship's favourite mistress."

Candide was thunderstruck; he sobbed for a long time; then he took Cacambo aside.

"My dear friend," said he, "this is what you must do. We each have in our pockets five or six million pounds worth of diamonds; you are more skilful than I am; go to Buenos Ayres and get Miss Cunégonde. If the governor makes any difficulties, give him a million; if he is still obstinate, give him two; you have not killed an Inquisitor so they will not suspect you. I will fit out another ship, I will go and wait for you at

Venice; it is a free country where there is nothing to fear from Bulgarians, Abares, Jews or Inquisitors."

Cacambo applauded this wise resolution; he was in despair at leaving a good master who had become his intimate friend; but the pleasure of being useful to him overcame the grief of leaving him. They embraced with tears. Candide urged him not to forget the good old woman. Cacambo set off that very same day; he was a very good man, this Cacambo.

Candide remained some time longer at Surinam waiting for another captain to take him to Italy with the two sheep he had left. He engaged servants and bought everything necessary for a long voyage. At last Mr. Vanderdendur, the owner of a large ship, came to see him.

"How much do you want," he asked this man, "to take me straight to Venice with my servants, my baggage and these two sheep?"

The captain asked for ten thousand piastres. Candide did not hesitate.

"Oho!" said the prudent Vanderdendur to himself, "this foreigner gives ten thousand piastres immediately! He must be very rich."

He returned a moment afterwards and said he could not sail for less than twenty thousand.

"Very well, you shall have them," said Candide.

"Whew!" said the merchant to himself, "this man gives twenty thousand piastres as easily as ten thousand."

He came back again, and said he could not take him to Venice for less than thirty thousand piastres.

"Then you shall have thirty thousand," replied Candide.

"Oho!" said the Dutch merchant to himself again, "thirty thousand piastres is nothing to this man; obviously the two sheep are laden with immense treasures; I will not insist any further; first let me make him pay the thirty thousand piastres, and then we will see."

Candide sold two little diamonds, the smaller of which was worth more than all the money the captain asked. He paid him in advance. The two sheep were taken on board. Candide followed in a little boat to join the ship, which rode at anchor; the captain watched his time, set his sails and weighed anchor; the wind was favourable. Candide, bewildered and stupefied, soon lost sight of him.

"Alas!" he cried, "this is a trick worthy of the old world."

He returned to shore in grief; for he had lost enough to make the fortune of twenty kings.

He went to the Dutch judge; and, as he was rather disturbed, he knocked loudly at the door; he went in, related what had happened and talked a little louder than he ought to have done. The judge began by fining him ten thousand piastres for the noise he had made; he then listened patiently to him, promised to look into his affair as soon as the merchant returned, and charged him another ten thousand piastres for the expense of the audience.

This behaviour reduced Candide to despair; he had indeed endured misfortunes a thousand times more painful; but the calmness of the judge and of the captain who had robbed him stirred up his bile and plunged him into a black melancholy. The malevolence of men revealed itself to his mind in all its ugliness; he entertained only gloomy ideas. At last a French ship was about to leave for Bordeaux and, since he no longer had any sheep laden with diamonds to put on board, he hired a cabin at a reasonable price and announced throughout the town that he would give the passage, food and two thousand piastres to an honest man who would make the journey with him, on condition that this man was the most unfortunate and the most disgusted with his condition in the whole province.

Such a crowd of applicants arrived that a fleet would not have contained them. Candide, wishing to choose among the most likely, picked out twenty persons who seemed reasonably sociable and who all claimed to deserve his preference. He collected them in a tavern and gave them supper, on condition that each took an oath to relate truthfully the story of his life, promising that he would choose the man who seemed to him the most deserving of pity and to have the most cause for being discontented with his condition, and that he would give the others a little money.

The sitting lasted until four o'clock in the morning. As Candide listened to their adventures he remembered what the old woman had said on the voyage to Buenos Ayres and how she had wagered that there was nobody on the boat who had not experienced very great misfortunes. At each story which was told him, he thought of Pangloss.

"This Pangloss," said he, "would have some difficulty in supporting his system. I wish he were here. Certainly, if everything is well, it is only in Eldorado and not in the rest of the world."

He finally determined in favour of a poor man of letters who had worked ten years for the booksellers at Amsterdam. He judged that there was no occupation in the world which could more disgust a man.

This man of letters, who was also a good man, had been robbed by his wife, beaten by his son, and abandoned by his daughter, who had eloped with a Portuguese. He had just been deprived of a small post on which he depended and the preachers of Surinam were persecuting him because they thought he was a Socinian.

It must be admitted that the others were at least as unfortunate as he was; but Candide hoped that this learned man would help to pass the time during the voyage. All his other rivals considered that Candide was doing them a great injustice; but he soothed them down by giving each of them a hundred piastres.

20

What happened to Candide and Martin at sea

So the old man, who was called Martin, embarked with Candide for Bordeaux. Both had seen and suffered much; and if the ship had been sailing from Surinam to Japan by way of the Cape of Good Hope they would have been able to discuss moral and physical evil during the whole voyage.

However, Candide had one great advantage over Martin, because he still hoped to see Miss Cunégonde again, and Martin had nothing to hope for; moreover, he possessed gold and diamonds; and, although he had lost a hundred large red sheep laden with the greatest treasures on earth, although he was still enraged at being robbed by the Dutch captain, yet when he thought of what he still had left in his pockets and when he talked of Cunégonde, especially at the end of a meal, he still inclined towards the system of Pangloss.

"But what do you think of all this, Martin?" said he to the man of letters. "What is your view of moral and physical evil?"

"Sir," replied Martin, "my priests accused me of being a Socinian; but the truth is I am a Manichæan."

"You are poking fun at me," said Candide, "there are no Manichæans left in the world."

"I am one," said Martin. "I don't know what to do about it, but I am unable to think in any other fashion."

"You must be possessed by the devil," said Candide.

"He takes so great a share in the affairs of this world," said Martin, "that he might well be in me, as he is everywhere else; but I confess that when I consider this globe, or rather this globule, I think that God has abandoned it to some evil creature—always excepting Eldorado. I have never seen a town which did not desire the ruin of the next town, never a family which did not wish to exterminate some other family. Everywhere the weak loathe the powerful before whom they cower and the powerful treat them like flocks of sheep whose wool and flesh are to be sold. A million drilled assassins go from one end of Europe to the other murdering and robbing with discipline in order to earn their bread, because there is no honester occupation; and in the towns which seem to enjoy peace and where the arts flourish men are devoured by more envy, troubles and worries than the afflictions of a besieged town. Secret griefs are even more cruel than public miseries. In a word, I have seen so much and endured so much that I have become a Manichæan."

"Yet there is some good," replied Candide.

"There may be," said Martin, "but I do not know it."

In the midst of this dispute they heard the sound of cannon. The noise increased every moment. Everyone took his telescope. About three miles away they saw two ships engaged in battle; and the wind brought them so near the French ship that they had the pleasure of seeing the fight at their ease. At last one of the two ships fired a broadside so accurately and so low down that the other ship began to sink. Candide and Martin distinctly saw a hundred men on the main deck of the sinking ship; they raised their hands to Heaven and uttered frightful shrieks; in a moment all were engulfed.

"Well!" said Martin, "that is how men treat each other."

"It is certainly true," said Candide, "that there is something diabolical in this affair."

As he was speaking, he saw something of a brilliant red swimming near the ship. They launched a boat to see what it could be; it was one of his sheep. Candide felt more joy at recovering this sheep than grief at losing a hundred all laden with large diamonds from Eldorado.

The French captain soon perceived that the captain of the remaining ship was a Spaniard and that the sunken ship was a Dutch pirate; the captain was the very same who had robbed Candide. The immense wealth this scoundrel had stolen was swallowed up with him in the sea and only a sheep was saved.

"You see," said Candide to Martin, "that crime is sometimes punished; this scoundrel of a Dutch captain has met the fate he deserved."

"Yes," said Martin, "but was it necessary that the other passengers on his ship should perish too? God punished the thief, and the devil punished the others."

Meanwhile the French and Spanish ships continued on their way and Candide continued his conversation with Martin. They argued for a fortnight, and at the end of the fortnight they had got no further than at the beginning. But after all, they talked, they exchanged ideas, they consoled each other. Candide stroked his sheep.

"Since I have found you again," said he, "I may very likely find Cunégonde."

21

*Candide and Martin approach the coast
of France and argue*

At last they sighted the coast of France.

"Have you ever been to France, Mr. Martin?" said Candide.

"Yes," said Martin, "I have traversed several provinces. In some half the inhabitants are crazy, in others they are too artful, in some they are usually quite gentle and stupid, and in others they think they are clever; in all of them the chief occupation is making love, the second scandal-mongering and the third talking nonsense."

"But, Mr. Martin, have you seen Paris?"

"Yes, I have seen Paris; it is a mixture of all these species; it is a chaos, a throng where everybody hunts for pleasure and hardly anybody finds it, at least so far as I could see. I did not stay there long; when I arrived there I was robbed of everything I had by pick-pockets at Saint-Germain's fair; they thought I was a thief and I spent a week in prison; after which I became a printer's reader to earn enough to return to Holland on foot. I met the scribbling rabble, the intriguing rabble and the fanatical rabble. We hear that there are very polite people in the town; I am glad to think so."

"For my part, I have not the least curiosity to see France," said Candide. "You can easily guess that when a man has spent a month in Eldorado he cares to see nothing else in the world but Miss Cunégonde. I shall go and wait for her at Venice; we will go to Italy by way of France; will you come with me?"

"Willingly," said Martin. "They say that Venice is only for the Venetian nobles, but that foreigners are nevertheless well received when they have plenty of money; I have none, you have plenty, I will follow you anywhere."

"Apropos," said Candide, "do you think the earth was originally a sea, as we are assured by that large book belonging to the captain?"

"I don't believe it in the least," said Martin, "any more than all the other whimsies we have been pestered with recently!"

"But to what end was this world formed?" said Candide.

"To infuriate us," replied Martin.

"Are you not very much surprised," continued Candide, "by the love those two girls of the country of the Oreillons had for those two monkeys, whose adventure I told you?"

"Not in the least," said Martin. "I see nothing strange in their passion; I have seen so many extraordinary things that nothing seems extraordinary to me."

"Do you think," said Candide, "that men have always massacred each other, as they do today? Have they always been liars, cheats, traitors, brigands, weak, flighty, cowardly, envious, gluttonous, drunken, grasping and vicious, bloody, backbiting, debauched, fanatical, hypocritical and silly?"

"Do you think," said Martin, "that sparrow-hawks have always eaten the pigeons they came across?"

"Yes, of course," said Candide.

"Well," said Martin, "if sparrow-hawks have always possessed the same nature, why should you expect men to change theirs?"

"Oh!" said Candide, "there is a great difference; free will. . . ."

Arguing thus, they arrived at Bordeaux.

22

What happened to Candide and Martin in France

Candide remained in Bordeaux only long enough to sell a few Eldorado pebbles and to provide himself with a two-seated post-chaise, for he could no longer get on without his philosopher Martin; but he was very much grieved at having to part with his sheep, which he left with the Academy of Sciences at Bordeaux. The Academy offered as the subject for a prize that year the cause of the redness of the sheep's fleece; and the prize was awarded to a learned man in the North, who proved by A plus B minus C divided by Z that the sheep must be red and die of the sheep-pox.

However, all the travellers Candide met in taverns on the way said to him: "We are going to Paris." This general eagerness at length made him wish to see that capital; it was not far out of the road to Venice.

He entered by the Faubourg Saint-Marceau and thought he was in the ugliest village of Westphalia.

Candide had scarcely reached his inn when he was attacked by a slight illness caused by fatigue. As he wore an enormous diamond on his finger, and a prodigiously heavy strong-box had been observed in his train, he immediately had with him two doctors he had not asked for, several intimate friends who would not leave him, and two devotees who kept making him broth. Said Martin:

"I remember that I was ill too when I first came to Paris; I was very poor; so I had no friends, no devotees, no doctors, and I got well."

However, with the aid of medicine and blood-letting, Candide's illness became serious. An inhabitant of the district came and gently asked him for a note payable to bearer in the next world; Candide would have nothing to do with it. The devotees assured him that it was a new fashion. Candide replied that he was not a fashionable man. Martin wanted to throw the inhabitant out the window; the clerk swore that Candide should not be buried; Martin swore that he would bury the clerk if he continued to annoy them. The quarrel became heated; Martin took him by the shoulders and turned him out roughly; this caused a great scandal, and they made an official report on it.

Candide got better; and during his convalescence he had very good company to supper with him. They gambled for high stakes. Candide was vastly surprised that he never drew an ace; and Martin was not surprised at all.

Among those who did the honours of the town was a little abbé from Périgord, one of those assiduous people who are always alert, always obliging, impudent, fawning, accommodating, always on the look-out for the arrival of foreigners, ready to tell them all the scandals of the town and to procure them pleasures at any price. This abbé took Candide and Martin to the theatre. A new tragedy was being played. Candide was seated near several wits. This did not prevent his weeping at perfectly played scenes. One of the argumentative bores near him said during an interval:

"You have no business to weep, this is a very bad actress, the actor playing with her is still worse, the play is still worse than the actors; the author does not know a word of Arabic and yet the scene is in Arabia; moreover, he is a man who does not believe in innate ideas; tomorrow I will bring you twenty articles written against him."

"Sir," said Candide to the abbé, "how many plays have you in France?"

"Five or six thousand," he replied.

"That's a lot," said Candide, "and how many good ones are there?"

"Fifteen or sixteen," replied the other.

"That's a lot," said Martin.

Candide was greatly pleased with an actress who took the part of Queen Elizabeth in a rather dull tragedy which is sometimes played.

"This actress," said he to Martin, "pleases me very much; she looks rather like Miss Cunégonde; I should be very glad to pay her my respects."

The abbé offered to introduce him to her. Candide, brought up in Germany, asked what was the etiquette, and how queens of England were treated in France.

"There is a distinction," said the abbé; "in the provinces we take them to a tavern; in Paris we respect them when they are beautiful and throw them in the public sewer when they are dead."

"Queens in the public sewer!" said Candide.

"Yes, indeed," said Martin, "the abbé is right; I was in Paris when Miss Monime departed, as they say, this life; she was refused what people here call the *honours of burial*—that is to say, the honour of rotting with all the beggars of the district in a horrible cemetery; she was buried by herself at the corner of the Rue de Burgoyne; which must have given her extreme pain, for her mind was very lofty."

"That was very impolite," said Candide.

"What do you expect?" said Martin. "These people are like that. Imagine all possible contradictions and incompatibilities; you will see them in the government, in the law-courts, in the churches and the entertainments of this absurd nation."

"Is it true that people are always laughing in Paris?" said Candide.

"Yes," said the abbé, "but it is with rage in their hearts, for they complain of everything with roars of laughter and they even commit with laughter the most detestable actions."

"Who is that fat pig," said Candide, "who said so much ill of the play I cried at so much and of the actors who gave me so much plea- sure?"

"He is a living evil," replied the abbé, "who earns his living by abusing all plays and all books; he hates anyone who succeeds, as eu- nuchs hate those who enjoy; he is one of the serpents of literature who feed on filth and venom; he is a scribbler."

"What do you mean by a scribbler?" said Candide.

"A scribbler of periodical sheets," said the abbé. "A Fréron."

Candide, Martin and the abbé from Périgord talked in this man- ner on the stairway as they watched everybody going out after the play.

"Although I am most anxious to see Miss Cunégonde again," said Candide, "I should like to sup with Miss Clairon, for I thought her admirable."

The abbé was not the sort of man to know Miss Clairon, for she saw only good company.

"She is engaged this evening," he said, "but I shall have the honour to take you to the house of a lady of quality, and there you will learn as much of Paris as if you had been here for four years."

Candide, who was naturally curious, allowed himself to be taken to the lady's house at the far end of the Faubourg Saint-Honoré; they were playing faro; twelve gloomy punters each held a small hand of cards, the foolish register of their misfortunes. The silence was pro- found, the punters were pale, the banker was uneasy, and the lady of the house, seated beside this pitiless banker, watched with lynx's eyes every double stake, every seven-and-the-go, with which each player marked his cards; she had them un-marked with severe but polite attention, for fear of losing her customers; the lady called herself Marquise de Parolignac. Her fifteen-year-old daughter was among the punters and winked to her to let her know the tricks of the poor people who attempted to repair the cruelties of fate. The abbé from Périgord, Candide and Martin entered; nobody rose, nobody greeted them, nobody looked at them; everyone was profoundly occupied with the cards.

"Her Ladyship, the Baroness of Thunder-Ten-Tronckh was more civil," said Candide.

However, the abbé whispered in the ear of the Marquise, who half rose, honoured Candide with a gracious smile and Martin with a most noble nod. Candide was given a seat and a hand of cards, and lost fifty thousand francs in two hands; after which they supped very merrily and everyone was surprised that Candide was not more disturbed by his loss. The lackeys said to each other, in the language of lackeys:

"He must be an English Milord."

The supper was like most suppers in Paris; first there was a silence and then a noise of indistinguishable words, then jokes, most of which were insipid, false news, false arguments, some politics and a great deal of scandal; there was even some talk of new books.

"Have you seen," said the abbé from Périgord, "the novel by Gauchat, the doctor of theology?"

"Yes," replied one of the guests, "but I could not finish it. We have a crowd of silly writings, but all of them together do not approach the silliness of Gauchat, doctor of theology. I am so weary of this immensity of detestable books which inundates us that I have taken to faro."

"And what do you say about the *Mélanges* by Archdeacon T——?" said the abbé.

"Ah!" said Madame de Parolignac, "the tiresome creature! How carefully he tells you what everybody knows! How heavily he discusses what is not worth the trouble of being lightly mentioned! How witlessly he appropriates other people's wit! How he spoils what he steals! How he disgusts me! But he will not disgust me any more; it is enough to have read a few pages by the Archdeacon."

There was a man of learning and taste at table who confirmed what the marchioness had said. They then talked of tragedies; the lady asked why there were tragedies which were sometimes played and yet were unreadable. The man of taste explained very clearly how a play might have some interest and hardly any merit; in a few words he proved that it was not sufficient to bring in one or two of the situations which are found in all novels and which always attract the spectators; but that a writer of tragedies must be original without being bizarre, often sublime and always natural, must know the human heart and be able to give it speech, must be a great poet but not let any character in his play appear to be a poet, must know his language perfectly, speak it with purity, with continual harmony and never allow the sense to be spoilt for the sake of the rhyme.

"Anyone," he added, "who does not observe all these rules may produce one or two tragedies applauded in the theatre, but he will never be ranked among good writers; there are very few good tragedies; some are idylls in well-written and well-rhymed dialogue; some are political arguments which send one to sleep, or repulsive amplifications; others are the dreams of an enthusiast, in a barbarous style, with broken dialogue, long apostrophes to the gods (because he does not know how to speak to men), false maxims and turgid commonplaces."

Candide listened attentively to these remarks and conceived a great idea of the speaker; and, as the marchioness had been careful to place him beside her, he leaned over to her ear and took the liberty of asking her who was the man who talked so well.

"He is a man of letters," said the lady, "who does not play cards and is sometimes brought here to supper by the abbé; he has a perfect knowledge of tragedies and books and he has written a tragedy which was hissed and a book of which only one copy has ever been seen outside his bookseller's shop and that was one he gave me."

"The great man!" said Candide. "He is another Pangloss."

Then, turning to him, Candide said:

"Sir, no doubt you think that all is for the best in the physical world and in the moral, and that nothing could be otherwise than as it is?"

"Sir," replied the man of letters, "I do not think anything of the sort. I think everything goes awry with us, that nobody knows his rank or his office, nor what he is doing, nor what he ought to do, and that except at supper, which is quite gay and where there appears to be a certain amount of sociability, all the rest of their time is passed in senseless quarrels; Jansenists with Molinists, lawyers with churchmen, men of letters with men of letters, courtiers with courtiers, financiers with the people, wives with husbands, relatives with relatives—'tis an eternal war."

Candide replied:

"I have seen worse things; but a wise man, who has since had the misfortune to be hanged, taught me that it is all for the best; these are only the shadows in a fair picture."

"Your wise man who was hanged was poking fun at the world," said Martin; "and your shadows are horrible stains."

"The stains are made by men," said Candide, "and they cannot avoid them."

"Then it is not their fault," said Martin.

Most of the gamblers, who had not the slightest understanding of this kind of talk, were drinking; Martin argued with the man of letters and Candide told the hostess some of his adventures.

After supper the marchioness took Candide into a side room and made him sit down on a sofa.

"Well!" said she, "so you are still madly in love with Miss Cunégonde of Thunder-Ten-Tronckh?"

"Yes, madam," replied Candide.

The marchioness replied with a tender smile:

"You answer like a young man from Westphalia. A Frenchman would have said: 'It is true that I was in love with Miss Cunégonde, but when I see you, madam, I fear lest I should cease to love her.'"

"Alas! madam," said Candide, "I will answer as you wish."

"Your passion for her," said the marchioness, "began by picking up her handkerchief; I want you to pick up my garter."

"With all my heart," said Candide; and he picked it up.

"But I want you to put it on again," said the lady; and Candide put it on again.

"You see," said the lady, "you are a foreigner; I sometimes make my lovers in Paris languish for a fortnight, but I give myself to you the very first night, because one must do the honours of one's country to a young man from Westphalia."

The fair lady, having perceived two enormous diamonds on the young foreigner's hands, praised them so sincerely that they passed from Candide's fingers to the fingers of the marchioness.

"I want you to pick up my garter."

As Candide went home with his abbé from Périgord, he felt some remorse at having been unfaithful to Miss Cunégonde. The abbé sympathised with his distress; he had only had a small share in the fifty thousand francs Candide has lost at cards and in the value of the two half-given, half-extorted diamonds. His plan was to profit as much as he could from the advantages which his acquaintance with Candide might procure for him. He talked a lot about Cunégonde, and Candide told him that he should ask that fair one's forgiveness for his infidelity when he saw her at Venice.

The abbé from Périgord redoubled his politeness and civilities and took a tender interest in all Candide said, in all he did, and in all he wished to do.

"Then, sir," said he, "you are to meet her at Venice?"

"Yes, sir," said Candide, "without fail I must go and meet Miss Cunégonde there."

Then, carried away by the pleasure of talking about the person he loved, he related, as he was accustomed to do, some of his adventures with that illustrious Westphalian lady.

"I suppose," said the abbé, "that Miss Cunégonde has a great deal of wit and that she writes charming letters."

"I have never received any from her," said Candide, "for you must know that when I was expelled from the castle because of my love for her, I could not write to her; soon afterwards I heard she was dead, then I found her again and then I lost her, and now I have sent an express messenger to her two thousand five hundred leagues from here and am expecting her reply."

The abbé listened attentively and seemed rather meditative. He soon took leave of the two foreigners, after having embraced them tenderly. The next morning when Candide woke up he received a letter composed as follows:

> Sir, my dearest lover, I have been ill for a week in this town; I have just heard that you are here. I should fly to your arms if I could stir. I heard that you had passed through Bordeaux; I left the faithful Cacambo and the old woman there and they will soon follow me. The governor of Buenos Ayres took everything, but I still have your heart. Come, your presence will restore me to life or will make me die of pleasure.

This charming, this unhoped-for letter, transported Candide with inexpressible joy; and the illness of his dear Cunégonde overwhelmed him with grief. Torn between these two sentiments, he took his gold and his diamonds and drove with Martin to the hotel where Miss Cunégonde was staying. He entered trembling with emotion, his heart beat, his voice was broken; he wanted to open the bed-curtains and to have a light brought.

"Do nothing of the sort," said the waiting-maid. "Light would be the death of her."

And she quickly drew the curtains.

"My dear Cunégonde," said Candide, weeping, "how do you feel? If you cannot see me, at least speak to me."

"She cannot speak," said the maid-servant.

The lady then extended a plump hand, which Candide watered with his tears and then filled with diamonds, leaving a bag full of gold in the arm-chair.

In the midst of these transports a police-officer arrived, followed by the abbé from Périgord and a squad of policemen.

"So these are the two suspicious foreigners?" he said.

He had them arrested immediately and ordered his bravoes to hale them off to prison.

"This is not the way they treat travellers in Eldorado," said Candide.

"I am more of a Manichæan than ever," said Martin.

"But, sir, where are you taking us?" said Candide.

"To the deepest dungeon," said the police-officer.

Martin, having recovered his coolness, decided that the lady who pretended to be Cunégonde was a cheat, that the abbé from Périgord was a cheat who had abused Candide's innocence with all possible speed, and that the police-officer was another cheat of whom they could easily be rid.

Rather than expose himself to judicial proceedings, Candide, enlightened by this advice and impatient to see the real Cunégonde again, offered the police-officer three little diamonds worth about three thousand pounds each.

"Ah! sir," said the man with the ivory stick, "if you had committed all imaginable crimes you would be the most honest man in the world. Three diamonds! Each worth three thousand pounds each! Sir! I would be killed for your sake, instead of taking you to prison. All strangers are arrested here, but trust to me. I have a brother at Dieppe in Normandy, I will take you there; and if you have any diamonds to give him he will take as much care of you as myself."

"And why are all strangers arrested?" said Candide.

The abbé from Périgord then spoke and said:

"It is because a scoundrel from Atrebatum listened to imbecilities; this alone made him commit a parricide, not like that of May 1610, but like that of December 1594, and like several others committed in other years and in other months by other scoundrels who had listened to imbecilities."

The police-officer then explained what it was all about.

"Ah! the monsters!" cried Candide. "What! Can such horrors be in a nation which dances and sings! Can I not leave at once this country where monkeys torment tigers? I have seen bears in my own country; Eldorado is the only place where I have seen men. In God's name, sir, take me to Venice, where I am to wait for Miss Cunégonde."

"I can only take you to Lower Normandy," said the barigel.

Immediately he took off their irons, said there had been a mistake, sent his men away, took Candide and Martin to Dieppe, and left them with his brother. There was a small Dutch vessel in the port. With the help of three other diamonds the Norman became the most obliging of men and embarked Candide and his servant in the ship which was about to sail for Portsmouth in England. It was not the road to Venice; but Candide felt as if he had escaped from Hell, and he had every intention of taking the road to Venice at the first opportunity.

23

Candide and Martin reach the coast of England;
and what they saw there

"Ah! Panglos, Pangloss! Ah! Martin, Martin! Ah! my dear Cunégonde! What sort of a world is this?" said Candide on the Dutch ship.

"Something very mad and very abominable," replied Martin.

"You know England; are the people there as mad as they are in France?"

"'Tis another sort of madness," said Martin. "You know these two nations are at war for a few acres of snow in Canada, and that they are spending more on this fine war than all Canada is worth. It is beyond my poor capacity to tell you whether there are more madmen in one country than in the other; all I know is that in general the people we are going to visit are extremely melancholic."

Talking thus, they arrived at Portsmouth. There were multitudes of people on the shore, looking attentively at a rather fat man who was kneeling down with his eyes bandaged on the deck of one of the ships in the fleet; four soldiers placed opposite this man each shot three bullets into his brain in the calmest manner imaginable; and the whole assembly returned home with great satisfaction.

"What is all this?" said Candide. "And what Demon exercises his power everywhere?"

He asked who was the fat man who had just been killed so ceremoniously.

"An admiral," was the reply.

"And why kill the admiral?"

"Because," he was told, "he did not kill enough people. He fought a battle with a French admiral and it was held that the English admiral was not close enough to him."

"But," said Candide, "the French admiral was just as far from the English admiral as he was from the French admiral!"

"That is indisputable," was the answer, "but in this country it is a good thing to kill an admiral from time to time to encourage the others."

Candide was so bewildered and so shocked by what he saw and heard that he would not even set foot on shore, but bargained with the Dutch captain (even if he had to pay him as much as the Surinam robber) to take him at once to Venice.

The captain was ready in two days. They sailed down the coast of France; and passed in sight of Lisbon, at which Candide shuddered. They entered the Straits and the Mediterranean and at last reached Venice.

"Praised be God!" said Candide, embracing Martin, "here I shall see the fair Cunégonde again. I trust Cacambo as I would myself. All is well, all goes well, all goes as well as it possibly could."

24

Paquette and Friar Giroflée

As soon as he reached Venice, he inquired for Cacambo in all the taverns, in all the cafés, and of all the ladies of pleasure; and did not find him. Every day he sent out messengers to all ships and boats; but there was no news of Cacambo.

"What!" said he to Martin, "I have had time to sail from Surinam to Bordeaux, to go from Bordeaux to Paris, from Paris to Dieppe, from Dieppe to Portsmouth, to sail along the coasts of Portugal and Spain, to cross the Mediterranean, to spend several months at Venice, and the fair Cunégonde has not yet arrived! Instead of her I have met only a jade and an abbé from Périgord! Cunégonde is certainly dead and the only thing left for me is to die too. Ah! it would have been better to stay in the Paradise of Eldorado instead of returning to this accursed Europe. How right you are, my dear Martin! Everything is illusion and calamity!"

He fell into a black melancholy and took no part in the opera *à la mode* or in the other carnival amusements; not a lady caused him the least temptation. Martin said:

"You are indeed simple-minded to suppose that a half-breed valet with five or six millions in his pocket will go and look for your mistress at the other end of the world and bring her to you at Venice. If he finds her, he will take her for himself; if he does not find her, he will take another. I advise you to forget your valet Cacambo and your mistress Cunégonde."

Martin was not consoling. Candide's melancholy increased, and Martin persisted in proving to him that there was little virtue and small happiness in the world except perhaps in Eldorado, where nobody could go.

While arguing about this important subject and waiting for Cunégonde, Candide noticed a young Theatine monk in the Piazza San Marco with a girl on his arm. The Theatine looked fresh, plump and vigorous; his eyes were bright, his air assured, his countenance firm, and his step lofty. The girl was very pretty and was singing; she gazed amorously at her Theatine and every now and then pinched his fat cheeks.

"At least you will admit," said Candide to Martin, "that those people are happy. Hitherto I have only found unfortunates in the whole habitable earth, except in Eldorado; but I wager that this girl and the Theatine are very happy creatures."

"I wager they are not," said Martin.

"We have only to ask them to dinner," said Candide, "and you will see whether I am wrong."

He immediately accosted them, paid his respects to them, and invited them to come to his hotel to eat macaroni, Lombardy partridges, and caviar, and to drink Montepulciano, Lacryma Christi, Cyprus and Samos wine. The young lady blushed, the Theatine accepted the invitation, and the girl followed, looking at Candide with surprise and confusion in her eyes, which were filled with a few tears. Scarcely had they entered Candide's room when she said:

"What! Mr. Candide does not recognise Paquette!"

At these words Candide, who had not looked at her very closely because he was occupied entirely by Cunégonde, said to her:

"Alas! my poor child, so it was you who put Dr. Pangloss into the fine state I saw him in?"

"Alas! sir, it was indeed," said Paquette. "I see you have heard all about it. I have heard of the terrible misfortunes which happened to Her Ladyship the Baroness's whole family and to the fair Cunégonde. I swear to you that my fate has been just as sad. I was very innocent when you knew me. A Franciscan friar who was my confessor easily seduced me. The results were dreadful; I was obliged to leave the castle shortly after His Lordship the Baron expelled you by kicking you hard and frequently in the backside. If a famous doctor had not taken pity on me I should have died. For some time I was the doctor's mistress from gratitude to him. His wife, who was madly jealous, beat me every day relentlessly; she was a fury. The doctor was the ugliest of men, and I was the most unhappy of all living creatures at being continually beaten on account of a man I did not love. You know, sir, how dangerous it is for a shrewish woman to be the wife of a doctor. One day, exasperated by his wife's behaviour, he gave her some medicine for a little cold, and it was so efficacious that she died two hours afterwards in horrible convulsions. The lady's relatives brought a criminal prosecution against the husband; he fled and I was put in prison. My

innocence would not have saved me if I had not been rather pretty.
The judge set me free on condition that he took the doctor's place. I
was soon supplanted by a rival, expelled without a penny, and obliged
to continue the abominable occupation which to you men seems so
amusing and which to us is nothing but an abyss of misery. I came to
Venice to practise this profession. Ah! sir, if you could imagine what it
is to be forced to caress impartially an old tradesman, a lawyer, a monk,
a gondolier, an abbé; to be exposed to every insult and outrage; to be
reduced often to borrow a petticoat in order to go and find some
disgusting man who will lift it; to be robbed by one of what one has
earned with another, to be despoiled by the police, and to contemplate for the future nothing but a dreadful old age, a hospital and a
dunghill, you would conclude that I am one of the most unfortunate
creatures in the world."

The monk looked fresh and vigorous; the girl was very pretty.

Paquette opened her heart in this way to Candide in a side room,
in the presence of Martin, who said to Candide:

"You see, I have already won half my wager."

Friar Giroflée had remained in the dining-room, drinking a glass
while he waited for dinner.

"But," said Candide to Paquette, "when I met you, you looked so
gay, so happy; you were singing, you were caressing the Theatine so
naturally; you seemed to me to be as happy as you say you are unfortunate."

"Ah! sir," replied Paquette, "that is one more misery of our profession. Yesterday I was robbed and beaten by an officer, and today I
must seem to be in a good humour to please a monk."

Candide wanted to hear no more; he admitted that Martin was
right. They sat down to table with Paquette and the Theatine. The
meal was quite amusing and towards the end they were talking with
some confidence.

"Father," said Candide to the monk, "you seem to me to enjoy a
fate which everybody should envy; the flower of health shines on your
cheek, your face is radiant with happiness; you have a very pretty girl
for your recreation and you appear to be very well pleased with your
state of life as a Theatine."

"Faith, sir," said Friar Giroflée, "I wish all the Theatines were at
the bottom of the sea. A hundred times I have been tempted to set fire
to the monastery and to go and be a Turk. My parents forced me at
the age of fifteen to put on this detestible robe, in order that more

money might be left to my cursed elder brother, whom God confound! Jealousy, discord, fury, inhabit the monastery. It is true, I have preached a few bad sermons which bring me in a little money, half of which is stolen from me by the prior; the remainder I spend on girls; but when I go back to the monastery in the evening I feel ready to smash my head against the dormitory walls, and all my colleagues are in the same state."

Martin turned to Candide and said with his usual calm:

"Well, have I not won the whole wager?"

Candide gave two thousand piastres to Paquette and a thousand to Friar Giroflée.

"I warrant," said he, "that they will be happy with that."

"I don't believe it in the very least," said Martin. "Perhaps you will make them still more unhappy with those piastres."

"That may be," said Candide, "but I am consoled by one thing; I see that we often meet people we thought we should never meet again; it may very well be that as I met my red sheep and Paquette, I may also meet Cunégonde again."

"I hope," said Martin, "that she will one day make you happy; but I doubt it very much."

"You are very hard," said Candide.

"That's because I have lived," said Martin.

"But look at these gondoliers," said Candide, "they sing all day long."

"You do not see them at home, with their wives and their brats of children," said Martin. "The Doge has his troubles, the gondoliers have theirs. True, looking at it all round, a gondolier's lot is preferable to a Doge's; but I think the difference so slight that it is not worth examining."

"They talk," said Candide, "about Senator Pococurante who lives in that handsome palace on the Brenta and who is hospitable to foreigners. He is supposed to be a man who has never known a grief."

"I should like to meet so rare a specimen," said Martin.

Candide immediately sent a request to Lord Pococurante for permission to wait upon him next day.

Visit to the noble Venetian, Lord Pococurante

Candide and Martin took a gondola and rowed to the noble Pococurante's palace. The gardens were extensive and ornamented with fine
marble statues; the architecture of the palace was handsome. The master
of this establishment, a very wealthy man of about sixty, received the
two visitors very politely but with very little cordiality, which discon-
certed Candide but did not displease Martin.

Two pretty and neatly dressed girls served them with very frothy
chocolate. Candide could not refrain from praising their beauty, their
grace and their skill.

"They are quite good creatures," said Senator Pococurante, "and I
sometimes make them sleep in my bed, for I am very tired of the ladies
of the town, with their coquetries, their jealousies, their quarrels, their
humours, their meanness, their pride, their folly, and the sonnets one
must write or have written for them; but, after all, I am getting very
tired of these two girls."

After this collation, Candide was walking in a long gallery and was
surprised by the beauty of the pictures. He asked what master had
painted the two first.

"They are by Raphael," said the Senator. "Some years ago I bought
them at a very high price out of mere vanity; I am told they are the
finest in Italy, but they give me no pleasure; the colour has gone very
dark, the faces are not sufficiently rounded and do not stand out
enough; the draperies have not the least resemblance to material; in
short, whatever they may say, I do not consider them a true imitation
of nature. I shall only like a picture when it makes me think it is
nature itself; and there are none of that kind. I have a great many
pictures, but I never look at them now."

While they waited for dinner, Pococurante gave them a concert.
Candide thought the music delicious.

"This noise," said Pococurante, "is amusing for half an hour; but if
it last any longer, it wearies everybody although nobody dares to say

so. Music nowadays is merely the art of executing difficulties, and in the end that which is only difficult ceases to please. Perhaps I should like the opera more if they had not made it a monster which revolts me. Those who please may go to see bad tragedies set to music, where the scenes are only composed to bring in clumsily two or three ridiculous songs which show off an actress's voice; those who will or can may swoon with pleasure when they see an eunuch humming the part of Cæsar and Cato as he awkwardly treads the boards; for my part, I long ago abandoned such trivialities, which nowadays are the glory of Italy and for which monarchs pay so dearly."

Candide demurred a little, but discreetly. Martin entirely agreed with the Senator.

They sat down to table and after an excellent dinner went into the library. Candide saw a magnificently bound Homer and complimented the Illustrissimo on his good taste.

"That is the book," said he, "which so much delighted the great Pangloss, the greatest philosopher of Germany."

"It does not delight me," said Pococurante coldly; "formerly I was made to believe that I took pleasure in reading it; but this continual repetition of battles which are all alike, these gods who are perpetually active and achieve nothing decisive, this Helen who is the cause of the war and yet scarcely an actor in the piece, this Troy which is always besieged and never taken—all bore me extremely. I have sometimes asked learned men if they were as bored as I am by reading it; all who were sincere confessed that the book fell from their hands, but that it must be in every library, as a monument of antiquity, and like those rusty coins which cannot be put into circulation."

"Your Excellency has a different opinion of Virgil?" said Candide.

"I admit," said Pococurante, "that the second, fourth and sixth books of his *Æneid* are excellent, but as for his pious Æneas and the strong Cloanthes and the faithful Achates and the little Ascanius and the imbecile king Latinus and the middle-class Amata and the insipid Lavinia, I think there could be nothing more frigid and disagreeable. I prefer Tasso and the fantastic tales of Ariosto."

"May I venture to ask you, sir," said Candide, "if you do not take great pleasure in reading Horace?"

"He has two maxims," said Pococurante, "which might be useful to a man of the world, and which, being compressed in energetic verses, are more easily impressed upon the memory; but I care very little for his 'Journey to Brundisium,' and his description of a bad dinner, and the street brawlers' quarrel between—what is his name?—Rupilius, whose words, he says, were full of pus, and another person whose words were all vinegar. I was extremely disgusted with his gross verses against old women and witches; and I cannot see there is any merit in his telling his friend Mæcenas that, if he is placed by him among the lyric poets, he will strike the stars with his lofty brow. Fools admire everything in a celebrated author. I only read to please myself, and I only like what suits me."

Candide, who had been taught never to judge anything for himself, was greatly surprised by what he heard; and Martin thought Pococurante's way of thinking quite reasonable.

"Oh! There is a Cicero," said Candide. "I suppose you are never tired of reading that great man?"

"I never read him," replied the Venetian. "What do I care that he pleaded for Rabirius or Cluentius. I have enough cases to judge myself; I could better have endured his philosophical works; but when I saw that he doubted everything, I concluded I knew as much as he and did not need anybody else in order to be ignorant."

"Ah! There are eighty volumes of the Proceedings of an Academy of Sciences," exclaimed Martin, "there might be something good in them."

"There would be," said Pococurante, "if a single one of the authors of all that rubbish had invented even the art of making pins; but in all those books there is nothing but vain systems and not a single useful thing."

"What a lot of plays I see there," said Candide. "Italian, Spanish, and French!"

"Yes," said the Senator, "there are three thousand and not three dozen good ones. As for those collections of sermons, which all together are not worth a page of Seneca, and all those large volumes of theology, you may well suppose that they are never opened by me or anybody else."

Martin noticed some shelves filled with English books.

"I should think," he said, "that a republican would enjoy most of those works written with so much freedom."

"Yes," replied Pococurante, "it is good to write as we think; it is the privilege of man. In all Italy, we only write what we do not think; those who inhabit the country of the Cæsars and the Antonines dare not have an idea without the permission of a Dominican monk. I should applaud the liberty which inspires Englishmen of genius if passion and party spirit did not corrupt everything estimable in that precious liberty."

Candide, in noticing a Milton, asked him if he did not consider that author to be a very great man.

"Who?" said Pococurante. "That barbarian who wrote a long commentary on the first chapter of Genesis in ten books of harsh verses? That gross imitator of the Greeks, who disfigures the Creation, and who, while Moses represents the Eternal Being as producing the world by speech, makes the Messiah take a large compass from the heavenly cupboard in order to trace out his work? Should I esteem the man who spoiled Tasso's hell and devil; who disguises Lucifer sometimes as a toad, sometimes as a pygmy; who makes him repeat the same things a hundred times; makes him argue about theology; and imitates seriously Ariosto's comical invention of fire-arms by making the devils fire a cannon in Heaven? Neither I nor anyone else in Italy could enjoy such wretched extravagances. The marriage of Sin and Death and the snakes which sin brings forth nauseate any man of delicate taste, and his long description of a hospital would only please a grave-digger. This obscure, bizarre and disgusting poem was despised at its birth; I treat it today as it was treated by its contemporaries in its own country. But then I say what I think, and care very little whether others think as I do."

Candide was distressed by these remarks; he respected Homer and rather liked Milton.

"Alas!" he whispered to Martin, "I am afraid this man would have a sovereign contempt for our German poets."

"There wouldn't be much harm in that," said Martin.

"Oh! What a superior man!" said Candide under his breath. "What a great genius this Pococurante is! Nothing can please him."

After they had thus reviewed all his books they went down into the garden. Candide praised all its beauties.

"I have never met anything more tasteless," said their owner. "We have nothing but gewgaws; but tomorrow I shall begin to plant one on a more noble plan."

When the two visitors had taken farewell of his Excellency, Candide said to Martin:

"Now you will admit that he is the happiest of men, for he is superior to everything he possesses."

"Do you not see," said Martin, "that he is disgusted with everything he possesses? Plato said long ago that the best stomachs are not those which refuse all food."

"But," said Candide, "is there not pleasure in criticising, in finding faults where other men think they see beauty?"

"That is to say," answered Martin, "that there is pleasure in not being pleased."

"Oh! Well," said Candide, "then there is no one happy except me—when I see Miss Cunégonde again."

"It is always good to hope," said Martin.

However, the days and weeks went by; Cacambo did not return and Candide was so much plunged in grief that he did not even notice that Paquette and Friar Giroflée had not once come to thank him.

How Candide and Martin supped with six strangers
and who they were

One evening when Candide and Martin were going to sit down to table with the strangers who lodged in the same hotel, a man with a face the colour of soot came up to him from behind and, taking him by the arm, said:

"Get ready to come with us, and do not fail."

He turned round and saw Cacambo. Only the sight of Cunégonde could have surprised and pleased him more. He was almost wild with joy. He embraced his dear friend.

"Cunégonde is here, of course? Where is she? Take me to her, let me die of joy with her."

"Cunégonde is not here," said Cacambo. "She is in Constantinople."

"Heavens! In Constantinople! But were she in China I would fly to her; let us start at once."

"We will start after supper," replied Cacambo. "I cannot tell you any more; I am a slave, and my master is waiting for me; I must go and serve him at table! Do not say anything; eat your supper, and be in readiness."

Candide, torn between joy and grief, charmed to see his faithful agent again, amazed to see him a slave, filled with the idea of seeing his mistress again, with turmoil in his heart, agitation in his mind, sat down to table with Martin (who met every strange occurrence with the same calmness), and with six strangers, who had come to spend the Carnival at Venice.

Cacambo, who acted as butler to one of the strangers, bent down to his master's head towards the end of the meal and said:

"Sire, your Majesty can leave when you wish, the ship is ready."

After saying this, Cacambo withdrew. The guests looked at each other with surprise without saying a word, when another servant came up to his master and said:

"Sire, your Majesty's post-chaise is at Padua, and the boat is ready."
The master made a sign and the servant departed. Once more all
the guests looked at each other, and the general surprise was increased
twofold. A third servant went up to the third stranger and said:

"Sire, believe me, your Majesty cannot remain here any longer; I
will prepare everything."

And he immediately disappeared.

Candide and Martin had no doubt that this was a Carnival mas-
querade. A fourth servant said to the fourth master:

"Your Majesty can leave when you wish."

And he went out like the others.

The fifth servant spoke similarly to the fifth master. But the sixth
servant spoke differently to the sixth stranger, who was next to Candide,
and said:

"Faith, sire, they will not give your Majesty any more credit nor me
either, and we may very likely be jailed tonight, both of us; I am going
to look to my own affairs, good-bye."

When the servants had all gone, the six strangers, Candide and
Martin remained in profound silence. At last it was broken by Candide.

"Gentlemen," said he, "this is a curious jest. How is it you are all
kings? I confess that neither Martin nor I are kings."

Cacambo's master then gravely spoke and said in Italian:

"I am not jesting, my name is Achmet III. For several years I was
Sultan; I dethroned my brother; my nephew dethroned me; they cut
off the heads of my viziers; I am ending my days in the old seraglio; my
nephew, Sultan Mahmoud, sometimes allows me to travel for my
health, and I have come to spend the Carnival at Venice."

A young man who sat next to Achmet spoke after him and said:

"My name is Ivan; I was Emperor of all the Russias; I was dethroned
in my cradle; my father and mother were imprisoned and I was brought
up in prison; I sometimes have permission to travel, accompanied by
those who guard me, and I have come to spend the Carnival at Venice."

The third said:

"I am Charles Edward, King of England; my father gave up his
rights to the throne to me and I fought a war to assert them; the hearts
of eight hundred of my adherents were torn out and dashed in their
faces. I have been in prison; I am going to Rome to visit the King, my
father, who, like me, is dethroned, and my grandfather, and I have
come to spend the Carnival at Venice."

The fourth then spoke and said:

"I am the King of Poland; the chance of war deprived me of my hereditary states; my father endured the same reverse of fortune; I am resigned to Providence like the Sultan Achmet, the Emperor Ivan and King Charles Edward, to whom God grant long life; and I have come to spend the Carnival at Venice."

The fifth said:

"I also am the King of Poland; I have lost my kingdom twice; but Providence has given me another state in which I have been able to do more good than all the kings of the Sarmatians together have been ever able to do on the banks of the Vistula; I also am resigned to Providence and I have come to spend the Carnival at Venice."

It was now for the sixth monarch to speak.

"Gentlemen," said he, "I am not so eminent as you; but I have been a king like anyone else. I am Theodore; I was elected King of Corsica; I have been called Your Majesty and now I am barely called Sir. I have coined money and do not own a farthing; I have had two Secretaries of State and now have scarcely a valet; I have occupied a throne and for a long time lay on straw in a London prison. I am much afraid I shall be treated in the same way here, although I have come, like your Majesties, to spend the Carnival at Venice."

The five other kings listened to this speech with a noble compassion. Each of them gave King Theodore twenty sequins to buy clothes and shirts; Candide presented him with a diamond worth two thousand sequins.

"Who is this man," said the five kings, "who is able to give a hundred times as much as any of us, and who gives it?"

As they were leaving the table, there came to the same hotel four serene highnesses who had also lost their states in the chance of war, and who had come to spend the rest of the Carnival at Venice; but Candide did not even notice these new-comers, he could think of nothing but of going to Constantinople to find his dear Cunégonde.

Candide's voyage to Constantinople

The faithful Cacambo had already spoken to the Turkish captain who was to take Sultan Achmet back to Constantinople and had obtained permission for Candide and Martin to come on board. They both entered this ship after having prostrated themselves before his miserable Highness. On the way, Candide said to Martin:

"So we have just supped with six dethroned kings! And among those six kings there was one to whom I gave charity. Perhaps there are many other princes still more unfortunate. Now, I have only lost a hundred sheep and I am hastening to Cunégonde's arms. My dear Martin, once more, Pangloss was right, all is well."

"I hope so," said Martin.

"But," said Candide, "this is a very singular experience we have just had at Venice. Nobody has ever seen or heard of six dethroned kings supping together in a tavern."

"'Tis no more extraordinary," said Martin, "than most of the things which have happened to us. It is very common for kings to be dethroned; and as to the honour we have had of supping with them, 'tis a trifle not deserving our attention."

Scarcely had Candide entered the ship when he threw his arms round the neck of his old valet and his friend, Cacambo.

"Well!" said he, "what is Cunégonde doing? Is she still a marvel of beauty? Does she still love me? How is she? Of course you have bought her a palace in Constantinople?"

"My dear master," replied Cacambo, "Cunégonde is washing dishes on the banks of Propontis for a prince who possesses very few dishes; she is a slave in the house of a former sovereign named Ragotsky, who receives in his refuge three crowns a day from the Grand Turk; but what is even more sad is that she has lost her beauty and has become horribly ugly."

"Ah! beautiful or ugly," said Candide, "I am a man of honour and my duty is to love her always. But how can she be reduced to so abject a condition with the five or six millions you carried off?"

"Ah!" said Cacambo, "did I not have to give two millions to Senor Don Fernando d'Ibaraa y Figueora y Mascarenes y Lampourdos y Souza, Governor of Buenos Ayres, for permission to bring away Miss Cunégonde? And did not a pirate bravely strip us of all the rest? And did not this pirate take us to Cape Matapan, to Milo, to Nicaria, to Samos, to Petra, to the Dardenelles, to Marmora, to Scutari? Cunégonde and the old woman are servants to the prince I mentioned, and I am slave to the dethroned Sultan."

"What a chain of terrible calamities!" said Candide. "But after all, I still have a few diamonds; I shall easily deliver Cunégonde. What a pity she has become so ugly."

Then, turning to Martin, he said:

"Who do you think is the most to be pitied, the Sultan Achmet, the Emperor Ivan, King Charles Edward, or me?"

"I do not know at all," said Martin. "I should have to be in your hearts to know."

"Ah!" said Candide, "if Pangloss were here he would know and would tell us."

"I do not know," said Martin, "what scales your Pangloss would use to weigh the misfortunes of men and to estimate their sufferings. All I presume is that there are millioins of men on the earth a hundred times more to be pitied than King Charles Edward, the Emperor Ivan and the Sultan Achmet."

"That may very well be," said Candide.

In a few days they reached the Black Sea channel. Candide began by paying a high ransom for Cacambo and, without wasting time, he went on board a galley with his companions bound for the shores of Propontis, in order to find Cunégonde however ugly she might be.

Among the galley-slaves were two convicts who rowed very badly and from time to time the Levantine captain applied several strokes of a bull's pizzle to their naked shoulders. From a natural feeling of pity Candide watched them more attentively than the other galley-slaves and went up to them. Some features of their disfigured faces appeared to him to have some resemblance to Pangloss and the wretched Jesuit, the Baron, Miss Cunégonde's brother. This idea disturbed and saddened him. He looked at them still more carefully.

"Truly," said he to Cacambo, "if I had not seen Dr. Pangloss hanged, and if I had not been so unfortunate as to kill the Baron, I should think they were rowing in this galley."

At the words Baron and Pangloss, the two convicts gave a loud cry, stopped on their seats and dropped their oars. The Levantine captain ran up to them and the lashes with the bull's pizzle were redoubled.

"Stop! Stop sir!" cried Candide. "I will give you as much money as you want."

"What! Is it Candide?" said one of the convicts.

"What! Is it Candide?" said the other.

"Is it a dream?" said Candide. "Am I awake? Am I in this galley? Is that my Lord the Baron whom I killed? Is that Dr. Pangloss whom I saw hanged?"

"It is, it is," they replied.

"What! Is that the great philosopher?" said Martin.

"Ah! sir," said Candide to the Levantine captain, "how much money do you want for My Lord Thunder-Ten-Tronckh, one of the first Barons of the empire, and for Dr. Pangloss, the most profound metaphysician of Germany?"

"Dog of a Christian," replied the Levantine captain, "since these two dogs of Christian convicts are Barons and metaphysicians, which no doubt is a high rank in their country, you shall pay me fifty thousand sequins."

"You shall have them, sir. Row back to Constantinople like lightning and you shall be paid at once. But, no, take me to Miss Cunégonde."

The captain, at Candide's first offer, had already turned the bow towards the town, and rowed there more swiftly than a bird cleaves the air.

Candide embraced the Baron and Pangloss a hundred times.

"How was it I did not kill you, my dear Baron? And, my dear Pangloss, how do you happen to be alive after having been hanged? And why are you both in a Turkish galley?"

"Is it really true that my dear sister is in this country?" said the Baron.

"Yes," replied Cacambo.

"So once more I see my dear Candide!" cried Pangloss.

Candide introduced Martin and Cacambo.

They all embraced and all talked at the same time. The galley flew; already they were in the harbour. They sent for a Jew, and Candide sold him for fifty thousand sequins a diamond worth a hundred thousand, for which he swore by Abraham he could not give any more. The ransom of the Baron and Pangloss was immediately paid. Pangloss threw himself at the feet of his liberator and bathed them with tears; the other thanked him with a nod and promised to repay the money at the first opportunity.

"But is it possible that my sister is in Turkey?" said he.

"Nothing is so possible," replied Cacambo, "since she washes up the dishes of a prince of Transylvania."

They immediately sent for two Jews; Candide sold some more diamonds; and they all set out in another galley to rescue Cunégonde.

28

What happened to Candide, to Cunégonde,
to Pangloss, to Martin, etc.

"Pardon once more," said Candide to the Baron, "pardon me, reverend father, for having thrust my sword through your body."

"Let us say no more about it," said the Baron. "I admit I was a little too sharp; but since you wish to know how it was you saw me in a galley, I must tell you that after my wound was healed by the brother apothecary of the college, I was attacked and carried off by a Spanish raiding party; I was imprisoned in Buenos Ayres at the time when my sister had just left. I asked to return to the Vicar-General in Rome. I was ordered to Constantinople to act as almoner to the Ambassador of France. A week after I had taken up my office I met towards evening a very handsome young page of the Sultan. It was very hot; the young man wished to bathe; I took the opportunity to bathe also. I did not know that it was a most serious crime for a Christian to be found naked with a young Mohammedan. A cadi sentenced me to a hundred strokes on the soles of my feet and condemned me to the galley. I do not think a more horrible injustice has ever been committed. But I should very much like to know why my sister is in the kitchen of a Transylvanian sovereign living in exile among the Turks."

"But, my dear Pangloss," said Candide, "how does it happen that I see you once more?"

"It is true," said Pangloss, "that you saw me hanged; and in the natural course of events I should have been burned. But you remember, it poured with rain when they were going to roast me; the storm was so violent that they despaired of lighting the fire; I was hanged because they could do nothing better; a surgeon bought my body, carried me home and dissected me. He first made a crucial incision in me from the navel to the collar-bone. Nobody could have been worse hanged than I was. The executioner of the holy Inquisition, who was a subdeacon, was marvellously skilful in burning people, but he was not accustomed to hang them; the rope was wet and did not slide easily and it was knotted; in short, I still breathed. The crucial incision caused me to utter so loud a scream that the surgeon fell over backwards and, thinking he was dissecting the devil, fled away in terror and fell down the staircase in his flight. His wife ran in at the noise from another room; she saw me stretched out on the table with my crucial incision; she was still more frightened than her husband, fled, and fell on top of him. When they had recovered themselves a little, I heard the surgeon's wife say to the surgeon:

"'My dear, what were you thinking of, to dissect a heretic? Don't you know the devil always possesses them? I will go and get a priest at once to exorcise him.'

"At this I shuddered and collected the little strength I had left to shout:

"'Have pity on me!'

"At last the Portuguese barber grew bolder; he sewed up my skin; his wife even took care of me, and at the end of a fortnight I was able to walk again. The barber found me a situation and made me lackey to a Knight of Malta who was going to Venice; but, as my master had no money to pay me wages, I entered the service of a Venetian merchant and followed him to Constantinople.

"One day I took it into my head to enter a mosque; there was nobody there except an old Imam and a very pretty young devotee who was reciting her prayers; her breasts were entirely uncovered; between them she wore a bunch of tulips, roses, anemones, ranunculus, hyacinths and auriculas; she dropped her bunch of flowers; I picked it up and returned it to her with a most respectful alacrity. I was so long putting them back that the Imam grew angry and, seeing I was a Christian, called for help. I was taken to the cadi, who sentenced me to receive a hundred strokes on the soles of my feet and sent me to the galleys. I was chained on the same seat and in the same galley as My Lord the Baron. In this galley there were four young men from Marseilles, five Neapolitan priests and two monks from Corfu, who assured us that similar accidents occurred every day. His Lordship the Baron claimed that he had suffered a greater injustice than I; and I claimed that it was much more permissible to replace a bunch of flowers between a woman's breasts than to be naked with one of the Sultan's pages. We argued continually, and every day received twenty strokes of the bull's pizzle, when the chain of events of this universe led you to our galley and you ransomed us."

"Well! my dear Pangloss," said Candide, "when you were hanged, dissected, stunned with blows and made to row in the galleys, did you always think that everything was for the best in this world?"

"I am still of my first opinion," replied Pangloss, "for after all I am a philosopher; and it would be unbecoming for me to recant, since Leibniz could not be in the wrong and pre-established harmony is the finest thing imaginable like the plenum and subtle matter."

How Candide found Cunégonde and the old woman again

While Candide, the Baron, Pangloss, Martin and Cacambo were relating their adventures, reasoning upon contingent or non-contingent events of the universe, arguing about effects and causes, moral and physical evil, free-will and necessity, and the consolations to be found in the Turkish galleys, they came to the house of the Transylvanian prince on the shores of Propontis.

The first objects which met their sight were Cunégonde and the old woman hanging out towels to dry on the line.

At this sight the Baron grew pale. Candide, that tender lover, seeing his fair Cunégonde sunburned, blear-eyed, flat-breasted, with wrinkles round her eyes and red, chapped arms, recoiled three paces in horror, and then advanced from mere politeness.

She embraced Candide and her brother. They embraced the old woman; Candide bought them both.

In the neighbourhood was a little farm; the old woman suggested that Candide should buy it, until some better fate befell the group. Cunégonde did not know that she had become ugly, for nobody had told her so; she reminded Candide of his promises in so peremptory a tone that the good Candide dared not refuse her.

He therefore informed the Baron that he was about to marry his sister.

"Never," said the Baron, "will I endure such baseness on her part and such insolence on yours; nobody shall ever reproach me with this infamy; my sister's children could never enter the chapters of Germany. No, my sister shall never marry anyone but a Baron of the Empire."

Cunégonde threw herself at his feet and bathed them in tears; but he was inflexible.

"Madman," said Candide, "I rescued you from the galleys, I paid your ransom and your sister's; she was washing dishes here, she is ugly, I am so kind as to make her my wife, and you pretend to oppose me! I should kill you again if I listened to my anger."

"You may kill me again," said the Baron, "but you shall never marry my sister while I am alive."

30

Conclusion

At the bottom of his heart Candide had not the least wish to marry Cunégonde. But the Baron's extreme impertinence determined him to complete the marriage, and Cunégonde urged it so warmly that he could not retract. He consulted Pangloss, Martin and the faithful Cacambo. Pangloss wrote an excellent memorandum by which he proved that the Baron had no rights over his sister and that by all the laws of the empire she could make a left-handed marriage with Candide. Martin advised that the Baron should be thrown into the sea; Cacambo decided that he should be returned to the Levantine captain and sent back to the galleys, after which he would be returned by the first ship to the Vicar-General at Rome. This was thought to be very good advice; the old woman approved it; they said nothing to the sister; the plan was carried out with the aid of a little money and they had the pleasure of duping a Jesuit and punishing the pride of a German Baron.

It would be natural to suppose that when, after so many disasters, Candide was married to his mistress, and living with the philosopher Pangloss, the philosopher Martin, the prudent Cacambo and the old woman, having brought back so many diamonds from the country of the ancient Incas, would lead the most pleasant life imaginable. But he was so cheated by the Jews that he had nothing left but his little farm; his wife, growing uglier every day, became shrewish and unendurable; the old woman was ailing and even more bad-tempered than Cunégonde. Cacambo, who worked in the garden and then went to Constantinople to sell vegetables, was overworked and cursed his fate. Pangloss was in despair because he did not shine in some German university.

As for Martin, he was firmly convinced that people are equally uncomfortable everywhere; he accepted things patiently. Candide, Martin and Pangloss sometimes argued about metaphysics and morals. From the windows of the farm they often watched the ships going by, filled with effendis, pashas and cadis, who were being exiled to Lemnos, to Mitylene and Erzerum. They saw other cadis, other pashas and other effendis coming back to take the place of the exiles and to be exiled in their turn. They saw the neatly impaled heads which were taken to the Sublime Porte. These sights redoubled their discussions; and when they were not arguing, the boredom was so excessive that one day the old woman dared to say to them:

"I should like to know which is worse, to be raped a hundred times by negro pirates, to have a buttock cut off, to run the gauntlet among the Bulgarians, to be whipped and flogged in an *auto-da-fé*, to be dissected, to row in a galley, in short, to endure all the miseries through which we have passed, or to remain here doing nothing?"

"'Tis a great question," said Candide.

These remarks led to new reflections, and Martin especially concluded that man was born to live in the convulsions of distress or in the lethargy of boredom. Candide did not agree, but he asserted nothing. Pangloss confessed that he had always suffered horribly; but, having once maintained that everything was for the best, he had continued to maintain it without believing it.

One thing confirmed Martin in his detestable principles, made Candide hesitate more than ever, and embarrassed Pangloss. And it was this: One day there came to their farm Paquette and Friar Giroflée, who were in the most extreme misery; they had soon wasted their three thousand piastres, had left each other, made it up, quarrelled again, been put in prison, escaped, and finally Friar Giroflée had turned Turk. Paquette continued her occupation everywhere and now earned nothing by it.

"I foresaw," said Martin to Candide, "that your gifts would soon be wasted and would only make them the more miserable. You and Cacambo were once bloated with millions of piastres and you are no happier than Friar Giroflée and Paquette."

"Ah! ha!" said Pangloss to Paquette, "so Heaven brings you back to us, my dear child? Do you know that you cost me the end of my nose, an eye and an ear! What a plight you are in! Ah! What a world this is!"

This new occurrence caused them to philosophise more than ever.

In the neighbourhood there lived a very famous Dervish, who was supposed to be the best philosopher in Turkey; they went to consult him; Pangloss was the spokesman and said:

"Master, we have come to beg you to tell us why so strange an animal as man was ever created."

"What has it to do with you?" said the Dervish. "Is it your business?"

"But, reverend father," said Candide, "there is a horrible amount of evil in the world."

"What does it matter," said the Dervish, "whether there is evil or good? When his highness sends a ship to Egypt, does he worry about the comfort or discomfort of the rats in the ship?"

"Then what should we do?" said Pangloss.

"Hold your tongue," said the Dervish.

"I flattered myself," said Pangloss, "that I should discuss with you effects and causes, this best of all possible worlds, the origin of evil, the nature of the soul and pre-established harmony."

At these words the Dervish slammed the door in their faces.

During this conversation the news went round that at Constantinople two viziers and the mufti had been strangled and several of their friends impaled. This catastrophe made a prodigious noise everywhere for several hours. As Pangloss, Candide and Martin were returning to their little farm, they came upon an old man who was taking the air under a bower of orange-trees at his door. Pangloss, who was as curious as he was argumentative, asked him what was the name of the mufti who had just been strangled.

"I do not know," replied the old man. "I have never known the name of any mufti or of any vizier. I am entirely ignorant of the occurrence you mention; I presume that in general those who meddle with public affairs sometimes perish miserably and that they deserve it; but I never inquire what is going on in Constantinople; I content myself with sending there for sale the produce of the garden I cultivate."

Having spoken thus, he took the strangers into his house. His two daughters and his two sons presented them with several kinds of sherbet which they made themselves, caymac flavoured with candied citron peel, oranges, lemons, limes, pine-apples, dates, pistachios and Mocha coffee which had not been mixed with the bad coffee of Batavia and the Isles. After which this good Mussulman's two daughters perfumed the beards of Candide, Pangloss and Martin.

"You must have a vast and magnificent estate?" said Candide to the Turk.

"I have only twenty acres," replied the Turk. "I cultivate them with my children; and work keeps at bay three great evils: boredom, vice and need."

As Candide returned to his farm he reflected deeply on the Turk's remarks. He said to Pangloss and Martin:

"That good old man seems to me to have chosen an existence preferable by far to that of the six kings with whom we had the honour to sup."

"Exalted rank," said Pangloss, "is very dangerous, according to the testimony of all philosophers; for Eglon, King of the Moabites, was murdered by Ehud; Absalom was hanged by the hair and pierced by three darts; King Nadab, son of Jeroboam, was killed by Baasha; King Elah by Zimri; Ahaziah by Jehu; Athaliah by Jehoiada; the Kings Jehoiakim, Jeconiah and Zedekiah were made slaves. You know in what manner died Crœsus, Astyages, Darius, Denys of Syracuse, Pyrrhus, Perseus, Hannibal, Jugurtha, Ariovistus, Cæsar, Pompey, Nero, Otho, Vitellius, Domitian, Richard II of England, Edward II, Henry VI, Richard III, Mary Stuart, Charles I, the three Henrys of France, the Emperor Henry IV. You know . . ."

"I also know," said Candide, "that we should cultivate our gardens."

"You are right," said Pangloss, "for, when man was placed in the Garden of Eden, he was placed there *ut operaretur eum*, to dress it and to keep it; which proves that man was not born for idleness."

"Let us work without arguing," said Martin; "'tis the only way to make life endurable."

The whole small fraternity entered into this praiseworthy plan, and each started to make use of his talents. The little farm yielded well. Cunégonde was indeed very ugly, but she became an excellent pastry-cook; Paquette embroidered; the old woman took care of the linen. Even Friar Giroflée performed some service; he was a very good carpenter and even became a man of honour; and Pangloss sometimes said to Candide:

"All events are linked up in this best of all possible worlds; for, if you had not been expelled from the noble castle by hard kicks in your backside for love of Miss Cunégonde, if you had not been clapped into the Inquisition, if you had not wandered about America on foot, if you had not stuck your sword in the Baron, if you had not lost all your sheep from the land of Eldorado, you would not be eating candied citrons and pistachios here."

"'Tis well said," replied Candide, "but we must cultivate our gardens."

LA PUCELLE
The Maid of Orléans

An Heroic-Comical Poem
in Twenty-one Cantos

English translation by W. H. Ireland, Lady Charleville, and Ernest Downson (1899)

1

The chaste Loves of Charles VII and Agnes Sorel.
Orleans besieged by the English. Apparition of Saint Denis, etc.

The praise of Saints my lyre shall not rehearse,
Feeble my voice, and too profane my verse;
Yet shall my muse to laud our Joan incline,
Who wrought, 'tis said, such prodigies divine;
Whose virgin hands revived the drooping flower
And gave to Gallia's lily ten-fold power;
Rescued its monarch from the impending fate
So dreaded from victorious England's hate;
Sent him to Rheims, where king before the Lord
The sacring oil upon his head was poured;
Although in aspect Joan was quite the maid,
Albeit in stays and petticoat arrayed;
With boldest heroes she sustained her part,
For Joan possessed a Roland's dauntless heart:
For me, much better should I like by night,
A lamb-like beauty to inspire delight;
But you shall see, if you peruse my page
That Joan of Arc had all a lion's rage;
You'll tremble at the feats whereof you hear,
And more than all the wars she used to wage,
At how she kept her maidenhead—a year!
O Chapelain! O thou whose violin
Produced of old so harsh and vile a din;
Whose bow Apollo's malediction had,
Which scraped his history in notes so sad;
Old Chapelain! if honouring thine art
Thou wouldst to me thy genius even impart,
I'll none of it—let it reward the pains
Of Motte-Houdart, who murdered Homer's strains.

Our good King Charles within his youthful prime
His revels kept at Tours, at Eastertime,
Where at a ball, (for well he loved to dance)
It so fell out, that for the good of France
He met a maid who beggared all compare,
Named Agnes Sorel, (Love had framed the fair).
Let your warm fancy youthful Flora trace,
Of Venus add her most enchanting grace,
The wood-nymph's stature and bewitching guise,
With Love's seductive air and brilliant eyes,
Arachne's art, the Syren's dulcet song—
All these were hers and she could lead along
Kings, Heroes, Sages in her captive chain.
To see her, love her, feel the increasing pain,
Of young Desire, its growing warmth to prove,
With faultering utterance to speak of Love;
To tremble and regard with dove-like eyes,
To strive and speak and utter nought but sighs,
Her hands, with a caressing hand to hold,
Till panting all the flames her breast enfold;
By turns each other's tender pains impart,
And own the luscious thrill that sways the heart;
To please, in short, is just a day's affair
For Kings in love are swift and debonnaire.
Agnes was fain—she knew the art to please
To deck the thing in garb of mysteries,
Veils of thin gauze, through which will always pry,
The envious courtier's keen, malignant eye.
To mask this business, that none might know
The King made choice of Councillor Bonneau;
A trusty man of Tours, skilled in device
Who filled a post that is not over nice,
Which, though the court, that always seeks to lend
Beauty to all things, calls the Prince's friend,
The vulgar town and every rustic imp
Are grossly apt to designate a *Pimp*.
Upon Loire's banks this worthy Sieur Bonneau
Stood seigneur of an elegant chateau,
Whither one day, about the time of shade,
In a light skiff fair Agnes was conveyed,

There the same knight King Charles would fain recline
And there they supped, while Bonneau poured the wine
State was dismissed, though all was served with care,
Banquets of gods could not with this compare!
Our Lovers their delight and joy confessed,
Desire inflamed and transport filled each breast,
Supremely formed by sprightly wit to please
Eager they listen and alternate gaze;
While their discourse, without indecence, free,
Gave their impatience fresh vivacity.
The ardent prince's eyes her charms devoured,
While in her ear soft tales of love he poured,
And with his knee her gentle knees deflowered.
The supper over, music played awhile,
Italian music—the chromatic style.
Flutes, hautboys, viols softly breathed around,
While three melodious voices swelled the sound;
They sang historic allegories, their strain
Told of those heroes mighty Love had slain,
And those they sang, who some proud Fair to please,
Quit fields of glory for inglorious ease.
In a recess this skilful band was set
Hard by the chamber where the good king ate;
As yet they sought their secret joys to screen
And Agnes fair enjoyed the whole unseen.
The moon upon the sky begins to glower;
Midnight has struck; it is Love's magic hour;
In an alcove begilt with art most sure,
Not lit too much and yet not too obscure,
Between two sheets of finest Holland made
The lovely Agnes' glowing charms were laid.
Here did Dame Alix leave her to repose;
But, cunning Abigail! forgot to close
The private door that ope'd an easy way
To eager Charles, impatient of delay.
Perfumes most exquisite, with timely care
Are poured already on his braided hair:
And ye, who best have loved, can tell the best
The anxious throbbings of our monarch's breast.
The sanctuary gain'd which shrines her charms,

In bed he clasps her naked to his arms.
Moment of ecstacy! propitious night!
Their hearts responsive beat with fond delight.
Love's brightest roses glow on Agnes' cheek;
In the warm blush, her fears and wishes speak.
But maiden fears in transport melt away,
And Love triumphant rules with sovran sway.
The ardent Prince now pressed her to his breast,
His eyes surveyed, his eager hands caressed,
Beauties enough which had been given her
To make a hermit an idolater.
Beneath a neck, whose dazzling whiteness shone
Pure and resplendent as the Parian stone,
With gentlest swell two breasts serenely move,
Severed and moulded by the hand of Love.
Each crowned with vermeil bud of damask rose,
Enchanting nipples, which ne'er know repose;
You seemed the gaze and pressure to invite,
And wooed the longing lips to seek delight.
Ever complying with my reader's taste,
I meant to paint as low as Agnes' waist;
To show that symmetry, devoid of blot,
Where Argus' self could not discern a spot;
But Virtue, which the world good manners calls,
Stops short my hand—and lo! the pencil falls.
In Agnes all was beauty, all was fair;
Voluptuousness, whereof she had her share,
Spurred every sense which instant took the alarm,
Adding new grace to every brilliant charm
It animated: Love can use disguise,
And pleasure heightens beauty in our eyes.
Three months on rapid pinions wing their flight
And leave our pair unsated with delight.
From Love's soft couch they seek the genial board
Where by rich food their wasted strength's restored.
Then eager for the chase on steeds of Spain
With deep-tongued hounds they sweep the echoing plain.
Returned, the bath's prepared, the rifled East,
Of essence sweet and perfumes yields its best;
As on the skin with softer polish shew,

Or teach the cheek with warmer blush to glow.
Dinner is served. How delicate the fare!
The bird of Phasis, and the heath-cock rare;
From some score stews the savoury odours rise;
They charm the nose, the palate and the eyes.
Wine d'Aï, whose froth in sparks died quick away
And goblets of the yellow-hued Tokay.
Warmed the young brain with fire that could not fail
In sallies of the liveliest wit to exhale;
Brilliant as liquor when the bubbles swim,
And sparkling dance around the goblet's brim:
When the good king, facetious, deigns to speak
Bonneau's fat sides with peals of laughter shake.
The dinner ended, mirth and jest went round,
Blind to their own, their neighbours' faults they found;
Verses of Master Alain loud were bawled,
And learned doctors of the Sorbonne called.
A harlequin who wore the motley shape,
Some squalling parots, and an antic ape,
A few selected friends at close of day,
Attend the jolly monarch to the play:
Who with the night returns again to prove
The tender inebriety of love.
Thus nurtured in the bosom of delight
To each blessed day succeeds more blissful night.
No lassitude, no bickering molests,
No jealous fear disturbs their tranquil breasts.
From each succeeding hour fresh pleasure springs,
Near Agnes, time and love forget their wings.
When Charles enraptured sank within her arms,
Kissed her ripe lips and revelled in her charms:
"Dear Idol of my soul, Agnes!" he'd cry,
"How fully, how supremely blest am I,
Whilst in thy snowy arms thus fondly pressed,
I reign sole monarch of thy tender breast.
To conquer and to reign is folly now,
My parliament disowns me, and I bow
To conquering England's haughty tyranny;
Well! let them reign, but let them envy me,
Kingship enough is to be king of thee!"

This speech was not heroic, may be said,
But when a hero haply lies in bed,
With a fair mistress, even a hero may
Speak as love guides and reck not what he say.
As thus he lived from every sorrow free
Just like an abbot in his rich abbey;
The English Prince, with whom war was the word,
In camp well armed, well-booted too and spurred,
With girded sword, and ever-ready lance
Victoriously strode through conquered France.
With rapid march the countryside he scours,
Nor walls withstand him nor embattled towers.
Slaughter and pillage mark his dreaded way,
Defenceless females fall his soldiers' prey;
Whole convents to their violation yield,
Whole caves are drained by many a vintage filled;
Gold they purloined, which relics had enchased,
Then into useful coin the ore debased:
Each sacred ordinance by them was spurned,
Churches and chapels into stables turned;
Just so when greedy wolves, with ravening eyes,
Spring 'mid the fold and seize the bleating prize,
Tear with their reeking jaws the victim's breast,
While in a distant meadow lulled to rest,
Colin, enfolded in Egeria's arms,
Sleeps undisturbed, contented with her charms,
While near him lo! his dog devours the meat
Which, at his supper, Colin could not eat.
Bright apogeum, golden gleam so high,
Mansion of saints beyond weak mortal's eye;
'Twas thence good Denis gazed on France, her woes,
The pangs inflicted by her victor foes,
Paris in chains and its most Christian king
For Agnes' kisses leaving everything.
Grieved to the soul, the good saint turned askance,
For Denis long had patron been of France:
As Mars was tutelary saint of Rome,
And Athens looked to Pallas of the loom.
But in our favour greatly were the odds,
One saint's worth more than fifty heathen gods!

"Ah, by my soul! he cried, it is not just
To see crash down an Empire so August,
Where I myself religion's banner bore;
And shall the Lilies' throne be seen no more?
Blood of the Valois! thy pains move my breast
Let us not suffer the aspiring crest
Of the fifth Henry's brothers without right
The lawful heir of France to put to flight;
I have, though Saint, as God may give me grace
A rooted hatred of the British race,
For if the book of destiny speak true,
The day shall some when this bold-thinking crew
Shall laugh the saints and their decrees to scorn;
The Roman annals will by them be torn
And yearly they'll in effigy destroy
Rome's sacred pontiff and the Lord's Viceroy.
Let us revenge this sacrilegious thought,
Punish the crime before the crime be wrought.
My beloved French shall all be catholics;
These haughty English all be heretics;
Chase hence these British dogs, leave not a man,
Let's punish them by some unheard-of plan,
For all the wickedness which they intend."
The gallic patron Denis, thus he quoth,
Spicing his *pater-noster* with an oath.
    While thus alone the saint reviewed the case,
At Orleans a council then took place,
Blockaded was the city round about,
Nor could it longer for the King hold out;
Some noblemen and counsellors of might,
Half of them pedants and half bred to fight,
All grieve their common fate in sundry tone,
Their only question: "What is to be done?
Let us, my friends, where Honour points the way
Sell them our lives as dearly as we may!"
Such the sad terms in which Dunois bewails,
To Poton and La Hire who bite their nails.
"By Heaven! cried Richemont, wherefore thus sit tame?
Let us at once set Orléans in a flame;
Let us deride the foe and then expire,

Leaving them nought but ashes, smoke and fire."
Trimouille exclaimed: "That moment vain I rue,
When parents made me native of Poitou;
To Orleans town from Milan fain to flee,
I left alas! my charming Dorothy;
Though reft of hope, fore Heaven, I yet will fight,
Yet must I die unblessed by her dear sight!"
Louvet, the president, great personage,
Whose grave appearance might have dubbed him sage,
Exclaimed: "'Twould previously be my intent
That we should pass an act of parliament
Against the British; and that in such case
Each point be canvassed in its proper place."
A mightly clerk was Louvet, though aright
He did not know his truly sorry plight,
How his fair lady was a rebel turned,
With mutual flame for gallant Talbot burned.
This had be known, his gravity, indeed,
Had soon found precedents how to proceed;
Louvet, unknowing of the fateful thrall,
Strives with male eloquence to rescue Gaul.
Amid this council of the wise and brave,
Were heard orations eloquent and grave
Virtue inspiring and the public good;
Foremost in flowing phrase is understood.
La Hire, who, though to long harangues inclined,
So ably speaks as to enchain the mind.
Much were their arguments with wisdom fraught,
Their words were gold but they concluded nought.
While thus haranguing, they beheld in air
A strange appearance most divinely fair;
A beauteous phantom with a vermeil face
Bestrode a sun-beam with celestial grace;
Which, as it through the expanse and aether sailed,
A saint-like odour all around exhaled;
Upon its head the spirit a mitre bore,
With double-points such as grave prelates wore,
By lambent flames its temples were confined.
Its gold dalmatic fluttered in the wind;
The embroidered stole was carried over all,

While the hand held the truncheon pastoral
That erst was known as *lituus augural*.
    Struck with the sight which they but ill discerned
Each his regard upon his fellow turned;
First Trimouille, a lecherous devotee,
Began to pray upon his bended knee.
Richemont, whose breast an iron heart concealed,
Blasphemer, and whose lips but oaths revealed,
Raising his voice exclaimed: "It is the devil
From Hell arrived, dread mansion of all evil;
I deem it pleasing pastime to confer
In friendly intercourse with Lucifer."
Louvet made off as fast as he could trot
To fetch in haste the Holy water-pot.
Bewildered Poton, Dunois and La Hire,
Opened their eyes all three appalled with fear;
Stretched on his belly every valet fawned:
The saint appeared in lustrous garb adorned,
Borne on bright gleam, descended to the ground,
Then dealt his holy benediction round.
They knelt and crossed themselves: the vision fair
Raised them from earth with a paternal air,
Then said aloud: "My sons, be not afraid,
My name is Denis, Sanctity my trade;
Your grandsires I both loved and catechized
But now mine honest soul is scandalized
To see my Godson Charles I loved so dear,
Whose land's in flames, whose subjects quake with fear,
Rather than seek to comfort the distressed,
Prefer to dally with a girl's white breast.
I am therefore come my utmost skill to try
And turn from France impending misery.
I wish to end the woes you have endured,
'Tis said all ills by contraries are cured;
If then king Charlie, for a harlot fain,
Will lose his kingdom and his honour stain;
I have resolved to save the king and land
And work by purpose by a virgin's hand;
If ye are Frenchmen tried and Christians true,
If for protection from on high you'd sue,

If ye are Frenchmen tried and Christians true,
Assist me in my sacred enterprise;
Show me the place where I can rouse the best
This veritable Phoenix from her nest."
    Thus spoke the venerable, sainted sire.
In one loud laugh his auditors conspire.
Young Richemont, born for pleasantry and joke
Anon the learned preacher thus bespoke:
"Ah, wherefore, good Sir Saint, take so much pains,
Abandoning for earth your heavenly plains,
Of us poor sinful mortals to enquire
For this bright jewel which you so admire.
To save a city I could never see
That there was magic in virginity;
Besides to seek it here seems hardly wise
When you've so much of it in Paradise;
Have you not more virginities at home
Than tapers at Loretto or at Rome?
But here in France there are, alas! no more
Our convents are all silent on that score.
Our Archers, Officers and Princes high
Have long since made the provinces run dry.
They stop at nothing, and—the Saints in spite!
Make bastards more than orphans, any night.
To finish good Sir Denis, our dispute,
Seek maids elsewhere; there's no one here will suit."
    Deep blushed the Saint to hear such lewd discourse,
And quickly mounted on his heavenly horse,
Upon his sunbean; not another word:
As through the air he sped, his steed he spurred.
In search of that inestimable toy
To crown his future hopes and present joy.
Well! let him go, and while he speeds his way,
Perched on the sunbeam which illumines day,
Dear reader, when on love you set your mind,
May you gain that which Denis went to find.

2

Thrice happy he who finds a maidenhead!
Great is the blessing, but who moves the heart
Is still more plainly to be envied,
And to be loved is the most pleasing part.
To tear up flowers—why, all can do't who start
It is another task to cull the rose!
Most learned clerks have ruined by their glose
So fair a text, by making duty war
With pleasure, and to Happiness a bar.
I'll write a book I'm positive will sell
To teach the precious art of living well.
And golden precepts in soft numbers sing
To shew how pleasures may from duty spring.
Denis shall quit his mansion in the skies
To aid me in my worthy enterprise;
Him have I sung, his hand shall be my stay.
Meantime it were as well that I should say
What came from his appearing, as saints may.
Close to the confines of wide Champaign's land,
Where full a hundred posts in order stand
On which are graven Martlets three to say
That on rich Lorraine's soil you wend your way,
By ancients little known there stands a town,
Which has in history acquired renown.
For thence salvation and great glory came
To the white lilies and the Gallic name.
Let us all sing of famous Dom Remy
And waft its praises down posterity.
O Dom Remy! though thy poor precincts hold

Nor muscadine, nor peach, nor citrons gold,
Nor damning wine, nor mines, nor precious stone,
Yet 'tis to thee France owes her glorious Joan.
There Joan was born! A curate of the place
Anxious that all his flock should merit grace
Ardent in bed, at table and at prayer,
And once a monk, was father of our Fair,
A chambermaid, robust and plump to view,
Was the blest mould wherein our pastor threw
This beauty who put off the English yoke.
At sixteen years, this damsel was bespoke
To serve the stable at an humble inn
At Vaucouleurs; where even then the din
Of her renown had stirred the countryside.
Her air was proud but gentle with her pride,
Her big, black eyes diffused a steady light
While two and thirty teeth all snowy white
Adorned a mouth that spread from ear to ear,
But red as ever ripest cherries were.
Firm were her breasts, although of colour brown,
Tempting the cowl, the helmet and the gown;
Both active, vigorous, and full of blood,
Her large plump hands for every work were good,
She'd carry burthens, empty cans of wine,
Serve peasant, noble, citizen, divine;
And while she worked, give many a lusty blow
To guests too pert, whose meddling hands would know
How her bare breast felt, or, perhaps her thigh.
From morn to eve she worked with laughing eye,
Watered her horses, tended, combed their hair,
Then brought them home, and, withal, rode them bare,
As any knight of Roman chivalry.
Wisdom Divine! O Providence profound!
Oft doth thy will presumptuous pride confound.
How trifling are the mighty in thine eyes,
How great the little are whom they despise.
Thy servant Denis went not to the Court,
Of nobles and princesses the resort;
No, nor to you dame duchesses so fair,
For well he knew the jewel was not there;

He ran—my friends, be not incredulous!
To seek for virtue in a public-house.
High time it was that to our maiden Joan
France's apostle made his wishes known;
Great was the danger of the public good.
Malice of Satan is well understood,
And had the Saint arrived one moment late,
Poor France indeed had had a sorry fate.
A Cordelier, whose name was Grisbourdon,
Arrived with Chandos late from Albion,
Had at this pot-house for a period staid;
And as his country he loved Joan the maid.
He was his order's boast, support and pride,
On holy mission sent on every side;
A confessor, a preacher and a spy,
And more, a learned clerk in sorcery,
Versed in that art which once was Egypt's boast,
That art by sages taught a mighty host,
Practised by Hebrew and by ancient sage,
Alas! unknown in this degenerate age!
   As he perused his books of mystery
He found how Joan should cross his destiny;
And her short petticoat should surely hide
The fate of England and of France beside.
The monk by aid of genie rendered bold,
Swore by his frock, the Devil and Saint Francis
He'd make to Joan such vigorous advances,
That he should soon that bright Palladium hold.
"As monk and Briton do I doubly stand,
Pledged to the Church and to my native land;
And much with patriotic zeal incline
To serve their purpose, when it answers mine."
Meantime, a boor in ignorance arrayed
With him disputed the illustrious maid.
His rival was a doughty muleteer
At least a match for any Cordelier;
Who sued both night and day Joan's heart to move
With clumsy offers of eternal love.
The occasion and the sweet equality
Made Joan regard him with complacency;

But chastity the flame could still control
Which through her eyes slipped straight into her soul.
Roc Grisbourdon beheld the kindling fire,
Better than Joan he knew her heart's desire.
His dreaded rival straight he came to find,
And thus bespoke him speciously and kind.
"O puissant hero! who in times of need,
Doth pass in force the comely beasts you feed
I grant such vigour may deserve the maid,
To whom my ardent vows are likewise paid.
Inveterate rivals steadfast both in love,
Thus must we still a mutual hindrance prove.
For her in amity let both agree,
Rivals no more, we'll friendly lovers be,
And both partake of the delicious treat
Which both might forfeit in the conflict's heat;
Conduct me to the couch where lies the fair,
The fiend of sleep anon I'll invoke there.
His poppies sweet will close her eyes in sleep
While we, alternately, Love's vigils keep."
The monk forthwith, bedecked with cord and cowl
By magic art invoked that demon foul,
Who anciently the name of Morpheus bore,
That leaden devil who in France will snore
When pleaders (as the matin ray gains force)
Speed to discant on *Cujas* till they're hoarse;
And next at church assists at the discourse,
By Massilon's poor journeymen preached o'er
On topics three, quotations by the store:
While even our theatre's in so sad a plight,
We seldom drive him from the pit at night.
Called by the monk, he mounts his ebon car,
Drawn by young screech-owls through the musky air.
With eyes half-closed he softly cleaves the shade
And stretches yawning o'er the sleeping maid.
Scatters his poppies, in narcotic wreaths,
And round a soporific vapour breathes.
So Father Girard who confessed the fair,
Breathed, it is said, on gentle Cadière,

And with his breath so lecherous and warm
Filled her with devils in a perfect swarm.
    Our two gallants, who watched this sweet repose,
Spurred on by waking thoughts, removed the clothes
That covered Joan, and on her bosom tried
With dice the anxious contest to decide,
Which should try first his courage in the breach:
The churchman won—magician's overreach!
Grisbourdon, eager to possess his prize,
Springs towards the fair—imagine his surprise!
Denis appears and Joan opens her eyes!
Heavens! how sinners tremble at a saint!
The monk and muleteer had like to faint.
Fear prompts to flight and both alike retire,
Their breasts still burning with perverse desire.
Have you not thus in crowded cities seen,
The frightened votaries of the Cyprian queen,
Scared by rough bailiffs, naked spring from bed,
And from the officers escape: so fled
Our quaking lechers most discomforted.
    Denis approached, the maiden Joan to cheer,
At the late dire attempt appalled with fear:
Then thus bespoke her: "Blessed maid elect!
The Gods of Kings by thee will France protect,
And Albion's chalky cliffs shall shortly mourn,
To see her vanquished squadrons homewards turn.
Wondrous the inexplicable ways of God!
The ruined world's refitted at his nod.
And at his breath, the reed no more does bend,
But, like the cedar, its rough arms extend.
Hills vanish at his voice and valleys rise,
His word the unfathomable Ocean dries!
Before thy steps his thunder shall go by,
And all around thee shall his terror fly;
Angels attend, of victory and wrath,
To open unto thee bright glory's path.
Quit then thine humble toil, and let thy name
Be henceforth written in the lists of fame."
At this discourse, so truly tragical,
So comforting and theological,

Our Joan, amazed, gaped wide with vacant look,
And thought 'twas Greek the saintly Denis spoke
But Grace—that august thing soon operates,
And in her mind its brightness penetrates;
Joan felt these flights which such a gift imparts,
Deeply its ardour struck into her heart.
No longer is she Joan, the chamber-maid,
Rather a hero for hot war arrayed.
As when we view some coarse, unpolished bear
Of an old miser's store become the heir,
Transformed his house is to a palace wide,
His timid look assumes an air of pride;
The great admire his pride; with one accord
The small rush eagerly to call him "Lord!"
Or rather such the happy, homely she,
Formed both by nature and by art to be,
The lover of a brothel's wanton joy
Or fill an opera dancer's loose employ;
Whose mother's circumspect, considerate head,
Had reared her for a wealthy farmer's bed,
But whom the hand of love expert in feats,
Transported to a monarch 'twixt two sheets
Her lively beauty bears the stamp of queen,
Armed with sweet majesty her eyes are seen,
Her voice at once assumes the sovereign sound,
And mounting with her rank her spirit is found.

    Wherefore to hasten the august intent
Joan and Saint Denis to the chapel went;
Where on the altar lay, to please the eyes,
(Oh, maiden Joan! how great was thy surprise!)
A handsome harness, dazzling to the sight,
Forth from the arsenals of the empyrean height.
Just at that instant's time the armour came
From the Archangel sent, Michael his name.
The head-piece, there, was seen of Deborah;
The pointed nail of fated Sisera;
The round, smooth stone the pious shepherd threw,
Which great Goliath's temples split in two;
The jaw wherewith the furious Samson fought,
Who snapped new cords, regarding them as nought,

When by his light o'love he was betrayed;
Those pots with which good Gideon dismayed
Of Midian, the unbelieving band;
The sword which graced the lovely Judith's hand;
That treacherous fair, most holy though beside
Who, for the Lord, did gallant homicide,
By stealing to her sleeping love in bed,
And whilst defenceless cutting off his head.

Astonished at these sights was Joan the maid,
Who in these arms was speedily arrayed;
Gauntlets, arm-coverings and helm she took,
Of thigh pieces and breast plate fixed each hook,
With stone, nail, dagger, jaw-bone, javelin, lance,
Marched, tried herself and burned for fame and France.

As coursers are by heroines required,
Joan of the muleteer a steed desired;
When instantly there stood before the lass
A fine gray-haired and loudly braying ass,
Well curried, bridled, saddled, while his head
A plumage bore; rich clothes his back o'erspread;
The ground he pawed, quite ready for the course,
Just like a Thracian or an English horse.
Two wings were carried by this noble gray
Wherewith he sometimes took an aerial way,
Like Pegasus who through Parnassian shades,
Conveyed of old the nine immortal maids,
Or Hippogriff, who carried to the moon
Astolpho on a visit to Saint John.
This ass who proffer'd thus his rump to Joan
To my kind reader shall be better known;
Another Canto may his worth declare,
And tell his journeys through the plains of air.
Till then, this happy ass I bid thee fear,
He has his mystery, tremble and revere!

Already Joan is mounted on her gray,
And Denis sits, astride upon his ray:
In haste they seek Loire's pleasant banks to bring
Tidings of joy to their enamoured king.
Sometimes the ass would trot and sometimes fly,
Winging its course 'mid regions of the sky.

Ever with lust inspired the cordelier,
Somewhat recovered from his shame and fear,
Using in short the dire magician's rule
Turned the poor muleteer into a mule;
Then mounting, spurred and very roundly swore
He'd follow Joan, all earth and ocean o'er.
The muleteer, concealed in mule's disguise
Thought by the change that he should share the prize;
His filthy soul was so devoid of grace,
As scarcely to discern its change of place.
Joan and Denis to Tours still bent their flight,
To seek the monarch plunged in soft delight;
And as at night near Orléans' walls they crossed,
They passed the encampments of the British host.
These haughty Britons, who had quaffed full deep,
Their wine digested in profoundest sleep.
Drunk was each soldier and each sentry found,
Nowhere was heard the drum or trumpet's sound;
Some sleep in tents, stretched naked on the floor,
And some promiscuous with their pages snore.
    Which Denis viewing, turned him to the maid,
And in a most paternal whisper, said:
"Have you not, Daughter of Election, heard
What Nisus once, in nightly battle, dared
To snatch Euryalus from the sleeping foe;
When the brave Rutuli in darkness bled,
And Turnus' troops were numbered with the dead?
So happened it with Rhesus, when of old
The son of Tydeus, vehement and bold,
Aided by famed Ulysses and the night
Sent, without hazarding the dangerous fight,
So many Trojans who had nobly bled
To the cold slumber of their kindred dead.
Say, will my Joan a like adventure try?"
Quoth Joan: "I'm not well read in history;
But strange would be the courage, in my sight,
Which slaughters enemies who cannot fight."
    Thus having spoke, the maid beheld a tent
Whereon the moon her silvery radiance bent,
Which to her dazzled eyes appeared to be

A chief's or some young lord's of high degree:
A hundred flasks of vintage rare being there.
Joan, whose assurance beggared all compare,
The ample remnants of a pasty seized,
And with Sieur Denis drank six bumpers down,
To France, and health and fortune of her crown.
The famous Chandos, he who owned the tent;
Stretched on his back lay, sleeping out his bent;
Joan promptly seized his redoutable sword
And slashed the velvet breeches of my lord.
As David, loved of God, had done of yore,
When he found Saul, and might have smote him sore;
He cut from off the sleeper with a knife
Part of his shirt, but did not take his life.
That to all potentates he might make plain,
What he dared do, and how he could abstain.
Near to John Chandos lay a youthful page,
Of fourteen years, but charming for his age,
Two globes displaying to the gazer's sight,
Which might have passed for loves, they were so white.
An *écritoire*, well furnished, stood hard-by,
Where the half-tipsy youth would sometimes try,
His slender talents at the rhyming trade,
In tender trifles for his favourite maid.
Joan takes the ink, her virgin hands design
Three *fleurs de lys* exactly 'neath his spine
This presage for the good of France was sent
'Twas of its monarch's love the monument.
When Denis saw his pleasure was not damped,
These English buttocks with French lilies stamped.

    Who with the sense of shame next morning shrunk?
'Twas Chandos, who the night before was drunk;
Waking, to see upon his pretty page
The *fleurs de lys*. Burning with proper rage,
He cries "Alarm!"; he thinks they are betrayed,
And seeks his sword which by his couch was laid
He sought in vain, is struck with grim surprise,
Gone are his breeches too, he rubs his eyes.
He grumbles, swears and vows with all his heart
In feats like these the Devil has had a part.

Ah! that a golden sunbeam and an ass
Which carried Joan, a gray and winged ass,
So quickly round the globe should thus have flown!
Arrived at Court are Denis and our Joan.
By long experience had the prelate proved
That joking at the court of France was loved,
The insolent remarks that Richemont threw
To him at Orléans he remembered too.
A similar adventure to escape
He thought it better to transform his shape,
Nor more the bishop's holy form expose;
Wherefore our Saint the grim resemblance chose
Of Roger, noble Lord of Baudricourt,
Brave warrior and a catholic most sure,
Bold speaker, loyal and to be believed,
And for all that at Court not ill received.
"God's day!" he cried, declaiming to the king,
"Why in a province are you loitering?
A slavish king, and fettered by love's chain.
What! can that arm from valiant feats refrain!
Quit myrtle wreaths with tinsel roses twined.
Let diadems your royal forehead bind!
You leave your cruel enemies alone
To govern France and occupy your throne!
Go forfeit life or once more gain that land
By robbers ravished from your rightful hand;
To grace your front the diadem was made,
Meet for your hand the laurel is arrayed.
God, who with courage has my soul inspired,
God, who my speech with energy hath fired,
Is ready now his favour to impart,
Dare but believe, dare rouse your softened heart,
Follow at least this Amazon elect,
She is thy stay, thy throne she will protect;
The King of Kings by her illustrious arm,
Will save our altars and our laws from harm;
Joan shall with thee, this family appal,
This English family; the scourge of Gaul.
Be but a man—and if, as I suppose,
Some girl must always lead you by the nose;

At least, fly her, whose soft but treacherous chain
Your heart subdues and is at once your bane;
And worthy so of this assistance strange
Follow the steps of her who will avenge.
'Twas but of late, my friend, you learned the truth
When Louis fled the arms of blooming youth,
That beauty exorcised by Linière
In the Low Country, on Rhine's bank so fair
He came to rouse him with fame's clarion breath,
And instant vanished every fear of death.
However vice Gaul's monarch may controul,
There's still a fund of honour in his soul."

 The veteran soldier's speech propitious proved,
And drowsy slumber from the monarch moved.
So an Archangel, on the last great day,
Appearing high, in terrible array,
Shall with trumpet's voice terrific, shake
The Universe and death's long bondage break,
From dreary tombs the sleeping ghosts invite,
And call re-animated dust to light!
Charles is awake, his soul with ardour warms,
His only answer is to cry: "To arms!"
He grasps his lance, and only longs to fight;
In war, not pleasure now, he finds his charms.
Recovered soon from transport's sudden heat,
When cooler reason reassumed her seat,
The maid he'd see, and judge of her intent,
Whether by Heaven or by Satan sent;
Whether as truth the prodigy to treat,
Or deem the whole a fiction and a cheat;
Turning his head toward the dauntless Joan
Thus spoke the King in a majestic tone,
Which any might have feared but she alone:
"Joan, hear me: Joan, if thou'rt a maid, avow!"
Joan answered: "Oh, great Sire, give orders now
That learned leeches, spectacles on nose,
Well versed in female mysteries to depose,
With clerks, apothecaries, matrons tried,
Be summoned here the matter to decide.

In such affairs whoever boasts of skill,
May truss up Joan, and forthwith gaze his fill!"
　　From this reply, which wisdom's help had fired,
The King perceived the maiden was inspired.
"Good!" said the King, "since this you know so well,
Daughter of Heaven, I pray thee, instant tell
What with my fair one passed last night in bed?
Speak free!" "Why nothing, Sire!" Joan promptly said.
Surprised, the king knelt down, and cried aloud
"A miracle!" then crossed himself, and bowed.
Immediately appeared the fur-capped band,
Their bonnets on, Hippocrates in hand,
Came to observe the bosom fine and pure
Of the Amazon who must their gaze endure.
Naked they stripped her, and the senior sage
Having considered all that could engage,
Above, below, on parchment then displayed
Certification that Joan was a maid.
　　This brevet bold, replete with sacred grace,
Joan took and marching on with measured pace,
Straight to the King returned, and on her knee
She showed her spoils of war triumphantly,
Which she had won from England in the night.
"Permit," said she, "Oh, monarch of great might,
That subject to thy laws thy servant's arm
Dare France avenge and banish her alarm;
Fulfilled shall be the oracles, I swear;
Nay, by my courage, in thy sight, I dare,
By this my maidenhead and this bright blade,
Vouch that at Rheims you soon shall be arrayed
Full King, anointed with the holy oil;
Of conquered English you shall reap the spoil,
Who now the gates of Orléans surround.
Come and fulfil thy destiny profound;
Come and abandoning the banks of Tours,
Count me henceforth a servitor of yours."
The courtiers pressed around her in amaze,
Some looked towards Heaven, some bent on Joan the gaze,
Each seconded alike the bold discourse,
And shouted joyously till they grew hoarse.

No warrior was there in the noble crowd
But as a squire to serve her had been proud,
Her lance to bear and gladly life resign;
Not one was there but owned the glow divine,
The thirst for fame and felt a wish most strong,
To ravish that which she had kept so long.
The knights make preparation to depart;
One greets the ancient mistress of his heart;
One to an usurer for credit prays,
One reckons with his host and never pays.
Denis unfurled the Oriflamme on high,
And at the sight proud grew the monarch's eye;
The Heaven-sent banner waving in his sight;
Filled him with hope coequal with his might;
Convinced a heroine and an ass with wings
Must bring him palms and rare immortal things.
Denis desired on quitting this retreat,
That the two lovers should by no means meet;
Too many tears their last adieux had cost,
Agnes still slept, although the hour was late
Little she thought of such a turn of fate;
A happy dream with soft illusive charms,
Gave her enamoured monarch to her arms;
Retraced the transports of the former day,
Too transient joys, that fled too fast away!
Deceitful dream to flatter thus the sense!
The lover flies and Denis leads him hence.
At Paris thus a Doctor of great skill
Will let the glutton eat but half his fill,
Inexorable prove to every wish,
And pitiless remove his favourite dish.
    No sooner could the saint succeed to win
The King of France from his delightful sin,
Than swift he ran to seek his pleasing care,
His valiant Virgin, his redoubted fair.
He had resumed his beatific air
His tone devout, his flat and short-cut hair,
The hallowed ring, the crozier pastoral,
The gloves, the cross, the cap episcopal.
"Go on," he cried; "thy monarch serve and France,

On thee shall ever fall my gracious glance
But with the laurel of high courage twine
The rose of modesty; let both combine.
Thy steps will I to Orléans safely lead.
When Talbot, mighty chief of miscreant breed,
By lust infernal fired, and heart enchained,
Shall think Dame President impure is gained,
Beneath thine arm robust shall end his fame;
Punish his crime, but never do the same;
Let true devotion with true courage vie!
I go—adieu—guard thy Virginity!"
The fair one made a solemn vow she'd try,
Whereat her patron started for the sky.

3

Description of the Palace of Folly—Combat near Orléans—Agnes
disguises herself in Joan's armour in order to rejoin her lover—
She is taken prisoner by the English and her modesty
is put to great straits.

'Tis not enough in courage to abound,
Or view with eye serene the battle's rage.
Men fit to lead a world of troops are found
In every climate, and in every age.
For in due turn each nation hath its share
Of horrid war, and Death's terrific dance
In equal portion. Nor doth aught declare
Britons out-done by the bold sons of France;
Nor is Iberia less than Germany:
Each has been beat and each shall beaten be!
Great Condé was o'ercome by brave Turenne;
And haughty Villars yielded to Eugene.
Whilst he, who for King Stanislas drew forth
His warlike bands, the Quixote of the North,
Whose valour seemed quite pure of human stain;
Did he not see, in depths of far Ukraine,
At Pultava, his laurels brought to naught
By a poor rival quite beneath his thought.
A happier secret far, might I advise,
Would be, to cheat and dazzle vulgar eyes,
In my esteem; 'tis far the surest way
To rank a God, thus leading foes astray;
The mighty Romans, to whose power all bowed
Europe subdued 'mid miracles a cloud.
Mars, Pollux, Jupiter, the gods all sought
To guide the eagle; each for Romans fought.
Great Bacchus, who all Asia rendered slave,
Old Hercules and Alexander brave,

That each with awe the vanguished might inspire,
Proclaimed alike great Jupiter his sire;
Wherefore, proud monarchs of the earth with dread,
When'er it thundered knelt and bowed the head.
    Denis full well these famed examples knew,
And to the marvellous had recourse too;
He vowed that maiden Joan, with Albion's race
Should pass for holy and a girl of grace:
That Bedford, Talbot famed for gallantry,
Tyrconnell, Chandos, man of mockery,
Should deem all supernatural in Joan
And in her arm, a force superior own.
To prosper in this enterprise so bold,
He sought a Benedictine friar old;
Not one whose labours famed were to enhance
The literary stores that blazon France;
A prior this, grown fat in ignorance,
Who ne'er enriched the libraries of France,
No controverted points disturbed his head,
Though but his missal Brother Lourdis read.
Hard by the moon, where erstwhile as they say
The Paradise of fools was held to lay,
Near that abyss profound, where endless night
And Erebus and Chaos meet the sight,
Which, ere the time the universe was made,
Knew no controul, and their blind power displayed,
To a vast, cavernous and dismal place,
Whose gloom the pleasant sunbeams never grace;
Where nothing but a light terrific gleams,
Diffusing pale, deceitful, trembling beams;
An *Ignis Fatuus* its only star,
Hobgoblins wanton in the peopled air.
Of this fell country Folly is the queen,
An aged child, who with gray beard is seen,
With mouth like Danchet, long-eared and squint-eyed,
Club footed, moving with a limping stride;
Of Ignorance, 'tis said, the child is she:
Around her throne is ranged her family,
Obduracy and Pride in Folly's dress,
Credulity and sluggard idleness.

Though vainly weak and impotent the while,
She's served and flattered in the regal style;
A forceless phantom, despicable thing,
Like Chilperic, that truly idle King.
Her greedy minister is one, Deceit,
And all is ruled by this official cheat;
Folly he deems his worthy instrument.
Her courts are furnished to her heart's content;
Folk, who astrology have studied long,
Sure of their art, but always proving wrong,
Though dupes and knaves, believed incontinent,
'Tis there you find the skilled in alchemy,
Producing gold but still in penury,
And Rosicrucians, and those mad-folk, all,
Who try their wits on points theological.
    Of all the brothers of fat Lourdis' sect,
Himself the Saint thought fitting to elect;
When night on clouds of curling vapour flew,
And o'er the Heavens her sable mantle threw,
Reposefully, with slumber on his eyes
He started off to Folly's Paradise;
Arriving there, he woke without surprise.
All pleased him there; 'twas just as it might be
Within the precinct of his monastery.
Here, in this antique dwelling, met his view
Symbolic paintings, excellently true.
Caco the Demon, who this temple graced,
Scribbled at pleasure and its walls defaced;
Depicting all our follies in burlesque,
Silly exploits, absurdities grotesque
Projects ill-planned and executed ill,
Though praised by monthly paper at its will.
In this strange mass of wonders which confuse,
Amidst impostors, who good sense abuse,
Was drawn a hero, who from Scotland came,
France's new monarch—Law his well known name.
Upon his head a paper crown he wore,
And Scheme was written legibly before,
Great empty wind-bags compass him about,
Which to all comers, he is doling out;

The priest, the warrior, lawyer and the whore
Bring him their gold, in hopes to make it more.
O what a spectacle! For there too are
"*Sufficient*" Molina, soft Escobar!
And Doucin too, whose little, chubby fist
Extends that bull to be devoutly kissed,
Framed by Le Tellier in such clumsy sort,
That even at Rome it served for secret sport;
That Bull, which since, the origin has been
Of the disputes and cabals we have seen;
And what is more, of books profoundly wise
Filled, I am told, with heresies and lies,
All acting on the sense, as poisons chill,
Infusing soporific draughts at will.
These combatants, like new Bellerophons
Chimeras ride instead of stallions;
With bandaged eyes, they seek their foes around,
And cat-calls shrill supply the clarion's sound;
And in their holy franticness of mind
They urge the war with bladders stuffed with wind.
Ye Gods! what scribbling then appears to view!
What precepts, orders, expositions too!
Which still explained are and by pedants scanned,
For fear mankind the truth should understand.
O Chronicler of great Scamander's tribe,
Thou, who of yore didst frogs and rats describe!
Who sang so learnedly their combats dire;
O! quit the tomb and strike thy frenzied lyre,
To celebrate the fierceness of this war,
Which for the holy Bull extended far.
The Jansenist, by destiny beguiled,
Of *efficacious grace* the ruined child,
A saint Augustin on his banner bears,
For numbers marches and for nothing cares;
While foes, bent double crawl to the attack,
Each riding on a little abbé's back.
O! cease vile discord, nor the land disgrace!
All soon must change, you idiot tribe give place.
A tomb with no rich ornament o'erspread,
Near to Saint Medard rears its lofty head,

France to enlighten; heaven above conceals
Beneath this tomb its power, not aught reveals.
Whither the blind his course unsteady wends,
Then stumbling home again, his footstep bends;
The lame appears, a loud *Hosanna* calls,
Halts by the sepulchre, jumps, capers, falls!
The deaf approaches, listens and hears nought,
Anon come others, with vast riches fraught,
True wonder-vouchers, lost in ease and bliss,
The sanctuary of abbé Paris kiss.
Lourdis his large eyes rolls; and, like a clod
Looks on the work, then renders praise to God;
Grins like a fool, and joins the applauding bands,
Well pleased with all, he nothing understands.
    Mark well that wise tribunal's sable rows,
Prelates one half, the other monks compose.
Behold the blessed inquisitorial band,
See their unnumbered sbirri round them stand,
Enthroned to judge, each holy doctor wears
For robe the plumage which the screech-owl bears.
Long asses' ears adorn their heads august;
And well to weigh the just with the unjust,
And try when truth or falsehood most prevails,
They hold a balance with two ample scales;
One filled, displays the gold by cheating gained,
The wealth and blood from penitents they've drained;
The other's filled with Oremus and briefs,
Chaplets and Agnuses and bulls and fiefs.
Do you not see, before the doctors sage
Poor Galileo, harassed in old age,
Sueing for pardon in a tone contrite,
Justly condemned for being in the right?
    Thy walls, Loudun, with new lit faggots fume!
A curate now the ruthless flames consume.
Twelve rogues doom Urbain Grandier to die,
And bid him roast, condemned of sorcery.
O! dearest Galigai, to fame well known,
Ill treated by the parliament and throne;
That stupid cohort, venal, insincere,
Consumed thee 'mid a fire both hot and clear,

For having with the Devil compact made.
How men of sense should be of France afraid!
Where you must pope and hell at once believe,
A *pater* all the learning you receive.
Beyond I see two more decrees authentic
For Aristotle and against emetic.
But come, good Father Girard, 'fore the throne,
For something should be sung of you alone;
Then hither come, my confessor of maids,
Preacher devout, well versed in double trades.
What say you of the penitential charms,
The tender fair converted in your arms?
'Tis not for me at such success to rail;
We are but men, Girard, and flesh is frail.
You ne'er transgressed 'gainst Nature's sovran laws,
Great devotees are blamed for truer cause.
Yet, my good friend, this I expected not,
To see you mix the devil in your plot.
Girard, O! Girard, 'midst the bitter foes,
Whose grievous accusations wrought thy woes;
Whether or Jacobin or Carmelite,
May try who best can judge, or worst can write;
Or proffer aid or enmity declare,
There's not a single conjuror, I'll swear!
Lourdis, in fine said our old parliaments
Of some score bishops burn the testaments,
And by decree exterminate the school
Of one Ignatius, a pernicious fool;
Yet they themselves were in their turn decried;
Ignatius laughed, though Quesnel deeply sighed!
Paris, disturbed, beheld this fortune's freak,
And solace sought in *opéra comique*.
   O Folly! fat and foolish deity!
Whose fruitful womb supplies more progeny,
And earth with flocks of fools more amply loads
Than erst Cybele crowded Heaven with Gods!
With what delight thy heavy eyes have scanned
Thy countless children in my native-land.
Compilers stupid and translators dull,
Authors and readers just as thick of skull.

Deign tell me of this idiotic host
Which of thine offspring dost thou cherish most?
Which are most skilled to write in heavy way,
Most competent to stumble and to bray?
Behold! the scribe the most beloved of you,
The author of the *Journal de Trévoux!*

Whilst Denis thus in moon-shine now prepares
'Gainst Britain's sons his inoffensive snares;
New scenes, that differ wide from these, engage
The fools who tread this sublunary stage.
King Charles to Orléans his march inclined,
His gaudy banners waving in the wind;
Beside him Joan, with helm upon her head
Vows that to Rheims he shall anon be led.
Ah! see you not the youthful squires advance,
Right loyal Cavaliers, the flower of France;
With couchèd spear, these nobles, every one,
Respectfully surround the Amazon.
Thus at Fontevraux, woman's rights prevail,
The female sex commanding there the male;
In madam's grasp, the ruling sceptre's pressed,
And by my Lady Father Anselm's blessed.

Now Agnes, all forlorn, her loss deplored
Abandoned by the prince her soul adored.
Excess of grief o'er nature's force prevailed,
And death-like languor every sense concealed,
Bonneau administered with anxious care
Restoring cordials to the swooning fair;
She opes her eyes, those eyes so sweet and clear,
Only once more to sigh and shed a tear.
On Bonneau then reclining her fair head,
"'Tis done, I am betrayed, the lady said.
Where strays he, and what will he undertake?
His vows and oaths he only meant to break;
Which were so often sworn, when first he strove
To gain my acquiescence with his love.
Without my lover must I rest at night,
Upon that couch the scene of our delight;
And yet, that dauntless female Warrior Joan,
Not England's enemy, but mine alone,

Against me strives to prepossess his mind
Heaven! how I loathe such creatures unrefined,
Soldiers in petticoats, hags turned to knights,
Of the male sex affecting valour's rites;
Without possessing all the charms of ours,
Of both pretending to usurp the powers,
And who the attributes of neither know."
Speaking she blushed as tears began to flow;
With rage she trembles and with grief she cries,
The gust of rage shot lightning from her eyes,
When, on a sudden, tender love benign
Instilled into her brain a new design.
To Orléans town anon her course she bent,
With her Dame Alix and good Bonneau went;
Fair Agnes gained an inn, where then at rest,
Slept Joan, who with hard riding had been pressed.
Agnes, till all were sunk to rest remained,
And craftily full information gained,
Where Joan was lying, where her armour lay;
Then soft approaching, bore with joy away
Chandos' breeches, into which she thrusts
Her tender thighs; the garment she adjusts;
In the bright breast plate her fair form arrays;
The stout steel forged expressly for affrays
Tears her white skin and bruises all her charms;
But Bonneau half supports her in his arms.
Then beauteous Agnes in a voice intense:
"O! Love, thou mighty master of my sense!
Endue with strength this little hand so frail,
Grant me to bear this heavy coat of mail,
To better win the author of my bale.
A female warrior now my lord requires,
Make Agnes warlike then for his desires;
I'll follow him, and grant whate'er betide,
This very day I combat at his side;
And if toward him war's tempest should be led,
And showers of English darts surround his head,
Let Agnes' sorry charms receive them all,
Let him, at least, be saved by my sad fall!
Let him live happy, so my latest sigh

Be wafted in his arms—content I die!"
Thus the fair prayed, while Bonneau led the way,
Where Charles the King at three miles' distance lay.
'Twas night, yet eager Agnes would depart,
To seek the darling monarch of her heart.
So thus arrayed and sinking 'neath her weight,
Cursing her arms and wailing her sad fate,
Perched on a horse, to find her love she strayed
Bruised her plump thighs, and her firm buttocks flayed.
Fat Bonneau on a Norman courser proud,
Rode heavy at her side, and snorted loud,
While tender Cupid trembling for the fair,
Saw her depart and sighed with anxious care.
    Scarce had sweet Agnes her escape made good
When straight was heard within a neighbouring wood
The noise of horses and the clash of arms
The noise redoubles: lo! the brave gendarmes
In scarlet clad; and to increase her pains,
'Twas Chandos' troop which that night scoured the plains.
One forth advancing cries: "Who passes there?"
At this commanding voice, the innocent fair
Thought of the King, and all evasion shed:
"'Tis Agnes, long live Love and France!" she said.
At these two names, which the just power on high,
Wished to unite by the most lasting lie,
Agnes and her fat confident they take,
And lead to Chandos, who, his wrath to slake
Had sworn great vengeance for his honour's sake,
Against the sneaking robbers, who had fled
Stealing his sword and breeches while in bed.
    Just as the power beneficent and wise
Dispels the balm of sleep that veils our eyes;
When tuneful birds begin the matin lay,
And man with strength renewed salutes the day,
When, with rekindled vigour all his fire
Within his bosom glows with love's desire;
Just then to Chandos was the fair one brought,
The lovely Agnes with each beauty fraught,
Which Phoebus boasts, when rising from the flood;
Chandos awake! how flowed thy boiling blood,

When at thy side thou saw'st the fair one sad
Bearing thy sword, and in thy small clothes clad.
The hero, started to renewed desire
Devoured the lady with a look of fire,
And Agnes quaked; she heard him, muttering, say:
"Anon, my breeches I shall bear away!"
First, on the bolster placing his sweet prize:
"Quit, my fair captive," said he, "this disguise;
Cast off these ponderous arms, unfit for thee,
And shine, arrayed in beauty's livery."
He ceased, then filled with hope and ardour too
Her helmet and her breast-plate quick withdrew;
Struggling, the fair defended each bright charm
And blushed, for modesty had ta'en alarm,
Thinking of Charles, but bowed to conqueror's will.
Bonneau by Chandos destined was to fill,
Within his kitchen the *chef's* high employ,
And thither instantly he speeds with joy,
Of puddings white, inventor famed was he;
And O French people! 'tis to him, that ye
Indebted are for eel pies which ye praise,
And that delightful *gigot á la braise*.

   Agnes exclaimed in tender, trembling tone,
"Oh, Monsieur Chandos, please leave me alone:
What are you doing? Prithee, Sir, forbear!"
"Ods Zooks!" quoth he (all English heroes swear),
"Someone hath done me very crying wrong
The breeches, which you wear, to me belong,
And when I find that which by right is mine,
I'll have it, I protest, by powers divine."
To argue thus and Agnes to strip nude,
Was the same thing; the fair one, handled rude,
Wept, struggling in his arms, 'gainst his intent,
"Never," she loud assured him, "I consent!"
   Just at this moment a loud din was heard,
To arms! To arms! is everywhere the word;
The trumpet's clamour death's portentous sound,
Called to the charge, and shrilly echoed round.
Joan, when awake, astonished, found no more
Those manly trappings which she lately wore;

Her helmet shaded by the rich aigrette,
The coat of mail, and eke the huge *braguette*,
Ne'er balancing in doubt, brave Joan anon,
A lowly squire's plain armour buckled on,
Vaulted her winged ass, and loudly cried:
"Come, cavaliers, support your country's pride."
Of knights one hundred straight obeyed her call
Six hundred and eke one score men in all.
From the gay palace where queen Folly reigns,
Lourdis just then alighted 'midst the plains;
And at that juncture critical appeared
Amongst the British phalanx so much feared.
His bulky figure atoms gross surround,
And on his broad back fooleries abound.
Dull ignorance and works of monks he bore;
Thus saddled he arrived, and then his store,
Forth from the full robe he contented shook,
And on the British camp dropped every book
Of filthy ignorance, his treasures vast,
Treasures throughout all France profusely cast.
As when of Night the sable deity,
Mounted on spangled car of ebony,
Charms with profoundest sleep our weary eyes,
And all our senses lulls 'midst dreams and lies.

4

Were I a King, I'd always justly deal,
Give peace at home, and guard the public weal;
And every day of my auspicious reign
Should some new benefit or grace attain.
If of Finance I had myself control
I'd give to men of sense; to men of soul
On every side my bounty I'd accord;
For, after all they merit due reward.
Or were I an archbishop I would seek
To tame the Jansenist and make him meek;
But if I loved a young and tender fair
To stay with her would be my constant care,
And every day my love fresh sights should see,
While banished thus dull uniformity,
Her heart I'd keep and she should live for me.
Say, happy lovers, can ye absence bear,
Or safely from your blooming mistress stay?
Ye risk, alas, if once ye quit the fair,
To be made cuckolds, twice or thrice a day!
Bold Chandos, fired with love and ripe for joy,
With his fair prey had scarce begun to toy,
When through the ranks Joan hurries, in a breath
To scatter blood around and carry death.
With Deborah's so long redoubted lance
She ran through Dildo, foe avowed of France
Who rifled the ripe treasures of Clervaux
And ravished all the nuns of Fontevraux.
Next Faulkner worthy of the gibbet, dies,
Struck through the temple and through both his eyes;
This brazen fellow, bred 'midst fogs and rime,

In the dark regions of Hibernia's clime,
Made love in France, three years, as if at home
Like a spoilt child of Florence or of Rome,
She overturns the great Lord Halifax,
His cousin too, the impudent Borax;
Midarblou, who his worthy sire denied
And Bartonay who had his brother's bride.
At her example there was not a knight,
A squire or soldier in this bloody fight,
Who did not with his lance run through some ten
Of these redoubted, hardy Englishmen;
Terror and death preceded their career,
No man but fought divested of all fear;
Their bosoms glowed with superstitious pride,
For each believed the Lord was on his side.
    Amidst this tempest and this bloody brawl,
Lourdis roured out as loud as he could bawl:
"She is a maid, so tremble, England's crew;
It is Saint Denis, who is armed 'gainst you!
She is a maid and miracles hath wrought,
Against her arm your prowess is as nought.
Quick on your knees, ye scum of Albion fall,
And humbly for her benediction call!"
Fierce Talbot, foaming at the mouth with ire
Seized instantly upon the babbling friar;
They bound him, yet the monk their rage defied;
He moved not, but with mouth distended, cried:
"Martyr am I, but, English, ye shall see;
She is a maid, she'll gain the victory!"
Man's credulous, and by his wavering mind
All is received; it is a clay refined;
And like that clay, it readily receives
The strong impression sudden terror leaves.
These words of Lourdis failed not to impart
More dread effect to every soldier's heart,
Than troop heroic and Joan's martial charms,
Aided by courage and their conquering arms.
That instinct old which prodigies believes,
Erroneous sense, which troubles and deceives,
Illusions and chill fear their poisons shed

And turn the sense of every British head.
Not yet had hardy Britons learned to vie
In deep researches of philosophy,
Most gallant knights were most illiterate;
And wits reserved to grace a later date.
    Full of assurance, Chandos to his band
Exclaimed: "My men, victorious in the land,
Wheel to the right!" The words were scarcely said,
Ere to the left they veered and swearing, fled.
Thus on the plain where famed Euphrates flows,
Presumptuous mortals did of old propose
To exert the utmost stretch of human power
And build proud Babel's heaven aspiring tower,
Till Heaven, which relished their approach no whit,
The tongue of man into a hundred split;
So, when one called for water or for food,
They brought him mortar or a piece of wood,
And this poor people of whom God made fun,
Were fain to part and leave their work undone.
    Soon at the ramparts of great Orléans town
Was clarioned of this combat the renown;
Thither, in winged flight went trumpet Fame,
And spread abroad of Joan the sainted name.
You know our folk's impetuosity,
How honour is their mad idolatry;
They go to battle just as to a dance!
Dunois, that Mars in Greece might personate
Dunois, so proudly illegitimate,
With Richemont, La Trimouille, Saintrailles, La Hire,
Sally from out the walls devoid of fear,
Presage success, and shout exultingly,
"Where, where are now these dastard enemy?"
They were not far, for near the gate we find
Stout Talbot, hero of capacious mind,
To check French ardour, this bold chief had laid
Ten stout battalions in snug ambuscade.
For one day past, Sir Talbot had aloud
To George (his patron saint) and Cupid vowed
To try each stratagem, essay each art,
Might gain the double object of his heart

Since the fat Louvet's most fastidious dame
With more than friendship met the hero's flame;
A double wreath he hoped might crown his care,
He'd sack the city and possess the fair.
Scarce through the gate had passed each cavalier
When hardy Talbot fell upon their rear;
Whereat our French were not surprised at all.
O plain of Orléans! noble stage though small,
From this brave conflict stubborn on each side,
Flowed human blood that all thy verdure dyed,
Which fattened for an hundred years the ground.
At Zama nor Pharsalia was there found,
Nor could Malplaquet's sanguinary field
For raging Mars a scene more glorious yield;
No, not e'en those where thousands found a grave
A combat fiercer boasted—feats more brave;
There, might be seen the mounted knights advance
And into splinters break each shivered lance;
Riders and palfreys sprawling on the plain.
Remounting straight and to the fight again;
From clashing swords bright scintillations play
That render doubly luminous the day.
On all sides flew and fell 'mid these alarms
Noses, chins, shoulders, legs and feet and arms.
      Angels belligerent, from heavenly height
Looked down with horror at the dubious fight,
Proud Michael and that other by his side
Erst the chastiser of the Persians' pride,
Michael, at length, the doughty balance rears
That counterpoised terrestrial affairs,
Those scales, wherewith mankind is weighed on high,
With steady hand to try the destiny
Of Albion's heroes and the sons of France.
Our knights thus justly poised, such proved the chance,
That Gaul unluckily was light of weight,
Great Talbot was the favourite of Fate;
Such Heaven's judgment, framed in secrecy
Le Richemont finds himself incontinently
Pierced through the haunch; Saintrailles upon the knee.
Le Hire was wounded where I dare not say

Alack! his lady-love will curse the day;
And La Trimouille could not escape from harm,
Plunged in a bog, he stuck with broken arm.
Thus wounded, back to Orléans were they led
And each, incontinent consigned to bed;
And may their punishment vain scoffers warn
Never again to treat a saint with scorn.
    God can or pardon or condemn, we know
Quesnel has said it, so it must be so,
And that the Bastard should be quite released
From other mockers' fate he now was pleased.
Whilst all the rest, on litters homewards borne,
Maimed and disfigured, their rash conduct mourn,
While each of fortune and of Joan complained,
Our brave Dunois without a scratch remained.
He shot like lightning to the hottest fray,
And through whole British Squadrons hewed his way;
Until he reached the quarters where the maid
Swept all before her, and great havoc made.
When rapid torrents their full floods unite,
Precipitating from some mountain's height,
Nought can the rage of mingled waves restrain,
They drown the rustic's hopes, deluge the plain.
But direr still were brave Dunois and Joan
When once they met and struck like one alone.
Such was their ardour, chasing England's host,
That soon to their own party they were lost;
The night-shades fall; our Bastard and the maid,
Nor French nor Chandos hearing in the glade,
Their converse closing, waved aloft the lance
And halting cried: "Forever flourish France!"
By moonlight, as drear silence reigned around,
A pathway leading through a wood they found;
Forward they sped, then turned, but all in vain;
O'ercome with toil and hunger's gnawing pain;
With searching tired, their palfreys wearied too,
Each 'gan alike the cursed adventure rue.
What use to win, when of no bed they knew?
Thus the light bark, her sails and compass lost,
Veers round, by Aeolus and Neptune tossed.

A dog just then appeared to our sad pair,
Seeming expressly sent to ease their care;
He barked, then wagged his tail and straight drew near
And fondled them, without a sign of fear;
And seemed in his odd dialect to say:
"Follow me, Gentlemen! This is the way,
Here's board and lodging for you, come away!"
Our heroes by such manners understood
This worthy dog was hither for their good,
Wherefore, with hope for guide, they followed straight,
Praying that France might share propitious Fate,
And lauding each the other's martial soul
Which nought terrestrial could e'er control.
With glance lascivious oft Dunois surveyed,
Spite of himself the beauty of the maid;
Though well he knew, that Gallia's fate must rest
With that choice jewel which the fair possest,
And ruin absolute had France to fear
If the fair flower was plucked within the year.
He stifled nobly, therefore, his desire
And for the State subdued love's wanton fire;
Yet ever when a roughness of the ways
The saintly ass to a false step betrays,
Dunois, officious and with ardour warm,
The valiant maid supported with his arm,
While Joan of Arc, and not without a wink,
On his left shoulder lets her head to sink.
Whence it arrived, that as they slowly went
Their lips encountered oft, but with intent
To speak more closely of what might relate
To theirs, or to the glory of the State.
    Report hath told me, Konigsmark so fair!
That the twelfth Charles, of humour passing rare,
He who could conquer Kings and love subdue
Ne'er at his brutal court dared suffer you;
Charles felt and feared to render thee the arms,
And in his caution shunned thy brilliant charms.
But Joan to clasp, and yet not touch the treat!
To sit at table hungry, and not eat!
A score-fold finer victory is to tell.

Dunois was like that Robert D'Arbrisselle,
That Saint who loved to lie at set of sun,
On either side of him, a tempting nun,
To squeeze four limbs and stroke the soft, white skin
Of four plump breasts—succeeding not to sin.
With dawn of day expands before their eyes
A sumptuous palace of tremendous size;
Reared were the walls of marble white and clear,
There lofty Doric colonnades appear,
Whereon was seen, with porcelain balustrade
A terrace wide of purest jasper made.
Enchaunted both beheld this edifice,
Believing they had entered Paradise.
The good dog barks, and twenty trumpets then
Were heard to sound; and forty serving-men
In doublets gay, with gold and silver bright,
Run to attend the maiden and the knight.
Two youthful pages of a gallant air
Led them within the palace-gate with care;
Hand-maidens come, and golden baths they try,
Then serve an ample breakfast when they're dry.
So on rich couches, buried in delight
Heroically, from morn they snored till night.
    'Tis fitting to my readers I record
Who of this sumptuous mansion was the Lord:
This edifice for master owned the son
Of one of those etherial sprights who run
A course eterne through heaven's regions bright,
Whose grandeur oft abandons such delight,
To humanize with our poor, feeble race;
This spirit, mingling then his flesh divine
With a young nun of Order Bernardine,
Unto this incubus and Dame Alix,
For issue came the noble Hermaphrodix,
Great wizard, worthy of his parentage.
The day he reached his fourteenth year of age,
From heights above his parent winged his flight,
Crying: "My child, to me you owe the light:
Make known the wishes of your heart, and I
To each and all will speedily comply."

Hermaphrodix, who had from childhood been
Voluptuous, worthy his high origin,
Replied: "My bosom glows with heavenly fires,
I know myself divine by my desires
All pleasures I would taste I must confess,
And glut my soul with hot voluptuousness.
'Tis my desire as either sex to love;
Wherefore by night, let me the female prove,
And with returning day, man's form resume."
The sire replied: "Be such, my son, thy doom!"
Since which the monster has by days and nights
Assumed of either sex the joys and rights.
Thus Plato, who to confidence aspires
With gods, pretends that our primeval sires,
Of pure clay formed and fashioned cunningly,
Were born complete and called Androgynae;
Each with the power of either sex supplied,
And with inherent virtues satisfied.
Higher than this, Hermaphrodix's lot:
For pleasure that in solitude is got
Is not a destiny divinely fair;
Better it is companion joys to share;
And thus celestial bliss in couples taste.
His courtiers vowed as he by turns embraced,
'Twas Venus now, performing tender rite,
Now Love, alloying wanton appetite.
In all directions girls they sought to find,
Young, lusty bachelors and widows kind.

But when Hermaphrodix this boon desired
He never asked what was the most required
A gift without which every joy must freeze,
A charming gift, and what? The art to please.
For this unruly wish 'twas God's decree
Uglier than Samuel Bernard, he should be;
No conquest ever could his glance command,
In vain were fêtes dispensed with liberal hand,
Long banquets, balls, and concerts to invite—
Nay, though he sometimes too would verses write;
Yet when, by day, the fair one he would see,
Or when, at night his female vanity

Subjected was to some audacious boy,
Fate still betrayed him, and curtailed his joy:
Nor aught return could his endearments gain,
Than insult and rebuff, disgust, disdain.
Just Heaven in sadness made him well confess
That grandeur is not always happiness.
"What!" he would cry, "the chamber-maid most vile
Enjoys upon her breast a gallant's smile,
Each ensign to some lovely sempstress runs,
The monks within their cloisters have their nuns,
Whilst I, a genie rich, who grace a throne,
I on this moving orb stand all alone,
Of bliss deprived while others boast a store."
By all the elements anon he swore,
That punishment on either sex he'd deal
Who should refuse for him Love's glow to feel;
And that examples bloody each should share,
The youth ungrateful and the obdurate fair.

    As king, he greeted each chance guest, I ween;
Of Sheba, erst the famous, tawny queen,
Talestris, who at Persia's court sojourned,
Presents less costly from those monarchs earned,
Who for each dame confessed himself Love's slave,
Than he to errant knights his largess gave,
To bachelors and every beauteous miss;
But when a restive soul denied him bliss,
Fell short in complaisance he might require
And shunned in trivial point his lewd desire;
For such affront his anger did not fail,
Alive the poor offender to impale.

    The night was come; and, owning female flame,
Four ushers from my lady's presence came,
Praying our amiable, bold Bastard straight
To come down stairs and have a *tête-à-tête*,
While squires and ushers in attendance wait
That Joan, in company, might dine in state.
The perfumed Dunois, by this escort led,
The *boudoir* entered where was supper spread,
Such as the sister erst of Ptolemy,
Yielding to every pleasure licence free,

To those illustrious Romans amply gave,
Heroes at once voluptuous and brave,
To Caesar, Antony, with passion drunk;
Such as myself once shared at board of monk,
Proclaimed the victor o'er each stupid foe,
And dubbed with tonsure Abbot of Clairvaulx.
Of such the feast that graced Heaven's conclave blue,
If Ovid and friend Orpheus tell us true,
And brother Homer, Hesiod and Plato,
When the great lord of infidels, you know,
With Semele, supped far from Juno's view,
With Isis and Europa, Danae too;
With dishes ranged upon the board's divinity,
By the fair hands of soft Euphrosyne,
And of Thalia and Aglai the young
As Graces three, of old so often sung,
Whose law our pedants seldom make their guide;
Of nectar Hebe served the luscious tide,
And the sweet son of him who founded Troy,
The famed Mount Ida's eagle-wafted boy,
His lord's cup-bearer and his secret joy;
Such of Hermaphrodix the feast was then
With Dunois shared 'twixt nine o'clock and ten.
  Madame with lavish hand had decked her head,
Surcharged the front, with diamonds overspread,
Her yellow neck, and arms of skin and bone
Circled by neck-laces and bracelets shone.
Adorned with precious pearls and rubies bright
She seemed more hideous to the hero's sight.
She gently pressed his hand, the supper o'er;
He trembled now, who never feared before!
Though famed for courtesy, he in vain prepares
To pay with kind returns his hostess' cares;
And when her hideous figure caught his view,
He said: "'Tis what in honour I should do!"
Yet nothing could—the bravest in such case,
May sometimes suffer similar disgrace.
Hermaphrodix, who keen affliction felt
For Dunois' plight, was almost fain to melt;
In secret she confessed a keen delight

At the great efforts of the cheerless knight
Nor was he doomed, without reprieve to bleed.
The will thus once was taken for the deed!
Quoth she: "The morrow for a feat so rare,
May offer you revenge. Go and prepare,
That to warm love your cold respect may bend;
Be ready, Lord! and better serve mine end."
    Already Day's advance guard from afar
In Orient had withdrawn night's murky bar,
The fates, you know, did to this hour affix
The male mutation of Hermaphrodix.
Burning with new desires he sought the bed
Where tranquilly reposed the doughty maid,
Drew back the curtain, and abruptly pressed,
With hand impertinent, her heaving breast,
Would burning kisses to her lips apply,
And thus attack celestial modesty;
As vile Hermaphrodix lascivious grew,
More hideous was his person to the view;
Joan, animated by celestial glow,
With nervous arm inflicts a mighty blow:
Amid my fertile plains, 'tis thus I've seen,
One of my mares upon a meadow green,
Unequal spotted of the tiger dye,
Possessing lightsome hoofs, dams bounding high,
With direful and avenging kick reprove
An ass's colt with crupper thus in love,
Which so caressing, grossly in the rear
Thought itself blessed, and high upraised the ear.
That Joan in this was faulty is most true;
Respectful feelings to her host were due;
I feel for modesty warm interest,
That virtue ne'er was banished from my breast.
Yet when a prince, or genie full of fire
For ladies' favours marks a strong desire,
When his swoll'n bosom with fond wishes glows,
'Tis hard to recompense such warmth with blows.
The son of Alix, though an ugly brute,
Had ne'er met maid dared thus his will dispute.
He cries, guards, pages; valets in a band,

Arch imps arrive, obedient to command;
One telling him, the maiden fierce could be
Less cruel to her friend in chivalry.
O Calumny! thou poison of all courts,
Malicious scandal, slander, false reports;
Cursed serpents, must your hissing's dire appal
The bliss of lovers, like the court of Gaul?
Our tyrant wronged thus, in a two-fold way,
Resolved upon revenge without delay;
Pronouncing to his myrmidons thus hailed,
The dreadful sentence: "Let them be impaled."
His words their law, the ready guards prepare
The implements of death with horrid care.
Joan and Dunois, the flower of Chivalry
Are thus condemned in life's gay spring to die.
Naked and bound the fair Bastard they take,
Shortly to seat him on a pointed stake.
And at that juncture, by a troop profane,
To scaffold, proud and beauteous Joan is ta'en,
Her tempting charms and her o'er-hasty blow
To expiate by infamy and woe.
From Joan's fair form the lily shift they tore,
And as she passed her lovely body bore
Stripes from the rods of those who carried her,
And passed her to the executioner.
Not all their rage could Dunois' firmness blast,
Though every hour he thought must prove his last;
Resigned he oft addressed th'omnipotent,
But when from time to time around he bent
A glance imperious, each was thrilled with dread,
All spoke the hero which he did or said;
But when Dunois beheld the Pride of France
Avengeress of its lilies, thus advance,
And death prepared for her his soul adored,
Then Fortune's fickleness he first deplored:
His eyes surveyed the graces of the Fair,
And while these men of death the stake prepare,
He wept, to see her like a victim led,
The tears which for himself he scorned to shed.
    Equal in charity and just as proud,

Attacks of fear the Maiden ne'er allowed,
On Dunois languidly she cast her eye,
For him alone her great heart heaved a sigh;
Their youth, their beauty and their nakedness
In their despite, awoke their tenderness.
A flame so constant, so discreet, so brave,
But blazed upon the borders of the grave;
The animal amphibious, at the sight,
Mingling his jealousy with bitter spite,
Straight to his minions gave the signal dire
That doomed on stakes the couple to expire.
A voice that moment, like the thunder's shock,
Making the earth and airy regions rock,
Cried: "Hold each executioner his hand;
Impale them not!" These words soon awed the band
The lictors gazed around and then withdrew,
For 'neath the gate a churchman met their view;
Whose cowl and frock, his girdle, sandaled shoon
Announced the reverend father Grisbourdon.
Thus when an hound within the neighbouring wood,
Reared for the chase, with nose both staunch and good,
Scents the fleet hart that courses o'er the lawn,
Roused by the echo of the bugle horn,
The dog runs lightly on the course intent,
Sees not the game, but follows by the scent,
Leaps the wide ditch and clears the hedge by force,
No other stag can then avert his course;
So—Saintly Francis of Assisi's son
Had on the traces of the maiden run,
Borne on his mule, and vowing, come what may,
No other scent should turn him from his way.
Arriving thus, he cried: "Hermaphrodix,
In Satan's name and by the flood of Styx,
And by the demon who has fathered thee,
And by thy mother's book of psalmistry,
Save her who hath my vows and plighted troth;
Behold me, I am come to ransom both.
So if this hero and this maid unskilled
Have not with thee their duty well fulfilled,
I will myself assume the place of two

And prove at once what feats a monk can do.
Nay more, this famous animal you see,
This mule so aptly formed to carry me,
Henceforth he's thine, for thee the beast was made,
Like monk, like mule, both follow the same trade.
Then send this clownish trooper to the wars,
And keep Joan here to soothe our mutual cares.
She is the price—we both demand no more
Than that rare beauty whom our hearts adore."
Joan shuddering, listened to a theme so fell:
Her holy faith, her cherished virgin spell,
Those thrills which love and grandeur's powers impart,
Were than her life, far dearer to her heart.
And Grace besides, of Heaven supremest dole,
Fought even Dunois' self within her soul.
She weeping to High Heaven her pangs disclosed,
And blushed, that naked she was thus exposed;
From time to time her eyelids shut would be,
Nought seeing, she believed that none could see.
     Despair, meanwhile, o'er came Dunois the brave,
"What!" he exclaimed, "shall this uncloistered knave,
Assisted by his impious arts alone,
Ruin my country and possess my Joan?
When I, condemned unheard-of ills to prove,
In modest silence hid till now my love!"
Of Grisbourdon, the offer thus polite
On the five senses of the infernal spright
A good effect produced; he calmed his ire,
And well content, exclaimed: "'Tis my desire
You and your mule tonight both ready be;
I pardon—set those French at liberty."
The friar gray possessed old Jacob's wand,
The ring that graced of Solomon the hand,
His clavicule, and the famed baton which
Sewed Pharoah's sorcerers as a magic switch,
And that same besom whereon rode of old
The toothless sorceress of Saul the bold,
When to that prince of kings imprudent most
At Endor once she summoned up a ghost.
The monk, who much as any of them knew,

First with his slender wand a circle drew,
Then backwards o'er his beast some ashes threw,
Repeating words with magic instance fraught,
By Zoroaster to the Persians taught.
At these big words, in Satan's language said,
(O power supreme! Marvel unparalelled!)
Our mule upon his hindmost legs uprose,
His oblong head, a rounder semblance chose,
His stiff black bristles little locks became,
But 'neath his cap his ears were still the same.
So in old times, that emperor so grand,
Whose proud obduracy by God's command,
Was punished by condemning him to pass
Seven years an ox, and feed upon the grass;
Yet when the guise of man anew he bore,
He proved no better than he was before.

From the blue summit of the vaulted sky,
Denis regarded with a parent's eye,
The piteous state of our afflicted Joan,
And willingly had to her succour gone,
But troubled was the saint and full of care,
His journey thither proved a bad affair;
Bold George, of England was the patron saint,
Against Saint Denis he had lodged complaint,
Of having without orders gone too far
Against his Britons thus declaring war.
'Twixt Denis and Saint George, high words arose,
Spurred to the quick, they almost came to blows;
A British saint has in his character
A certain something, harsh and insular:
The nature of our soil holds strong control,
In vain may rest in Paradise the soul,
All is not pure, provincial accents still
At princes courts can not be dropped at will.

Reader, 'tis time I pause a little here,
Since I must furnish out a long career,
My breath is short; yet I were fain to sing
This wondrous business's unravelling,
What Joan performed, and what to all befell
Upon the Earth, in Heaven, and e'en in Hell.

5

Oh, let us keep the Christian path in view!
'Tis the best scheme, believe me, to pursue;
Each must at length his bounden duty own;
As for myself, in youth my mind was prone
To stews; and oft I loved the dance to grace,
Ne'er casting thought upon the Holy place,
Supping and sleeping with the nymphs of love,
And mocking those who serve the powers above.
What happens then? Death, fatal Death appears
With his flat nose, and his sharp scythe uprears,
And cuts quite short the *bons mots* of the wits;
The ardent fever, with unequal fits,
Bailiff of Atropos, ascendant gains;
Daughter of Styx she wrecks the puny brains.
At the bed-side the nurse and lawyer stay,
Crying: "The time is come, you must away!
Where would you, Gentleman, your bones should lay?"
As tardy issues the repentant breath,
Still lingering to proclaim its wish in Death;
Some call Saint Roch, Saint Martin to their aid,
Another to Nitouche devoutly prayed,
One singeth psalms, or Latin groans with pain,
They sprinkle holy water, all in vain.
At the bed's foot the evil one displays.
His hungry fangs till soul from body strays;
Then carries it to depths profound of Hell
Fit sojourn for perversities to dwell.
    'Tis time, dear reader, I should now record,
How Satan of infernal realms the lord,
To all his vassals banquet gave in state;

His hellish mansion-house was all in fête:
A vast recruiting had of late been made,
And demons quaffed to brethren of the trade,
A well known pope, a cardinal with a paunch,
A Northern king, and fourteen canons staunch,
Intendants three, and lazy monks a score,
Trios of councillors to swell the store,
All from the mortal places freshly sent
The stoves that burn below to supplement.
The horned King his black imps shouting hears,
And yields to mirth, surrounded by his peers.
Tipsy with that infernal nectar strong,
They sit and roar a hellish drinking-song,
When at the gate a sudden cry is heard:
"Good day—arrived—what here!" was straight the word,
"Brothers, 'tis he, the envoy whom we send;
'Tis Grisbourdon, our very faithful friend,
Welcome, great Grisbourdon, our ally tried,
Come in and warm yourself by our fire-side;
Doctor of Lucifer, great Grisbourdon,
Hell's high apostle, and our Satan's son."
Then was he hugged, caressed and kissed by all,
And led triumphant to the festive hall.
    Satan arising, cried: "O Hell-born child!
Pride of all debauchees, by sin defiled,
Thus soon I did not hope thy face to see,
On earth thou hast so useful been to me.
Who more than thee made realm populous?
Through thee France was a seminary for us;
For while in Gaul, thou gavest sin full scope:
To view thee here extinguishes my hope;
But fate's omnipotence we can't command,
So drink and set thyself at my right hand."
The cordelier with saintly horror kneels.
Kisses the gaffs on his great master's heels;
Then rising sorrowfully, casts his sight
On the dire regions of eternal night;
Dire realms of fire, wherein forever rest
Death, crimes and those by torments fell opprest;
Eternal throne on which the fiend was hurled,

Abyss immense which swallows up the world;
Entombing hoar antiquity so sage,
Love, talent, wit, grace, beauty, every age,
That crowd unnumbered and immortal crew,
True heaven-born race, but, Satan! made for you.
You know, my reader, in the flames of Hell,
The best of kings with the worst tyrants dwell.
Aurelius there, there Antonine we place,
And Trajan, model of each princely grace,
The gentle Titus, by mankind revered;
Two Catos, who as plagues of vice appeared;
Scipio, who well against temptation strove,
Who conquered Carthage, and who conquered Love.
There too you broil, learned and wise Plato,
Homer divine and eloquent Cicero;
You Socrates, the child of sapiency,
Martyr of God 'mid Greece's profanity;
Just Aristides, virtuous Solon, giv'n
All to the flames because they died unshriv'n.
But greater far was Grisbourdon's surprise,
When 'midst the glowing coals he cast his eyes
On king and saints, who graced a former age,
Renowned in legends and the historic page.
The first he saw was Clovis, our good king!
Start not, O Reader, for the truth I sing.
Much may you marvel, that a king so wise
Who pointed out the path of Paradise
To all his subjects, should forsake the road,
Nor see the great salvation he bestowed.
Who'd think the first of Christian kings must die,
Damned like a Pagan to eternity?
But Reader, thou wilt call to mind I'm sure
That being washed in font with water pure,
Cannot from soul corrupt efface the stain,
And Clovis was so linked in vice's chain,
Within his breast an heart so direful beat,
Of bloody deeds inhuman 'twas the seat,
Therefore Saint Remi strove to cleanse in vain
From Gallia's king the black and gangrened stain.
    Amongst these great ones, sovereigns of the world

Promiscuously into darkness hurled,
Appeared famed Constantine at sight of whom
Our monk in gray, astonished at his doom,
Exclaimed aloud: "O Lord, O cruel fate!
Can this be true? What he! who shone so great!
This hero who first made the world obey
The Christian creed and chased false gods away!
Is he alike subdued to Satan's yoke?"
When to the monk, thus Constantine bespoke:
"The worship of false gods I overturned,
And on the ruins of their temples burned
Incense to God above, with hand profuse,
But in such show external what's the use?
My cares for the supreme, though none could see,
Were not for Heaven, they centred all in me;
The holy shrines were but a stepping-stone
In my intention to the Caesar's throne.
Ambition, madness, mundane joys I made
My Gods, to whom my sacrifice I paid;
While Christian blood and treasure freely poured
Cemented fortune and my state secured.
To guard this throne, so idolized through life
I murdered next the father of my wife;
In blood and pleasure plunged, my jealous mind,
Where madness, weakness, cruelty combined,
Drunken with love, and to distrust a prey
Hurried to death my queen and son away;
O, Grisbourdon, no more astonished be,
That Constantine should be as damned as thee!"
Still more and more the Cordelier admires
The secrets veiled in Pandemonium's fires.
He views on all sides learned preachers there,
Doctors and those who filled the casuist's chair,
Right wealthy prelates, bigot monks of Spain,
Italian nuns, and to increase the train
Of every King the confessor was seen;
Ghostly advisers of the fair, I ween,
Whose Paradise 'mid mundane joys was past,
In dormitory somewhat overcast.
He next perceives enrobed, half black and white,

A monkish form, whose hair appeared to sight
A circle raised; but when his pious mien,
By fierceness marked our Cordelier had seen,
He, laughing, could no more his thoughts keep in,
But softly said: "This man's a Jacobin."
Then sudden cried: "Thy name I fain would learn."
When melancholy thus the shade in turn,
To his interrogator made reply:
"Alas, my son! Saint Dominic am I!"
Our Cordelier some paces back retired,
To hear this name august, on earth admired;
Then crossed himself, for he could not believe:
"How!" he exclaimed, "and shall this gulf receive
A saint, a doctor and apostle too?
Thou, great promoter of the monkish crew,
Preacher evangelic, inspired by God,
Bend'st thou, an heretic, 'fore Satan's rod?
Can grace so sadly inefficient prove?
Poor mortals! how ye are deceived above!
Go, and perform your ceremonies quaint,
And sing the litanies of every saint."

  Whereto replied, with feelings on the rack,
The dolorous Spaniard, in his white and black:
"No more the vanities of man discuss,
What is the hubbub of their crimes to us?
Cursed and tormented here, why care a jot
For psalms and praises sung where we are not?
Many who roast here, in these realms of night,
On earth are honoured with a chapel bright,
While with impunity, by men are cursed
Victims on earth, who rank in Heaven the first.
For me I suffer by a most just hand
For persecuting the poor Albigeois land,
My mission to convert, not to condemn,
I'm roasted here for having roasted them!"
Oh, was I gifted with an iron tongue
That wagged forever, still would ne'er be sung,
My gentle reader, still I could not tell
Of all the Saints, who have abode in Hell.
When the black cohort of the sons of woe

Had done the honours of the realms below,
As with one voice, they, all of them constate,
"'Tis Brother Grisbourdon who must relate,
What has conduced to his so sudden end:
What direful accident? recount, good friend!
Retail the deed that hurled thy hardened spright,
Thus fathoms deep amid chaotic night?"
"Good sirs, your will, he answered, I'll obey,
And my adventure strange will straight display,
But if what I recount excites surprise,
Oh! let me still find favour in your eyes;
Since, when we're dead, we deal no more in lies!

     "I was, you know, apostle yours, above,
And for my habit's honour and your love,
I did as gallant, and as doughty deed,
As ever monk performed, from cloister free'd.
The noted animal, my muleteer,
O wondrous man! in all things my compeer,
Most dutiful, he gave his powers such scope
As to surpass Hermaphrodix's hope,
I, without vanity, had strove amain
The female monster's plaudits to obtain,
Till Alix's daughter did, quite ravished, own
For once, she was content, and gave up Joan.
Joan, the rebellious, Joan of nought afraid,
Was soon to lose the envied name of maid;
Already circled in my steady arms,
She struggled stoutly for her virgin charms,
The muleteer beneath, our damsel pinned,
The while Hermaphrodix, delighted, grinned.
     "But will ye credence to my story yield,
The air op'd wide, when from that azure field,
Called Heaven—(a place which neither you nor I
Shall ever see—ye know the reason why)
I saw descending, O most fatal stroke
The long-eared beast that once to Balaam spoke,
When Balaam bold would o'er the mountain pass;
O direful messenger! Terrific ass!
A velvet saddle on his back he bore
And from his saddle-bow, hanging before,

Suspended, was a trenchant sabre seen,
With ample blade and either edge most keen;
Two wings upon his shoulders were combined
Wherewith he flew, and far outstripped the wind."
When Joan perceived what thus had come to pass,
"Praised be the Lord!" she cried: "behold mine ass!"
At these her words, I shrunk benumbed with fear!
The long-eared animal in haste drew near,
And bent before Dunois on suppliant knee,
As if he wished to say, "pray mount on me!"
Dunois obeys, the animal takes flight,
And rears and prances overhead, dire sight!
While mounted Dunois, with his glittering blade,
Prepares to charge on wretched me, afraid:
Just as 'tis said, O Satan, my liege Lord!
When with Omnipotence you vainly warred,
Archangel Michael met you fatally;
Fell instrument of vengeance heavenly.

 "Thus forced my threatened carcass to defend,
I courted magic as my surest friend.
The heavy brows and self-sufficient pride
That marked the cordelier I cast aside:
Assumed the charming form and blushing air
Of a young damsel, gentle, fresh and fair.
Tresses of flaxen hue adorned my breast,
Mine ivory skin a gauze transparent pressed,
Through which transpired, the warrior to deceive,
A bosom thrilled by love's convulsive heave;
All graces of the female sex were mine,
I strove to give my look a glance divine,
All spoke that innocence which charms the view,
Ever deceiving as its wiles subdue.
And though mine outward parts such candour showed,
A certain languor, so voluptuous glowed
With such enticing warmth through every part,
It must have softened the most savage heart
I could have ta'en the wary by surprise,
And have seduced to folly the most wise,
Since all was mine that could ensure success,
Thus doubly armed with beauty and finesse.

My knight incontinent confessed the charm,
One moment more I'd fallen 'neath his arm,
For in his grasp upreared, the glittering steel,
Now half descending was my fate to seal,
And trembling Grisbourdon, with pallid hue,
Already thought his skull was cleft in two.

    Dunois beholds, is moved, his hand he stays:
Thus seen, Medusa's head in ancient days,
The gazer changed into the senseless rock;
But gallant Dunois felt far different shock,
His soul was made a prisoner through his eyes,
I saw him drop his sabre in surprise.
I saw my charms produce their full effect,
He burned with passion tempered with respect.
Who then had thought my victory could fail;
But lo! here comes the worst part of my tale.

    "The muleteer, who, urged by passion's flame,
Pressed in his arms of Joan the sturdy frame.
Beholding me, so lovely and so sweet,
Sudden was taken with a new conceit.
Alas! my heart no thought had entertained
That he by tender charms could be enchained—
A boorish mind inconstancy to own!
I was preferred, and straight he left alone
The direful Joan—a fatal fair to me:
No sooner Joan enjoyed her liberty,
When, lo! her eye enquiring, so it chanced;
On Dunois' lately fallen sabre glanced;
She seized the steel, just as the faithless hind
Joan's peerless charms for mine had left behind,
And at that moment, aiming one back blow,
Severed my collar-bone and laid me low.
Since then I've had occasion none to hear,
Of cruel Joan, or of the muleteer,
Whether the monster or the ass prevailed;
May they be all, a hundred times impaled!
And may kind Heaven, which sounds the sinner's knell,
Send the whole company forthwith to Hell!"

    Thus spoke the monk, concluding angrily;
Whereat the hosts of Hell laughed mightily.

6

*Adventure of Agnes and Monrose–The Temple of Fame–
The Tragical Episode of Dorothy.*

Let us quit Hell! quit the abyss impure
Leave Grisbourdon with Lucifer to burn;
Wing to the realms of day our flight secure,
And to the busy scenes on earth return!
That Earth alas! which is another Hell,
Where innocence no longer dares to dwell,
Where hypocrites make good appear as bad;
Where sense, refinement, taste are run stark mad,
While all the virtues, being led astray,
Have joined the party, and are flown away,
There empty policy, as weak as loud,
Takes the first place, the one desert allowed.
Wisdom must yield to superstition's rules,
Who arms with bigot zeal the hand of fools;
And interest, earth's king, for whom the trade
Of peace and war by potentates was made,
Pensive and sad beside its coffer dwells,
And to the stronger's crimes the weaker sells.
O wretched, guilty, senseless mortals, why
Your souls debase with crimes of such a dye?
Unhappy men! who void of pleasure, sin,
Be wise at least, when you the course begin,
And since you needs must to damnation speed,
Be damned for pleasure, 'tis the wisest deed.
    Oft Agnes Sorel would this precept prove,
Whom none could blame except for sins of love.
On her forgiveness I with joy bestow,
And trust that God will equal mercy show:
Not maiden, every saint of Paradise,
And penitence the virtue is of vice.

When, in defence of honour, Joan was led
To sever with her heavenly sword the head
Of Grisbourdon, our winged ass, whose flight
Bore through the air Dunois, the gallant knight,
Conceived the thought, profane caprice I own,
To bear the hero far away from Joan.
What was it urged the wish? Love's ardent fire—
Love's tenderest flame, the soul's new-born desire.
Another time, kind reader, shall be told
The ardent fancy and the notion bold
That 'gan the Arcadian hero to uphold.
The holy animal resolved to fly
Towards the plains of pleasant Lombardy.
Good Denis had so counselled it, indeed,
This escapade unto his winged steed,
Wherefore, you ask?—Because he read each thought
Wherewith his ass and Dunois' breast was fraught;
Each burned with wishes that would, soon or late
Have proved subversive of the realm and state,
Have hurled destruction on the Gallic throne,
And marred the fortune and the fame of Joan.
Absence and time the saint conceived would prove
Sufficient to dispel their dawning love!
Denis had further views in this affair,
Another aim, a second pious care:
Abstain then, Reader, from all rash complaints,
And view with reverence the acts of Saints!
    The ass celestial, Saint Denis' pride
On Loire's fair banks no longer would abide,
Made straight toward the Rhone, while in his fright
Dunois could scarce sustain that dizzy flight.
From high above, his Heroine he beheld;
Naked she was, a sword her fingers held,
While her breast swelling with celestial ire
Through streams of blood gave proofs of sainted fire.
Hermaphrodix her flight would fain impede,
His myrmidons could not effect the deed;
In vain the cohort would her course withstand,
Joan humbles all with her courageous hand:
As when some giddy youth in forest sees

The waxen palace of industrious bees,
Admires the labour, and with daring strives
To pry still closer in the sugared hives;
Forth, on a sudden, bursts the winged race,
And settle fiercely on the intruder's face,
Who, by their stings assailed in every part,
Screams, runs and plunges to evade the smart;
Strikes, scatters, crushes hundreds 'neath his feet,
Of these winged hoarders of each luscious sweet.
'Twas thus with dauntless Joan, who chased afar
This puny phalanx, apeing men of war.
    Now at her feet, the caitiff muleteer,
Dreading the same fate as the Cordelier,
Trembles and cries, "O maiden, O my fair!
Whom once to serve in stable was my care,
What fury urges thus thy bosom's strife;
Have mercy, spare at least my wretched life,
Let not thine honours change thy clemency;
Behold my tears, O Joan! in truth, I die!"
    Whereto the maid replied: "I yield thee grace;
Thy recreant blood shall not my sword disgrace;
Vegetate still, and let thy clumsy mass
This very instant, serve me as an ass:
For though to mule, I can not change thy frame
Thy figure matters not; 'tis just the same;
Dunois has got mine ass, so I'll take thee,
Or man or mule, you are a mount for me,
Crouch then, directly!"—Quick the brute obeyed,
Submissive stooped his old and clumsy head,
Went on all-fours, whilst Joan his back bestrode,
And to face Heroes off the Heroine rode.
The genie swore by his ethereal sire
Frenchmen should henceforth feel his ceaseless ire.
His bitter thoughts inclined towards Britain's race,
And in this just revenge, he swore to efface
His wrongs on any Gaul whose sorry fate
Should lead him to encroach on his estate.
Forthwith was reared a castle at his will
Of structure strange, new architectural skill,
A trap, a labyrinth wherein might fall
The noblest heroes of this hated Gaul.

Yet soft we'll now recur to Agnes' state;
Dost thou not call to mind her cruel fate,
As when, quite senseless, Chandos sinewy arms
Entwined with rapture all her naked charms?
This same John Chandos at the martial cry
Left love and Agnes for the enemy;
Who, thus abandoned to her own sweet will,
Conceived she had escaped the threatened ill.
Scarcely recovered from the peril past,
She made a vow that it should prove the last;
And swore to love but good King Charles alone,
Who loved her better than he loved his throne,
And die ere tarnish once her faith so fair;
All this was wrong, for ladies should not swear.
    Amidst this crash of foes, formed to astound,
From camp attacked inseparable sound,
Where officers and soldiers join the fray,
Some fighting hard as others run away;
While coward lackeys, marching in the rear,
Plunder the baggage through excess of fear.
'Mid fire and smoke and yells of the distrest,
Agnes, perceiving she was quite undrest
To noble Chandos' ward-robe instant hied,
With fitting raiment there to be supplied;
And having seized on robe and shirt to boot,
Even his night-cap to complete the suit,
Silent and tremblingly she bent her way,
When lucky chance produced a dappled bay,
Bridled, and with a saddle on its back;
Of doughty Chandos 'twas the attendant hack.
A squire, an aged sot of courage bold,
Dozing, kept station there the steed to hold;
The wary Agnes stealthily there crept,
And took the bridle from the squire who slept.
Uttering harsh sounds suspicion to defeat,
She sprang with martial prowess to the seat,
Clapped spurs and t'wards a forest bends her way,
While joy and fear usurp alternate sway.
Bonneau endeavoured to stump off the while,
And cursed his heavy paunch at every mile

Damned this fine journey, courts and wars' alarms,
The English nation, love and Agnes' charms.
    Meanwhile, of Chandos the most faithful page,
(By name Monrose, such was the personage)
As early home with diligence he hied
From far his master's gown and night-cap spied:
Divining ill the cause of this strange sight,
Firmly believed his lord was put to flight.
Astonished at a scene so wondrous new
Monrose whips hard his loved lord to pursue;
Crying: "My Lord, my master, halt and say,
Are you pursued? Can Charles have won the day?
I'll follow you, where'er your course you bend,
One common fate my days and yours shall end."
He spoke and flew, as if the winds conveyed
Him and his horse as well as what he said.
Agnes, conceiving some pursuer near,
Entered the wood, appalled with chilling fear;
Monrose still followed, and the quicker she
Strove to escape the quicker galloped he;
The palfrey stumbled, and the fainting fair
Wafting a shriek that echoed through the air,
Fell lifeless by her panting courser's side,
In all the liveried hues of terror dyed.
Swift as the wind arriving, Monrose stared,
For at the sight his wondering wits were scared;
As 'neath his master's robe, then floating wide
The lovely charms of Agnes he descried:
Bosom of snow, and beauty *sans* compare,
Which bounteous nature lavished on the fair.
    Favoured Adonis, such was thy surprise
When the beloved of Mars forsook the skies;
What time the condescending queen of love,
Offered to bless thee in the conscious grove.
Venus, there's little doubt was better 'rayed,
Her lovely frame fatigue had not essayed;
No decent vestments did her body lack,
Nor had she tumbled from a palfrey's back;
Her ivory buttocks had felt no sharp thorn,
Nor did a night-cap her fair brows adorn;

Yet had our Agnes met Adonis' view,
His choice had surely wavered 'twixt the two.
The British youth immediate felt the smart,
Respect and fear by turns subdued his heart;
Trembling, he raised the fair one in his arms
Then cried: "The shock hath wounded sure these charms."
Upon him Agnes turned her languid eyes,
And then exclaimed, in broken faltering sighs:
"Whoe'er thou art that hast my course pursued,
If thou be not with innate crime endued,
Take no advantage of my hapless state,
To guard mine honour be it now thy fate;
O save me, give me freedom!" Agnes sighed,
Nor words spoke more, for words were then denied;
She turned away her face in silent grief,
And found a melancholy, short relief
In promising that, come what might, she'd be
True to her royal lover steadfastly.
Monrose in silence sympathized a while,
At length in accents soft, with gentlest smile,
"O thou! by nature framed to bear the sway,
Illuming hearts with thy celestial ray,
Behold thine humblest slave—on me rely,
For you alone I'll live, or dare to die.
Accept my service, my fond cares approve;
'Tis happiness to succour what we love!"
Then forth he drew a flask of *Eau des Carmes*;
And bathed, with timid hand, those injured charms
The saddle or the cruel fall had bruised,
Where rose and lily their soft tints confused.
Fair Agnes blushed, yet felt no undue rage,
Nor checked the hand of the adventurous page,
Nor well knew why she stole the side-long glance,
Still swearing faith to royal Charles of France.
The page, his bottle soon exhausted, cries:
"Rare beauty! let thy faithful swain advise
To take yon devious path, whose windings meet
A neighbouring hamlet's safe and calm retreat,
Retreat which no fierce warriors possess,
Accessible within an hour—or less.

Money I have—Oh, let it serve to pay
For petticoat and cap thy form to ray;
To deck in decency and elegance
A beauty worthy of a king of France."
    The lady-errant this advice approved
So soft Monrose, so worthy to be loved;
So handsome he, so tender, so well-bred,
The fair was not unwilling to be led.
Some cynic here, perhaps, may check my tale,
Demanding how it chanced a page should fail;
This youthful Englishman, so full of blood,
Should near a mistress prove so passing good,
And no improper conduct e'er betray?
Be peaceful, thou censorious babbler, pray,
The stripling loved, and if mere gallantry
Makes bold, true love begets timidity.
    Monrose and Agnes, towards the hamlet move,
Now make fine speeches, now converse of love,
Of war's exploits, and feats of chivalry,
And old romances stuffed with gallantry.
Our squire, at every hundred steps would stand,
Approach the fair, and kiss her lily hand,
All with an air of such respectful love,
'Twere vain in beauteous Agnes to reprove;
But nothing more—the gentle youth enslaved,
Though much desiring, nothing further craved.
The lovely pair, the hamlet once within,
The squire conducts the beauty to an inn:
When lovely Agnes quitting fond Monrose,
Seeks modestly in bed desired repose.
Now, out of breath, the page runs round and buys
Such food and raiment as the place supplies;
Whate'er or ease or comfort could impart,
To the dear idol of his doating heart.
Sweet youth in whom honour with love combined!
'Twas all his joy to let them sway his mind.
Where are they found, whose studied arts compare
With thy soft blandishments and gentle care?
    At this same Inn (it cannot be denied)
John Chandos' almoner lodged close beside;

And every almoner in every age,
In impudence surpasseth every page.
No sooner doth this wicked churchman hear,
How such transcendent beauty sleeps so near,
Than lewd desire inflames his heated blood,
Swells each distending vein, a madding flood,
Fires his foul body, flashes from his eyes,
Till to her room in rage of lust he flies,
And like a madman, as he enters, swears,
Makes fast the door, and the two curtains tears.
    But, gentle reader, it is meet I tell,
What likewise at this point of time befell
Our brave Dunois, long borne through air, alas!
Far from brave Joan, by her unruly ass.
Where hoary Alps their snow-crowned summits rear.
Divide the clouds, and seek a purer air;
Where yielding rocks to Hannibal supplied,
That passage fatal to the Roman pride;
Where bending skies describe an azure bow,
While blackening tempests breed and roll below;
A palace of transparent marble stands,
No roof, no door, the wondrous pile commands,
Open on every side and free to all;
Unnumbered mirrors grace the interior wall,
That thro' this structure, whosoe'er shall pass,
Reflected in some faithful looking-glass,
Or passing old, or young, or fool or fair
His veritable face is figured there.
    A thousand paths conduct by divers ways
To this bright Empire, where such numbers gaze;
But awful precipices hang in view,
And fraught with danger is each avenue.
This new Olympus many have attained,
Unconscious how the glorious heights they gained:
Yet few, indeed, the wished-for goal attain,
For one who mounts, there are a hundred slain.
The mistress of this palace perched so high,
Is that same old and prating Deity,
Called Fame, to whom since suns have light displayed
Even modesty hath gentle tribute paid.

The sage affects, 'tis true, a proud disdain,
And treats the triumphs of renown as vain,
Declares no poison to the soul like praise:
Wherein he lies, and folly what he says.
    Fame then is stationed on this giddy height,
To pay their court her minions take delight;
Kings, warriors, pedants, churchmen too are there,
Vain multitude; puffed up with nought but air;
On bended knee, each supplicates and cries:
"O Fame! most puissant goddess, ever wise,
Who knowest all, whose speech is ever free,
For charity, I pray thee, speak of me!"
To satisfy each indiscreet demand
Fame holds two trumpets, one in either hand;
This to her lips, with justice, see her raise
To celebrate some noble hero's praise;
While t'other, strange to tell is oft applied
(Since I must say it) to her broad back-side;
And serves in sounds sonorous to express
The name of the last rubbish from the press:
Productions of each mercenary quill,
Ephemeral insects of Parnassus Hill;
That each by each eclipsed, in turn decay
Labours of months that perish in a day,
Buried with college pedants, men of schools
Themselves worm-eaten by their verse and rules.
    Here would-be authors, a malicious band,
Detractors of all real genius stand;
Here La Beaumelle, Fréron, Nonnotte we view,
Guyon, and he, the refuse of the crew,
Savatier, the instrument of fraud,
Who sells his pen and lies to swell his hoard.
These shameless hucksters of reproach and blame,
Here crowd around and dare solicit fame;
Bedaubed with filth, they've yet the vanity
To shew themselves to this divinity:
Still from her presence chased with stripes unkind,
Scarce have they seen the goddess's behind.
Still on thine ass, Dunois, thou keep'st thy seat,
And art transported to this bright retreat;

Thy virtuous deeds, which were so justly famed,
The goddess with her decent trump proclaimed;
What must have been thy pleasure at the sight,
When gazing there upon each mirror bright,
To view in those reflectors purely clear,
Of all thy virtues the resemblance dear;
Not simply feats of arms which victors crown,
Sieges and battles that create renown,
But virtues far more difficult to see;
For wretches in the asylum due to thee,
Bless and record thy generosity;
With honest men, protected at the court
By thee, and orphans righted through thy thought.
    Dunois with honest pride some time surveyed
His gallant actions on those walls portrayed:
And little less delighted seemed the ass,
Who pranced and capered round from glass to glass.
Meanwhile, was heard through air the clarion sound
From one of Fame's two trumpets so renowned,
These words proclaiming: *"'Tis the dreadful day,*
When Dorothy to stake must wend her way,
And die in Milan; such is the behest,
Weep every mortal whom dear love hath blest."
"How now?" exclaimed Dunois, "condemn the fair?
What hath she done? Why burn a beauty rare?
If old or foul, 'twere well; but why conspire
To punish youthful loveliness with fire?
By all the Saints! such cruelty is too bad!
Ye men of Milan, have ye all gone mad?"
Yet as he spoke, the Trumpet made reply:
"This hour, the hapless Dorothy must die,
Unless some hardy knight the adventure take
To snatch the damsel from the fatal stake!"
    These sounds the bosom of Dunois inspired;
The lady's rescue straight his heart desired;
For, well ye know, as soon as chance displayed
Occasion for his courage, he obeyed;
To punish injuries, and wrongs redress,
He thoughtless hurried, summoned by distress.
"Bear me, my faithful ass, to Milan's walls,

Direct thy flight," he cries, "where honour calls."
His ample wings the beast obedient plies,
Less rapidly four-winged cherubim flies.
Now near the city by whose same consent
Justice decrees tremendous punishment,
Already they observed base slaves prepare,
The stake and faggots in the ample square.
Three hundred archers, their joy others' pain,
Their stations took the rabble to restrain
The gentry wait at windows, bathed in tears:
The archbishop in robes of state appears,
From a balcony with his priests on high,
Who view the scene with firm complacent eye.
    Four Alguazils lead Dorothea round
Stripped to her shift, in galling fetters bound.
Wildness and horror mark her mournful air,
Shame and confusion heighten her despair.
Before her grieving eyes a cloud is shed
And bitter tears adown her cheeks have spread,
She scarce discerned death's instruments revealed;
The direful stake whereon her fate is sealed;
And through her sobs at last her sad words start:
"O lover mine! O thou who in mine heart,
Reignest always, ev'n in this hour of dread—"
The suppliant ceased, for no more could be said,
And stammering forth of him she loved the name,
Speechless she sank to earth, a senseless frame,
Her forehead spread with a pale mortal hue;
Still lovely was she in that state to view.
Before the crowd stepped forth a caitiff wight,
The prelate's champion, Sacrogorgon hight;
Tow'rds the dire pile, behold him straight advance,
Armed at all points, with steel and arrogance.
Then cried: "My friends, a vow to God I make
That Dorothy hath well deserved the stake;
Will here present risk his life,
And for her wage 'gainst me in mortal strife?
If so, let him his daring strength display,
That with my look I strike him with dismay;
And show him that, which soon shall smart his brain."

Thus having spoke, he fiercely paced the plain,
Wielding a sharp edged sword of massive size,
Twisting his mouth and rolling his huge eyes;
They shudder who behold his aspect dire
Nor in the town was found a single squire,
Who to defend fair Dorothea dared,
So are they all by Sacrogorgon scared.
From fit reply withheld by abject fear,
All pay the tribute of a ready tear.
While the fierce Prelate from his seat on high,
Applauds his champion's arrogant defy.
Dunois, still hovering o'er the ample square,
Is shocked to meet audacity so rare.
And lovely Dorothea bathed in tears,
So beautiful in horror's 'midst appears,
Her deep despair lends such soft languishment;
To see her was to hold her innocent.
To ground the Hero vaults, and cries: "Behold,
My courage shall chastise thy vauntings bold;
Prove Dorothy as virtuous as she is wise,
And thine assertions, recreant braggart, lies!
But I would first from Dorothea know,
The imputed crime, the pretext of her woe;
Hear her sad story, learn what horrid plan,
Condemns to flames the beauties of Milan!"
He spake, and all the multitude gave scope,
Combining mingled shouts of joy and hope,
The trembling Sacrogorgon, terror's slave,
Strove all he could to act the part of brave,
While vain the prelate sought to lull to rest
Those fears that stole upon his dastard breast.

　　Dunois advanced with noble, courteous grace
To hear fair Dorothy's most piteous case;
She, casting down her eyes, her story told
With sighs and tears and pauses manifold.
The ass divine judged meet his form to perch,
Beholding all from steeple of the church;
While Milan's devotees, in ardent prayer,
Gave thanks to God who takes of girls due care.

7

How Dunois rescued Dorothy condemned to death by the inquisition.

When, in the spring-time of my youth, some fair
Abandoned me to be the slave of care,
My wounded heart indignant spurned love's reign,
And left his empire fraught with just disdain:
But to offend the fair, with rage thus fraught,
In word or act, ne'er entered once my thought;
'Twas not my mode to force a stubborn heart.
I pardoned one who Love's great law abused,
Who played a fickle and a faithless part:
A cruel fair I sooner had excused.
A generous lover ever must disdain
To persecute the maid he cannot gain.
Therefore, if she, for whom thy passions burn,
Doth not with equal love thy love return,
Seek elsewhere for some mistress less severe,
Sufficient numbers thou wilt find, ne'er fear!
Else take to drink; it is a course most wise.
And would to God, that being in such guise,
That tonsured prelate, barbarous and rude
Whose brutal love so cruelly pursued
And plunged in woe a maid of beauty rare,
Had been advised by me on this affair.
    Soon hath Dunois the fair afflicted maid
Inspired with courage and in hope arrayed;
Yet was it just that he the charge should hear
Which doomed the beauty to this lot severe.
    "O thou!" she blushing cried with downcast eyes,
"Bright angel, who descendest from the skies,
Heaven sent, it seems to fight in my defence,
To thee, at least, is known my innocence!"

"By some strange chance unknown," Dunois replied,
"I come, though not with heavenly power supplied,
To shield thy life from death's relentless dart,
Omnipotence alone can read thy heart;
I know thy soul is virtuous and white,
But, prithee tell the reason of thy plight."
Fair Dorothea, weeping thus replied:
"Love is my crime, and Love alone!" she cried.
Big tears, while yet she spoke, bedewed her face;
"'Tis love betrays me to this sad disgrace;
Of La Trimouille has the name crossed your ear?"
Dunois exclaimed: "My friend, of all most dear!
Few heroes have a soul of finer steel,
Nor has my king a warrior more leal,
Britain has no more dreaded enemy,
No cavalier more worthy love can be!"
"Too true your speech, sir knight," she cried, "'tis he.
Nor yet elapsed is one revolving year,
Since he from Milan hied, and left me here.
Here first for me he felt Love's pleasing pain,
Here first he sighed, nor sighed he long in vain;
O may the youth still fond and faithful prove,
He should love well, for far too well I love!"
"Judge of his faith," Dunois replied, "by yours—
Such wondrous charms his constancy ensures;
I know him: as myself he'll guard the trust,
True to his love, as to his sovreign just."
"Yes," she exclaimed, "I credit what you say,
And still shall bless the kind auspicious day,
Gave to my sight the idol of my soul,
And lit a flame no reason could controul.
To me appeared the loveliest of mankind,
Of less attractive form, than gracious mind;
Him I adored with feeling's fervid glow
Scarce conscious whether yet I loved or no.
     "'Twas at the Archbishop's board—entrancing hour!
He made confession of love's conquering power;
Ah! then an unknown fever seized my blood,
And through my veins rushed on the crimson flood;
Mute was my tongue and dim my glazy sight,

No more the banquet spurred my appetite;
'Twas thus I felt the powerful impulse move,
Nor dreamt of dangers that await on love.
Next morn he came, but transient was the view,
His stay was short, too soon he bade adieu!
And, as he went, my heart recalled his sight,
My tender heart, which after him took flight.
Next day, indeed, we had a *tête-à-tête*,
A little longer but no less discreet.
Next day he stole a kiss, I can't tell how,
And offered next to plight the marriage vow;
Next day again more boldly he beguiled,
So that the next day he got me with child!
What do I say? and need I thus proclaim
Through every stage my sorrow and my shame,
Unknowing yet, O knight of martial pride,
In what great hero thus I dare confide."
Mute on the subject of his birth and deeds,
The courteous knight obedient thus proceeds:
"I am *Dunois!*" It was enough to say.
"Then Heaven," she cried, "has answered when I pray;
Yes, pitying fate dispatches to my aid
The great Dunois, whose arm must be obeyed.
Ah, 'tis apparent whence your birth you owe
Enchanting Bastard, warmed with godlike glow!
Of tender Love I was the victim true,
And Love's own child my saviour proves in you;
Kind Heaven is just, and hope springs forth anew.
Know then, Dunois, thou brave and courteous knight,
Ere many months elapsed, my soul's delight
Heard the loud voice of duty from afar,
And left my arms, to join the ranks of war.
Ah! horrid war, and England, cursed land!
My love's despair you well can understand.
A state like this you doubtless have confest,
And know the anguish of the sufferer's breast;
'Tis thus imperious duty blights love's ray;
I proved it as in tears I spent that day;
Restraint too added torture to my pain,
And agonized, I dared not to complain.

A curious bracelet of his golden hair,
Dear Relic! guarded with religious care!
His portrait too he parting gave, whose powers
In absence cheated oft the heavy hours.
Last to my care he left a precious scroll,
Whereon was firmly traced Love's glowing soul;
It was, Sir Knight, a promise justly made,
Dear surety of his tenderness displayed,
And thus it ran: 'By mighty Love I swear,
By all the bliss my ravished soul can share,
Ere long great Milan's court again to see,
And give my hand and heart to Dorothy.'
    "Alas! he listened to stern duty's call,
Perhaps is still near Orléans' lofty wall.
Ah, could he now my matchless sorrow know,
Or once suspect my complicated woe!
But no, just Heaven, in ignorance let him rest,
Why pain with bootless grief his noble breast?
Trimouille departed, thus, surmise to drown,
I left the confines of a tattling town,
And in a lone retreat seclusion sought
Framed to indulge my bosom's anguished thought
My parents dead, I gave my sadness rein,
Hid from the world, no eyes discerned my pain;
'Twas thus I starved in secrecy my fears,
My ripening pregnancy and ceaseless tears;
But ah! sad truth destructive of my peace
Alas! I chance to be the Archbishop's niece."
At these sad words her sobs and tears increase.
Uprearing then her streaming eyes to heaven,
"To light," she cried, "I now my babe had given;
Pledge of a furtive love, that in mine arms,
Consoled my griefs and banished mine alarms;
Thus anxious I my love's return implored,
My mind's eye dwelling on his form adored.
'Twas then the Archbishop took into his head
To come and pry into the life I led;
The palace quitted, pomp and grand parade,
He came to greet his niece in forest's shade.
Ill fated hour! O why did form like mine

To Love abhorred my uncle's breast incline?
Detested gift, which now my hate inspires
Features that kindle passion's foulest fires;
He breathed his flame—Heaven, what was my surprise!
I placed his rank and duties 'fore his eyes,
His sacred calling, and what further stood,
Great bar—the consanguinity of blood!
Just portrait of the horrid act I drew,
Repugnant to the church and nature too;
Alas! to talk of duties was but vain,
A hope chimerical had fired his brain.
He fondly thought my heart was still to tame,
As yet untroubled by an alien flame;
In fine that passion was to me unknown,
And triumph therefore soon would be his own.
To practise hateful arts he ceaseless toiled,
Attentions loathed, desires forever foiled.
    "One day, alas! as oft had been before,
My eyes perused the plighted promise o'er;
As tears bedewed the page with fervour fraught,
Thus reading, was I by my uncle caught,
His hostile hand detained the fatal scroll
In which he read the secrets of my soul;
He saw me plighted as another's bride,
Nor could I long my darling infant hide:
And what in others might have damped desire
Did but add fuel to his wanton fire.
He seized the advantage which my secret gave:
"'Tis me,' he cried, ''tis me alone you brave,
While you reserve such favours he finds good
To the rash knave who slew your maidenhood?
Think twice before you dare resist me still;
Beware, judge wisely, you deserve but ill
That love which has enslaved me to your will.
Yield on the instant or my vengeance meet.'
I sank affrighted at my uncle's feet,
I called on God: with tears I strove to move
His heart grown mad with rage and slighted love,
But in my tears he fresh incentives found,
He seized and threw me struggling on the ground,

And would have ravished me by brutal force.
My cries for succour were my last resource!
When obstinate I dared his lust oppose,
O Heavens! I suffered from my uncle's blows!
Rejected love to sudden hatred rose.
The neighbours came, roused by my piercing cries;
A prompt excuse his ready wit supplies;
Fresh crime makes that crime still more hideous.
'Christians!' he says, 'my niece is impious;
I excommunicate, abandon her
Whom a damned heretic and seducer
Has brought to flagrant and to open shame!
Adulterous is the child, without a name.
Then may the mother and the child God curse;
They have my malediction which is worse;
And let the Inquisition be their nurse!'
        "No threat the traitor thus pronounced in vain:
Scarce had he entered Milan than a train
By grand Inquisitor was forthwith sent,
Which seized and dragged me straight to punishment,
In dungeon, where my mind was left to brood
And anguish, sighs and tears my bitter food;
Those horrid vaults whence light and wholesome air
Excluded, yield fit dwellings to despair!
Three days expired, mine eyes beheld the light
Till tortures closed them in the realms of night;
You see the stake, amid the fire's fierce rage,
There must I die at twenty years of age;
This is the bed for my expiring hour;
'Tis there, 'tis there, without your vengeful power,
With life, my honour I must quickly yield:
Though many a knight for me had ta'en the field,
And couched the lance, defending my just cause,
Had not my uncle chained them by the laws
Of mother church, 'gainst which none dares depart:
Ah! there's no valour in the Italian heart!
They tremble at the mere sight of a stole;
Whereas your Frenchman boasts a dauntless soul,
And braves the Pope in his own Capitol."
        This honour-goading theme stirred Dunois' breast,

Who felt acutely for the fair opprest,
Fraught with just rage against her deadly foe,
He thirsted to inflict the vengeful blow,
And felt an easy conquest would ensue,
Till, sudden gazing round, were seen in view
An hundred archers fierce, despising fear
Investing him most nobly from the rear.
With bonnet square, a caitiff, sable-clad
Declaimed in terms as *Miserere* sad:
"From Holy church, to all whom it may concern!
From Monsignor, and for God's glory, learn:
To Christians, blessed by the eternal Sire,
That we condemn to faggot and to fire
This foreign champion, who dares brave the fight
Of Dorothy, the sacrilegious knight.
As heretic, magician, infidel:
Let him be burned forthwith, his ass as well!"
Cruel priest! O Busiris, in cassock rayed,
Wretch, 'twas a trick of thine insidious trade,
This warrior's arm thou didst not dare discount,
So with the Holy Office took account,
Beneath the name of justice to oppress,
Him who stood forth the champion of distress,
And drew that dreadful veil from human sight,
Which scarfed from mortal eyes the deeds of night.
Of Holy Office now the recreant crew,
Their murderous purpose keeping still in view,
To seize Dunois, brave knight of chivalry
Two steps advance, then backwards measure three,
March on again, then cross themselves and stand;
When Sacrogorgon, leader of the band,
Trembling exclaims: "We'll die or conquer now;
This dire magician to our arms shall bow."
The sacristans and deacons of the town,
Amongst the rest, in solemn file troop down;
These bore *Aspergers*, these the holy urns,
Whence salted water sprinkled each by turns.
The Fiend they curse and greatly exorcize;
While the proud prelate with his anxious eyes;
All round his benedictions lavishes.

Dunois felt shocked, though godly his intent
That any should esteem him Satan-sent;
With one stout hand his trusty sword he took,
The other a most pious object shook,
Salvation's pledge, a holy rosary;
Then called his ass, who still sat perched on high.
The ass descends, astride the hero sprung,
And dealt thick blows the caitiff crowd among;
Of one the *sternum* and the arm he hit,
Another pierced where *atlas* bone is knit;
One drops a nose, his jaw's in piteous plight,
One sinks forever into gloomy night;
Here falls an ear and here a *humerus*,
And some run howling out an *oremus*:
Our ass, amidst this carnage shows his might,
Supporting gallantly his errant knight;
He flies, kicks, bites and tramples in the dust
These vagrant foes of the defenceless just.
Now Sacrogorgon close his vizor wears,
While still retreating, lustily he swears;
Dunois arrives, he cleaves the *os pubis,*
The bloody blade passed out by the *coccis,*
The wounded miscreant falls, the people roar,
"Blessed be God! The villain lives no more."
Still on the dust the ruffian struggling lay,
When thus exclaimed the hero: "Prithee, say,
Most treacherous soul, whom Hell waits and the grave,
Confess, the archbishop is but a mitred knave?
A ravisher, and proved a perjured elf,
While Dorothy is innocence itself,
To her one lover constant proved and true:
The worthless and besotted fool is—you!"
"Yes, yes," he cried, "my Lord is in the right,
I am a fool, the thing's as clear as light,
Your doughty sword has proved your precept well."
He spoke: his caitiff soul went down to Hell.
As the vile, graceless braggart's soul took flight,
To join fell Satan in the realms of night,
A squire was seen amid the crowd to advance,
A helm he wore and waved a gilded lance:

Two couriers gay in yellow livery
Preceded still this gallant equerry,
Sure symbol that some noble knight was near.
No sooner did these unknown forms appear,
Than Dorothy at the unlooked-for sight,
Exclaimed aloud: "It is, it must be, he!
Kind Heaven's too gracious to my misery."
    This squire through Milan town caught every eye.
The folk are cursed with curiosity!
    Say then, dear Reader, are you not ashamed
To indulge this silly fault I just have named;
And let this squire who caused such strange surprise
Usurp your spirit and engross your eyes:
Is this the aim and purpose of my song?
Oh, think of Orléans and its warlike throng,
Of cruel besiegers, Charles who holds the throne,
And of our amazon, the illustrious Joan,
Who, without bonnet, petticoat or gown,
Like Centaur scours the country up and down,
Placing more confidence in Heaven's high will
Than all the courage nature can instill;
Addressing now and then a fervent prayer
To good Saint Denis, whose assiduous care
To the affairs of France was wholly given;
Who now caballed against Saint George in Heaven.
Above all, Reader, Agnes ne'er forget,
But on her charms your fervid fancy set:
Is there a man so sullen and austere
Could look on Agnes with an eye severe?
Each honest man must love to linger there.
And now, my friend, I frankly would enquire,
If Dorothy was sentenced to the fire;
Or did the author of all things on high
Rescue this victim of calamity?
Such case but seldom finds its parallel:
But that an object you love passing well
For whom your constant tears prove love's alarms
Should find repose in some stout chaplain's arms,
Or with a youthful page share fond embrace—
You must allow it no uncommon case.

Such accident more common is no doubt,
Nor needs a miracle to bring about.
I love, I own, adventures to pursue,
That still keep Human Nature full in view:
For I'm a man, and I am proud to say,
Had share of human weakness in my day:
Of old I've clasped my mistress in my arms,
And still the pleasing recollection charms.

8

How the gallant La Trimouille met an Englishman at Notre Dame de Lorette, and the Sequel of the story of his Dorothy.

How wise, how interesting proves our page;
The heart and mind at once formed to engage!
Virtue triumphant here we always view,
Each knight has courage, aye, and conduct too;
The rights of kings, chaste feelings of the fair
All are displayed; it is a garden rare,
Whose whole contour is pleasing to the eye,
At once by culture and variety.
And fairest flower that ever garden graced
Here blooms supreme, the virtue that is chaste;
Like the white lily, Heaven's peculiar care
Lifting its head immaculate to the air.
Youths, maidens all, my lays assiduous read,
Of heavenly virtue the divinest creed.
The learned Picard, abbé Tritemus,
Pride of his age has written it for us;
Our Joan and Agnes for his theme he took.
How I admire him! and with pleasure look
On times now past, when I alone preferred
His wholesome modest page, and then averred
How much the sense surpassed those rapid strains
That flow in torrents from romancers' brains,
From whose dull wits abortive themes appear,
Born but to perish in one short-lived year.
The wonder of our Joan's portentous fate
Shall triumph over time's remotest date;
And baffle envy. 'Tis the truth I tell,
And truth alone is really durable.
    But yet, dear Reader, 'tis not in my power,
To occupy with Joan the present hour;

Since Dorothy, Dunois, her champion,
And La Trimouille who all her love had won,
Each have upon my verse a rightful claim;
And I must here confess, devoid of shame,
That with just cause, the reader may enquire
What was the sequel of their tender fire.
   Near Orléans (recall the scene to view)
Brave La Trimouille, the glory of Poitou,
While for the king performing valour's feat
Neck-deep in ditch enjoyed a muddy treat.
His squires extracted him, with pain, I trow,
From the foul bottom of the filthy slough;
Our hero galled by many a direful stroke,
Had shoulder shattered and his elbow broke;
So was conveyed the sore afflicted knight,
Within the ramparts, in this piteous plight;
But Talbot, keeping vigilance in view,
Had to the city barred each avenue;
By secret path then silent they conveyed
Our Paladin, of ambush sore afraid,
To ancient Tours, on litter safe reclined,
City most faithful and to Charles resigned.
There a Venetian quack, just come to us,
Adroitly put to rights the *radius*,
And in its socket set the *humerus*.
His squire informed him that all thoughts were vain,
Of now returning to the king again,
Since every road was guarded by the foe.
The hero, ever thrilled by passion's glow,
At length resolved, consumed by dire ennui,
That he would speed his lady-love to see.
Through throng and dangers fared the knight to gain
The Lombards spoil, the fair and pleasant plain;
And gaining Milan's walls, with soul elate
There found advancing to the city's gate,
Like flood resistless, a besotted band,
Collected from the circumjacent land,
Crowding to Milan, citizen and clown;
Monk, Benedictine hurried to the town;
Parents and children, noisy rabble train,

Whose eagerness the barrier could restrain,
Forward they press and cry: "Let's hurry there,
We do not every day such pastime share!"
    Soon learned our knight with horror and dismay
What made these worthy Lombards' holiday,
The spectacle prepared to meet his sight.
"My Dorothy!" he cried, then took his flight;
His courser vaulting o'er each vagrant's head
Quick bounded forward; so the knight was led
From suburbs and the city to the square;
When lo! he saw the conquering bastard stand,
The mob subduing with his valorous hand;
While Dorothy, quite speechless from surprise,
Scarce dared from earth to raise her timid eyes.
Abbé Tritemus, I must truly say
Though great his talents, never could portray
What wells of ecstacy, surprise, delight
Filled her pure bosom at the sudden sight,
Of her love's coming on that direful day.
What colour or what pencil could convey
That mélange soft, so pleasant and so keen
Of joy ensuing where her pain had been,
Of thrilling ecstasy, the blissful tide?
Confusion, virtue, shame she could not hide,
While by degrees, soft passion overcame.
Trimouille impelled by the resistless flame
Within his ardent arms her form entwined,
By bliss subdued, to tenderness resigned;
And thus embraced in turn, with transport mute,
Dunois, his mistress and the long-eared brute.
The fair sex at their windows saw the sight,
And clapped their hands with rapturous delight;
The cassocked gentry o'er the ruins fled
Of the dire pile and place bestrewed with dead.
Amidst the débris, reeking still with blood
The gallant knight, the dauntless Dunois stood,
But now fair Dorothy in honour rode,
Borne in a litter to a safe abode,
The air and port of Hercules maintained,
Who once beneath his feet grim death enchained,

And bound Eumenides the furies fell
And Cerberus, three-headed hound of hell,
Yielding Alcestis to her husband's arms,
Who still in secret felt some jealous qualms
Whilst the two heroes closely rode behind:
Next morn our Bastard led by feelings kind,
Approached the bed whereon the lovers lay:
"I feel, he cried, how useless 'tis to stay,
Since your sweet pleasures I can not enhance;
Joan and King Charles require my aid in France.
I'll now rejoin them, for I know that Joan
The absence of her ass doth much bemoan.
Denis, the patron of our realm, revered,
To me this night in person hath appeared;
Denis I saw as plain as you I see;
Denis, who lent his mount divine to me;
To succour kings and dames afflicted sore,
He ordered me to visit France once more.
Thank Heaven, I've rendered service to the fair,
The monarch Charles, in turn, demands my care;
Taste now the pleasures that fond lovers share.
I seek the king, obedient to the fates;
I yield my life—time flies—mine ass awaits."
     "My steed I'll mount, and after you I'll ride!"
The ever-courteous La Trimouille replied.
The fair one said: "Such is my project too.
I long have felt a lively wish to view
Gay Charles the Seventh and his gallant court,
Where knights unequalled in renown resort;
Gentle Agnes, who governeth his heart,
And fiery Joan who chose the warrior's part.
My cherished lover, and my saviour friend
Would safe conduct me to the world's far end.
But on the point of roasting, sore distressed,
Unto the Virgin I my prayers addressed;
And vowed if rescued from impending woe,
On pilgrimage I'd to Loretto go.
Forthwith God's mother, as this came to pass,
Dispatched you hither on your heavenly ass;
From the dread stake you brought security,

I live through you; my vow must sacred be,
Or justly will the Virgin punish me.".
     "Your converse is discreet and wondrous sage,"
Exclaimed Trimouille, "and such a pilgrimage
Becomes a sacred duty which you owe.
I will alike on this excursion go;
Loretto warms me with a zealot's ray;
Thither I'll lead thee; Dunois, speed thy way;
Through starry realms, pursue thine airy flight,
Till fertile plains of Blois appear in sight;
I hope and purpose to rejoin you soon
Ere the completion of another moon.
You, Madam, hieing to Loretto straight,
Fulfil the pious vow you contemplate.
Whilst I make one that's worthy your fair face,
To prove at every time, in every place,
To every comer, or with sword or lance
The fond affection which I here advance,
That you surpass in beauty and in grace
All maids and women of whatever race."
The fair one blushed; from earth the gray ass springs,
Spurning the ground, he spreads his ample wings,
And soon beyond the near horizon flown,
Seeks the pure sources of the rapid Rhone.
     The Poitevin with his fair dame so gay,
To rich Ancona took the nearest way.
The pilgrim's staff their pious purpose tell,
And palmer's hat bedecked with cockle shell;
While blessed rosaries from their waists depend,
Where pearls and gold in beads alternate blend.
Oftimes the Paladin these beads would tell;
Ave, he said: the fair responded well,
Anon with sighs, with litanies again;
But still *I love you* was the sweet refrain
Of th'orisons thus chanted by these twain.
They travelled through Placenza and Modena,
Through Parma, through Urbino, through Cesena,
And lodged each night within the sumptuous walls
Of Princes, Dukes and Counts and Cardinals.
Our knight this grand advantage too possessed

Upholding of all dames his fair the best,
For wisdom, beauty and celestial grace,
To Dorothy assigning sovereign place;
Which bold opinion no one dared dispute
Avouched by knight so famed; each tongue was mute
Such the good breeding and sage policy,
Of all these noble lords of Italy.

    Along Musona's banks near Riconate,
Rising amidst Ancona's marquisate,
Afar the pilgrims saw where brightly shone
The lofty mansion of the bless'd madonne;
Those walls which tutelary angels bore
From holy Palestine in days of yore,
Fending the air with an impressive sweep,
As a ship ploughs the billows of the deep.
Loretto was the ending of their way;
And of themselves the walls resolved to stay:
And ever since succeeding Popes have vied,
(Vicars of Heaven, and Lords of Earth beside)
In heaping what most precious could be got,
To ornament that highly favoured spot.
Our lovers from on horseback here descend,
And on both knees, with due contrition bend;
Then both, to ratify the vow they made,
Most sumptuous offerings on the altar laid;
Accepted all with gratitude profound,
Both by the Virgin and the monks around.

    Unto the inn our lovers went and dined,
Where as a fellow-guest, whom should they find,
But a bold Briton, careless, rough and free,
For pastime come the Virgin's shrine to see;
A sorry joke to his contemptuous view,
Appeared Loretto, and our Lady too;
True Briton, travelling he knew not why,
New-made *antiques* he *dearly* loved to buy,
His sweeping air all haughtily comprised;
The saints and all their relics he despised.
Of every Frenchman the opponent fell;
His name was Christopher of Arundel;
Through Italy he made a dismal tour,

But still his *ennui* did not find a cure;
While with him went the mistress of the wight,
Proud as himself and even less polite;
Little she spoke, though formed of finest clay,
Loving at night, yet insolent by day;
In bed, at board, capriciously perverse,
In all things was she Dorothy's reverse.
   The baron bold, Poitou's bright ornament
First greets him with a well-turned compliment;
But the rude Briton deigned not to reply!
Still would the courteous knight new matter try;
Told how the Virgin Mary lent her aid,
Told of his vow amidst the Lombards made,
To great Saint Denis, in each time and place,
To prove his mistress' superior grace;
Addressing thus the Briton full of scorn:
"I do not doubt your Lady nobly born;
Doubtless with beauty virtue's joined to it;
Nay more, I trow she hath a pretty wit,
Though she has so far nothing had to say;
Her Dorothy surpasses any day.
You'll own to it, and grant her second place;
With such a rival, none can deem disgrace."
   The British knight from head to foot surveyed
The gallant lord, and this rough answer made;
"God damn me if I care one pinch of snuff
For vows to Denis or such silly stuff;
And for that girl of yours, what boots it me
That wise or foolish, foul or fair she be!
Each his own property should cherish most,
Nor make of what he has an idle boast;
But since you thus have had the insolence
To dare assume a sort of preference
O'er Briton born, I'll teach you soon to know
The duty which to England's sons you owe;
For in such case, we islanders ne'er prate,
But give each upstart Gaul a broken pate;
And so my mistress, both in figure, size,
Colour and plumpness, bosom, arms and thighs
In virtuous sentiments, and charms of mind

Leaves your much vaunted pilgrim far behind.
And so my king (for whom I little care)
Discomforture can, when he will, prepare,
Both for your master and your clumsy Fair."
"'Tis well!" the champion of Poitou replied.
"Hence let us go, and let the sword decide,
To your dismay, perhaps, I'll shortly prove,
How much you wrong my country, king and love.
But since in courtesy we still should vie
The choice of combat at your will shall lie;
Whether on foot or horseback, prithee say;
Your inclination o'er my wish shall sway."
"On foot, by God!" the Englishman declared,
"I would not that a horse my glory shared;
Throw the cuirass, throw the strong morion by,
Let coward breasts to steel for shelter fly.
It is too hot; I like to be at ease,
But being stripped I'll argue as you please;
The strokes our rival beauties shall decide."
"Just as you please," the Gallic hero cried.
The challenge troubled his dear Dorothy,
Though in her heart she felt the flattery,
Of being subject of such deadly feud;
Trembling the while, lest Arundel imbued
With deadly steel the bosom of her dear
Which she then moistened with a piteous tear.
Meantime the British dame her champion warmed
With a proud glance conscious of how she charmed.
Her cheeks were never sullied by a tear,
Contention to her haughty heart was dear;
Her nation's cock-fights were the games which she
Had always cherished with avidity.
Judith of Rosamore was styled the dame,
Bristol admired her, Cambridge told her fame.
    Behold our hardy knights strip off their clothes,
And in close fight prepare for study blows,
Each gallant with his noble quarrel charmed,
In maintenance of love and country armed;
The front erect, well poised the glittering steel,
The arm extended, body in profile,

Rapid they join their swords, in quart and tierce,
Each by the other struck in contact fierce;
'Tis pleasant to observe them stoop, advance,
Rise and recoil, or active turn askance;
Parry and feint, then with address leap back,
And boldly recommence the rude attack.
Thus we may view in the celestial plains,
Beneath the Lion, or when the Dog-star reigns,
The horizon flames and burns with sudden light,
A thousand fires attract the dazzled sight;
Whilst universal conflict seems decreed,
And vivid lightnings flash to flash succeed.
  A blow right well directed by the Gaul,
Straight at the Briton's chin he now let fall;
And lightly springing back preserves his guard,
While Arundel in turn then presses hard,
And dashing on in tierce, assails his foe
Whose thigh incontinent receives a blow,
When streaming blood the polished flesh imbrues,
The ivory tinged with variegated hues;
Whilst these assaults our combatants enrage,
Each glad to die, so he may but engage
A mistress' plaudit, and at once decide
The fair one, who shall reign the victor's pride,
Arrived a bandit from the Papal Power
With troops dispatched the country wide to scour,
Who gives with promptitude his mission scope
To pay his pure devotion to the Pope.
This rascal bore the name of Martinguerre,
Thief night and day, and always a corsair;
But duly on the Virgin's service set
To tell his rosary he'd ne'er forget,
That purged from every sin his soul might be.
He chanced within the close our dames to see,
Their steeds and the bright trappings that they wore,
Their mules which *agnuses* and treasure bore:
Which when he saw, our heroes saw no more;
For off he carried Judith Rosamore,
And Dorothy, and all the baggage too;
Horses and mules swift vanished from the view.

Still in the dubious strife, our hardy pair,
Brandished their shining faulchions in the air,
And death and danger for their ladies braved;
It was the Poitevin who first perceived
The Fair had vanished from the scene of war,
And saw their esquires galloping afar.
He stood amazed—his sharply pointed brand,
Remained effectless in his feeble hand.
Lord Arundel was seized with like surprise;
They stand with gaping mouth and staring eyes,
Gazing around till Christopher exclaims:
"As God's my judge, they've carried off our dames!
Why stand we madly thus like mortal foes
Inflicting on each other cruel blows?
Better pursue them; and renew the attack,
To prove who's fairest when we bring them back."
They both agree the quarrel to postpone
And like good friends depart to seek their own.
But e'er an hundred yards our heroes move,
"In arm and thigh what pain," cried one, "I prove!"
While similar complaint the other made
Of his scarred breast and of his wounded head.
Those animal spirits which make heroes fight
Now rushing round the heart no more excite;
Nor could they more impetuous ardour boast
Which with their loss of blood was also lost.
Both bruised and languishing from many a wound,
Together fell upon the blood-stained ground;
And far away their trusty squires the while
Pursued the robber many a tedious mile.
Our Paladins extended on the plain,
Naked and moneyless, in grief and pain
Life's latest moment they believe at hand,
When worn with years and traversing the land,
A dame beheld them in such plight arrayed,
And in a litter had them both conveyed
To her own homestead, where within a trice
She cured their wounds by medical device!
Her lenient remedies at once repair
Exhausted strength, and give a healthful air.

This ancient dame was a reputed Saint,
Highly respected wheresoe'er she went;
Nor round Ancona was there one could vie
With her in pious works and sanctity.
She could foretell the weather, foul or fair,
Cure slighter wounds with oil and holy prayer;
And had more times than once obtained the praise
Of turning sinners from their wicked ways.
    Our heroes to the dame their tale confess,
And claim her counsel in this dire distress;
The half decrepit beldam shook her head,
Prayed to the Virgin, opened mouth and said:
"Depart in peace, and love your ladies gay,
Provided always, in an honest way!
Cautioned by me this wholesome counsel take,
Never to kill yourselves for either's sake.
The tender subjects of your ardent love
Are now subjected rude assaults to prove;
Your ladies fair now suffer trials rude,
I mourn their woes and your solicitude.
Dress yourselves quick, to horse without delay,
And take good care you do not miss your way.
Through me Heaven sends this information kind,
That you must follow what you wish to find."
The Poitevin admired her energy,
The sombre Briton said: "Your prophecy
Is true; this flying robber swift and sure
We'll follow if fresh steeds we can procure,
And be with doublets and with arms supplied."
"I'll furnish them," the withered hag replied.
It chanced a son of Isaac luckily,
Well circumcised and bearded stood hard-by;
Of the deprepuced race he was the flower,
Ready to proffer service any hour.
This worthy Jew most generously lent
Two thousand crowns at forty-five percent.
According to the *uses* of that race,
Whom Moses led into the promised place;
The profit of this monetary affair
The saintly dame and Jew agreed to share.

9

*How La Trimouille and Lord Arundel overtook their Ladies
in Provence, and of the strange adventure
which befell them in Sainte-Beaume.*

Two cavaliers who well the fight have waged,
Mounted or in a fencing match engaged,
Whether with broad sword, pointed rapier thin,
Armed *cap-à-pie*, or naked to the skin,
Reciprocal esteem in secret feel,
As both their meritorious acts reveal;
And, when from anger free, they laud each blow
Ably inflicted by the gallant foe;
But when the conflict's o'er, should fate's decree
Involve the champions in calamity,
A common misery unites the twain,
And friendship springs from enmity again;
Of such a case occurred true parallel
With La Trimouille and spleenful Arundel.
This Arundel was cast in roughest mould,
Haughty and fierce, indifferent and cold;
Yet could his heart, though tempered like his steel,
For his polite opponent kindness feel;
And Poitou's knight with ease sustained his part,
For Nature formed him with a tender heart.
Said he: "Your friendship cheers my drooping soul,
Some villain has my Dorothea stole;
Help to regain the beauty I adore,
And I'll brave death to rescue Rosamore."
    Thus half consoled, the foe became a friend,
Their rapid course tow'rds Leghorn's walls they bend,
Led by some false intelligence astray:
The ravisher had ta'en the opposite way;
And while the knights depart on vain surmise,

He takes with ease his rich and noble prize.
Safely and unmolested soon he gains
A lonely castle on the sea-girt plains,
Betwixt Gaeta and imperial Rome;
A stately mansion once, but now become
Of fierce banditti the retreat obscure,
Where rapine, filth and gluttony impure,
With all the horrors that make up their train,
Rage, blood and murder for the love of gain,
The deadly feuds which drunkenness excites;
Days of debauch and blood-polluted nights,
Infernal lusts, that quench the gentle fires
Of Love's pure torch and delicate desires,
United rule and rage without control;
While each excess that stains the vilest soul,
Shows how unbridled passion may debase,
Degrade and vilify the human race.
Oh man, of thy creator, shape and shade,
Consider then, 'tis thus that thou art made!
    Duly arrived, the insolent corsair,
Sat down to table with the indignant fair,
One on each side; and ate and drank and laughed,
And many a bumper to their beauty quaffed;
At last he cried: "My damsels, 'tis but right,
That you should choose who lies with me to-night;
All's good alike, it's all the same to me,
Or black or blonde, England or Italy,
Christian or Infidel, *petite* or tall,
—Another glass!—It matters not at all."
At this proposal a soft blush o'erspread
Fair cheeks of Dorothy with sudden red;
Her gentle bosom swelled with heaving sighs,
And floods of anguish gushing from her eyes,
Fell on her dimpled chin, where Cupid's kiss
Had left the soft impression of his bliss
One day caressing her; and thus distressed,
With poignant anguish was the fair oppressed.
Judith, a moment, wrapped in thought remained,
Her lofty port and dignity maintained;
Till with a smile and air of haughty pride,

"Be mine to yield your midnight prey," she cried,
"Then learn when robbers undertake to woo,
What in their beds an English dame can do!"
A clumsy kiss anon our robber gave,
And thus made answer Martinguerre the brave:
"I always dearly loved an English lass."
Another kiss, and then another glass;
To be refilled—and while he sings and swears,
And eats and drinks, his hand audacious dares,
Finger at random, with scant ceremony
The forms of Rosamore and Dorothy.
The latter weeps, the other with disdain
Ne'er changing colour, nor evincing pain,
Sat quite unmoved, apparently resigned
And let the ruffian act as he inclined.
At length from table with a yawn he rose,
With foot unsteady and an eye that glows,
And with a gesture of his corsair's trade,
He claims fulfilment of a bargain made;
Still flushed from rosy Bacchus' sparkling rites
Ready he is for Cythera's soft delights.

    The modest Milanese with down-cast eyes,
Bespoke the British dame: "Dare you," she cries,
"Grant the detested wretch his odious suit?
So proud a beauty yield to please a brute?"
"My purpose is to give him different fare,"
Said Rosamore; "you shall find all I dare;
Well I'll avenge my glory and my charms,
True to my honour and my lover's arms.
Know then that God, of His consummate grace,
Gave me stout arms as well as a fair face,
And *Judith* is the christian name I bear.
Await my coming in this loathly lair,
Leave me to act, but spend your time in prayer."
She then passed onwards, holding high her head,
To place herself beside her host in bed.

    The night now covered with a veil of gloom
The mildewing turrets of this place of doom;
The rabble of banditti snoring lay
And slept in barns the fumes of wine away;

And Dorothy in such a wretched plight
Was left alone and almost died of fright.
 The buccaneer, in that dense part his head,
Whence springs the thought, was almost numb and dead,
With vines of Italy; his heavy mind
Less upon love, than slumber, was inclined;
And half asleep, his torpid hand he throws
O'er the proud charms for which his bosom glows;
While Judith lavish of her tenderness
Envelops him in many a false caress;
Death's toils she spreads; the wearied debauchee
Yawns, turns his head, and slumbers peacefully.
Beside his bed the formidable blade
Of long-redoubted Martinguerre was laid;
Our British dame the trenchant weapon drew,
Invoking every war-like name she knew:
Judith and Jael, Deborah the fell,
Aod, and Simon Peter called as well,
Simon-Barjona, who cut off an ear.
The robber's hair she seizes, stifling fear,
In her left hand, and lifting up his head,
That ponderous skull incasing nought but lead,
She gathers nerve; her stroke profound and deep
Cleaves off the miscreant's head in snoring sleep.
Mixed streams of blood and wine, a dire display,
Deluged the couch on which the robber lay;
Whilst spouting from the trunk the impurpled gore
Bespattered the fair face of Rosamore,
From out of bed the Amazon repairs,
And in her hands the bleeding head she bears,
Speeding her trembling friend anon to seek,
Who, in her arms, forgets the power to speak;
But cried at once, upon recovery:
"O gracious God! what woman can you be!
O what a deed, a blow! What danger too
Attends our flight if any should pursue!
Should they awake, our lives they'll take away."
Said Rosamore: "Speak not so loudly, pray!
My mission's not yet ended, banish care!"
The other dame grew valiant from despair.

Their lovers wandering still at hazard round,
Sought every where in vain and nothing found.
At length the walls of Genoa they gain
And having sought by land their loves in vain,
They choose to try their fortune on the main;
Demanding news of every wind that blows,
Of the fair nymphs who trouble their repose.
The veering winds waft their light vessel o'er,
Now to the confines of that happy shore,
Where he, whose laws the Christain world obeys,
Of Paradise right humbly bears the keys;
Now to that gulf where Thetis' aged spouse
With feeble prow the Adriatic ploughs;
Now to gay Naples with her vine-clad steeps
Where Sannazar too nigh to Virgil sleeps.
The vexing Gods who wanton pinions ply,
Who are no more Orythias' progeny;
O'er the green billows of old Ocean's tide,
With force impetuous our lovers guide;
Where fell Charybdis bellows now no more,
Where Scylla's howling waves forget to roar,
And giants, crushed by Etna's fiery glow,
Ashes and flame commingled cease to throw;
Such change with time our little world can show!
Not far from Syracuse, the wandering pair
To Arethusa's limpid fountain fare,
Whose rushy bosom now no more receives
Alpheus, thy gentle and enamoured waves;
Borne onward thence, the classic shores they sought,
Where Carthage flourished, and Augustine taught;
A fearful region which the living see
By rage infected and rapacity
Of mussulmans, children of ignorance.
At last our knights by Heaven's blessed chance
Attain the smiling skies of fair Provence.

There, on the shore, adorned with olive bowers,
Of Marseilles town arise the ancient towers;
O noble city! Greek of old and free,
These two-fold blessings have been lost by thee!
Fairer thou findest kingly servitude,

Which is—who doubts?—a great beatitude,
Yet to thy confines boast a holy hill,
More marvellous and salutary still.
Who knows not Magdalene, who in old time,
To love devoting beauties in their prime,
Grown old, repented, bowed to Heaven her knee,
And greatly wept her mundane vanity?
From Jordan's banks in this repentant mood,
To fair Provence her journey she pursued;
Where with a scourge she sought to purge her sin
Ofttimes beneath the rock of Maximin;
Since when, rich odours all diffused around
Sweetly embalm the consecrated ground
And many an harlot, pilgrims not a few
Climb to that rock, with purpose to eschew
The God of Love—a devil in their view.
     The contrite Jewess on a day, 'tis said,
Requested grace upon her dying bed,
Of Maximin, her pious confessor:
"Obtain for me, if ever on this shore,
About this rock, adventure lovers two,
Their time to spend in private *rendezvous*,
Their impure flames no longer here may burn,
But all their ardour to aversion turn";
The blest adventuress thus having said,
Her confessor to grant her prayer was led;
Since when, who climb this holy rock, detest
The objects heretofore they loved the best.
     Marseilles inspected by our curious knights,
Its port, its roadstead, all the wondrous sights,
With which its citizens their ears assail,
Forthwith they start the sacred rock to scale,
That rock amongst the cassocked crew so famed,
Which is by them the Holy Balm surnamed;
Whose odour wraps the realm in sanctity.
The handsome Gaul was led by piety,
The haughty Briton by curiosity.
As up the rock they climbed they soon espied
Two female travellers on its rugged side,
One on her knees, hands clasped in ardent prayer,
The other on her feet with scornful air.

O cherished objects! unexpected hour!
Each knight discerned and owned his fair one's power;
Behold them then, these sinful men and dames,
Within the shrine which love supremely shames;
The English lady briefly tells her tale,
How her strong arm was able to prevail
O'er Martinguerre, by heavenly impulse led,
Thus to avenge the honour of her bed.
The prudent fair one, as a slight resource,
Had seized the slaughtered robber's heavy purse;
For gold, though current in this world—she knew
Was useless in the world she sent him to.
Then clearing in the horror of the night
The walls ill-fitting of that fearful site,
With sword in hand to the adjacent shore
Her fellow victim, trembling still, she bore;
Then went on board a craft which lay in view,
And woke the captain and his drowsy crew,
Who, highly bribed, the fugitives to please,
Consent to navigate Tyrrhenian seas.
Till favoured by the winds' capricious blast,
Or else by Heav'n whose wisdom's unsurpassed,
To Magdalena's feet they come at last.
    O sovran virtue! Mighty miracle!
At every word Judith was fain to tell,
Her warrior's noble heart felt love abate;
Disgust, soon turning to a deadly hate,
Succeeded to love's former ecstasy;
Nor is he paid in different currency.
While La Trimouille who had esteemed more bright
His Dorothy than even morning light,
Conceived her ugly, wit she seemed to lack;
So with contempt he turned on her his back.
Whilst she beholds in him a prince of fools,
Her scorn increasing as his ardour cools.
From out her cloud the Magdalen surveyed
With joy the swift conversion she had made.
But Mary Magdalen was much deceived,
When from the Saints in glory she received
This grace, that, every lover come her way

Should cease to love his fancy from the day,
That brought him to her rock's vicinity.
Alas! the Saint, by slip of memory,
Had never asked that once the lovers healed,
They should not to a newer mistress yield.
Saint Maximin had not the case foreseen,
Wherefore the English infidel, I ween,
To Poitou's knight extended wide her arms,
While Arundel was ravished by the charms
Of Dorothy, enamoured as of old.
The abbé Tritemus has even told,
That Magdalen at such an unforeseen
Result, from Heaven's height to smile was seen.
I quite believe it, and excuse the *trait*;
Virtue is good, but rule us though it may,
To old pursuits our thoughts are prone to stray.
It chanced our lovers scarce Saint Balm had left
Ere of its spell, each heart anon was reft;
No charm it boasts when once the precincts past;
The shrine alone commands the spell to last.
Trimouille was much confused when down below,
To think he had disliked his mistress so;
He found her even sweeter than before,
And sang her praises ever more and more;
While Dorothy to bitter grief a prey,
With love renewed her error wiped away,
Contrite Arundel's arms his fair enfold;
Each loved again as they had loved of old.
And I'll avouch that Magdalen above,
On viewing them, forgave this mutual love.
The Briton stern and Poitou's knight so kind,
Each with his dame on pillion behind,
To Orléans their steady course inclined.
Each hero burning fierce with martial flame,
Eager to vindicate his country's fame.
Lovers discreet, and generous enemies
Together they advance in friendly guise;
In honour of their kings they fight no more,
Nor of the rival beauties they adore.

10

How Agnes Sorel is pursued by the almoner of John Chandos—
Lamentations of her lover—What happened to the fair Agnes
in a convent.

And shall I then to every canto stick
A preface? Moralizing makes me sick;
For sure I am, a story frankly told,
Where simple truth we undisguised behold,
Narrated brief, from false refinement free,
Or too much wit or too much pedantry,
To parry censure must at least prevail—
So let us, reader, roundly to my tale.
When pictures merit from ressemblance claim,
To Nature true, we disregard the frame.
    Now good King Charles for Orléans departs,
Inspires fresh courage in his soldiers' hearts,
Raises the drooping destiny of France,
And bids his troops with joyous hope advance.
Of nought he spoke but marching to the fight,
He nothing seemed to feel but war's delight;
Yet secretly the soul-drawn sigh found vent,
For from his mistress far his course was bent;
Her for a moment only to have left,
Of Agnes for an hour to be bereft!
This was an act that virtue might conceive,
'Twas of himself the dearer half to leave.
    When in his chamber Charles was left alone,
And calm within his heart resumed the throne,
Which glory's demon planted in his soul
The other demon who owns love's control,
Rushed to his mind and in his turn explained;
He pleaded best, the victory was gained.
With absent air, the good prince lent an ear

To all the projects he was forced to hear.
Then sought in privacy some short relief,
And there to ease an heart depressed with grief,
His pen portrayed the ardour of his soul,
While big tears blotted oft the impassioned scroll.
Nor was Bonneau at hand those tears to dry.
A stupid gentleman in ordinary,
With the soft missive was in haste dispatched,
And ere the enamoured Prince an hour had watched
(O bitter, bitter grief! O! King forlorn!)
He saw his courier with the note return.
With dire and dread forebodings on the rack,
"Alas!" the monarch cried, "what brings you back?
How's this, my note returned?" "All's lost," he said,
"These Britons Sire . . . we're ruined, we're betrayed;
Sire . . . they have taken Agnes and the Maid."
     At such rough tidings so abruptly told
The swooning monarch's sluggish blood ran cold;
Fainting he falls, nor do his powers revive
But to keep keener agonies alive.
He, who with courage such a shock could bear,
Has never been true lover of a Fair;
And such was Charles, who with this tale opprest,
By turns felt rage and anguish rive his breast;
His loyal knights bestowed their cares in vain
In mitigation of his bitter pain,
Which in its strength was like to turn his brain:
For slighter cause his royal Sire ran mad!
"Let them take Joan," he cried in accents sad,
"My knights, my clergy, the remaining land,
Fortune still spares to my supreme command,
Take all—ye cruel Britons, but restore
To my fond arms the beauty I adore.
O Love! O Agnes! O unhappy king!
But what relief can lamentations bring?
She's lost, O let me lay me down and die!
She's lost and while I impotently cry,
Perhaps some Briton rude enjoys those charms
Designed to bless a gentle Frenchman's arms.
Shall that sweet mouth, with other kisses pressed

Inspire such ecstasies as fired my breast?
Another!—Heaven, to dream it is despair!
Who knows but at this moment terrible,
She shares his transports and enjoys as well?
Alas! with her warm temperament she may
Quite possibly her luckless love betray!
The king could bear incertitude no more,
But sought adepts well versed in mystic lore
Sorbonne professors, all the magic set
Of Jews and all, who know the alphabet.
 "Sirs," said the king, "'tis fitting ye make known,
If Agnes guards for me her faith alone,
If for her lover, still her bosom sighs,
Take heed, nor dare deceive your king with lies,
Reveal the truth, for all must come to light."
The wizards, amply paid, begin out right;
In Latin, Syriac, Hebrew and Greek;
The one of them the monarch's palm will seek,
Another draws a figure in a square,
Some upon Mercury and Venus stare,
And one turns o'er his psalter for a prayer,
Pronounces loud *Amen*, then mutters low;
Others in empty glasses omens show,
And one describes a circle on the floor:
For thus the truth was sought in days of yore.
The eager king their futile labours viewed,
Till, praising Heaven, they all at once conclude,
And bid him set his jealous heart at rest,
Calm the suspicious tumult in his breast,
Since gracious Heaven, most singularly kind,
A faithful mistress to his arms assigned,
For constant Agnes ne'er had stepped astray!
Henceforth confide in what such prophets say.
 The Almoner, inexorable brute
That very moment chose to crown his suit:
Spite of her tears, in spite of Agnes' cries,
He rudely makes her youthful charms his prize;
Imperfect pleasure though was all he stole,
Embraces coarse, that never touch the soul,
Detested union delicacy mourns,

Degrading transports real passion scorns;
For who within his arms would press with pride
A mistress who should thrust her lips aside,
Whose tears of bitterness the couch bedew?
The generous soul has other bliss in view;
No thrill of happiness imbues his heart,
Save he can transport to his fair impart;
An almoner is not so nice, indeed,
But with a spur mounts his unwilling steed;
Nor heeds the feelings of his fair a jot,
Regardless if she pleasure feels or not.
The page o'ercome with love, yet timid too,
Who forth had hurried as a gallant true,
To honour and to serve the goddess bright
Destined his ardent hope to cheat or blight,
At length returned! alas, returned too late,
Entering in haste he views the churchman's state,
Who with his brutal pleasure, all a-fire
Tames and compels his prey to his desire.
Monrose springs sword in hand, with horror pale,
To castigate the beastly animal.
The almoner's impure concupiscence
Yields to the urgent calls of self defence;
From bed he starts, and grasps his staff in rage,
Parries a while then grapples with the page.
Both are right bold, courage and love inspire
Monrose, the priest mad rage and sensual fire.
    Those happy folk who taste 'midst verdant fields,
That calm which innocence unclouded yields,
Have often seen, near thickets spreading wide,
Greedy for prey, a wolf with carnage dyed,
Whose fangs the fleece destroy, while smoking blood
Of the poor sheep he ravenous laps for food;
If a strong mastiff with stout heart, cropped ears
And well set jaws now suddenly appears,
Like a winged arrow darting from afar,
Resolute, active and prepared for war;
Soon the carnivorous offender drops
The bleating victim from his foaming chops,
Flies at the dog and summoning his might

Sustains an obstinate and sturdy fight;
The wounded wolf soon feels infuriate glow
And thinks to strangle his determined foe;
While the poor panting sheep beside them lays
And for its champion dog sincerely prays.
'Twas thus the sinewy priest with iron heart
And Herculean arm played savage part
Against the page, while Agnes lay half-dead,
The victor's worthy prize upon the bed.
The Host and Hostess, valets, chambermaid,
In fine the family one will obeyed,
Roused by the noise, they mount and straight in view,
The combat seeing rush between the two.
The audacious churchman from the chamber drive,
For the fair page, all feelings are alive,
Since youth and grace combined, can never fail
To waken pity and o'er lust prevail,
Monrose so brave thus ended his affair,
Remained alone beside his beauteous fair.
His scouted rival with a front of brass,
Marched slowly off to say his morning mass.
   Agnes ashamed and torn with pangs acute
To think a priest should thus her charms pollute,
But more so that the gentle page should spy
How she was vanquished so unworthily;
Shed tears, and dared not look him in the face;
Nay, such her sorrow at this dire disgrace,
She then had wished grim Death with sudden aim,
To close her eyes and terminate her shame.
"Kill me," was all she said, "and end my woes!"
"What! would you die?" exclaimed the young Monrose.
"And shall I lose you by this recreant priest?
Oh no! Suppose you even had transgressed,
'Twere better live and expiate the offence.
Say, is 't our part to practise penitence?
The unwilling victim of superior force,
Agnes divine, what need of such remorse?
Or wherefore suffer for another's crime?"
If his discourse could not be called sublime,
His speaking eyes emitted such a fire,

As in the fair one's bosom served to inspire,
Of late detested life some faint desire.
'Twas time to dine—for in despite of woe,
As we poor mortals, from experience know,
The wretched find in abstinence no treat,
In raging fury still the sufferers eat;
For this sage reason all the scribes divine,
Good Virgil, babbling Homer—all, in fine
Who still are honoured by our thinkers deep,
Though o'er their page they gape and fall asleep—
Before the din of conflict is o'erpast,
Love to expatiate on a rich repast.
Know then fair Agnes and her gentle guide,
Dined *tête-à-tête* by the fair one's bed-side,
Where such at first their shy embarrassment,
Both on their plate their timid glances bent;
Then bolder grown they dared a stealthy look,
And bolder still a fresh occasion took.
   Reader, thou know'st that in youth's flowery days,
When all our senses own health's vivid blaze
A hearty meal excites within each vein
Those seeds of passion which we can't restrain,
Attuned to joy our quickened pulses move,
We yield to the necessity of love.
Our bosoms with soft, thrilling transports glow,
The flesh is frail, and Satan tempts us so.
   Monrose in moments with such danger fraught,
Unable to resist the glowing thought,
Falls at the feet of the afflicted fair,
And kneeling so, prefers his amorous prayer.
"Beloved object! Idol of my soul!
Death is alone henceforth my aim and goal;
What! Can my fervent passion fail to gain,
That which a ruffian's force has dared obtain?
Ah, if a crime ensured another's bliss,
What's due to him who does not act amiss?
When love no sentiment save virtue knows;
'Tis Love who speaks—you ought to hear his woes."
   Good was the argument which he preferred;
The voice of reason Agnes quickly heard;

Yet a long hour would with resistance coy
Retard the moment of expected joy;
By such soft dalliance does lady's guile
Pleasure and virtue seek to reconcile;
Right well they know resistance oft will please
A great deal better than excessive ease.
At length Monrose, the fortunate Monrose,
The fondest rights of favoured lovers knows!
The truest happiness is surely his,
When in her arms he tastes supremest bliss;
The English prince increase of glory brings
Only by humbling of rival kings;
Though haughty Henry had e'en conquered France,
Superior still I deem the page's chance.
Alas, how transitory are our joys!
How soon mischance felicity destroys!
Scarce had the gentle page love's torrent owned,
Scarce had voluptuousness his soul enthroned,
When English troops arrive with warlike din,
They rush the stairs, the door is beaten in.
Enraptured pair! that with love-transports burn,
The Almoner had played ye this foul turn.
Agnes, who terror-struck lost every sense,
Was with her lover to be hurried thence
Anon to Chandos both were to be ta'en;
If Chandos dooms them, what must be their pain?
These tender lovers had already proved,
How seldom pity his rough bosom moved!
Shame and confusion their bright eyes expressed,
Despair and grief their air forlorn confessed.
And yet they languished on and ogled too,
Blushing at pleasures which were still so new.
To cruel Chandos what will either say?
But as it chanced while still upon their way,
A score of cavaliers of Charles' train
They met, who vigilantly scoured the plain,
To ascertain if any news was known,
Concerning Agnes and the maiden Joan.
  When mastiffs, fighting cocks or lovers twain
Meet nose to nose upon the open plain,

Or some stout prop of efficacious grace,
Comes with a sturdy Jesuit face to face,
Or one who Luther's, Calvin's doctrine holds,
An ultramontane priest by chance beholds,
Without much loss of time begins the fray,
Tongue, pen or lance wage fight in fell array;
'Twas even so when chivalry of France
Beheld the British, then began the dance;
No sooner seen, than as a falchion light,
They rushed impetuous to the sudden fight,
The hardy sons of Britain stand their ground,
And many a sturdy blow is dealt around.
　　The fiery steed that Agnes chanced to bear,
Was active, young and mettlesome like her,
He plunged, curvetted, reared with eager heat,
While Agnes jumped and bounded in her seat,
And when the clang of arms increased his might,
Swallowed the bit and spent his head-strong flight;
Vainly awhile the timid Agnes tried
With feeble hand his rapid course to guide;
Too weak to rule, she must at length comply,
And to her horse remit her destiny.
Monrose perceived not 'midst the fierce affray,
Whither the fugitive now bent her way;
Her courser flew as swiftly as the wind,
And left the combatants six miles behind,
Nor halted ever till he stood before
An ancient convent's solitary door.
A forest stood, the monastery near
And close beside there flowed a streamlet clear,
With many a devious turn meandering,
It took its course where flowers were blossoming.
Green rising hills the distant landscape bound,
Whose vine-clad steeps perennially were crowned
With gifts wherewith the race of man was blest
When Father Noah left his cumb'rous chest,
The void in human nature to replace;
And weary of beholding watery space,
He haply chanced the secret to divine
By a new process to produce good wine.

Flora, Pomona and their Zephyr train
With fragrant breath perfume the healthful plain;
Unwearying the scene which meets the eyes,
Our primal parents' very Paradise
Ne'er to the view more smiling vales portrayed,
More fortunate was Nature ne'er displayed;
The air, with balmy influence could impart
Calm and contentment to the ruffled heart,
Soften the sorrows of solicitude
And make vain worldlings sigh for solitude.
    Agnes beside the rippling streamlet lay,
Her fine eyes pleased the convent to survey;
And soon no agonizing pains she felt.
It was, my friend, a convent where nuns dwelt.
"Ah! charming sanctuary," cried the fair.
"Resort where Heaven hath shed its blessings rare,
Sweet spot of innocence and peace the fane,
By prayer, perhaps, I may its grace obtain.
Perchance expressly am I hither brought,
To weep the sins with which my life is fraught.
Spouses of God, these sainted sisters meet,
Embalm with virtue their sequestered seat,
While I, of sinners the most famous known,
My days have spent to every weakness prone."
Thus spoke the fair aloud, and as she gazed,
Observed the cross high o'er the portal raised;
Then prostrate in humility adored
Salvation's emblem to lost man restored;
And feeling o'er her soul compunction press,
She straightway thought of going to confess;
From love to piety, the ways not wide,
So closely each to weakness is allied.
    It chanced the saintly Abbess of this pile
To Blois had journeyed there to stay awhile,
Her convents' privileges to maintain,
Who, while thus absent had consigned the reign,
To sister *Busy*, of the holy crew.
This nun now promptly to the parlour flew;
The gate, to welcome Agnes, opened wide.
"Enter, O welcome traveller," she cried.

"What fostering patron, or what joyous day
Hath to our altars prompted thus to stray,
This beauty dangerous to human sight?
Or art thou Saint or Angel full of love,
Who soft descending from bright realms above,
Long by the voice of innocence implored,
Deigns't to console the daughters of the Lord?"
"Too flattering, holy sister, your report,"
Agnes replies, "a sinner seeks support;
With grievous sins are all my days o'ercast,
And if to Paradise I win at last,
'Twill be by Magdalen's authority.
The strange, capricious hand of destiny
God, my good angel—not to count my horse
Have to this spot designed my errant course.
Remorse now fills my agitated soul,
Nor yet doth hardened vice usurp control.
I honoured virtue e'en when most I strayed,
And now to find her crave your pious aid;
Led as I think by wisdom infinite,
For my soul's safety here to rest this night."
    The prudent *Busy* with a pious care
Gently encouraged the repentant fair;
She ceases not the charms of grace to tell,
And escorts Agnes to her private cell;
A cell well-lit, and decked with flowers and neat,
Of gallant ornaments the charming seat,
Ample and soft was the commodious bed,
As Love himself some bridal couch had spread.
Agnes beheld, and praising Providence,
Saw there were sweets in pious penitence.
    The supper done (I ne'er could think it fit,
A matter of such moment to omit.)
Busy the charming stranger thus addressed,
"Thou knowst, my love, night rears her sable crest;
'Tis now the time when wicked spirits prowl,
To tempt on every side the saintly soul.
'Tis fitting we a worthy feat perform,
Let's sleep together, that should Satan's storm

Against us rise, we may thus being two
Give to Beelzebub himself his due."
    Can I, O Reader, without too much shame
What sister *Busy* truly was proclaim?
I must be candid, and reveal the truth;
My sister *Busy* was a lusty youth;
He joined with Hercules his force, the grace
And winning softness of Adonis' face;
Nor yet his one and twentieth year he knew,
As white as milk and fresh as morning dew.
The lady Abbess for some private end
Lately selected him to be her friend,
Thus sister Batchelor lived within the Gate,
Nor spared his pretty flock to cultivate;
So great Achilles, as a maiden drest
At Lycomedes court was greatly blest,
And by his Deidamia's arms carest.
The penitent had scarce on couch reclined
With her companion, when she seemed to find
In nun a metamorphosis most strange.
Doubtless she benefited by the exchange.
To scream, complain, the convent to alarm
Had proved a scandal only fraught with harm;
To suffer patiently, be silent too,
To be resigned was all that she could do.
Besides on such occasions it is rare
For much reflection to find time to spare.
But when the sister's cloistered fury ceased,
(For all require some interval at least),
Fair Agnes, not without a certain shame,
Found time this silent sentiment to frame;
"'Tis then in vain I try," she thus pursued,
"To shape my course as honest woman should;
'Tis vain on aspiration's wing to rise,
One is not always virtuous though one tries."

11

How the Convent is sacked by the English—
Combat of Saint George, Patron of England
with Saint Denis, Patron of France.

No useless preface shall I here employ,
But tell, how wearied with forbidden joy,
Clasped in each others arms, exhausted quite
The lovers slept, inebriate with delight.
  Sudden a dreadful din drives sleep afar,
On all sides gleams the horrid torch of war;
Death, grisly death now blazes on their view,
And streams of blood the convent's site bedew.
This filibustering and British horde,
The Gallic troops had routed in discord,
The conquered, sword in hand, scoured o'er the plain
By victors followed who pursued amain,
Striking, destroying, shouting out of breath:
"Yield Agnes or prepare for instant death!"
But none had any tidings of the fair,
Till hoary Colin, who of flocks had care,
Said: "Sirs, my sheep while tending yesterday,
A miracle of beauty came my way,
And gained admittance in yon convent's gate."
"'Twas she," the Britons cry, with joy elate,
And instant scale the sacred walls—behold!
The famished wolves 'midst the defenceless fold.
  Searching from cell to cell the convent round,
Thro' chapel, dormitory, cave profound,
These enemies of those who serve God's name,
All things assail *sans* scruple and *sans* shame.
Ah! sisters Agnes, Ursula, Marton!
Why lift your hands to Heaven and vainly run?
Poor moaning doves with trouble in your eye,

Death in your bosom, whither shall ye fly?
Would ye to Altar's dread asylum get,
Of holy chastity the amulet?
Vain and unheeded are your fervent vows,
In vain you invocate your heavenly spouse.
Before His eyes, nay, at His very shrine,
Vile ravishers compel you to resign
That pure and sacred faith, which heretofore,
Your pretty lips so innocently swore.
Some mundane readers, prone to silly fun,
May ridicule the sacred name of nun;
Frivolous wits, a shameless mocking crew,
Who jest at rapes and ravished maidens too;
Let them say on—Alas! my sisters dear,
Full well I recognize your grief and fear;
I see your simple graces, timid charms
Struggling, in vain, in blood-polluted arms;
I see your lips become disgusted food
Of felon's kisses, reeking still with blood,
Who by an act detestable and dire,
Their lips blaspheming and their eyes on fire,
Mingle voluptuousness with injury
And offer love in all ferocity!
Whose hateful breath emits a poisonous stench,
Whose beards are hard, whose hands are formed to wrench
The hideous forms, the bloody arms, smoke-stained,
Suggested death, caresses only feigned;
And from their savage wrath one might have said,
Devils these were who angels ravished!
  Crime had already to their shameless view,
Tinged front of each chaste fair with crimson hue,
Sister Ribondi so devout and wise,
Had fallen to the haughty Shipunk's prize.
Wharton the infidel and stern Barclay too
Poor sister Amidon at once pursue.
They weep, they pray and swear; press, push and run;
When in the tumult's seen, *Busy*, the nun.
Struggling with Bard and Parson, who employ
Their utmost force—not knowing she's a boy!
Nor was't thou Agnes, 'mid the sorrowing band,

To be neglected by the assailer's hand.
Tender, enchaunting object, 'twas thy lot
Always to sin, whether thou wouldst or not;
The blood-stained chief of this unholy crew,
Courageous victor, he sped after you;
While troops, obedient, in their passions still,
Resigned this honour to his potent will.
    But Heaven, just e'en in its severe decrees
Will sometimes limit human miseries,
For whilst these gentlemen of Britain's isle
With foul pollution thus had dared defile
Of Holy Sion this most sacred place,
From Heaven's high vault Gaul's patron full of grace,
Good Denis, to bright virtue always kind,
Found means to escape from thence and leave behind
Fierce turbulent Saint George, of France the foe.
From Paradise he bent his course below;
But, in descending to our earthly sphere,
No more on sun-beam did he dare appear;
Too clearly thus might men his march descry.
    He sought him out the God of mystery,
The God of cunning, foe of noise and light,
Who flieth everywhere and goes by night.
He favours (more's the pity!) rogues that steal,
But leads the man impressed by wisdom's seal;
To church and court he hies; at all times there;
While anciently of love he had the care.
He first enveloped in a cloud obscure
The worthy Denis, with him made the tour,
By secret path which no one had descried;
They talked in whispers, marching side by side.
The faithful guardian of Gaul's goodly set,
Not very far from Blois, the Maiden met,
Who by a little, winding path drew near,
Still mounted on the clumsy muleteer;
Praying some lucky chance might guide her way
Where her late lost and much loved armour lay.
When Denis from afar the maid espied
In tone benign, the pious patron cried:
"O maiden mine! O Virgin most elect!

Still destined kings, and damsels to protect,
O come! and succour virtue in distress,
O come! and mad, licentious rage repress;
Come, let that arm, that guards the Fleurs de Lys,
To blessed sprigs of promise bring release.
Yon convent view—they violate, time flies,
Come then, my Maid!" He spoke; she thither hies,
While the good patron, as her squire in rear,
With lusty stripes whips on the muleteer.

    Behold then Joan, amongst the ignoble throng
Who dare treat venerable dames with wrong!
The maid was naked; a rude British knight
Losing his head at such a tempting sight,
He covets her; and, thinks some maiden gay
Has sought the sisters to enjoy the fray;
To her he runs and on her nakedness
Seeks to indulge his filthy nastiness;
But he was answered by a lusty blow,
Which cleft his hose and laid the villain low;
Swearing that oath by Frenchmen all revered,
Expressive word, to pleasure's feats endeared;
Though in their anger oft the herd profane
Are known to take this blessed word in vain.
Trampling his corpse, with crimson current dyed,
Joan to this wicked people forthwith cried;
"Cease cruel troop, leave innocence alone,
Fell ravishers, and fear both God and Joan."
Each miscreant till the mighty work was done,
Gave heed to naught, intent upon his nun;
Young asses thus will crop the verdant glades,
Spite of the cries of masters or of maids.
Joan, who their deeds audacious thus descries,
Transported feels a saintly horror rise;
Invoking Heaven and backed by Denis' power
With glaive in hand, of blows she deals a shower,
From nape to nape and thence from spine to spine,
Cutting and slashing with her blade divine;
Transpiercing for intended crime the one,
The other striking for offences done;
Right well her blade the felon cohort mowed,

She stabbed each wretch whilst each his nun bestrode,
And as in ebb of lust the soul took flight
Sent them to Hell expiring in delight.
    Unblushing Wharton whose lubricious fire,
Had to its acme spurred his foul desire,
First of the troop was Wharton's business done,
He first got disentangled from his nun;
Then seized his arms and with undaunted look,
Awaiting Joan a different posture took.
O! thou great Saint, the state's protecting shield,
Denis, who saw this well-contested field,
Deign to my faithful muse those feats indite,
Which Joan enacted to thy reverend sight;
Joan trembled first and cast a wondering stare;
"My saint, dear Denis, what do I see there?
My corset and celestial armour too,
The valued present I received from you,
Upon that felons' back insults my view!
See my gay casque, behold my hauberk bright."
'Twas very truth and maiden Joan was right.
Agnes had changed her silken petticoat,
For Joan's bright helm and strongly mailed coat;
When Chandos stripped her, Wharton dared aspire
To these fair spoils, as Chandos' trusty squire.
O Joan of Arc! redoubted heroine!
You combat to regain those arms divine,
For your great monarch Charles so long abused,
And scores of Benedictine nuns misused,
To please Saint Denis and correct his foes.
Denis, who saw you lavish lusty blows,
On your own helmet gay in crested shade,
And cuirass ringing from your trenchant blade.
When Vulcan for the Thunderer supplies
Those mighty cannon men too lightly prize,
His blind companions labour underground,
And Etna's caverns far and wide resound;
The sparkling anvils ring with hearty blows,
Less heavy, less reiterate than those.
    Encased in iron, our Briton, full of pride,
Falls back, his soul with wonder stupefied,

To find himself so vigorously beset,
By a young, tempting, fresh, and plump brunette.
To view her naked filled him with remorse,
To wound that body robbed his arm of force,
He but defends himself and backward moves,
Admiring in his foe the charms he loves;
Those treasures which impel his heart to scorn
The martial virtues which her soul adorn.

When in the 'midst of happy Paradise
Denis of France no longer met his eyes,
Saint George of England harboured little doubt
What schemes his brother Denis was about.
Through all the ways of the celestial plain,
He turned his anxious scrutiny in vain,
Nor wavered long, but called his gallant steed,
That horse whereof in legend much we read.
His charger came, Saint George the saddle pressed,
His sabre by his side, his lance in rest;
And journeyed through the dreadful space that man
With vain audacity desires to span;
Through divers Heavens, 'midst globes emitting light,
That bold Descartes in wild romantic flight,
Saw through a mass of shifting atoms move,
In giddy vortex difficult to prove,
Which Newton, greater dreamer still, descried,
Turning themselves, of compass reft, and guide,
Around mere nothing through the vacuum wide.

Saint George inflamed, his rage then boiling high,
Traversed this void in twinkling of an eye,
To where Loire's gleaming waters smoothly run,
And Denis thought the victory was won.
Some comet thus doth in deep night appear,
Marking with horrid light its long career;
The people tremble to behold its tail,
The Pope's appalled, the superstitious quail,
And all foretell that vintages shall fail.

As in the distance valiant George descries
His confrère Denis, swift his passions rise;
And brandishing his deadly lance the while,
These things he said in true Homeric style,

"O Denis! Denis! weak and peevish foe,
Timid support of party doomed to woe,
Is 't thus to earth in secret you descend
To bring my English heroes to sad end?
Think you the destinies you can disarm
With a winged jackass and a woman's arm.
Nor fear you the just vengeance of my lance,
Which soon shall punish you, your drab and France!
Your sour sconce shaking on your twisted neck
Has once before your carcass ceased to deck:
I wish to crop, e'en in your church's face
Your bold pate set but badly in its place,
And send you packing to your Paris walls.
Fit patron whom each tender cockney calls,
In your own suburbs where your mass is said,
There bide and let them once more kiss your head."
    Good Denis lifting slowly to the skies
His pious hands, in noble tones replies,
"O puissant George! O brother saint most sage,
Will you be ever blinded thus by rage?
Since first we met in the celestial hall,
Your heart devout has overflowed with gall I
Befits it us who rank amongst the bless'd,
Enshrined saints, so much on earth caress'd;
We, who to others should example set,
Must we in quarrels thus ourselves forget?
Is it your wish to carry discords rude
Into the land of pure beatitude?
How long shall saints who from your nation rise
Carry confusion into Paradise?
O Britons! nation fierce; too bold by far,
Just Heaven in turn will wage the watchful war;
And of your mode of acting weary grown,
Will to your jealous cares no more be prone,
For devotees from you are never known.
Ah! wretched saint, the pious, choleric,
Damned patron of a race of blood ne'er sick;
Be tractable for once and let me bring
Safety to France and succour to my King."
    At this harangue, George with redoubled ire

Felt his blood boiling, and his cheek on fire.
The cockney patron he surveyed a while,
Then (taking Denis for a coward vile)
His courage rose and at the saint he drove,
Much as a hawk might at a timid dove.
Denis retreats and prudently commands
His faithful ass to wait on his demands,
His winged ass, his joy and aid in strife,
"Come," he cries loud, "once more defend my life."
Using such words, good Denis had forgot
A saintly life's a thing one loseth not.
From Italy our dapple of grey hue,
Just then arrived and I, narrator true,
Why he returned already have displayed.
To Saint he bent his back with saddle 'rayed.
Our patron with delight his charger viewed,
And felt his courage and his strength renewed.
With subtile malice he from earth had ta'en
A sword but lately grasped by Briton slain;
Then brandishing the glittering blade on high,
At adverse George he doughtily let fly.
The British Saint by indignation led,
Aims three dread blows at his devoted head;
All three are parried, Denis guards his sconce,
Directing in return his blows at once
Upon the horse and eke the cavalier
From clashing swords the vivid sparks appear;
From hilt to point their clashing sabres meet,
With dread intent in the dire combat's heat;
Seeking the neck with scaly armour bound,
Or casque, where lambent glory played around;
Or aiming at the still more tender point,
Where cuirass meets the plated codpiece joint.
These fruitless efforts but increase their spleen,
And Victory stood balancing between.
When lo! the ass's tones discordant sound,
As grating octaves, harshly bray around.
The Heavens tremble; and the woods reply
With shuddering echoes to the grating cry.
Saint George grew pale; the other active saint

Managed adroitly a celestial feint;
A back stroke slit Saint George's nose in twain;
The bleeding lip fell on the ensanguined plain.
George keeps his courage, though he lost his nose;
Forthwith to venge his outraged face he goes;
And with an oath conformant to the way,
In which men swear in England to this day,
What Peter cut from Malchus long ago
He lopped from Denis with a dexterous blow.
    At such a sight, and at the voice so fell
Of the holy ass; at cries so terrible,
Great the commotion that prevailed on high;
And the wide portal of the starry sky
Flew open and from the vaults where seraphs dwell
Issued, at length, the angel Gabriel;
Extended wings his placid course sustain,
He soared majestic through the aerial plain
In his right hand that mystic wand he bore,
Which Moses stretched aloft, in days of yore,
When the obedient sea piled wave on wave,
O'erwhelmed whole nations in a watery grave.
"What's this?" he cried in anger; "what a sight!
Two patron saints, the heirs of joy and light,
Participators of eternal grace,
Adopt the quarrels of the mundane race!
O! let the foolish sons of women feel
The rage of passion, and the force of steel;
Abandon them to their profaner souls,
Their sickly bodies and their grosser souls,
In vice created and to death consigned;
But ye, immortal sons of Heaven refined,
Nourished forever with ambrosia pure,
Would ye such blissful scenes no more endure?
Are ye stark mad? Good Heavens! an ear, a nose;
Ye, who on mercy and sweet grace repose,
Whose duty 'tis the reign of peace to teach,
Can ye in some kings' cause—I know not which—
A mortal quarrel and dispute embrace?
Either renounce the bright, empyreal space,
Or instant yield submissive to my laws;

Let charity within plead her own cause;
You, insolent Saint George, pick up that ear,
And you, good master Denis, also hear,
Pick up that nose with saintly fingers blest;
Let all things in their proper places rest!"
  Obedient Denis straight restores the point
Of nose he put so lately out of joint;
Whilst fiery George did Denis' ear restore,
And either Saint to Gabriel muttered o'er
Oremus soft, whilst he replaced with care
Those bits of gristle as at first they were.
Blood, fibres, flesh unite with little pain,
Nor did a vestige on the Saints remain
Of the decapitated nose or ear;
The flesh of Saints is e'en so firm and fair.
  Then Gabriel with presidential air
Bade them embrace and end this strange affair.
Denis, all gentleness, sincerely kissed
His rough and rancorous antagonist,
But fiery George with an insidious kiss,
Swore Denis should in future pay for this.
The bright Archangel, (things thus reconciled),
Took my two saints and with deportment mild,
Led them, one on each side, to Heaven, where
Bumpers of nectar banish strife and care.
  Few readers will believe this combat brave;
But round the walls Scamander's waters lave,
Have we not known two bands in martial pride,
From high Olympus fight on either side?
Have we not seen in English Milton's song,
Whole legions of the winged angelic throng,
Redden celestial plains with sanguine tide,
Mountains by hundreds scatter far and wide;
And what is worse have big artillery?
If Michael and the Devil, anciently
Fought thus—why might not George and Denis too,
These precedents with emulation view?
Excited by examples of such note.
To meet and try to cut each other's throat?
  But while in Heaven peace was hovering;

On earth alas! it was a different thing,
Fell scene accursed of discord and of blows.
Good Charles went every where, nor knew repose,
Sighed Agnes' name, and sought and wept her plight;
Meanwhile the thundrous Joan with constant might,
And bloody sword that owned no victors will,
Prepared to give fierce Wharton straight his fill;
A mighty blow those monstrous parts destroyed
Which to defile the convent he employed;
From his numbed hand the useless weapon fell,
He reeled and still blaspheming sunk to Hell.

    The aged nuns their maiden champion greet.
Viewing the slaughtered Briton at her feet;
And said with *Aves*: "'Tis the justest case,
His punishment has struck the *sinning place.*"
Sister Ribondi, whom in sacristy
He had o'ercome with impious victory,
Wept for the traitor, whilst she thanked the skies;
And measuring the culprit with her eyes,
Exclaimed in charitable tones: "than he,
Alas! alas! none could more guilty be."

12

*Monrose slays the almoner–Charles discovers Agnes who consoled
herself with Monrose in Cutendre's Castle.*

True, I had sworn to moralize no more,
To narrate brief, avoiding long discourse,
But garrulous the God-head I adore,
And who is proof against Don Cupid's force?
His inspiration fires my fevered brain,
And my pen scribbles on the unequal strain.
Young beauties, maidens, widows, wives enrolled
Upon his charming banners' ample fold;
Ye who alike receive his flames or darts,
Now tell me, when two glowing youthful hearts,
Equal in talents, merit and in grace,
When both would court you in the fond embrace,
Pressing alike, and fanning rapture's fire,
Awakening in the breast each keen desire;
Does not a strange embarrassment ensue?
Perhaps this simple tale is known to you;
An ass, in school illustrious, who lay
Stabled between two equal loads of hay,
Alike in form, they drew him either way.
He pricked his ears and dubious long delayed,
By potent laws in *equilibrio* swayed,
Till loath to choose, unable to decide
From fatal doubt, the ass with hunger died.
Oh! never follow such philosophy,
But rather honour intermittently,
Your rival swains, with all the joy you will;
To risk your precious life is always ill.
    Not far removed from this monastic pile,
Polluted, sad and stained with bloodshed vile,
Where nuns a score that morn from sorrow's spell,

Our amazon had but avenged too well,
Hard by the Loire, there stood a castle old,
Which turrets, loop-holes and drawbridge uphold,
A current level with its margin flowed,
Meandering round this turretted abode;
While twice two hundred, bow-shots served to mark
The broad enclosure of the spacious park.
A Baron old, Cutendre intitulate
Was Seigneur of this fortunate estate,
Each stranger there became a welcome guest,
The ancient lord, whose heart was of the best,
Made it a refuge for the country round;
English and French a like reception found.
Stranger in coach, in boots, in gaiters 'rayed,
Prince, nun or monk, or Turk or priest by trade,
Were welcomed there with amity most true;
But those that came, must enter two by two;
For every lord his fantasy must feed,
And this same Baron firmly had decreed,
That even numbers only stayed with him,
Odd numbers never; such his crazy whim.
When two and two assailed his mansion's gate
All things went well; but woe betide the fate
Of him who single sounded at his port;
He badly supped—was fickle fortune's sport
Till some companions came to glad his view,
Making the perfect number—two is two.

The martial Joan, who had reta'en her arms,
Which loudly rattled on her sturdy charms,
With Agnes, bland and fair, at setting day
She here, confabulating, bent her way.
The Almoner who followed close behind,
The Almoner of ardour unconfined,
Reaches full soon the hospitable door.
As some dire wolf, his chaps distained with gore,
Mouths the soft down of some late-rescued lamb,
Who bleating walks beside the sorrowing dam
Whilst he from recent disappointment bold
Watches to scale the well-defended fold;
So with an ardour nothing could deter,

And eye on fire, the priestly ravisher
Went prowling after his departed prey,
In moment of enjoyment snatched away.
He rings, he calls; those who attending wait,
Perceive a single stranger at the gate;
And lo! the two substantial beams above,
To whose ascendant force responsive move
The trembling rafters of the ponderous frame,
Rose up—and up the heavy drawbridge came.
At such a sight, expected not the least,
Who cursed and swore, if not the scurvy priest!
He seeks the soaring rafters with his eyes,
He lifts his hand, and voiceless gives no cries.
Thus have I seen from leaden spouts on high
A cat steal down to some gay aviary,
And pass her trait'rous paws through slender wires
That screened the songsters from her fell desires;
Pursuing with her eyes the feathered race
Who safely perched, elude her cruel chase.
But our lewd Almoner was more dismayed
When, from beneath an elm's high tufted shade,
A handsome youth he saw, with golden hair,
With eye-brows black and an assured air,
His eyes were lustrous and his downy chin,
And eke the graces had adorned his skin;
He shone with colours of a brighter age;
'Twas Love himself, or else the handsome page;
'Twas young Monrose, who all the day had roved
In search of that dear object whom he loved.
When at the convent the lost fair he sought,
(Some holy comforter the sisters thought)
The blooming youth to their too partial sight
Than th' Angel Gabriel appeared more bright,
Come down to bless them from the Heavens' height.
The gentle sisters when they saw Monrose,
Their faces dyed in colours of the rose.
And thus each whispered, "Where, alas, was he,
Merciful Father, when they ravished me?"
Forming a ring their tongues incessant go,
They press upon him and no sooner know,

That this sweet page in search of Agnes hied,
When straight was given a courser and a guide,
In order that no ill might him befall,
In journeying to Cutendre's castle wall.
He saw upon the road, arriving there,
Hard by the bridge the brutal Almoner.
With joy and rage, he felt his bosom swell;
"Ah, then 'tis you," he cried, "vile priest of Hell.
By Chandos and my soul's salvation now,
And more, by her I swear who has my vow,
That thou shalt expiate thy damning deeds."
The chaplain's wrath his power of speech impedes;
He loaded pistol, the nice trigger drew,
The cock obeyed, pan flashed and bullet flew;
Subservient to the ill directed glance
Wide of the mark, it whizzed a line of chance.
His pistol now the royal page presents,
Lodging with surer aim its dire contents,
Full in that front, where nature's hand designed
The rugged outline of a wicked mind.
    Down fell the Almoner, the Page's breast
Some sparks of pity for his foe confesst;
"Alas!" he cried, "a christian die, at least,
Te Deum say; you lived a very beast.
Ask Heaven's forgiveness for your luxury,
Pronounce Amen, and seek eternity."
The tonsured villain cried: "I am damned, I know,
And to the devil I am forced to go."
He spoke and died, and his perfidious spright
To swell the infernal cohort flew outright.
    While thus impenitent, this monster hied
On brimstone flames of Satan to be fried,
King Charles, o'erloaded with his grief profound
His errant mistress anxious sought around
And as he strolled along Loire's pleasant tide
His kind confessor journeyed by his side.
Now in few words I must my readers tell,
In what a pious doctor should excel
Whom a voluptuous prince in youthful pride
For etiquette appoints to be his guide.

'Tis one who to indulgence sets no line,
Who in his hand knows gently to incline
Of good and ill the most perfidious scales,
Who leads you up to Heaven by pleasant vales.
Who, (surest thus his master's heart to win),
Instructs him conscientiously to sin
Composing still his actions, eyes and face,
Observing all and flattering with grace,
The master, mistress and the confidant,
Ever alert and always complacent.
The confessor, of whom I now shall speak,
Was a true son of good Saint Dominic.
Whom Father Bonifoux we'll henceforth call;
He could accommodate himself to all.
His lord he thus bespoke, devout of heart:
"I pity you, alas! your grosser part
Has got the upperhand—fatal affair.
Agnes to love is sinful, I declare,
But venial sins like that were much in vogue
With the old Hebrews of the decalogue.
His servant Agar Abraham beguiled
And proved the father of his handmaid's child;
Bright were the eyes caused Sarah's jealous pain,
And righteous Jacob married sisters twain.
The patriarchs all loved variety
In the exchange of amorous mystery.
Boaz, the veteran, after harvest led
The young and lovely Ruth to his old bed
And not to mention Bathsheba the fair,
His full seraglio was King David's care;
Where his brave son for flowing locks renowned
Withal to stay his matchless vigour found.
Of Solomon, the judgment sage you've heard:
Like oracle men listened to his word,
Wisest of Monarchs, tutored in all things,
He was alike the most gallant of kings.
If you the track of these dear sins pursue,
If love must all your youthful years subdue,
Console yourself—wisdom will have its turn,
We sin in youth; grown old, to grace return."

"Ah!" cried Charlot, "this lecture's good to con,
Alas! how far am I from Solomon!
Three hundred mistresses his ample store
I had but one, and she is mine no more.
His happiness does but augment my woe."
All down his nose his piteous tear-drops flow,
And interrupt his voice plaintive and low,
When turning towards the river's banks his eyes,
On palfrey mounted, trotting hard, he spies
A scarlet cloak, an ample paunch and round,
The judge's band; good Bonneau then was found.
Now each must own, that after his adored,
Nought to her lover can such bliss afford,
As once more his true confidant to greet;
The breathless monarch 'gan his name repeat,
Crying: "What demon brings thee here, Bonneau?
Where is my love?—Whence camest thou? Let me know.
What spot she graces, where her bright eyes reign?
How shall I find her?—Tell me quick!—Explain!"
    To all these questions prompt by Charles proposed,
Anon good Bonneau in due turn disclosed;
How doublet he had been compelled to wear,
How kitchen service eke had been his care;
How, by a trick, he had escaped well,
Eluding Chandos as by miracle,
When all were occupied to join the fight;
How each was in pursuit of Agnes bright;
Omitting nought he thus the tale went through,
Recounting all: whereas he nothing knew:
He did not know the fatal destiny
Of the English churchman's brutal luxury,
Nor how the page had loved—and been loved back,
Nor of the convents most incestuous sack.
Over and over they explained their dread;
And reassumed an hundred times the thread
Of their complaints; blamed fate but England more,
Till both became as pensive as before.
'Twas night and Ursa Major's car on high
Towards the Nadir had his course gone by,
The Jacobin his pensive prince addressed:

"Darkness is near, let memory warm your breast,
That every mortal prince or monk, thus late,
Must seek some roof, where he in happy state,
May sup and pass the hours of night away."
The tristful king was ready to obey,
Without reply—and dwelling on his pain,
With head reclined he galloped o'er the plain;
And soon before the moat of the chateau
Stood Charles, his confessor and eke Bonneau.

In the canal his rival's carcass thrown,
Still near the bridge the page remained alone,
Forgetting not at all his journey's goal,
He hid within, the anguish of his soul,
Viewing the bridge that barred him from his Dear;
But when, beneath the moon, he saw appear
The Frenchmen three, once more within his heart,
He felt hope's fire its cordial glow impart;
And with a grace as rare as his address,
Hiding his name, and more, his eagerness,
His very sight excited tenderness.
And when he spoke, the king himself he pleased,
And the good monk the soft contagion seized;
Who leering piously with aspect bland,
Patted his downy cheek with open hand.

An even number thus composed of four,
The beams which late aloft the drawbridge bore,
Slowly descend; the cavaliers pass on,
Beneath their coursers' hoofs the madriers groan.
Fat Bonneau puffing to the kitchen went,
His thoughts, as ever, on good cheer intent:
Nor Bonifoux required him to entreat,
But on devoutly passed to bless the meat.
Charles, with the name of simple *sieur* arrayed,
Cutendre sought ere *somnus* he obeyed.
The worthy Baron courtesy expressed,
Then to his chamber led the royal guest.
Charles now required the balms of solitude
To relish all his deep solicitude.
Agnes he wept; but shedding thus the tear,
He little dreamt her charms reposed so near.

More than the king, Monrose already knew,
And with address from prating pages drew
Full information where fair Agnes lay;
Discreetly reconnoitering his way,
Just as a cat when quiet lies the house,
Watches the stealthy passage of a mouse,
And stealing forth the feeble foe to meet,
Lets not the earth feel the impress of her feet,
But once in view upon the prey she springs;
Monrose alike, impelled by love's own wings,
With arms extended onward cautious steals,
Planting the toes, and raising high the heels;
O Agnes! Agnes! in thy room he kneels.
Less quickly fly to amber lightest straws,
Less quickly steel obeys magnetic laws,
Than on his knees the bold Monrose we find
Beside the couch where the fond belle reclined.
For words they had nor leisure nor desire,
Sudden as thought bright blazed the amorous fire
In an eye's twinkling, one warm amorous kiss,
Their half-closed mouths united straight in bliss;
Their dying eyes the tender fires disclose,
Their soul comes floating to their lips of rose;
Their lips, which kissing, closer contact seek
And eloquently thus their passion speak!
Mute intercourse, the language of desire,
Enchanting prelude, organ of love's fire:
Yet for a trice, 'twas fitting to forget
This concert sweet, this exquisite duet.
    Fair Agnes' hand assists to disengage
The cumbrous garments of the impatient page,
Who casts aside his troublesome attire,
Disguise averse to nature and desire,
To mortals in the golden age unknown,
Shunned by the God who still hath naked gone.
Ye Gods, what treasures! Is it Flora say,
With youthful Zephyrus in wanton play?
Or is it Psyche fair caressing Love?
Or is it Venus in the Idalian grove

Clips fast the boy afar from the emprise
Of garish day, while Mars is wrath and sighs?
    The Gallic Mars, Charles, in the same chateau
Sighed at this moment with his friend Bonneau,
He eats regretful, drinks with sadness 'rayed.
An ancient valet, garrulous by trade,
To render gay his Highness taciturn,
Informed the king, who nothing sought to learn
How two young beauties, one robust and bold,
With raven locks, and mien that Mars foretold,
The other gentler, coloured-fresh, blue-eyed,
Slept at that moment at the other side.
Astonished Charles, suspicious at this strain,
Bade him repeat it o'er again;
What were the eyes, the mouth and what the hair,
The converse tender, and the modest air,
Of that loved object which his heart adored;
'Tis her at length, his all in life restored.
Assured he is and quits the gay repast:
"Bonneau, adieu, I seek her arms at last."
He spoke, he flew—reckless of noise was he,
Being a king, he sought not mystery.
    Full of his joy, he called through every ward,
On Agnes' name, till Agnes frightened heard.
The happy couple on their couch of bliss,
Were much embarrassed: how escape from this?
When lo! the youthful page his card thus played:
Beside the canopy, a niche displayed
Itself, wherein an oratory stood
A *pocket-altar*; whereto any could.
(If any wanted such a thing at all)
For fifteen pence a good Franciscan call.
And in the altar-piece, device so quaint,
Was scooped a niche which waited for its saint.
This niche, from eyes profane was covered o'er
With a green curtain, wide displayed before.
What did Monrose? with happy thought impress'd,
He of the sacred place became possess'd;

And leaping up, behind the curtain goes,
To play the saint, *sans* doublet, cloak or hose.
   Charles flew; no barrier his course could check,
Entering, he clasped his loved one round the neck,
And would indulge in many nameless things,
Which lovers claim, especially when kings.
The curtained saint at such a sight was shocked
He made a noise and straight the altar rocked,
The Prince approaching, then his hand applied,
He felt a body and retiring cried:
"Love and Saint Francis, Satan, Lord of night!"
Half overcome by jealousy and fright
He pulled, and on the altar down pell-mell,
With clattering sound the rods and curtains fell;
Squatted behind, a figure shewed as fair
As nature ever formed with partial care.
His shoulders turned in modesty displayed
That part, which Caesar shamelessly betrayed,
To Nicomedes in his youthful prime,
That part which the Greek hero of old time
So much admired in his Hephestion,
Which Adrian set up in the Pantheon:
On heroes' frailty, Heaven, compassion!
   If my kind reader has not lost the thread
Of my narration, he will mind to have read,
How in the British camp courageous Joan
Traced on his baser part (I blush to own)
With hand conducted by Saint Denis keen
Three lilies as expert as e'er were seen.
This rump, these lilies, three within a shield,
Astonished Charles: his knees began to yield;
He thought Beelzebub had played the trick;
Struck with repentance and with sorrow sick,
Devoured by grief and fear, fair Agnes faints,
Which much the anguish of her lord augments:
"Succour," he cried, whilst her soft hand he pressed,
"Hither come all, alas, my love's possest!"
The confessor, by the king's cries upset,
Deserts his supper not without regret;

Bonneau came puffing up, quite out of breath;
Joan waking, seized with hand that dealt in death,
That sword which ever brought her victory,
And sought the place from whence had come the cry,
While 'spite of all, Cutendre's ancient lord
Slept at his ease, and never heard a word.

13

*The sally from the Castle of Cutendre–Combat between the Maid
and John Chandos–Strange law of Combat to which the Maid
is obliged to submit–Father Bonifoux's vision, and the
miracle which saves the honour of Joan.*

'Twas just that brilliant season of the year,
When Sol, to ope anew his bright career,
Curtails the night to lengthen out the day;
Delighted, as he slow expands his ray,
To view the happy climate of our land;
Till gained the Tropic, lo! he takes his stand:
O! great Saint John, thy festive morn now smiled,
First of all Johns! who preached in desert wild,
And crying everywhere, in olden day,
Proclaimed the path, where man's salvation lay;
Thee do I love and serve, O herald great!
Another John, though, had the better fate
To travel to the country of the moon
With Astolphe, giving reason's gracious boon
To Paladin, Angelica's lover true:
(O, John the second, give me back mine too!)
Thou, patron of that singer rare and bright
Ferrara's lords' perpetual delight
Who didst forget the sallies terse which he,
In comic couplets dared address to thee;
Extend supporting succour to my song;
I need such aid; for well thou knowst the throng
Is far less tolerant, and far more rude,
Than was that age with genius deep imbued,
When Ariosto honoured Italy.
Against those surly sprites, O, succour me,
Who thunder 'gainst my light frivolity!
If jesting innocent, once on a while,

Happen my work with laughter to beguile,
I can be solemn, when it is required;
Only, I would not make the reader tired.
Guide then my pen, and please convey for me,
To brother Denis all my courtesy.
As onward, haughty Joan with ardour hied,
She, through a lattice in the park, espied
Twice fifty palfreys, a right glittering troop
Of knights behind, each bearing dame on croup;
Attended these by faithful squires who bore
All the appanages of dreadful war;
An hundred bucklers that reflected bright
The quivering beams of Cynthia's silver light;
An hundred-golden helms which plumage shade,
And lances tipped with sharp and pointed blade,
And ribboned knots befringed with gold, I ween,
That pendant hung from weapon's point so keen:
Great Joan, alarmed at this unusual sight,
Believed Cutendre's walls begirt at night
By British vigilance; but erred in this:
Warriors, like other folk, may judge amiss.
Our heroine was often so deceived,
Nor had Saint Denis e'er this fault relieved.
'Twas not of Albion's sons an hardy band,
Which thus surprised Cutendre's smiling land;
But Dunois, who from Milan safe had flown,
The great Dunois, to Joan of Arc well known;
And La Trimouille with Dorothy, his fair,
With love and joy transported, happy pair!
And in her case the joy was justified:
Her faithful La Trimouille was by her side,
Love urged him on and honour was his guide;
She followed him, nor deigned from truth to stir,
And feared no more the grand Inquisitor.
　　This splendid troop, in pairs arriving right,
Within the castle were received at night;
Joan thither flew: the king who saw her go
Conceived she hurried on to meet the foe;
He hastened after, eager to engage
And left once more his Agnes with the Page.

O happy page! more blest in everything
Than the most mighty and most Christian King,
How piously you thanked the saint whose place
You occupied with such becoming grace!
But now 'tis needful you your clothes resume,
Pourpoint and variegated hose assume;
   Agnes, with timorous hand affording aid,
Which, from the toil direct, full often strayed.
How many kisses on her lips of rose
Were pressed, as she was dressing up Monrose!
While her bright eyes beholding him in dress
Seemed still desirous of voluptuousness!
Monrose in silence to the park then hied;
The saintly confessor, in secret sighed,
That such a handsome youth should e'en pass by,
Was certainly distraction for the eye.
The tender Agnes then composed her mien,
In eyes, air, port and speech, a change was seen;
To join his monarch Bonifoux was led,
Encouraging, consoling, thus he said:
"Within the niche an envoy from on High,
Came to announce from the supremest sky,
That Albion's baneful power anon will bend,
And Gallia's sufferings soon shall have an end.
Shortly the king shall victory achieve."
Charles credence yielded; anxious to believe.
This argument was favoured by the Maid:
"Accept," she cried, "this precious Heavenly aid.
Come, let us, mighty Prince, rejoin the camp,
Where your long absence has infused a damp."
Dunois and La Trimouille, who wavered not,
Of this advice were partisans most hot,
And by these heroes Dorothy outright
Was duly ushered to the royal sight.
Agnes embraces her, then, one and all,
The noble party leave the Baron's hall.
But Heavenly Wisdom oft looks down and smiles
On sublunary cares and human wiles.
In order due this gallant troop appears,
Accomplished dames and warlike cavaliers.

By Agnes' side the amorous monarch rode,
Her hand was locked in his and still she showed
How much her honour was concerned to prove,
She still was constant to her royal love.
Yet shame to tell! the involuntary glance
Oft turned aside and eyed the page askance.
The worthy confessor brought up the rear,
And chaunted forth the proper form of prayer,
Yet paused beholding such attractions nigh,
Gazing alike with a distracted eye,
On page, king, Agnes and his breviary.
Glittering in arms, the gallant court's gay pride,
Trimouille, with Dorothea by his side,
Came prancing forward; while the gentle dame,
Inebriate with joy, avowed her flame,
Called him her dear deliverer, her guide,
The idol of her heart, her joy, and pride.
Whereto he answered: "When the wars shall cease,
On my estates we'll spend our days in peace;
Adored one, I am mad for love of you,
When shall we both be settled in Poitou?"
　　Not far from these appeared redoubted Joan,
Doughty supporter of the Gallic throne,
Whose front was decked with velvet bonnet green
Enriched with gold, o'er which a plume is seen;
Her strapping charms the donkey fierce bestrode
Cant'ring and chatting, as with Charles she rode;
She bridled oft and heaved a tender sigh
When she perceived the brave Dunois draw nigh.
Her fancy still portrayed in liveliest hue,
His nakedness, which once assailed her view.
　　Bonneau, with patriachal beard arrayed,
Perspiring, blowing, closed the cavalcade.
Oh! precious servant of so great a king,
His care was such, he thought of everything;
Two mules he furnished, charged with vintage old;
Long sausages, pies luscious to behold,
And fowls, or trussed to roast, or cooked and cold.
Onward they went, when Chandos full of rage,
Who sought fair Agnes and his truant page,

And sword in hand the fugitives pursued,
Met our gay heroes near a little wood.
Of sturdy Britons with Joan Chandos came
A gallant troop, in numbers much the same,
With those attendant on the amorous king;
But different looks and different arms they bring:
Nor were there heaving bosoms nor bright eyes.
"O, ho!" cries he, in voice that thunders high,
"You gallant Gauls, with hate whom I pursue,
Ye have three girls to go along with you,
While I, the Chandos, have not even one:
To combat, let the will of fate be done,
And fortune show who best can face the foe,
Who surest wounds, who strikes the deadliest blow.
Who best can make the legions dance,
Who strongest is with battle-axe and lance;
Come on, your bravest warrior I defy,
Against this arm his boasted strength to try;
Let him who proves superior skill in arms,
Enjoy the nymph who most his fancy charms."
Piqued at the cynic offer of the knight,
The King stepped forth, and claimed the champion's right.
But Dunois cried: "Great sire, let me advance,
To vindicate the cause of love and France."
He rushed to arms—Trimouille arrests his course
And claims an equal right to test his force.
Each to the honour of the fight pretends
Till kind Bonneau, to pacify the friends,
Proposed by lot the question to decide,
As in heroic times was often tried:
E'en in some modern commonwealths we find
The dice decide who best may rule mankind.
Did I but dare, in these my flights so high
Quote some whom mortal men would ne'er deny,
I'd state that such was saint Mathias' case,
Who by this means of Judas gained the place.
Fat Bonneau takes the box, he quakes and sighs;
For Charles he fears; he tosses, throws the dies;
Saint Denis from the rampart of the skies,
Regards the warriors with paternal eyes;

On Maiden and on Donkey bends his glance;
'Twas he directed what we construe—*chance*,
Which proved propitious—Joan obtained the lot.
Joan, it was time to make that cast forgot,
That wicked hazard, when the cordelier
Raffled thy beauties with the muleteer.
Joan to the monarch sped, to arms then flew,
And modestly behind a hedge withdrew
To doff her petticoat and, eke unlace
And on her limbs, her sacred armour place,
Prepared all ready by her faithful squire;
Her ass then vaulted fraught with glowing fire—
Closing her knees, she brandishes her lance,
Evoking tutelary saints of France,
And those eleven thousand maidens dead
In honour of their precious maidenhead.
As for John Chandos—faith in him was faint,
He went to fight invoking ne'er a saint.

    John, to encounter Joan, with fury drove;
Equal the valour was of each that strove;
In iron cased and barbed, the ass and steed,
Goaded by spur eclipsed the lightning's speed;
'Gainst either hardened head, how dire the stroke,
Front against front, piece-meal the armour broke;
Fire flashed, the courser's blood with crimson seal
Dyed flying remnants of the battered steel;
From the fell shock the echoes wide resound
As all the coursers' eight hoofs spring from ground,
And both unhorsed at once the riders lay.
Thus when two ivory balls suspended play,
By cords of equal length, with force alike
In arch cycloidal they move and strike,
They clash, they flatten at the dreadful knock,
When each remounts urged by repellant shock,
Their weight augmented in a like degree,
As each redoubles in velocity.
The gazers judged each courser dead outright,
And either party trembled for its knight.
Now Gaul's august protectress, own we must,
Had not the flesh so firm, nor so robust

Bones so well knit, muscles or limbs so tight,
As had the proud John Chandos, England's knight.
Compelled in dread encounter to resign
The equilibrium, central point and line,
Her quadruped those parts to heaven displayed
Which Joan unveiled upon the verdant glade,
Her well turned back, plump thighs, in one word all—
She fell in short as maidens ought to fall.

   When Chandos saw his adversary low
He thought Dunois or Charles had been his foe,
Sudden he stoops, his conquest he surveys;
The helm removed to Chandos' view displays
The humid lustre of two big, black eyes.
That languishingly shone; he next unties
The strings that bound her cuirass to her breast;
He sees with rapture not to be exprest,
Ye Gods! two breasts as plump as they are round,
Elastic, firm, with blushing rose-buds crowned.
'Tis said that then, his voice he deigned to raise,
And for the first time breathed to Heaven his praise.
"The famous Maid of France is mine," he cried,
"Content am I, revenge is satisfied,
Grace be to Heav'n, I've doubly earned the blow
Which prostrate lays the haughty beauty low.
Let Denis look and blame me from above,
I'll use my double rights—of Mars and Love."

   His squire exclaimed: "Proceed, my Lord, proceed,
Proclaim the might of England by the deed.
In vain would Lourdis strike our souls with dread,
In vain he vaunts this sacred maidenhead,
This grand Palladium of the Gallic state,
This Latian buckler, that secures their fate,
Shall mock the efforts of our love and hate:
'Tis yours, my Lord! by one stout effort try
To wrest the *Oriflamme* and victory."
"Yes," answered Chandos, "and I have in view
The best of gifts, glory and pleasure too."
Shocked at this language of the British chief,
Joan chastely prayed to Denis for relief,
Made vows a thousand—all there was to do.

Dunois, who kept heroic deeds in view,
Would in its course this triumph vile arrest;
But how proceed? In every state the best
Was to submit to combat's stern behest;
The heavenly ass, as on the ground he lay,
With hanging ears and looks of deep dismay,
Confus'dly, languishingly, viewed the scene,
And haughty Chandos's triumphant mien.
Long had he felt for Joan the softest fire,
The purest flames of delicate desire;
A chastely noble, sentimental glow,
But little known to asses here below.
The confessor of Charles was fraught with fear,
Hearing the speech of England's graceless peer;
But trembled most lest his royal penitent,
His passions roused by such a strange event,
To assert his country's honour and his own,
With Agnes should engage; nor he alone:
Trimouille might feel the sympathetic flame,
And he and Dorothea do the same.
Beneath an oak he knelt himself in prayer,
And pondered with a meditative air,
The cause, effects, originality
Of the sweet sin that some call lechery.

    While thus the monk pursued his reverie,
He saw a vision full of mystery;
Resembling much that visionary view
Of Jacob, blessed for having spoke untrue;
Whose skin was smooth, who had a frugal mind,
And sold his lentils of the Jewish kind.
Old father Jacob I mystery sublime!
Euphrates near, one night upon a time,
A thousand rutty rams, in sleep he saw,
Upon their ewes obeying nature's law.
More pleasant sights awaited the monk's eyes:
He saw, advancing to the same surprise,
The heroic persons of posterity,
Admired the charms in all variety,
Of beauties who in combats full of mirth
Chained and enslaved the masters of the earth.

Each was established at her hero's side,
With Paphian reins his willing steps to guide.
Thus when returning Zephyrs gently play
And wake the flowers that deck the lap of May,
The feathered songsters agitate the groves,
And recommence their half-forgotten loves;
The gaudy butterflies on beds of flowers,
Caress the partners of their happy hours;
E'en savage beasts the genial warmth invades
And softened lions seek the conscious shades.
    Francis the First now in his dream appears,
The flower of monarchs and of cavaliers;
Whom Anne d'Etampes, a willing slave detains,
Forgetful of Pavia's shameful chains.
And Charles the Fifth, who bay with myrtle shared,
And for *la Maure* as well as *Flamande* cared.
Just Heaven, what monarchs! in this glorious course,
One gained the gout—the other—something worse.
Diana's near, he sees her wrinkles move,
As she is stirred by the sweet joys of love,
When in her arms she fondly rocks to rest
The second Henry, panting on her breast.
The fickle Charles the Ninth next mounts the stage,
Who laughing leaves his Chloris for a page,
Heedless of warfare which Parisians wage.
But ah! what feats our friar's vision told
When Borgia's amorous pastimes stood unrolled;
Oh, how shall I in numbers meet express
The countless pastimes of His Holiness?
There, with Vanoza joined in converse sweet,
His triple crown neglected at his feet;
While later, the same Sanctity he spies,
Who for his daughter Lucrece yearns and sighs.
O mighty Leo! O transcendent Paul!
You rival monarchs, nay! surpass them all.
Henry the Great, to you alone they yield,
Victorious both in Mars and Venus' field;
By Gabrielle's love made more illustrious far,
Than by full twenty years of toils and war.
    A glorious spectacle now rose to view,

The age of pleasure and of wonders too,
Great *Louis* and his sumptuous court now move,
Where all the arts were instigate by love.
Love reared the structure of Versailles renowned,
By Love the dazzled multitudes were crowned,
From flowery couch Love formed great Louis' throne,
Spite of the clash of arms and battle's groan;
Love, to the chief and sun of all his court
Led the most charming rivals to resort,
Impatient all and glowing with desire;
First Mazarin's fair niece, her eyes on fire,
Then generous and tender Vallière,
Then Montespan, more proud and debonnaire.
One yielding to ecstatic rapture's power,
The other waiting pleasure's promised hour.
Now mark the Regency's auspicious time,
The pleasant reign of license had its prime,
As folly, tinkling loud her bells in hand,
With lightsome step tripped over Gallia's land,
Where to devotion not a soul was prone,
And every act save penitence was known,
While the kind Regent from his palace walls,
To gay voluptuous mirth the people calls.
This charming bidding, one responsive greets,
Young Daphne—she that rules the courtiers' suites;
Who from the Luxemburg, wherein she dwells,
Whom Bacchus and the god of festivals,
Lead to the bed, Love going as her page.
        But let me pause—for of this latter age
I dare not point in verse the semblance true,
Those flattering charms too potent ills pursue
Time present as the Lord's own ark we see;
Who dares invade it with a touch too free
By Heaven is punished with a lethargy.
I will be mute—yet, reader, might I dare
Of *belles* that live, I'd trace the fairest fair,
Of tender creatures, noble, touching, sweet,
And more than Agnes constant and discreet;
Before your round, plump knees—Ah, might I dare
That incense breathe, which Venus well might share,

If I Love's weapons in due order laid,
If I the soft, the tender link displayed;
If I—but no, there shall be nothing said,
Your charms, above me, lie so far o'erhead.
At length the dreaming monk, of sable hue,
Beheld at pleasure what I dare not view.
His eyes, though modest, somewhat agitate,
The spectacle celestial contemplate
Of lovers twain arranged in a row:
The second *Charles* with *Portsmouth* fair below,
The second *George* with buxom *Yarmouth* lies.
"Alas! if grandees of the earth," he cries,
"In two and two perform such practices,
If such the universal law of all,
Why should I murmur if John Chandos fall
Upon the beauties of his nut-brown maid?
Let not the will of Heaven be gainsaid!
"*Amen, amen.*" A swoon his sense destroyed:
He thought that all he'd seen, he had enjoyed.
    But distant was it from Saint Denis' thought,
That he should see performed what Chandos sought,
That Joan and France should hear destruction's word:
Friend reader, thou hast doubtless sometimes heard,
That short clothes anciently by tags were braced:
A dreadful custom this and much misplaced;
So cruel a resource no Saint should try,
Unless in case of great emergency.
The hapless Swain no longer fondly burns,
But hot desire to icy coldness turns;
Consumed, unnerved, unable to enjoy,
He fails astonished on the brink of joy;
E'en as a flower that scorching rays have spent,
Its head reclining and its stalk down-bent,
Seeketh in vain moist vapours to inhale,
And waft its fragrance to the passing gale;
Such was the method Denis took to blight
The valiant Briton in his conquest's right.
Joan thus escaping from her conqueror crost,
Regains those senses which himself has lost.
Then cries with terrible imposing tone,

"Invincible thou art not—straightway own
That in the most important fight of all,
God helps thee not but lets thy courser fall:
Some other day I will avenge my land.
Denis so wills it, and he is my stand;
At Orléans' walls thy prowess shall be tried."
"I'll meet thee there," the great Chandos replied:
"Maid or no maid! In George I do believe,
And there I vow mine error to retrieve."

14

How John Chandos would abuse the devout Dorothy—
Combat between La Trimouille and Chandos—
How the doughty Chandos is overcome by Dunois.

O thou voluptuousness, in whom we see
Nature's true source—Venus' bright Deity,
By Epicurus erst in Greece revered,
'Fore whom, through Chaos darkness disappeared,
Who givest life and brings fecundity,
And soft emotion and felicity.
To those innumerable tribes, that live
By thy command, and at thy call revive;
Thou, painted as disarming, in thine arms,
Great Jove and Mars, the God of dire alarms;
Thou, whose sweet smile can lull the thunders' dint.
Becalm the air, and 'neath whose foot's light print,
Soft pleasures spring that all the earth control,
Goddess descend: of blissful days the soul;
Come in thy car, surrounded by thy loves,
While, with their downy wings thy constant doves
Awake the Zephyrs that afford thee shade,
As billing through the floods of air they wade:
Descend, the universe to animate,
And calm; while at thy voice, suspicion, hate
And dire *ennui* than those, more noxious ill,
And dark and leering envy, blacker still,
Replunged by thee into the depths of Hell,
Shall there in chains eternal ever dwell.
Be all on fire; uniting at thy call,
Let universal love control us all,
To flames our codes and flimsy laws consign,
We only follow one; and that is thine.
    O tender Venus! Guide to sure estate

The King of France who combats for his State.
And safe from every peril deign to guide.
The lovely Agnes ever by his side.
In earnest, for those lovers I entreat.
For Joan of Arc, no invocation's meet,
She's not yet subject to thy gentle sway:
'Tis Denis' part to lead her on her way;
A maiden she, the saint her patron friend.
To thy soft favours let me recommend
Trimouille the gallant and his Dorothy,
Let peace reward their sensibility;
That 'neath her own true lover's fostering care,
No more her former enemies may dare,
Nor sad disaster longer be her share.
And thou Comus! due recompense obtain
For Bonneau, worthy seigneur of Tourraine,
He, who pacific truce knew how to end,
'Twixt cynic Chandos and King Charles, his friend;
And planned most dexterously each force should bide,
On either margin of the current's tide,
That no reproach or quarrel should ensue,
To right and left, Loire's stream between the two.
He to the Englishmen his cares made known,
Rend'ring their manners, tastes and wants his own;
A big sirloin, with butter seasoned fine,
Plum-puddings and a noble Garonne wine,
All these were offered him; more dainty meat,
Ragouts with sauces which the lips entreat,
With partridges, their red leg offering,
For the fair dames, the seigneurs and the king.
Proud Chandos, therefore, having quaffed his drink,
Proceeded onward o'er the Loire's clear brink,
Swearing the first time he could Joan attain
He'd use the rights of such as victory gain;
Meantime, he with his pretty page returns,
While Joan, near great Dunois, for combat burns.
      The King of France, with guards in bright blue gear,
Agnes in front, the confessor in rear;
Had now a league proceeded on the way,
O'er verdant meads bedecked with flowrets gay;

By limpid Loire, its banks extending wide,
With tranquil current and inconstant tide.

On boats appeared, supporting half-worn planks,
A bridge that served to join the river's banks,
And at the farther end a chapel lay.
'Twas Sunday, and a voice was heard to pray,
An hermit's voice that through the valley rung,
Chaunting the Mass; a child responsive sung.
One Mass, the King of France and his escort,
Had heard already ere they left the fort;
But Dorothy must now hear this at least,
Her pious faith had been so much increased,
Since Heaven, the guardian of innocence
The Bastard sent to fight in her defence,
And so protected that true love which trusts.
She quick dismounts, her fluttered dress adjusts,
Three times, from holy source her forehead signs,
Folds hands, bows neck and pious knees inclines;
The holy hermit seeing her come there,
Turned round, confused, and quite forgot his prayer.
He should have said, "Let's pray for Heavenly grace,"
But cried instead, "Oh, what a heavenly face!"

To this same shrine with no devout intent,
But for mere pastime British Chandos went,
And head erect, with high, imperious air,
Saluted, as he passed, Trimouille's fair,
Then whistling still, he knelt himself behind;
No *pater*; not an *ave* crossed his mind.
With heart contrite, and grace within her eyes,
Prostrate was Dorothy, in charming guise;
Her forehead low, her buttocks rather high,
Her coats were raised from inadvertency,
Discovering still to Chandos' ravished eyes,
Such legs and such rotundity of thighs,
Such polished ivory, so smooth, so white,
So exquisitely moulded for delight,
As once Diana showed the Theban boy,
Who paid full dear that ecstasy of joy.
Chandos, who of oraison made small case,
Felt a desire, befitting not that place

So consecrate; and swift his hand steals in
Beneath the coat which hid that satin skin.
I would not with a cynic's pencil draw,
To strike my reader's modest sight with awe,
Nor e'en presume suggestion of the extent,
To which the audacious hand of Chandos went.
      Meantime Trimouille, who missed the lovely Fair,
The constant object of his amorous care,
Forth to the chapel straight his steps inclined—
Oh, whither will not love direct the mind!
Trimouille arrived just as the priest turned round,
And Chandos insolent his rude hand found
Near the most perfect of all backs below,
As fainting Dorothy with terror's glow
Emitted piercing screams, loud, echoing wide;
Fain would I have some modern painter guide
His pencil to portray this scene so strange,
And on their faces four with skill arrange
The fell astonishment that mantled there—
With cries the knight of Poitou rent the air:
"O durst thou," quoth he, "most discourteous knight,
Impious profaner of each sacred rite,
These holy walls with profanation blast?"
With bantering air, as haughty look he cast,
Adjusting dress—when near the door he drew,
Fierce Chandos said: "What is it, sir, to you?
Are you the sexton? Is this church your care?"
"A higher charge," Trimouille replied, "I bear;
I am the favoured lover of the Fair,
Whose habit is to deal out vengeance meet,
On those who dare her honour to entreat."
"In such a case you well might risk your own,"
The Briton cried, "to each the other's known,
And what he's worth, and how John Chandos may
Ogle a back, but ne'er his own display."
      For jeering Briton and the handsome Gaul,
Were steeds caparisoned for combat's thrall;
Each from his squire receives his spear and shield,
And takes his station in the dusty field.
Firm in their seats, terrific they appear,

Pass and repass, and tilt in full career.
Nor tears nor sighs of Dorothy can charm
Or check the blow of either's direful arm:
Her tender lover cried, "My lady true,
I combat to avenge or die for you."
Wrongly he judged: his valour and his lance,
Glittered in vain for tender love and France.

    Twice having pierced John Chandos' battered mail,
And well assured that victory would, not fail,
His palfrey stumbled, rolling o'er his corse,
And plunging, struck his casque with dreadful force,
Inflicting on his front an ample wound;
The crimson tide bedewed the verdant ground.
The hermit ran in haste the knight to bless,
In manus cried, and begged him to confess.
O Dorothy! then, what was thy despair,
Beside him kneeling, with a lifeless air,
Thine heavy heart could no more silence break;
But what thy words when thou, at last, couldst speak!
"My lover dear! Oh, have I killed thee—I,
The assiduous partner of thy Destiny?
Who never should thy side revered have left,
For quitting thee, of comfort I'm bereft:
This chapel ruined me, wherein I strayed,
And my Trimouille, and Love as well, betrayed,
Seeking to hear two masses in one day!"
So speaking, melted she in tears away.

    Chandos, at his success, gave vent to jeers
"My pink of Frenchmen, flower of cavaliers,
And also you, devoutest Dorothy,
Adoring couple, shall my prisoners be;
Of knightly combats, 'tis the laws' decree.
Some fleeting moments Agnes was my prey,
And 'neath me, Joan, the captive maiden lay;
I must avow, I failed in duty there,
I blush to say it—but with you, my Fair,
I'll well regain whatever then I lost.
Trimouille himself may witness if I boast."
The hermit, knight and Dorothy with fear,
Tremble all three, such horrid threats to hear.

So to a cavern's depths when dreads oppress,
Confused, entreating, flies the shepherdess;
Her flock in trembling owns the rueful cause,
The poor dog struggling in the wolf's fell jaws.
    But Heaven is just, though in its vengeance slow;
Such insolence could not unpunished go;
John Chandos' many sins reiterate,
Who boys and maidens oft would violate,
His blasphemous and unrepentant days,
His impiousness, at last, Death's angel weighs.
The great Dunois had from the other side
The combat and Trimouille's defeat espied,
He saw a damsel with disordered charms,
Clasping the languid hero in her arms,
Close by the hermit muttering on the ground,
While British Chandos wheeled triumphant round.
Fired at this sight he gives his steed the rein,
And quick as lightning darts across the plain.
    'Twas Albion's custom then, that foul or fair,
All objects should their appellations bear;
Having the bridge's barrier now past through,
Straight to the conqueror our Dunois flew,
When these rude accents struck his haughty ear:
"Son of a whore!" he heard, or seemed to hear.
"Yes," he exclaimed with pride, "that name is mine,
Such bore Alcides, Bacchus the divine,
Perseus the happy, Romulus the grand,
Who purged the earth of rapine's fateful band;
'Tis in their name, I'll do as much with you.
Remember how a Norman, bastard too,
With hand victorious made England fall.
Then O, ye sons of Thunder, Bastards all,
Direct my lance, each doughty blow decree,
Honour commands, avenge yourselves and me!"
This prayer was hardly fitting, 'twill be said;
The hero was in fable so well read;
For him the Bible lore less charm possessed;
He spoke, he flew; the golden trowel pressed;
The armed teeth are urged, until they bleed
The noble haunches of his fiery steed;

The first blow of his barbed lance amain
John Chandos struck, and burst the links in twain,
And scales are shattered of his armour bright,
Where the steel helm is joined to corselet light.
The gallant Briton deals a lusty blow
Full on the brazen buckler of his foe;
The buckler rings, but guiltless of a wound,
The weapon turns oblique. The shores resound:
With rage redoubled, and increasing force,
The closing warriors grapple in their course.
In the fierce shock, each quits the horse he rode,
Who disencumbered of his shining load,
No longer guided by coercive rein,
Turns round in peace to graze upon the plain.
As in some fearful earthquake, one has spied
Two mighty rocks detached from mountain side,
Fall on each other with a thundrous sound;
So, when these haughty warriors touched the ground,
They grip together in a fierce embrace;
The shock awakes the echoes of the place,
The air is stirred with the nymphs' mournful sighs.
E'en so when Mars, before whom Terror flies,
Covered with blood, with fury in his eyes,
Descended raging from Olympus' height,
For Troy's proud walls to mix in mortal fight;
And when the lance against him Pallas reared,
To her support an hundred kings appeared,
The fixed earth to its centre trembling stood,
Troubled was Acheron's infernal flood,
And turning pale, upon its margin dread,
E'en Pluto shook for empire of the dead.
    Now fiercely from the ground both heroes rise,
And view each other with indignant eyes,
Forth from the sheath their shining swords they drew,
At every stroke their mail in shivers flew;
The purple streams, that issued from each wound
Stained their bright armour, and bedewed the ground.
Anxious spectators the dire conflict viewed,
And round the combatants encircling stood;
With neck outstretched, eyes fired, and mind intent,

They scarcely breathed while trembling for the event.
Courage augments, when crowds are standing by,
Keen spur of glory is the public eye;
The former efforts of their martial might
Were but the preludes of this dreadful fight.
Achilles, Hector, demi-gods of old,
The Grenadiers more formidably bold,
And lions, who are redoubtable as well,
Less cruel are, less proud, implacable,
Less given to blood—The Bastard ever great
Conjoining force with art and blessed by fate,
Seized on the Briton's arm, who struck awry,
And with a back-blow smote his glaive on high,
Then with a leg advanced, his point to gain,
Chandos o'erthrew upon the gory plain;
Who, falling, dragged his foe alike to ground,
Where struggling clouds of dust their forms confound;
So in the sand for masterdom they move,
The Briton under and the Gaul above.
　　The noble victor, whom all virtues guide,
At least when fortune's favour's on his side,
His adversary pressing with one knee,
Exclaimed: "O, yield, yield Briton unto me!"
Whereto John Chandos cried, "An instant wait,
Hold!—it is thus, Dunois, I yield to fate."
　　As last resource of his infuriate mind,
A dagger drawing, he throws out behind
His sinewy arm, and striking while he swore,
Stabs in the neck his clement foe once more
The mail uninjured there, and firm of joint
Bends back and blunts the dagger's murderous point;
Dunois exclaimed: "Wretch, art resolved to die?
Then have thy will." He waited not reply,
But having no more scruple for his part
He plunged his bloody weapon in his heart.
Expiring Chandos, caught in throes of death,
"Son of a whore!" cried, with his latest breath.
So to the last, retained its character,
That proud, fierce heart which pity could not stir.
His eyes, his front infused dark horror's thrill,

His hand seemed threatening the victor still;
His soul, so godless and implacable,
Had gone to brave the Devil down in Hell.
Thus died as he had lived, this British knight,
Slain by the Gallic chief in single fight.
    To spoil the vanquished foe Dunois disdained,
Though by the usages of Greece maintained,
The law of arms; Trimouille his mind engrossed;
He lifted him, and once again could boast,
His aid had saved the days of Dorothy.
Along the road she helps him presently,
Her tender love, whom, when her hands surround,
He lives again and no more feels his wounds.
He feels but those of his adored one's eyes,
At them he looks; his strength and force arise,
His lovely mistress, snatched from depths of woe,
Found in her breast reviving pleasure glow.
The tenderness of an agreeable smile
Begins to dawn—though still tears fall awhile.
So a black thunder-cloud one oft has seen,
Illuminate by ray of sun serene.
The Gallic king, his Agnes, fraught with grace,
And Joan illustrious, all by turn embrace
The happy Dunois, whose triumphant hand
Had love avenged and his own native-land;
But chiefly was admired the modesty
Of his demeanour, of each repartee.
Easy it is, yet beautiful no less,
Modest to be, when one has won success.
    Some jealousy Joan stified in her breast,
Her heart upbraiding Destiny's behest.
That 'twas not granted to her maiden hand
Of such a miscreant to rid the land:
Bearing forever two-fold wrongs in head,
Which, near Cutendre dyed her cheeks with red,
When braved by Chandos, in the combats' list,
She was, at once, thrown on her back—and missed.

15

Of the great banquet at the Town-House of Orléans, followed
by a general assault–Charles attacks the English–
What befell the lovely Agnes and her travelling companions.

Malignant critics, you're despised by me,
Mine own defects I better know than ye.
In this fair history 'twas my design,
In gold engraven upon memory's shrine,
Nought to present but facts of high renown;
Of how the king in Orléans won a crown,
By Love and Glory and the Maid sublime.
'Tis grievous thus to have misused my time,
Singing of Sire Cutendre and a page,
Of Grisbourdon and his licentious rage,
Of muleteer, and many an incident
That to my flowing theme does detriment.
But all these narratives that greet your eyes,
Were written down by Trimetus the wise,
I simply copy, not one trait invent;
On facts, my reader, cast a look intent,
If sometimes your stern sense of gravity
Judges my sage with keen severity:
If at some traits your brow to scowl inclines,
The knife and pounce-box may efface my lines;
Half of my verse obliterate if you will,
But oh! respect that Truth which guides my quill.
O sacred Truth! thou virgin ever pure,
When wilt thou reverence deserved procure?
Divinity who mak'st us wise, why dwell,
In palace placed at bottom of a well?
Ah, when wilt thou from out those depths appear?
When will your learned men their voices rear,
From gall exempt, and from all flattery free,

To detail lives in full fidelity,
And all the exploits of our errant knights?
Prudent was Ariosto in his flights,
When Archiepiscopal Turpin he cites,
For testimony of such sacred lore,
The faith of every reader must restore.
Anxious his future destiny to know,
Charles t'wards Orléans town was fain to go,
Surrounded by his knights, with gilded crest,
The brave Dunois for his advice he pressed;
Like other kings, misfortune made him tame,
In happier times he was not quite the same.
Charles thought that Agnes followed in the rear
With Bonifax: well-pleased with hope so dear,
His glance the royal lover often turned,
And stopped to see if Agnes was discerned;
And when Dunois presaging his success,
Named Orléans, the monarch named—Agnes.
The Bastard fortunate, whose prudent mind
To serve his country more and more inclined,
A fort beheld about the fall of eve,
Which Bedford's worthy Duke thought fit to leave;
This structure near the beleaguered city lay;
By Dunois ta'en, Charles there thought fit to stay—
When fortified anon the fort was seen,
Made by besieging host their magazine.
The God of blood who victory decides,
The pimply God who o'er the feast presides,
To stock this fort, their mutual cares combine;
One cannon brings, the other noble wine:
War's dreadful implements are treasured here,
While all the apparatus of good cheer,
This little castle equally could show:
What a success for Dunois and Bonneau!
All Orléans town at such great news uprise,
And thanks to God return in solemn wise.
Te Deum they sing, with drone from *serpent-bass*,
Before the noble chieftains of the place;
Next was the dinner served for judge and mayor,
The bishops, prebends, warriors all were there:

With glass in hand each falls upon the ground;
Fire from the river casts its flashes round,
Illuminates the sombre, nocturn skies;
The cannons thunder and the people's cries
Loudly announce that Charles is come again,
The kingdom he had lost soon to regain.
    These shouts of glory and each blissful strain,
Were followed by the lengthened yells of pain,
As Bedford's name was heard from every breath;
Fly to the walls! Defend the breach—to death!
The Britons taking vantage of this chance,
When citizens engaged with wine and dance
Extolled their prince, in songs and couplets graced,
Beneath a gate two sausage forms they placed,
Not puddings such as Bonneau had in view,
When he produced them for a new *ragoût*,
But sausages, filled with the fatal force
Of gunpowder, which like the rapid course
Of lighting flash confuses heaven and earth;
Dire, murderous engines of infernal birth,
Which in their iron entrails bear the brand,
Kneaded by Lucifer's destructive hand;
By means of match, arranged with careful art,
The fell combustions quick as lightning part,
Spread, mount and to a thousand yards convey
Bars, hinges, bolts in splintery, torn away;
Fierce Talbot onward rushes with full speed,
Success, rage, glory, love excite the deed,
From far emblazoned on his arms, the eye,
In gold, a Louvet's cypher could descry.
For Louvet ever was the dame that taught
His soul to love, and swayed his haughty thought.
His was the wish to clasp her beauty's pride,
On walls demolished and with carnage dyed.
    This handsome Briton, chosen child of war
Cries to the braves who follow 'neath his star:
"Go there, my gallant conquerors, go here,
And flame and flashing steel cast everywhere,
Let's drink the wine of Orléans' coward race,
Their gold purloin, and all their wives embrace."

Not Cæsar's self, so eloquent of speech,
Such honour and audacity could preach
To martial spirits, as this fiery strain,
Instilling fury through the warlike train.
Upon the spot, where the gate as it burned,
For fumes of sombre smoke was not discerned,
A rampart high, of stone and turf appeared,
By order of La Hire and Poton reared,
From whence projected forth a parapet
Thickly with ranged artillery beset;
To check the first shock of th' assailant's rage,
And Bedford's fierce assault awhile engage.
There straight La Hire and Poton took their stand,
Of citizens behind them strove a band;
The cannons roar—the horrid order—*kill*
Re-echoes when the mouths of Hell are still,
And from their iron jaws the thunders cease,
Leaving incontinent the winds at peace;
Against the ramparts scaling ladders rose,
Bearing already legions of the foes,
With foot on step, and grasped in hand the glave,
Each soldier urges on his fellow-brave.
In such a case, nor Poton nor La Hire
Forgot their foresight which all men admire,
They had foreseen each dire emergency,
And each resource of art resolved to try.
There was the molten pitch, the boiling oil;
Of stakes, a forest to make foes recoil;
Large cutting scythes in sharp array were seen,
Emblems of death, destructive weapons keen;
And muskets launching forth their storms of lead,
Tempestuous rattling round each Briton's head.
All that necessity combined with art,
Misfortune, intrepidity, impart,
And fear itself, alike were planted there,
The deeds ensanguined of that day to share.
How many Britons then were boiled, pierced, riven,
Dying in crowds, and ranks on ranks hard driven:
So the ripe corn beneath the reaper's hand
Promiscuous falls and covers all the land.

Still this assault they furiously maintain,
The more they fall, the more they come again.
Like horrid Hydra, fierce heads fall to earth,
Only to be created in another birth;
Yet this affrighted not the son of Jove;
The English thus through fire and carnage drove,
After their check more formidable fall,
And bravely stern the numbers which appall.

Fierce Richemont, hope of Orléans in the fight,
Thou rushest onward to the ramparts' height;
Five hundred burgesses, a chosen band,
Reeling, march forward under thy command;
The potent wines their souls illuminate,
And with its sap their veins are animate:
As gallant Richemont bellowed out amain,
"Your legs, good folks, your weight can not sustain;
But I'm with you, 'tis fit we come to blows";
He spoke, and rushed 'mid thickest of the foes.
Talbot already had carved out a way
Along the ramparts, urged by fury's sway;
One direful arm hurled foes to death's drear night,
The other urged his phalanx to the fight;
"Louvet," he cried, with strong, stentorian voice.
And Louvet heard him, flattered at his choice.
Thus *Louvet* sounds from all the British band
Though not a soul the cause could understand;
O stupid mortals, with what ease we teach
Your tongues those things which are beyond your reach.

In sadness Charles within his fort was locked,
Fast by another English cohort blocked;
To the beleaguered town he may not go,
He suffocates with weariness and woe;
"What," he exclaimed, "and must I thus stand by,
Nor succour those, who in my service die;
With joyous hymns their sire's return they hailed,
I should have entered, fought, perhaps prevailed,
And saved them from inhuman British bands;
But here grim Destiny enchains my hands!"
"Not so," quoth Joan, "'tis fitting you be seen,

Come, signalise your blows; let vengeance keen
These Britons place 'twixt you and Orléans town;
March on, the city save, and reap renown;
Though small our band, we thousands boast in you."
"What," quoth the monarch, "can you flatter too?
My worth is small; to merit, I will try,
France's esteem and yours, impartially—
And England's too": he spoke, spurred on for fame,
Before his person streamed the Oriflamme;
Joan and Dunois both galoped at his side,
Horsemen behind, to list his orders ride;
And 'midst a thousand cries is heard to ring,
Long live Saint Denis, Mont-Joye and the King.
    Charles and Dunois and eke the martial fair
Attack the British squadrons in the rear;
As from those mounts which in their breasts confine
The reservoirs of Danube and the Rhine,
The haughty eagle with his pinions spread,
And piercing eyes, and eight sharp talons dread
Poised in 'mid air, on falcon darts in turn,
Who gorged the neck of the expiring hern.
'Twas then that British valour highest rose,
As purest steel upon the anvil glows,
By fire attempered and attuned by blows.
See, Albion's youth all emulous of praise,
See heirs of those who fought in Clodion's days;
Inflamed and fierce, insatiate each of gore,
They flew like winds, that through the vacuum pour,
In contact joined, immovable they're seen,
Like rook amidst old Ocean's empire green,
Foot against foot, the crest opposed to crest,
Hand to hand, eye to eye, and breast to breast,
Onward they rush, oaths breathing that appall,
While rolling o'er each other dead they fall.
O! wherefore can not I in sounding lays,
Of feats heroical prolong the praise?
'Tis only Homer hath a right to tell
All these adventures and on such to dwell,
To lengthen out and feats anew expose,

To calculate the several wounds and blows,
To add to Hector's battles, still a store
Of mighty deeds, and join to combats more.
That such a course were sure to please is plain;
'Tis not my way, and I will e'en refrain.

16

How Saint Peter appeased Saint George and Saint Denis,
promising a noble prize to him who should produce
the best Ode—Death of the lovely Rosamore.

O Heavenly palace! open to my lay,
Bright spirits who six pennons wide display!
Ye feathered Gods! whose tutelary hands
People and kings encircle in Fate's bands;
Ye, who, expanding wide your wings, conceal
The blaze eternal farthest Heavens reveal,
Deign for a little time apart to stand;
Let me behold, as war thus wields the brand,
What's done in sanctuary's depth of Heav'n,
And be my curiosity forgiv'n.
    This prayer Tritemus breathed: My dazzled eye
Never presumed to pierce the ambient sky,
Nor dared the depths of court supreme to see;
I should not have so much temerity.
    The rough Saint George and our apostle kind,
Were both in Heaven's etherial realm confined:
All they beheld, yet neither could extend
His hand, those earthly combats to befriend;
They both caballed, to this all folks resort,
And such the practice ever is at court:
Both George and Denis, turn by turn complain
To worthy Peter in the empyrean plain.
    This porter famed, whose Vicar is the Pope,
Closes in net, of all our fates, the hope,
His double keys rule life and death below.
To them thus Peter said: "You doubtless know
The dire affront, my friends, I had to bear,
When from one Malchus I removed an ear.
Right well I call to mind my master's word;

He bade me in my scabbard sheath my sword;
Deprived was I of lustrous right of arms;
Another mode, I find, with novel charms,
To heal your breach and settle your alarms.
You, Denis, from your district, forth shall draw
The greatest Saints that ever Gallia saw;
You, Master George, repair with equal speed,
And call those Saints that sprung from Albion's seed:
Let either troop incontinent compose
An hymn in verse, but not an ode in prose;
Houdart was wrong: at such a height, one must
One's tongue to language of the gods adjust;
Let each, I say, Pindaric ode indite,
In which my virtues rare be brought to light;
My rights, my attributes, supremacy;
To music set the whole immediately;
The race of mortals oft takes time enough
To rhyme its verses—e'en the poorest stuff:
We quicker go in these abodes of joy.
Proceed, I say, your talents well employ;
The better ode the victory shall obtain;
Thus shall the fortune of the foes be plain."

    Thus from the heights of his etherial throne
To rivals spoke the infallible Barjone;
Two words, at most, the sense of it supplies,
The language of the Saints is so concise.
Forth in a twinkling both the Saints are gone,
To summon bards before Saint Peter's throne;
Saints who as mortals for their wit were known.

    The patron Saint in Paris' walls adored,
Invited to his round and ample board
Saint *Fortunatus*, little known on earth,
Said to have given *Pangé linguas* birth;
And Saint *Prosper*, of epithets the bard,
Though somewhat Jansenist, as well as hard;
The name of *Gregory* on his list was placed,
Who with his mitred see of Tourraine graced,
Dear to the soil, where Bonneau saw the light.
Bernard—antithesis was his delight—
He had no rival in his famous time,

With other saints to form the council prime;
As trusty councillors he summoned these;
Without advice we rarely learn to please.
   George, hearing of Saint Denis, all this din,
Disdainful eyed him, with sarcastic grin,
Amidst enclosure saintly; then espied
The noted preacher *Austin*, Albion's pride,
And thus addressed him, calling him aside.
"Good fellow Austin, I am formed for arms,
And not for verse, which has for me no charms;
Right well I know my trusty blade to wield,
And scatter trunks and heads about the field;
You versify—come, set to work and rhyme,
Support our country's fame in lays sublime;
One Briton on the plain of deadly thrall,
With ease can triumph o'er three sons of Gaul:
Oft have we seen upon the Norman plain,
In Guienne, Picardy and Upper Maine,
These pretty gentlemen with ease laid low;
If in the fight we stronger arms can shew,
Trust me where hymn and ode or aught's required,
Where rhyme and thinking are the points desired,
In all such things we have as good a might;
Enter the lists then, Austin; promptly write;
Let London rule forever and a day,
In the two arts to do well and well say:
Denis of rhymers will collect an host
Who in the mass but little genius boast;
Toil thou alone, old authors thou canst weight—
Courage, proceed, sound from thine harp the lay;
The sacred strain shall Albion's name adorn,
And laugh his dull academy to scorn."
   Austin, to whom the labour was consigned,
Thanked him, as author blest by patron kind:
Himself and Denis in a snug abode,
Squatted themselves, and each composed his ode;
When all was done, the flaming Seraphim,
The bloated chubby heads of Cherubim,
Near Barjone in two ranks were perched aloft,
Angels beneath nestled in aether soft;

While all the saints, considering their ranks,
Await to hear upon the judgement banks.
    Austin begins the wonders to impart,
Which made obdurate the Egyptian's heart;
Moses, and the ensuing company,
Equal to him in holy sorcery;
The waves of Nile, beneficent of yore,
By incantation turned to fluid gore;
The magic wand, a winding snake becomes,
Again the rod its wonted form resumes;
Day changed to night; cities and deserts wild
By swarms of gnats and vermin foul defiled;
Mange in the bones; thunder in airy space,
And all the first born of a rebel race,
All butchered by the Angel of the Lord;
Egypt in mourning and the faithful horde
Its patrons of their silver plate bereaves;
They earn salvation by becoming thieves:
For forty years they wander to and fro,
These twenty thousand for a calf laid low,
And twenty thousand more to graves consigned,
For having found the other sex too kind:
Then came the Hebrew Ravaillac, Aod,
Murdering his master in the name of God;
And Samuel, who seized the kitchen knife
With holy hand from altar, and of life
Agag bereft, whom he anatomized
Because this Agag was uncircumcized;
Of Bethulia was praised the saviour fair,
Pure folly acting with her charms so rare;
The good Baasha who massacred Nadad,
And impious Ahab dying like the bad,
Because he had not slain Levi Benhadad.
Blood of Athalia's queen by Joad spilled,
And princely Joas by Josabad killed.
    Dull was the litany and somewhat long;
While interspersed these brilliant traits among
Were mighty deeds detailed in sounding lays.
Those acts so cherished in the olden days;
Videlicet—the Sun dissolved in smoke,

Recoiling seas, the moon in fragments broke,
The globe forever quaking and on fire,
And God an hundred times awoke in ire—
Ruins and tombs were seen, and seas of blood,
Yet still beside the silvery current's flood,
Milk flowed beneath the olive's verdant shade,
Like very rams the mountains skipped and played,
The hills like little lambs kept skipping too.
Unto that lord, good Austin gave full due,
Who threatened loud the conqueror of Chaldie,
And left his people still in slavery;
But always broke the teeth of lions dread,
And trampled on the rampant serpent's head:
Though at his word the flowing hill was stayed,
Leviathans and basilisks obeyed.
Austin was silent; his Pindaric strain
Called forth amid the bright empyrial train
A doubtful murmur; whispers were bestowed
Not altogether flattering to the ode.
    Denis arose, low bent his eyes serene,
Which straightway reared, displayed his modest mien,
Before his auditors then bending low,
As if surprised at their celestial glow,
Thus seemed he to address the sacred host,
Encourage that one who admires you most.
Thrice with humility he lowly bent
To counsellors and the first president;
Then chaunted with a tender voice and clear
This hymn expert, which ye anon shall hear:
"O Peter, on whom Jesus deigned to found
His holy church, from age to age renowned,
O Heaven's Porter, Pastor of sheep true!
Master of kings, who bend their knee to you,
Doctor Divine, Priest, Saintly Father just,
Of all our Christian Kings support august,
To them your salutary air extend,
Their rights are just, and you their rights befriend.
At Rome, the Pope ranks chief of sceptered men,
None doubt it, and if his lieutenant then
Bestows on whom he lists this present small,

'Tis in your name, for you dispense them all;
Alas! alas! our men of parliament
Have banished Charles; and their hands insolent
Have placed an alien on the throne of France,
Taking from son the sire's inheritance:
Porter divine, your benefits oppose
To this audacity, to ten years woes,
On your benignity our sufferings ease,
And of the *Palace Court* restore the keys."
    Such was the prelude of Saint Denis' strain;
He paused awhile, then read with studied pain,
Glancing askance in Simon Peter's eyes,
Reluctance feigned within his bosom rise:
Cephas content lets show upon his face,
Of flattered vanity sufficient trace;
And thus the scattered wits well to release
Of the skilled singer, put him at his ease:
"Continue,"said he, "you are sure to please."
With prudence Denis once more struck the lyre:
"Mine adversary may have charmed the choir,
The God of vengeance he hath loudly praised,
Whereas my sounding plaudit shall be raised
To praise the God of mercy: if you will,
To hate is good, to love is better still."
Denis more confident in voice and mind
Then sang in pleasing verse the shepherd kind,
Who when his flock to other pastures roam,
Is glad to follow them, and bear them home;
The farmer bland, whose kindness dared dispense
Still to the sluggard workman recompense,
Who came too late, that diligent for pay,
He might his toil renew with blush of day:
The worthy patron, who with loaves but five
And fishes three, could thousands keep alive;
He, with more sweetness than austerity,
Forgiving her found in adultery—
That Magdalen; nor were his feet denied,
But by the fair repentant, bathed and dried.
"Fair Magdalen, the type of fair Sorel."
(This stroke of light allusion answered well.)

The great etherial hall the trait observed
And thought that Love its pardon had deserved.
The ode of gentle Denis, its worth perceived,
The prize, with no demurring voice received;
Of England's Saint was foiled the boldness dread,
Austin blushed deep, and forthwith skulking fled:
One and all laughed; through Paradise they bawled:
E'en so in Paris hooting once appalled
A pedant dull, like Thersites in face,
Informer vile, of hypocritic race,
Whose recompence was hatred and disdain,
As in style vulgar, he dared waft his strain,
His brothers damn, and arts of honour stain.
Peter of Agnuses gave Denis two,
He kissed them rev'rently, and straight to view,
Subscribed by twelve elect was seen decree,
That Albion's host upon that day should flee
'Fore Gallia's bands, to glory's conquest led
By sovereign Charles in person, at their head.
    That moment then the Amazon of Bar
Beheld in air, athwart dense cloud afar,
The form and likeness of her donkey gray,
As oft a cloud imbued by sunny ray
Receives impression, and reflects the hue.
"This day," she cried, "is glorious for you;
All, all is ours; my ass is in the skies."
Bedford at this fell marvel in surprise
Halted and was invincible no more;
But read, astounded, in that heavenly lore,
That by Saint George he was deserted quite:
The Briton thinking he beheld outright
An host, rushed forthwith from the town alarmed;
Its citizens with sudden valour armed,
Viewing them urged to flight by terror's spell,
Forth rushing straight, pursue them all pell-mell;
Charles at a distance amidst carnage strove,
And to their camp a noble passage drove;
Besieged in turn besiegers now appear,
Assailed and slaughtered in the front and rear,
In crowds they fall, the dykes are choked with slain,

And arms and dead and dying load the plain.
'Twas even there, upon that fateful plain,
Thou cam'st to give thy dauntless valour rein,
Bold Christopher, by surname Arundel,
Thy cold indifference, visage hard and fell,
Tended thy lofty vigour to enhance.
From 'neath that haughty brow, the silent glance
Examined shrewdly how they fight in Gaul;
From his important look it seemed to all,
He loitered there Time's heavy hours to kill;
His Rosamore, attached and faithful still,
Like him was cased in steely war's attire,
As she had been some page or faithful squire;
Gold was her casque, and steel her coat of mail,
Her nodding crest a parrot's gaudy tail,
Its lofty shade obedient to the gale.
For since the day her hand had dared assail,
And severed head from trunk of *Martinguerre*,
Her chief delight had been war's deeds to dare,
Pallas she might have been in all her bloom,
For arms abandoning the inglorious loom;
Or Bradamant, or even very Joan.
She spoke to her loved wanderer alone,
Deploying sentiments sublimely grand;
When lo! some fiend, fell foe of Cupid's band,
For their mishap toward Arundel decreed
That young La Hire and Poton should succeed,
And Richemont of no pitying thrill the slave.
Poton beholding mien so fierce and grave,
To see him babbling, right indignant grew
And at the Englishman his long lance threw;
Pierced in the flank to earth the Briton rolled,
In copious streams flowed blood alas! too cold:
He fell, he died; the shivered lance still seen
Plunged in his corse, and rolling on the green.
At this dread sight, this moment of distress,
No eye saw Rosamore her lover press,
Nor tear away the gold of her blonde hair,
Nor with her cries of sorrow rend the air,
Nor rail infuriate 'gainst high Heaven's decree;

Not e'en a sigh; "Vengeance," she cried, "for me";
But, at the very moment Poton leant
Forward to grasp his battered blade and bent,
Her naked arm, that arm of power so dread,
Which with one stroke had severed, when in bed,
From bandit's trunk the grim and hoary head,
Now lopped with nimble and with nervous blow
The guilty right hand from the exulting foe.
Those hidden nerves beneath the fingers five
For the last time with motion are alive:
Poton has written nought since then, I trow.
The brave and fair La Hire comes forward now,
To aid his vanquished friend, and aims a blow,
A mortal thrust transpiercing through the heart;
Falling, the straps of the gold helmet part,
Discovering neck of rose and lilies' hue,
Nor was there aught concealed her front from view,
Her long, long hair streams down upon her breast,
Her big, blue eyes are closed in deathly rest;
And all confessed to his astonished sight
A lovely woman formed for all delight.
La Hire thus gazing, breathes full many a sigh,
And weeping wafts this lamentable cry:
"Just Heaven, as vile assassin I appear,
A black hussar and not a cavalier;
My heart and sword foul infamy display,
Is it permitted thus a dame to slay?"
But Richemont, always scoffing, always rough,
Cries to him: "This remorse is pretty stuff;
She was an English dame, the harm is small,
With, unlike Joan, no maidenhead at all!"
While thus indulging in such speech profane,
From arrow's barbed point he felt the pain,
Wounded he turned, still more provoked and dread,
His thrusts, both right and left, increased the dead:
Foes rushing torrent-like surround his form;
Himself, La Hire, and nobles brave the storm,
With soldiers, citizens, all strive their best,
They kill, they fall, pursue, retire, hard pressed,

Of bleeding trunks a mountain was displayed,
And Britons, of their dying, ramparts made.
  'Mid all this sanguinary, dreadful fray,
To Dunois thus the King was heard to say:
"Prithee, dear Bastard, where may she be gone?"
"Who?" cried Dunois. The worthy King went on,
"Do you not know what time she last was seen?"
—"Who then?"—"Alas, I think it must have been
Last night ere lucky fortune brought us all
Before the doors of Bedford's castle wall."
"Ne'er fear," quoth Joan, "restored she soon shall be."
"Heaven grant," quoth Charles, "that she rest true to me,
For me preserve her." With such discourse fair,
He still advances, fighting everywhere
Soon night, embracing our wide hemisphere,
Spread her broad mantle through the murky air,
And terminated with the close of day
The novel ardour Charles would fain display.
  Whilst thus escaping from the combat dread
The anxious monarch, sudden heard it said,
Three tender specimens of womanhood
Were seen that morning in a neighbouring wood;
Amidst the rest, a form divinely fair,
Two big blue eyes, and dainty, infant air;
The smile most tender, skin like satin soft,
Whom sermonized a Benedictine oft.
Brilliant esquires, equipped in proud array,
In steel adorned, and gold and ribbands gay,
Tended the fair horse-women on her way,
Till soon the errant troop perceived in view
A noble edifice that no one knew
Till this adventure, in that spot to be:
No pile more curious the eye could see.
  The King amazed at such a wondrous thing,
To Bonneau cries: "Who loves, follows his King!
Tomorrow with the dawn I will repair
To view the constant object of my care,
Agnes regain, or cast my life away."
Small time within the arms of sleep he lay,
And when Phosphor, with face ensanguined,

The roses of Aurora well had led,
While yet in Heaven, unharnessed were the steeds
That wheel bright Phoebus on to blazing deeds,
The monarch, Dunois, Joan and eke Bonneau,
Their saddles vaulted with a joyous glow,
Hieing this sumptuous palace to explore.
As Charles declared: "My fair, let's see before;
There's time enough to join the British host,
Her to be with, is now what presses most."

17

How Charles VII, Agnes, Joan, Dunois, La Trimouille, all became fools—
and how they recovered their senses by the exorcisms of the most
reverend Father Bonifoux, the confessor of the King.

Oh, what enchanters does this world display!
(Nothing of fair enchantresses I say.)
That page is turned, where weakness writ the page,
Dear folly's spring-time, error's lovely age;
Yet still deceivers come at every hour,
Real sorcerers, seducers of much power,
Bright glory beaming and in purple dight,
Escorting you at first to Heaven's height,
Then plunging you within the black wave's brink,
Where bitterness and death is all you drink.
Then, whatsoe'er your rank, I much entreat
Your care when necromancers such you meet,
And if you seek some high enchantments' stir,
Neglect the mightiest of kings for—Her.
    Hermaphrodix expressly chose to build
This happy castle which fair Agnes held,
O'er all the fair of France to prove his rights,
O'er donkeys also, saints and simple knights,
Whose deeds by Heaven inspired, whose modesty
Had dared resist his magic potency.
Who ever entered this abode so fell
Could not, incontinent his best friend tell;
His senses, wit and memory all fled.
Lethean waters whereof quaff the dead,
Or scurvy wines which living men infect,
Have far less an extravagant effect.
    Beneath vast columns of a portico,
Which modern and antique in medley show,
A brilliant phantom was seen to parade,

Light footed; in his eyes fire-flashes played;
Quick-gestured, nervous-stepping, still erect
He held his head; in tinsel he was decked;
Unsteady motion ever moved his frame,
Imagination was the phantom's name;
Not that same goddess, ever fair and glad,
Who over Rome and Greece dominion had,
Who spread the colours of her high estate
On works of many authors and so great,
Who diamonds and immortal flowers would rain
On the great painter of Achilles' strain;
On Dido erst by Virgil celebrate,
Who Ovid's skill was wont to animate;
But she whom reason ever has abjured,
Flighty and impudent and most absurb,
Who leads so many authors at her side,
Who serves as inspiration and as guide
To Desmarets, Le Moine or Scudéris.
She sheds abundant of her charity.
On our new operas and romantic stuff;
(I think her empire's lasted long enough
Over the stage, the pulpit and the bar!)
A certain *Bombast* followed not afar,
A most loquacious monster, whose arms hold
Him, the *Seraphic Doctor* called of old,
Deep, subtile, versed in energy's bold page,
Imagination's commentating sage,
Creator of confusion's dire epoch
Of late producing *Marie à la Coque*;
Around him bad *bons mots* were seen to flit,
And dull conundrums, which are folly's wit;
Dreams, blunders, prejudices and lies immense,
And all the other things which outrage sense;
As near the mouldering walls of some old house,
Are heard the screech-owl and the flitter-mouse.
Howe'er that be, this damnable resort
Was fabricate with art of such a sort,
That all who entered, were anon bereft
Of any scrap of reason they had left.
    Hardly had Agnes with her fair escort

Come to the precincts of the palace court,
Than Bonifoux, that confessor of fame
Became the object of her faithful flame;
From France's king she could not him design.
"Mine hero," cried she, "only hope of mine!
O, by just Heaven to my arms restored
Have the proud Britons fallen 'neath your sword?
Some wound perchance you haply have received;
Be now by me from armour's weight relieved."
With tender care, and with affection true,
Anon she sought to unfrock Bonifoux,
With eyes on fire, bent neck, her willing charms,
Gladly she had abandoned to his arms;
A kiss she seeks to take and then repay.
O charming Agnes, what was thy dismay!
A chin fresh-shaved was doubtless what she sought,
A frowsy, unkempt beard was what she caught.
Long and uncombed; right well it tickled her.
The confessor departed in a stir,
The entreating fair he did not recognize;
Whilst Agnes, grieved that he should thus despise,
Runs after him, with tears in her fair eyes.
        As each amid the vast enclosure sped,
One signing cross, while tears the other shed,
Lugubrious cries excite them to alarm.
A youthful creature, touching, full of charm
Crouched on the ground, in terror dire embraced
Knees of a cavalier in armour laced,
Who soon had dealt her out chastisement sore.
In such a savage case, one knew no more
La Trimouille, lover unparalleled,
Who, at all other times, his life had held
Cheap price for Dorothy, whom he mistook
For proud Tyrconel, though not any look
Of that proud Briton had she: him she sought,
Her valiant hero, then with fury fraught,
Dear object of a love that could not die:
Him she addressed, not knowing he was nigh;
And thus she cried: "Have you seen anywhere,
That knight who is my master and my Dear?

Who hither came that he might rest with me,
My Trimouille, alas, where can he be?
Where is he now? Ah, wherefore doth he fly?"
The knight of Poitou heard this touching cry,
But did not know his faithful love was there;
A Briton proud and fierce he seemed to hear,
Who, rushing on him, sought that life to end
Which sword in hand he started to defend,
Towards Dorothy he moves, with paces slow:
"Another face," he says, "I'll make you show,
Briton disdainful, arrogant, severe,
Rough islander, drunk ever with strong beer,
Well it becomes you in such way to prate,
And thus revile a man of my estate!
I, Poitevin, with grand-sires of renown,
Whose doughty deeds have often hurried down
To the dark places British not a few,
Brave, fierce and great, more generous than you.
What! does your hand refuse the sword to wield,
To what vile terrors does your bosom yield?
Coward in deed! Loquacious at your ease!
You English goat! You British Thersites!
Fit in your Parliament to brawl at home;
Quick, draw our broad-swords and to action come,
Unsheath then quick, or with my hand I go
To mark your face, the ugliest face I know,
And with a whip upon your large behind,
Apply as many scores as suits my mind."
At this discourse, in fearful wrath expressed,
Pale, fainting and with fear of death distressed:
"I am no Briton," Dorothy cried out;
"O, far from that, how does it come about,
That you should so mistreat me in this place:
Why am I fall'n in such a direful case?
To search for Poitou's knight was my intent,
Alas! it is a girl that you torment,
With tearful kisses suppliant at your knees."
She spoke, but no whit listening was he,
And La Trimouille, whose madness knew no check,
Already caught the lady by her neck.

The confessor who in his nimble speed,
Thus sought from Agnes Sorel to be freed,
Tripped as he ran and fell between the pair;
The squire of Poitou strove to grasp his hair,
But finding none, rolled with him on the ground,
The arms of Agnes straight his form surround,
Who on him falling uttered shrieks of fear,
And sobs that stayed the course of sorrow's tear,
While Dorothy beneath them struggling lay,
In sad disorder and in torn array.
    Just in the middle of this novel fight,
Led by Bonneau, King Charles appeared in sight,
With Dunois bold and Joan the maid of Fate,
Who just had past this castle's dreadful gate,
With fond intent his faithful fair to view;
Oh! mighty power, oh, wonder, strange and new;
On ground from steeds they'd hardly set their feet,
That portico had barely time to greet,
When each incontinent was left of brain,
Of doctors furred in Paris, thus the train
With arguments replete 'neath bonnet square,
Gravely to antique Sorbonne all repair;
Resort of strife, that theologic cell,
Where disputation and confusion dwell,
And reason hath no longer any right.
One after t'other comes each reverend wight,
Steady in mind and air to casual sight;
Each, when at home, a very sage is seen,
Who well might pass for gentle and serene,
Not quarrelsome and not extravagant,
Nay, even some looked quite intelligent;
Yet on their benches fools to all intent.
    Charles with joy drunken and with soft desire,
His eyes all wet, yet glistening with fire,
Feeling impetuous his heart inflamed,
In tones of languor and of love exclaimed:
"My mistress chaste—my Agnes ever dear,
My paradise, of every joy the sphere,
How often have I lost thy form adored!
To my desires thou art at length restored.

Tell me of love, now thee I see and hold;
O, how thy face is charming to behold;
But thou no longer hast that slender waist,
That erst with my ten fingers I enlaced.
What thighs! what plumpness! and oh, what a paunch!
This is the fruit of our embraces staunch:
My teeming Agnes bears the fruit of joy,
And soon will bless me with a bouncing boy.
O let me graft again, so great my glee,
This novel fruit upon the mother tree.
Love so ordains it, for the feat I'm wild,
To rush to meet this dear, expected child."
    To whom breathed thus the monarch's glowing strain?
To whom addressed he this pathetic vein?
Whom in his amorous arms did thus he hold?
'Twas Bonneau, puffy, sweating, dry and old—
'Twas Bonneau; man to earthly scenes allied
Soul ne'er possessed so deadly stupefied;
Charles, by an ardent passion hotly pressed,
With nervous arm his courtier huge caressed,
Down threw him, and our pond'rous Bonneau fell
Upon the troop already there *pell-mell,*
Which his great bulk by no means relishes.
O Heavens! what clamour, and what piercing cries!
The confessor with germ of sense now graced,
His paunch so corpulent precisely placed,
Agnes above and Dorothy below—
He rose, then ran as fast as he could go.
While scarcely breathing, worthy Bonneau fled,
Seized by a fit La Trimouille was led
To think those arms sweet Dorothy embraced,
And Bonneau's steps, thus bawling out, he chased;
"My heart, my life, O torturer restore;
Stop, hear my speech"—nor words he uttered more,
But with huge sabre dealt on back rude stroke.
Bonneau, then galled by breast-plate's ponderous yoke,
Gave out a clatter which resembled much
That of the steel, when at the hammer's touch.
Upon the potent anvil it resounds:
Fear drove his hurried course in heavy bounds.

Joan thus beholding Bonneau at full trot,
And the dire strokes he from assailant got,
Joan, in her helm and armour bright arrayed,
Followed Trimouille and with good interest paid
All that on kingly confidant was poured.
Dunois, of noble knights the puissant lord,
Will not endure that one should strive to stop
La Trimouille's days; he is his dearest prop;
For him it is his destiny to fight—
That he knew well—the maid was to his sight
An Englishman: he falls on her amain,
He thrashes her, as he thrashes again
The knight of Poitou, pricking in his turn
Friend Bonneau, who to fly did greatly yearn.

    The good king Charles, in this confusion dire,
In worthy Bonneau saw his soul's desire,
His Agnes—what condition for a king,
The prince of lovers, ever languishing!
Her to defend he would an army face,
And all his men of war who Bonneau chase,
Blood-thirsty ravishers to him appeared:
His lifted sword against Dunois he reared—
The handsome Bastard turns and renders back
Full on his visor a tremendous whack;
Ah, had he known it was the King of France,
How he had looked upon himself askance!
With sheer remorse and shame his life had failed.
His sword alike the warrior Joan assailed,
Whose potent blade was not slow to requite;
The Bastard, quite incapable of fright,
Attacks at once his king and mistress too;
About their heads his good sword flashed and flew,
A thousand times its strokes tempestuous blew.
Stop, gallant Dunois, stop, O beauteous Joan!
What tears, what fell regrets your breast will own,
When whom your arms assailèd either knows,
Whom you had struck, with whom you came to blows.

    The knight of Poitou in this dread alarm
Let fall from time to time his doughty arm,
Assaulting all the beauties of the Maid;

Friend Bonneau followed not this soldier's trade,
His thick head, than the rest, less trouble felt,
All he received, but never one blow dealt;
As running, Bonifoux, impelled by dread,
Maintained the van and thus the cohort led,
The hurricane that with their rage prevailed,
Sent all pell-mell, assailants and assailed.
Beating and beaten, each in skirmish vile
Crying and bawling, traversed the vast pile;
Agnes in tears, and Dorothy, fear-chilled,
Screamed out for help: "My throat is cut, I'm killed."
While the confessor, with a contrite heart
In the procession took the leading part.
Now, at a certain window, he espyed
This mansion's master in his evil pride,
Hermaphrodix, whose glance was gay, to see
Gaul's sons tormented with barbarity;
He held his sides, he laughed and laughed again;
Bonifoux saw then that this fell domain
Was without doubt some foul device of Hell,
A little reason he retained as well;
His tonsure broad, his ample cowl and great,
Had served indeed for armour to his pate.
He knew Bonneau possessed a slender store
(A frugal custom used in days of yore,
Dear to our fathers, ne'er to be in fault)
Cloves, nutmeg, pepper, cinnamon and salt;
For Bonifoux, he had his missal there.
Hardly he chanced to see a fountain clear,
Whither he sped, with salt and mass-book fraught,
Resolved the demon should this time be caught;
Anon he 'gan mysterious rite so rare,
To exorcize, and imps of sin to scare;
He muttered low: *Sanctam catholicam,*
Papam Romam, aquam benedictam.
In Bonneau's cup the holy water placed,
Thus armed by Heaven he onwards cunning paced,
And ere the fiend guessed what was to be done,
Sprinkled of Alix, the Hobgoblin son.
Less fatal far the Stygian current rolled

To guilty souls in Pagan days of old.
Straight his tanned hide with sparkles was o'erspread,
A funny vapour sailed around his head,
Covered the palace and its master too,
Hiding the combatants in night's dark hue:
While one after the other fast they run,
Just at that time the palace is undone;
With combats ceased mistakes and errors too,
They saw aright, their friends each other knew,
And every brain resumed its wonted place;
Thus to each hero a short second's space,
Restored the little sense one moment lost.
Folly, alas! or wisdom, to our cost,
Has little count in our poor human-kind.
It was a mighty pleasure then, to find
These Paladins who to the black monk fall,
Who bless him well, sing litanies, and all,
For all their follies seek his pardoning.
O La Trimouille! And you, oh amorous King!
Your raptures then, oh, who can well declare!
Where nought was heard but such like cries: "My Fair!
My all, my King! Mine angel true and rare!
'Tis you, 'tis thou! sweet moments, hours of bliss!"
And then embraces, then the tender kiss;
Questions by hundreds, and in haste replies;
Faulty their tongues to utter thoughts that rise;
The monk aloof and with paternal glance
Muttered his prayers and eyed them all askance:
The mighty Bastard and his lady blest,
In modest terms their tenderness express'd;
And the companion of their loves so rare
Raising the head as well as voice in air,
Voiced a discordant octave, loud and new,
A strain so bold no goat-herd ever blew.
At this octave, at this most heavenly bray,
All things were moved, and Nature 'gan to sway;
Quite horror-struck, as Joan beheld amazed
The magic bastions of this palace razed,
An hundred towers of steel and gates of brass;
As erst to Moses' horde it came to pass,

When word was given for loud trump to blow,
Down, instant, fell the walls of Jericho,
Reduced to powder, to the prone earth bowed—
Such practices no longer are allowed.
    The palace then, with brilliant gold enchased,
Sublime in structure and by sin debased,
Became an ample, holy monastery.
The hall was turned into an oratory;
The boudoir, where this mighty lord of crimes,
Wallowed in vice, or slept in former times,
Transformed was to a sanctuary straight.
The potent order was of ruling fate,
The Hall of Banqueting unchanged should be,
Thenceforth entitled, *The Refectory*,
Where all was blest before they drank and ate.
Joan, with her heart by all the Saints elate,
With thoughts of sacred Rheims and Orléans' walls,
Cries to Dunois: "Propitious fortune calls,
In love as well as in our great designs
Let's hope always; be sure the fiend resigns,
He's done his worst, and now can do no more."
Yet speaking thus, Joan was mistaken sore.

18

Disgrace of Charles and his Golden Company.

I know not in this world's historic page
Nor hero, man of wealth, or even sage,
Prophet or Christian, ranking faith his forte,
Who has not of some rascal been the sport,
Of evil sprites, or of the jealous sort.
 High Providence at every time would press
The good King Charles with manifold distress;
Sadly from cradle was he reared in truth,
Pursued by the Burgundian from his youth;
Him of his rights his father had deprived,
And Paris parliament, where Gonesse thrived,
Tutor of kings, adjourned their pupil there,
And bound on English brow Gaul's lilies rare.
Of mass and weal deprived, he'd errant stray,
And scarcely ever would prolong his stay,
His mother, uncle, mistress, state and church
In turn betrayed and left him in the lurch.
An English page partakes his Agnes' smiles;
Hell sends Hermaphrodix with fateful wiles,
Dire magic spells to turn his store of brains;
On every side he shuns misfortune's banes,
Yet suffers all, to Heaven's decree resigned;
Thus Fate forgives his sins, humanely kind.
 Our lover's cavalcade, as proud as gay,
Far from the fatal castle took its way,
Where Beelzebub, the cause of all their woe,
Deranged the knights, fair Agnes and Bonneau.
Along the gloomy forest they repair,
Which still the name of Orléans doth bear,
While Tithon's spouse new-decked in Orient light,
Shed purple radiance through the shades of night.

Soon from afar are seen some archers there,
In short-cut gerkins and in bonnets square,
On corselet half way down, the eye might see,
Quartered with powdered lilies, leopards three:
The monarch halted and with care surveyed
A troop, that squatting near the forest laid;
Some paces onward moved Dunois and Joan:
Sweet Agnes, with her fair arms outward thrown,
Charles thus bespoke: "Let's go, let's fly, my sire."
Joan onward sped, still nearer to enquire,
And saw a wretched troop in couples bound,
With fronts abashed and eyes enchained to ground.
"Alas! a band of gallant knights," cried she,
"Captives, our duty I conceive to be,
From bondage straight to free this faithful train:
Come, Bastard, come and let's anon make plain,
What Dunois is, and what the virgin maid!"
With lance in rest—these words were quick obeyed,
They charge the troop which guard these heroes true;
Joan's aspect fierce no sooner struck their view,
With the brave Dunois, and still more the ass,
Than hurriedly these scurvy warriors pass,
And scud like hunted hares across the plain.
Thus the glad maiden hails the captive train;
"Brave cavaliers, whom the proud English chain,
First thank your king, who saves you from this thrall,
His hand salute, then follow one and all,
And on these peevish English, vengeance meet
Ye shall obtain"; at such a promised treat,
Their eyes bent low, a sullen air proclaimed;
Impartial readers, would you have them named,
Would ye enquire what was this noble crew,
By Joan impelled these valiant deeds to do?
These knights were miscreants from Paris strayed,
Who had reaped their deserts, if there they'd stayed,
And gone to plough the back of Amphitrite,
Their trapping's well betrayed them to the sight.
Good Charles the pitying sigh could not control:
"Alas!" said he, "these objects in my soul
Have deep implanted the keen shaft of pain;

What! shall the Britons in my empire reign?
'Tis their decrees my subjects now obey,
For them alone the multitude must pray;
And shall my subjects then at their intent
From Paris to the galleys e'en be sent?"
Charles, who compassion's thrill could not withstand
Moved courteous to the leader of the band,
Who was the foremost in the cavalcade;
No scoundrel could more plainly show his trade;
His long chin shaded by a beard uncouth,
His shifting eyes more lying than his mouth,
The red and twisted tufts upon his brow,
Of fraudulent imposture make avow;
On his broad front, daring and cunning lies,
Of those who laws ignore, remorse despise;
Foamed his wide mouth, pestiferous his breath,
And with perpetual rancour gnashed his teeth.
    The sycophant beholding thus his prince,
Seemed humbly his devotion to evince,
Bent low his eyes, then softened and composed
That visage, which his haggard crimes disclosed;
Just so, the mastiff that with haggard gaze,
Its thirst of blood with sudden growl betrays,
His master views and fawns about him gay,
And licks his hand, discoursing in his way;
And for a crust a very sheep will grow.
Or as a fiend escaped from gulfs below,
His grisly beard, and his foul tail conceals,
Amongst us comes, and tone and visage steals
Of some young hermit; tonsured head he shows
Better to tempt Sister Discreet or Rose.
    The King of France, by arts like these deceived,
This grisly ruffian pitied and relieved,
And as his gentle converse fear allayed—
"Tell me," quoth Charles, "poor devil, what's thy trade,
Thy name and origin, and for what deed
The Châtelet has indulgently decreed
That henceforth thou shouldst row on Provence main?"
Whereto the culprit thus made known his pain:
"O bounteous monarch, Frélon is my name,

And from the néighbourhood of Nantes I came.
Jesus I love with pure and true desire,
And in a cloister I was sometime friar,
Their morals as of old my mind retains,
To save young children I took wondrous pains;
Passed were my days in virtue's pure intents.
'Neath Charnel house, 'yclept of Innocents
Of my rare genius Paris saw the feats,
Dearly to *Lambert* I sold all my sheets;
Full well I'm known in *Maubert's* famous square,
And justice, above all was done me there;
The impious, sometimes, maliciously
My frock have e'en reproached with frailty,
With mundane vice, to cheating near allied—
But I have always conscience on my side."
     The monarch heard with pity all he said;
"Console thyself," he cried, "and nothing dread:
But tell me, friend, if all thy company,
To Marseilles speeding on such embassy,
Were like thyself, of good and honest race?"
"Ay," Frélon cried, "I swear by Christian grace,
For each, as for myself, I'll answer bold,
Since every one is cast in self-same mould.
Abbé *Goyon*, who marches at my side,
Say what they will, of love is justified;
Never absurd, fictitious nor perplext,
No calumnies degrade his manly text.
Here is *Chaumé*, with sanctimonious grace,
Whose haughty heart belies his humble face;
For doctrine too he'd suffer whipping sound;
There's famous *Gauchat*, who might well confound
Jew rabbis all—on text and note rare chief;
See yonder advocate without a brief,
Who left for heavenly bliss the wrangling bar,
Sabotier 'tis, than honey sweeter far:
Ah, choicest wit! saint, priest and tender heart!
'Tis true he played his lord a traitor's part,
But for so little gold and without vice;
He sold himself, but for the highest price.
Like me, his traffic was in libel writs;

And where's the harm? we live but by our wits;
Employ us and we all will faithful be.
Laurels and glory in these times we see,
Devolve on those who Charnel Houses write:
But great success much envy must excite.
Of scribes and heroes such the fate we view,
Of brilliant wits and devotees a crew,
Since virtue ever was lampooned, poor thing,
Who knows this better than my noble King?"
Whilst breathing thus his soft, seductive lays,
Two melancholy forms met Charles' gaze,
Each, with two hands, concealed his heavy head.
"Who may these bashful oarsmen be?" he said.
"Behold," replied the weekly gazetteer,
"Two of the justest, most discreet who are here,
Of all who on the limpid sea must row.
One is *Fantin*, a preacher you must know;
Proud to the poor, but cringing to the great;
His piety spares those in life's estate,
But all his store of goodly deeds to hide,
Those he confessed and robbed just ere they died.
The other's *Brizet* who his nuns confessed
And for their favours had but little zest,
But sagely piled up hoards for Heav'n above,
His soul replete with pure and saintly love,
He self despised, yet owned of fear the thrall,
Lest to ungodly hands the gold should fall.
Beaumelle, the hindmost of the train is he,
His kindly care endears him most to me,
Best of six rascals who their voices sold
Is he, though lowest in the lists enrolled.
Though, in a fit of absence, while he pored
On those high mysteries by Saints adored,
He, for his own, a neighbour's purse mistook;
Besides you find such wisdom in his book,
For feeble wits he also knows so well,
How dangerous 'tis the naked truth to tell,
That light deceptive is to feeble eyes,
Which thus are hoodwinked; wherefore, scribe so wise,
So horrible beholding her to sight,

Resolved he never would her themes indite:
For me, I have aver, most gracious Sire,
In you I see a hero I admire;
This from my pen posterity shall learn,
Save those whom calumny would make you spurn,
Whose fetid breath all blackens and besets.
Save honest men from fell impiety's nets.
O free us and avenge us, pay us well,
By Frélon's faith, your praises we will tell!"
      Then a pathetic argument he'd draw,
'Gainst Englishmen, and for the Salic law;
Proving that soon, without war's slaughtering ill,
The state he'd rescue with a goose's quill.
The king admired this doctrine so profound;
Dispensing sweetest smiles on all around,
And with compassion, full assurance gave,
That each might henceforth his protection crave.
      Agnes, who heard this touching interview,
Felt tenderest sympathy her soul imbue;
Her heart is good; a woman prone to love,
To simple impulse will more often move,
Than one to martial deeds or prudery prone.
"My king," quoth she, "this day you needs must own,
Propitious proves to this most wretched race,
Since on contemplating your loyal face,
Bliss they enjoy and broken are their chains;
Your's is a front where grace celestial reigns,
Too much these men of law presume to do,
Who make decrees in any name but you!
'Tis thee, my love, they should alone obey,
Pedants they are, in judges' false array.
I know them well, heroes of scrivening,
Pretended guardians of a noble king,
These haughty cits, tyrants arrayed in black,
Their wards of all their revenues they rack;
Cite them before them in most formal state
Gravely their crown and all to confiscate.
These worthy people crouching at your knee,
Like you are treated by this bold decree,

Protect them, then; yours is a common cause,
Avenge their wrongs, proscribed by self-same laws."
    This argument had touched the monarch's mind,
To clemency his soul was aye inclined.
But Joan whose heart more doughtily was strung,
Insisted still 'twas best, that all were hung;
That Frélon, and all those to such trade born,
Were only good a gallows to adorn.
Dunois, on wisdom more profoundly bent,
Thus spoke, like able soldier, his intent:
"Often," he said, "in war, we soldiers lack,
Are scant of men of arms and legs and back;
These fellows have them: in adventures fell,
Assaults, long marches, combattings pell-mell,
We little stand in need of such as write;
Enlist them all, and by tomorrow's light,
Instead of oars a musket let them bear;
Paper they've spoiled enough of, and to spare—
Let them prove useful now on Mars' great plain."
The monarch relished well brave Dunois' strain,
As at his knees appeared this worthy crew,
Sighing and bathing them in sorrow's dew;
To pent-house of the fort they went enrolled,
Where Agnes, Charles and all his troop of gold,
The dinner o'er—agreeable evening spent;
With Bonneau, Agnes on good deeds intent
Took heed that each should share of food an hoard,
The ample refuse of the royal board.
Charles and his escort having amply fed,
With Agnes soon he hied him to his bed;
When each, awak'ning, from the couch arose,
Surprised they found nor doublet, cloak nor clothes;
For ruffles Agnes vainly turned the eye,
And necklace boasting pearls of yellow dye;
The portrait of her lord she found no more.
Fat Bonneau, treasurer of all the store,
In narrow purse confined with skilful care,
No longer finds his master's money there.
Clothes, vesses, linen, vanished to a rag;
The scrawling cohort 'neath the unfurled flag

Of Nantes' famed pamphleteers, with zealous pain
Had in the night performed their legerdemain;
Easing of equipage thus light, their Sire—
Pretending warriors fraught with real fire,
As Plato said, but little luxury need.
To 'scape secure, by winding paths, they speed
And at a way-side inn their spoil divide;
Then take their rest, but write and read beside
A moral treatise, with a Christian view,
On the contempt of pleasure, virtue too.
It proved that men as brothers were allied,
Born equal, all good things they should divide;
And miseries too, dispensed from Heaven above,
Living in common to share social love.
This saintly book, which since has met our eyes,
Contains a commentary, wond'rous wise,
To tutor and direct the *heart and mind*,
With preface, and to reader counsel kind.
    Our clement monarch's household thus amazed,
To grief abandoned, on each other gazed.
Through woods and plains the band they sought to trace,
As good Phineas, erst the Prince of Thrace,
And as Aeneas famed for pious mind,
Were quite aghast with fright and short of wind.
When to their very teeth, just at mid-day,
The glutton Harpies, ravenous for their prey,
From caverns rushing, borne on outstretched wings,
Pouncing, devoured the dinners of those kings.
    Timid was Agnes, Dorothy in tears;
To veil their charms, no ready means appears;
Bonneau the treasurer so roared his pain,
From peals of laughter they could not refrain;
"Ah," Bonneau cried, "a loss so fell before
Was ne'er experienced in the battle's war;
The rascals all have ta'en, I die with grief
Why did my king afford them kind relief?
Such is the recompence indulgence gains,
'Tis thus we're paid by men of brilliant brains."
Agnes commiserating, Agnes kind,
Forever courteous, always bland of mind,

Anon replied: "My dear and fat Bonneau,
Fore Heaven, take heed, nor let this ill-starred blow
With new disgust inspire you 'gainst those men
Who wield in letters the most: doughty pen.
Good writers have I known, of that I'm sure,
Possessing hearts; just like their hands as pure;
Who, without robbing, love their master dear,
Doing all good, nor suffering soul to hear;
Lauding bright virtue, or in prose or verse,
Her feats in acting, abler to rehearse;
Their fruit, the public good is recognized,
In pleasantness their lessons are disguised,
They touch the heart, ears own the dulcet sound,
Cherished are they, and if Hornets are found
In this our era, bees alike abound."
"Alas!" quoth Bonneau, "what care I for these,
Such trifles vain, your *Hornets* and your bees,
'Tis meet to dine, and I my purse have lost."
Each now essayed to calm his temper crost,
Like heroes to all usage rough inured,
Prepared to soften all the ills endured.
Towards the town they forthwith take the road,
To castle fair, secure and firm abode
Of all those knights and Charles, the mighty King,
Furnished with generous wines and everything.
Our gallant Cavaliers but half equipped,
And fair ones too, of richest vesture stripped,
A sorry crowd that castle came to view,
One foot quite bare, the other *sans* a shoe.

19

Death of the brave and gentle La Trimouille and of the charming Dorothy—The ruthless Tirconel becomes a Carthusian.

O direful war! of Death the sister dread
The cut-throat's right, or heroes', as 'tis said;
Thou monster bloody from the loins derived
Of Atropos: how have thy crimes deprived
This earth of souls! 'tis thou inspirest fears,
Wide spreading devastation, blood and tears.
But when the pangs of gentle Love combine
With those of Mars, ah, when the hand benign
Of lovers kind by favours quite subdued,
With stream from heart adored becomes imbrued,
And that her breath to save, he'd life lay low,
An ill-directed dagger deals the blow,
Piercing that bosom, glowing lips so oft
Have sealed with love's ecstatic transports soft;
Thus seeing, closed on light of radiant day,
Those eyes that erst beamed nought but love's pure ray;
A scene like this more terror far imparts,
To bosoms blessed with sympathetic hearts,
Than hosts of watriors earning mundane doom,
By monarchs bribed to gallop to the tomb.
 Charles, now surrounded by his royal train,
The fatal gift of reason had reta'en,
(Present accurst which men so loudly boast.)
But to encounter the opposing host,
To city ramparts now they wend their way,
This castellated pile their surest stay,
Wherein of Mars the magazines were stored.
Of glittering lances pointed spears an hoard,
And cannon cast by Hell's infernal spite,
To hurl us headlong to the realms of night.

Already now the turrets greet their view,
Fast trotting there, the knights their course pursue,
Replete with hope and warmed by valour's glow;
But La Trimouille, in whom the chief we know
Of Poitou's knights and lover the most kind,
Now slowly ambling with his Dame behind,
And of his flame conversing on the way,
Thus from the path direct was led astray.
  In valley watered by a limpid flood,
Deeply embosomed in a cypress wood,
By nature reared in Pyramidic form,
Whose tops a century had braved the storm,
Was found a cave where oft the Naiads fair
And the Sylvani breathed the cooling air;
A crystal stream, which subterranean strayed,
And formed a sheet, where twenty cascades played,
Near which was spread a carpet ever green:
The wild thyme there, and balmy mint were seen;
The fragrant jonquil, and the jasmin white,
Seemed all the neighbouring shepherds to invite,
Whisp'ring "Upon this couch of Love recline."
Our youth of Poitou heard the call benign
From heart's recess; sweet Zephyr's sighs engage—
The time, the place, his tenderness, his age,
But more than all, his lady fanned the fire:
Their steeds they left; both glowing with desire,
Each on the turf towards the other turns,
Flowers and kisses sweet they cull in turns:
Venus and Mars regarding from above,
Objects ne'er saw more worthy of their love;
From forest's deep recess echoed around
Of gazing wood-nymphs the applauding sound.
The sparrows, too, and pigeons of the wood,
Example took and found that love was good.
  In this same wood a chapel's structure rose,
Sacred to such as in Death's arms repose;
And thither, evening come, to grave was borne
The corpse of Chandos, from earth's region torn;
Two parish clerks in surplices all white,
Of *De Profundis* long rehearsed the rite;

To this sad service Paul Tirconel sped
Not from a taste for pure devotion led,
But from affection for the vanished knight.
Brother he ranked of Chandos, bold in fight,
Haughty like him, debauched and void of fear,
Stranger to love, nor ever shedding tear,
He still for Chandos certain friendship bore,
And in his violent anger now he swore,
By the just God, his vengeance should be wrought,
More spurred by passion than with pity fraught.

   He from the corner of a casement spied
The palfreys twain, then grazing side by side;
T'wards them he goes; they turn and run away
Straight to the fountain where our lovers lay,
Yielding in secret to the soft control,
Themselves excepted, seeing not a soul.
Bold Paul Tirconel, whose inhuman mind
To neighbours' pleasures ever proved unkind,
Grinding his teeth, exclaimed: "Ye souls most vile,
'Tis thus with transports base you must defile
A hero's tomb, insulting his remains,
Refuse of courts, which nothing pure retains,
Base foes, when some brave Briton yields to fate,
'Tis thus the rare event ye celebrate,
To outrage his loved Manes you presume,
And act your wanton frolics on his tomb.
Speak, is it thou, O knight discourteous,
Made but for courts, and born voluptuous,
Whose feeble hand by fluke of fortune gave
Death to the bravest warrior of the brave?
What! no reply, and ogling still thy fair,
Thy shame thou feelst, thine heart can nothing dare."

   To this discourse Trimouille at length replied:
"No sword of mine with his life's blood was dyed,
Heav'n, that conducts all heroes to renown,
Can as it list accord the victor's crown;
'Gainst Chandos I with honour sought to shine,
Fate willed a hand more fortunate than mine
Should seal on martial plain its dread decree,
And there cut short at once his destiny.

But since that day I have not ceased to yearn,
Some Englishman to punish in my turn."
　　As freshening breezes which in murmurs creep,
And whistling ruffle surface of the deep,
Swell high their roar, and wrecking barks on strand,
Spread horror o'er the surface of the land;
So fierce Tirconel and Trimouille in rage
Prepared in direful duel to engage.
By these remarks of wrath and rage unmanned,
Helmless alike, without cuirass they stand.
The Poitevin upon the flowery glade,
Had near his dainty dame of Milan laid
Lance, morion, breast-plate, glaive, his limbs to free,
And trappings all, the more at ease to be.
Who, to make love, requires a ponderous blade?
Tirconel ever went in armour 'rayed;
But he beside the catafalque had placed
His cuirass and his helm with gold enchased,
In charge of squire—with costly brassarts too;
The shoulder belt alone appeared to view,
Appendant, bearing his broad glittering brand;
He drew it—La Trimouille was quick at hand,
Prepared the brutal islander to brave.
Springing with lightsome bound he grasped his glaive,
And brandished it, and bubbling o'er with hate
Cried, "O, thou cruel monster, do but wait,
What merit thy deserts, thou soon shalt feel,
Cut-throat that in hypocrisy can deal;
Thus coming with impertinence to view
And eke molest a lover's rendezvous."
So saying, on the Briton bold, he burst:
In Phrygia, Menelaus, Hector erst,
Threatened each other and would death devise,
Before fair Helen's sad and guilty eyes.
　　From cave, air, heav'n and forest, echoes rose
Responsive to sad Dorothea's woes,
Love never with such thrills her breast had fired,
Nor had she felt her tender heart inspired
With equal pain: what, on the very green,
Of pure voluptuousness so late the scene:

"All potent Heav'n! and must I even here
Lose what I hold on earth supremely dear?
Adored Trimouille! barbarian, stay thy rage,
And let my timid breast this wrath assuage."
Saying such words, with rapid feet she came,
She flew with outstretched arms, and eyes aflame,
And rushed betwixt the combatants distrest;
Her gallant lover's alabaster breast,
Soft as the satin, idolized, adored,
Was by a grievous wound already gored
From blow terrific, parried off with pain;
The knight thus galled, his rage could not retain,
And headlong rushed the Briton to subdue,
But Dorothy was just between the two.
O! God of love! O! Heav'n! O! direful blow!
What faithful lover e'er the truth can know,
And not with tears my script pathetic lave,
When of all lovers the most fair and brave,
Graced with all favours that she could bestow,
Could deal his charming mistress such a blow!
That fateful steel, that dread, ensanguined blade
Transpierced the heart for love's soft transports made,
Which ever burned for him her soul desired:
She staggered, sighing forth, as she expired,
Name of "Trimouille—Trimouille!" then direful death,
Grim spectre, seized upon her fleeting breath,
She felt it, turning once more on the light
Those eyes unclosed, which an eternal night
Was soon to seal her feeble hand, the breast
Once more of her fond lover fondly pressed.
Vowing to cherish an immortal glow,
Forth ebbed her life in sobs and sighing low.
"I love—I love!" in falt'ring accents broke.
Such the last words this faithful lady spoke.
'Twas vainly said, alas! for Trimouille too,
Nought but death's shadows understood or knew,
They wrapped him round; he falls upon her charms,
Unconsciously, and lies within her arms,
Bathed in her blood, and yet not knowing aught:
At sight so tender and with horror fraught

Aghast and chilled, awhile Tirconel stood,
His senses fled, and frozen was life's flood:
So, erst if heathen records tell us true,
Was Atlas, whom no feeling could subdue,
When for obduracy 'twas Heaven's decree,
Changed into flinty rock his form should be.
    But pity, gentle nature's soft behest,
Dispensed to quell the fury of the breast,
Awoke at length within his hardened heart;
He joined the fair, assistance to impart,
And found two portraits as her person fair,
Portraits preserved by Dorothy with care,
For times long past, thro' adventures rare.
The one, blue eyes of La Trimouille portrays,
His tresses blonde, his proud and gentle traits,
Where noble courage, grace the most refined,
In happy unison are well combined.
Tirconel said: "He well deserved her heart!"
But at the second picture does he start!
Himself he gazed at, trait for trait designed;
O! what surprise!—as straight he called to mind,
That journeying once to Milan's famous town,
He Carminetta knew, of fair renown,
Gallant and noble, kind to Albion's race,
When quitting after months' elapse that place,
Finding herself with child already great,
He gave her, absence to alleviate,
This portrait traced by the accomplished hand
Of great Bellini, of the Lombard band.
'Twas Dorothy's own mother—Truth, how dire!
All is explained, Tirconel is her sire!
    Though haughty he, indifferent and cold,
His heart, if probed, would generous germs unfold;
When by such characters the bitter draught
Of poignant agony is amply quaffed,
Its dire effects impressions strong impart,
Which ne'er assail an ordinary heart,
Too open to receive warm passion's flow;
As brass or steel more powerfully flow
Than rushes burnt, when trifling flame they meet.

Our Briton viewed his daughter at his feet,
Who Death had glutted with her cherished blood,
Her he considered, as from eyes a flood
Of tears flowed fast, he ne'er had wept before.
With streams he bathed her, kissing o'er and o'er,
His loud cries echoing thro' the woods around,
As fraught with anguish, he breathed grief profound;
And cursing fortune, war and direful death,
Felt quite o'ercome, bereft of voice and breath.

Thy lids unclosed at sounds so fraught with fate,
Trimouille, once more thou saw'st the day, and straight
For the remaining light possessed no charm;
Shudd'ring thou didst withdraw thy murd'rous arm,
Which had with agonizing fervour prest
The lily beauties of that cherished breast.
His sword hilt placed he on the ensanguined plain,
Then on its cruel point he rushed amain;
The mortal blow transpierces: soon a tide
Of crimson blood his prostrate mistress dyed.
The horrid screams that came from Tirconel,
Attract the squires, the priests run up as well;
Affrighted, gazing at the cruel deed,
Their stony hearts as well as his could bleed,
And, but for them, Tirconel by self-doom
Had followed the poor lovers to the tomb.

At length, the horrors of his anguish o'er,
And master of his faculties once more,
He caused the clay-cold lovers to be placed
Upon a litter made of spears enlaced;
Thus were they borne by knights in sad array,
To the King's Court, while tears bedewed the way.
Tirconel, who made violence his guide
Was ever prompt on matters to decide,
And from the hour this fatal deed took place,
Women he hates and all the woman race.
His beard grew long, no valet with him sped,
Mournful his eye, nor word he ever said;
His heart sore pent, and in this sombre mood,
He roamed to Paris, leaving Loire's bright flood;
Ere long he gained, at Calais, ocean's strand,

Embarked, and safely trod his native land;
'Twas there he took the robe monastical
Of Holy Bruno: ennui to dispel
Betwixt the world and him the Heavens he set,
And would himself as well as men forget.
And thus with thoughts on melancholy bent.
His days were past in everlasting Lent;
'Twas there he lived, no sentence e'er breathed he,
And yet, he never proved a devotee.

As Charles and Agnes and the martial Maid
Behold thus pass this doleful cavalcade,
No sooner they the generous pair espied,
Happy so long, and erst bright beauty's pride,
All bathed in blood, their forms with dust besmeared,
Than struck with dread each personage appeared,
While every eye the glistering drops distilled;
Each sympathetic heart with anguish thrilled.
In Troy, they wept not thus, the bloody day
When Hector of grim Death became the prey;
And when Achilles, gentle victor he,
Bid him be dragged with so much charity,
His feet in bonds, with poor down-trailing head,
Behind his car which trampled o'er the dead;
Alive, at least, was fair Andromachê,
When her spouse crossed the stream of agony.

Agnes, the lovely Agnes, shook by fears,
Whose arms the King entwined, with bitter tears
Exclaimed: "My love, alas! we both some day
Thus to the charnel house shall pass away;
Ah, that my soul, as well as body too,
In death's domain may be at one with you."

At their complaints, which in their bosoms bear
A faint affliction and a gloomy fear,
Joan, who assumed that martial tone and loud,
The happy organ of her courage proud,
Cried out: "'Tis not by wailings and by sighs,
By tears, by sobbings and such doleful cries,
That we may vengeance for Love's sufferers take,
'Tis blood, let's arm tomorrow for his sake;
Behold, O King, of Orléans, yonder walls,

Sad ramparts, subject now to Britain's thralls,
Its plains still smoking, by fell carnage fed
Of those, who by your royal prowess bled,
As in your suite the Gallic legions went.
Let us prepare, pursue the grave intent,
This debt deserve the bleeding shades we see,
La Trimouille and his dear-loved Dorothy:
'Tis meet a King should conquer and not weep;
Sweet Agnes, in oblivion, prithee, sleep
Those soft emotions of a tender heart;
Agnes to her royal lover should impart
Thoughts worthier of his crown and station high."
"Leave me alone!" quoth Agnes, "let me cry."

20

*How Joan fell into a strange temptation—The gentle audacity
of her ass; the noble resistance of the Maid.*

Woman, like man, is but a vessel weak;
To put your trust in virtue never seek:
Fair is the vessel but it's made of clay,
A nothing breaks it; mend it though you may,
The enterprise is often somewhat hard;
With due precaution such a vase to guard
Without a spot, is but a vision vain,
Which, from Eve's husband onwards, none attain;
As witness Lot, Samson who lost his eyes,
David the Saint, and Solomon the wise,
And you, sweet sex and fair, of soft intent,
Or in the new or in the ancient Testament,
In history or legend though you live!
O pious sex, I easily forgive
Your little ruses and your light caprice,
Your sweet refusals, charming artifice;
But there are certain cases I confess,
And certain tastes I can excuse no less,
I've seen, sometimes, a puppet, very ape,
Fat, stunted, red, all hairy 'neath his cape,
Caressed, like some fair gallant in your arms;
Then I grieved greatly for your tender charms.
Perhaps, worth ten times more a winged ass,
Then fop in clothes arrayed, or dandy crass.
O sex adorable, to whom I've vowed
The gift of verse with which I've been endowed;
For your instruction, meet 'tis to display
Our Joan's mistake, and how her handsome grey
A moment eke had caused her wits to stray.

It is not I, but Tritemus the wise,
That worthy Abbé, who this story cries.
    Of Grisbourdon, the spirit damned and rude,
Who, as you know, within his copper stewed,
While he blasphemed, would still occasion seek,
Upon the maiden proud, vengeance to wreak,
Through whom, in realms above, by broad-sword crost,
His patron's body its head sadly lost.
"Beelzebub, my father!" thus he cried,
"In some foul sin, oh, can you not decide
This Joan, to fall, albeit so austere?
For me, I think, your honour's rooted there."
Just as he spoke, alive with Fury's flame,
Hermaphrodix to the dire river came,
With holy water moist his visage yet,
The amphibious animal on vengeance set,
Came to address the author of all ill.
Behold them there, all three, conspiring still
Against a woman! Yet we often see
For a seduction, there's no need of three.
Long to this trio had it been revealed
That Joan beneath her petticoat concealed
The keys of the beleaguered town; that more,
The fate of France, afflicted then so sore,
Was to the fortune of her mission knit.
The Devil has a most inventive wit,
And went with speed upon the Earth to spy
What did the friends of England occupy,
And to what state of body and of mind,
After that conflict fierce was Joan resigned.
The King, Dunois, Agnes at that time true,
The Maid, the ass, Bonneau and Bonifoux,
Within the fort at length in shelter were,
Waiting till some fresh succour should be there.
The breach of the besieged once more restored,
Was shut 'gainst entry of the assaulting horde;
Into retreat is sped the hostile sword.
The citizens, King Charles and Bedford too,
Supped hastily and to their couches flew.

Muses! now quake at the adventure rare,
Which to posterity ye shall declare.
And Readers! ye, to whom the Heavens ensure
Tastes virtuous and tenderness most pure,
To Dunois and to Denis vows submit
That a most heinous sin was not commit.

My former promise, you remember well,
The marvels and the gallant feats to tell
Of long-eared Pegasus, who for the Maid
And for Dunois, the enemy dismayed;
You saw him, with his wings all golden, soar,
When Dunois to the Lombard plain he bore:
Jealous was he when he returned once more.
You are aware that, when he bore the Maid,
Within his heart he felt the fire was laid
Of that fair spark, that's not so sweet as keen,
Soul, source and spring of all things that have been,
Which in the air, where woods or waters dwell,
Bodies produces and inspires as well.
That sacred fire of which there rests to-day,
Within this worn-out world so scant a ray,
From Heav'n was stolen, Pandora to inspire,
And since that time the torch has no more fire:
All things are withered; force which fades away
Of nature in this most unhappy day,
Imperfect loves can only now create.
If still there lives a flame that's animate,
One germ of those high principles divine,
Venus. Urania has not the sign;
Nor look for it in weak humanity—
The heroes rather seek of Arcady.

Fair Celadons, whom your victorious flames
Have wreathed in flowery bands, whom passion tames,
Soft lovers in cuirass, or cassocked sirs,
Priests, prelates, colonels or councillors,
Folk well to do, eke cordeliers, alas!
Where love's concerned, distrust ye of an ass.
That famous *Golden Ass* the Latins found,
By metamorphosis so well renowned,

To this, our ass, in sooth, resembled naught:
That was a man, a thing of small import.

Abbé Tritemus, wise mind of his age,
Than pedant Larchet more discreet and sage,
When this fair history he dared display,
Was terrified far more than one can say,
That he must need to dim posterity
Of such excess transmit the memory.
With fingers three he'd hardly dare engage
His agitated pen upon the page;
So let it drop; then 'gan his soul assuage
Of its alarm, as he would meditate
Upon the Devil's power and evil state.

Of all the race of man, this guilty foe
Is, by profession, tempter as you know.
The folk he meets, he's very prone to win;
This formidable father of all sin,
Rival of God, seduced my mother dear
At evening, a woodland's corner near,
Within his garden. This deceitful snake,
An apple, with a curse on't, bid her take;
That he did worse than this, some even say.
From blessed Eden she was chased away;
And since that time, at home, the Prince of Hell
Has ruled our daughters and our wives as well,
Sooth instances good Tritemus has set
Of this effect which his own eyes have met.
Thus the great man relates how came to pass,
The shameless insolence of the holy ass.

The sturdy Joan, all vermeil to the view,
Her face by poppied sleep refreshed anew,
Between her sheets secluded modestly,
Resumes her life and her high destiny.
Her young heart flattered by so much success,
Did not to Denis all the fame confess;
She 'gan conceive a certain vanity.
Vexed was Saint Denis, as he well might be;
To punish her he left her for a while,
That all unwatched, her senses might beguile.

Denis, who loved her well, desired his Joan
Should feel what it is like to be alone,
And know that woman, in whatever case,
A patron needs, if she would keep in grace.
She was just ready to become the prey
Of a dread snare the Demon sent her way:
One wanders far, when once one goes astray.

    The great Deceiver, who neglecteth naught,
Seized his occasion, seized it with forethought.
He's everywhere; and now with skill he came
Within the ass's skin his wits to frame;
His tongue he taught of sound significance,
And tuned his raucous bray to eloquence,
Instructing him in that most subtile art,
Which Bernard, like old Ovid, knew by heart.
The enlightened ass put modesty away,
And softly from the stable made his way
To the bedside where Joan, reposeful, lay,
And dreamed of all the labours of the day;
Then squatting very gently by her side,
He praised her for the heroes who had died;
Invincible she was and fair no less:
Thus did of old the snake's seductiveness,
When our first mother he desired to gain,
A flatt'ring compliment began the campaign.
The arts to please and praise are surely one.
"O Heavens!" cried Joan, "alas! I am undone.
Saint Luke! Saint Mark! What is it that I hear?
Is it mine ass? What prodigy is here?
Mine ass—he speaks! he even speaks me fair."

    The ass still kneeling with a tranquil mien,
Cried to her: "D'Arc! no miracle is seen;
In me the ass of Canaan you behold;
Nourished and bred long time by Balaam old;
Balaam was priest amongst the Pagan horde;
I was a Jew, and but for me, my lord
Had cursed that elect people with good will,
Whence, doubtless, had arrived exceeding ill.
The Heavens just, my zeal did recompense!

To Enoch next, passed my obedience:
Enoch with life immortal was endowed,
I, with the same; the Master then allowed
That scissors of the Parcae cruel should spare
The thread which bound me to my years so fair.
Immortal spring was at that time my share.
Our garden's master, ever debonnaire
All things save one permitted: understand,
A life of chastity was his command;
For any ass, oh, what a piteous case!
Young and unfettered in so fair a place,
Master of all, I had o'er all things right,
Save over love, whether by day or night.
Better obeyed I, than that witless one
Who, for an apple's sake lost everyone.
I fought my temperament victoriously,
Subdued my flesh, had no more frailty;
Virgin I lived; now, know ye by what grace?
There was no single she-ass in the place!
Thus I saw pass, contented with my life,
A thousand years and more, without a wife.
When from the heart of Greece came Bacchus fair,
The thyrsis, glory, drunkenness to bear;
In lands o'errun by Ganges' gentle rain
My trumpet followed in that hero's train:
And still the Indians, civilized by us,
Sing their defeat and my name glorious:
I am Silenus, more renowned in song
Than all the rest whom Bacchus led along.
It is my worth alone, my single name
Which is the crown of Apuleius' fame.
    "At last above, in plains of azure blue,
When English George, who little loveth you,
Saint George the proud, who ever loves to fight,
Would have an English steed for his delight;
When Holy Martin, famous for his cloak,
A courser e'en more beautiful bespoke;
Denis, not wishing to be left behind,
Like them, must have a courser of some kind:

He chose me out and called me to his side,
And of two shining wings made gift beside;
Upon which wings to Heavenly vaults I glide,
There was I fêted by Saint Roch's huge hound,
Anthony's pig a faithful friend I found—
O pig Divine, emblem by monks confest!
With a gold curry-comb my coat was drest;
Nectar I drank, ambrosia was my food:
But oh, my Joan, a life so great and good
Is far beneath the ecstasy which warms
My veins, in contemplation of your charms.
Denis nor George, nor dog nor pig compare
With the rich treasure of your beauty rare.
Above all other occupations far,
Whither has called me my benigner star,
Know, that the happiest, most to my will,
Which most, perhaps, I worthy am to fill,
Is but to serve 'neath your august commands.
When I left Heav'n and the empyrean strands,
In you my fortune and my honour met;
Nay, verily, I've not left Heaven yet,
I still am there; for in your eyes 'tis set."

At such discourse, that modesty might blame,
Joan felt within her breast quick anger's flame.
To love an ass, and yield to him her pride!
There was dishonour she could not abide,
Who lived, her innocence preserved to tell,
From muleteers and knights of France as well,
Who had, supported by high Heaven's grace,
In mortal fight brought Chandos to disgrace!
Yet, Heavens! this ass has a deserving air,
Can he not with the loved she-goats compare,
Whom the Calabrians with flowers array?
"Nay," said she, "put these horrid thoughts away."
Yet in her heart, these thoughts a tempest formed,
And all her mind was troubled and deformed.
So, on the ocean deep, one oft may spy.
The haughty tyrants of the waves and sky,
One rushing from the distant Austral caves,
While one from icy Boreal regions raves,

Some wandering ship on Ocean to appal,
Seeking Ceylon, Sumatra or Bengal:
Anon the hull seems lifted to the sky,
Then near the rocks is hurried perilously;
Then comes the abyss with its engulfing swell
Seeming to issue from the jaws of Hell.
    That cunning boy, to whose rule is consigned
Asses and gods, the whole of human-kind,
From heights of Heaven, his bow in hand the while,
Looked down upon the Maid with sweetest smile.
Now secretly much stirred was Joan's great heart,
And flattered that her form should thus impart
So great effect; that on her so should brood
Such heavy senses and a soul so rude.
She stretched her lily hand towards her swain,
With scarce a thought; then drew it back again.
She blushed, afraid, condemns herself, alas!
Then reassured, exclaims to him: "Fair Ass,
Chimerical the hope you entertain;
Respect my duty and my glory's chain;
Too broad the differences that us divide:
I never could your tenderness abide;
O have a care, and urge me not too far!"
The ass replied: "Love levels every bar:
Think of the Swan, by Leda not disdained;
Nathless, an honest woman she remained.
Know you the daughter unto Minos born,
Who for a bull's sake heroes held in scorn,
And for her comely beast bore many a pain?
Know, by an eagle Ganymede was ta'en,
How Philyra her lavish favours threw
On the Sea-God, whom as a horse she knew."
    The Devil, while thus he argued from his store,
The Devil, first author of all fabled lore,
Furnished him fresh examples, for the case,
So that the ass might take our *Savants'* place.
Whilst thus his subtile phrases meet her eat.
The great Dunois, whose bed-chamber was near,
Hearing, was seized with wonderment immense

At the bold strains of so much eloquence.
What hero speaks, he straightway longed to see,
And whom Love sent to him in rivalry.
He enters, sees (O, wonder! prodigy!)
Two lengthy ears adorn the swain who sighs:
He sees, but cannot yet believe his eyes.
Venus of old felt thus of shame the dread,
When o'er her wiry net of brass was spread,
And the wretch Vulcan to the gods afar
Showed her all naked 'neath the god of war.
Joan after all was not subdued, 'tis plain;
Denis to comfort her was always fain,
Near the abyss, her steps he guarded still,
And snatched her from the dire effects of ill.
Indignant Joan within herself retired,
As at his post will sleep the sentry tired,
Who, as the first alarms his senses greet,
Springs up and sudden stands upon his feet,
Rubs either eye, attires himself and lo!
Seizes his arms, prepared to meet the foe.

Of Deborah the most redoubted lance
Stood by the pillow of the Maid of France.
It rescued her from perils every day;
She seized the stock, the fiend's power to dismay,
Who ne'er could stand against its might divine.
Dunois and Joan attacked the fiend malign;
Foul Satan fled, and while he hideous cried,
The woods of Orléans, Blois and Mantes replied,
And Poitou's donkeys who in meadow strayed,
In harsh tones answering, discordant brayed.
The Devil sped, fain in his course so fleet
The British to avenge and his defeat.
So flew like arrow into Orléans straight,
And passed of Louvet president the gate.
Then entered snug the body of the dame
Sure of controlling there the mental flame;
It was his chattel and he knew full well
The secret sin whereof she owned the spell,
He knows she loves, that Talbot fascinates;
The wily snake her conduct indicates,

Spurs and inflames her, hoping in the end,
Some friendly succour he may thus extend,
And thro' the gates of Orléans lead amain
The valiant Talbot and his fiery train;
Yet while he works for England which he likes,
He knows 'tis really for himself he strikes.

21

The chastity of Joan demonstrated—Malice of the Devil—
Rendezvous given to Talbot by the wife of Louvet, the President—
Services rendered by Brother Lourdis—Repentance of the Ass—
Exploits of the Maid—Triumph of King Charles VII.

Experience hath taught my reader's mind,
That the sweet Deity as boy designed,
Whose sports, an infant's gambols ne'er unfold,
Two different quivers hath, his shafts to hold;
One, only filled with tender, striking darts,
Void of all pain and danger, wounds imparts,
Which, time increasing, penetrate the breast.
Like fire consuming are the darts which rest,
All on a sudden their fell course they wing,
And to the senses five destruction bring;
With lively red, the face illuminate,
Seems with new being to be animate;
With fresher blood the body gleams and glows,
The eyes grow bright; one nothing heeds or knows.
Water boils noisily upon the fires,
Escapes above its limits and expires,
But gives no echo, faithful at the last,
Of those desires you follow over fast.
  Blasphemers, all unworthy to be known,
Who have defiled the glorious name of Joan,
Vile scribes who, fascinated by your lies,
Corrupt the wisest writings of the wise—
Pretend my Joan, of ever maiden fame,
For a gray ass conceived an evil flame:
In print you say she fought a losing fight,
At once her sex and virtue you indict.
Ye scurvy writers, scribes of infamy,
To honest dames, pray, more respectful be,

Nor ever tell that Joan had gone astray!
No learned man in such an error lay.
The actions and the times you do confuse,
The very rarest miracles abuse;
The ass and his amazing feats respect,
Talents the like of his, you can't expect,
E'en if your ears be longer than his own.
And if, in such a case, the maiden Joan
Saw, with an eye that satisfaction fired,
The fresh incentives that her form inspired,
'Twas but that like her sex she's passing vain;
'Twas love of self, not love that loves again.

     To set before you in its fullest light,
Lustre of Joan, untarnishable, bright;
To prove to you, how to the Devil's wiles,
And ass's fire, whose eloquence beguiles,
Her noble heart was never overthrown,
Know that another lover had our Joan.
It is Dunois, as nobody ignores,
The gallant bastard, whom her heart adores.
A donkey one may heed without disdain,
And e'en to please him feel a pleasure vain;
So innocent and light an escapade,
Love that is constant never yet betrayed.

     'Tis an admitted fact in history,
That gallant Dunois, famed in chivalry,
Was wounded with a golden shaft Love drew
From his first quiver, and unerring threw.
But ever his vain fondness he'd subdue;
His haughty heart no weakness ever knew;
Too well the Kingdom and the King he served,
Their interest the one law he observed.

     He knows thy precious maidenhead, O Joan!
Of victory is the reward alone;
Both Denis he respected, and thy charms;
Like faithful hound, courageous 'mid alarms,
Who nobly struggling against hunger's stings,
The partridge he might eat to master brings.
Yet seeing that the ass of heavenly fame
Had spoken and confessed his direful flame,

Dunois conceived that he might speak in turn:
Sages forget themselves sometimes, we learn.
　　No doubt a flagrant folly it had proved,
To sacrifice the state for her he loved.
'Twas all to lose, and Joan still wrapped in shame
That thus an ass had dared confess his flame,
Resisted ill her hero's ardent speech;
Love in her soul was fain to make a breach.
All had been done, when lo! her patron bright,
His ray detachèd from the heavenly height.
That golden beam, his glory and his steed,
Bearing his Saintly form in time of need,
As when he sought, impelled by pressing call,
A virgin flower to rescue Orléans' wall;
This heavenly ray that pierced Joan's better sense,
All sentiment profane removed from thence.
"Dear Bastard stop": she cried, "O! shun the crime,
Our Loves are reckoned, 'tis not yet the time;
Let us naught mar, nothing of our destiny,
My solemn faith is plighted but to thee,
Thine I protest the virgin bud shall be:
Let us await until your vengeful arm,
Your virtues, which in Britons strike alarm,
Have driven the usurper from the land:
Then over laurels our soft bed may stand."
　　At this address the Bastard calmed his rage,
He heard the oracle, submitted sage;
Joan then received his hommage, pure and sweet,
And modestly returned him, for a treat,
Of kisses thirty, eloquent though chaste,
Such as fond brothers with their sisters taste.
Each bridled in the torrent of desire,
And modestly agreed to quench the fire:
Denis looked on; the Saint was satisfied,
And straight his projects hastened to decide.
　　That night bold Talbot, chief of high renown,
By ruse resolved to enter Orléans' town,
A new idea in haughty British breast,
To courage more than cunning owing zest.
O God of Love! O power by frailty known!

O fatal love! how nearly hadst thou thrown
That citadel of France in hostile hands,
Success unhoped of those who hate our lands;
What Bedford, in experience grown old,
And Talbot, sought to do, albeit bold,
And failed at last, O Love you did essay!
Dear Child, you're all our ill, and still you play.

If, in his course of conquering career,
A gentle shaft to heart of Joan could veer;
Another arrow from his bow-string flew,
Dame President's five senses to subdue.
With hand he struck her, which triumphant rules,
Directing dart that turns us all to fools.
You've seen already that grim escalade,
Assault of blood and horrid cannonade,
Those brave attempts and all those desp'rate fights,
Within, without and on the ramparts' heights;
When Talbot and his fiery following train,
The ramparts and the gates had burst and ta'en;
When on them from the houses' tops there broke
Sword, flame and grisly death at one fell stroke.
The fiery Talbot, with his agile walk,
Tramples the dying, through the town to stalk;
He upsets all things, crying out aloud,
"My Britons, enter and disarm the crowd!"
Much he resembled then to War's great God,
Beneath his footsteps, echoing the sod;
When Discord and Bellona and high Fate,
As minister of Death, arm him with hate.

Dame President, within her walls, a breach
That looked upon a ruined cot could reach,
And through this hole her gallant could espy;
His golden helm, where feathers curl and fly,
His mailed arm, and those live sparks of flame
Which from his pupils' orbits darting came,
That carriage proud, that demi-god's great air:
Dame President was almost in despair,
With shame dumbfounded and bereft of wits.
As once, when in her grated stage-box sits
Madame Audon, whom love has sore inflamed,

And ogles Baron, actor justly famed;
With ardent eyes she feasts upon his face,
His rich adornment, gestures and his grace;
Mingled with his, her accents in tones low
Love's flames received, her senses owned the flow.
    In Dame Louvet the fiend was throned in state,
Acquiring post, though not importunate;
And that archangel black, Hell's ravenous King,
The Devil or Love, which means the self-same thing,
In cap and traits of Suzon was arrayed;
(Long time within that house she'd been the maid)
A girl both active and instructed too,
Dressing and frizzing, bearing *billets-doux*,
In double *rendezvous* a careful elf,
The one for mistress, t'other for herself;
Satan, concealed beneath her semblance well,
Thus held harangue with our important belle.
"Alike my heart and talents you must know,
I wish to aid your bosom's ardent glow;
Your interest now alone concerns my mind.
This night, my own first cousin, as I find,
Stands sentry at a certain postern gate,
Where naught against your fame can doubt create;
In secret there bold Talbot you may meet;
Dispatch a note, my cousin is discreet,
Your message, trust me, he'll perform with care."
Dame President then penned a billet fair,
Impassioned, tender words that strike the goal,
And with voluptuous ardour fire the soul;
Devil's dictation in it well was seen:
Talbot was amorous, his wits were keen,
He swore his fair at rendezvous to meet,
But vowed alike, that in this conflict sweet,
The path of pleasure should to glory lead;
All things were ready for the purposed deed;
Thus springing from the couch 'twas planned that he.
Should leap into the arms of Victory.
    Our Reverend Lourdis, you well know, was sent
By holy Denis with the wise intent
Of serving him 'mid Britain's cohorts dire.

In action free, he sang the chant of choir,
Said mass and even to confession hied.
Talbot upon his plighted faith relied,
Ne'er thinking one so dull, a rustic vile,
A brainless monk, dross of conventual pile,
Who'd had a public scourging at his will,
Could e'er outwit a general of skill.
But righteous Heav'n in this judged otherwise,
In its decrees strange whims will oft arise,
To mock and make the greatest merely tools,
Sages confounding by the means of fools.
From Paradise dispatched, a ray of sense
Beamed to illumine Lourdis' pate so dense.
The mass of thickened brains within his skull
Lighter became anon and far less dull,
Amazed, he felt new mind his head endow;
Alas! we think, the Lord above knows how!
Let us for springs invisible enquire,
That, more or less, with thought the brains inspire:
Those divers atoms, let our wits descry,
That from sound sense, or reason turned awry;
In that sly nook of pericranium's placed
An Homer's genius and a Virgil's taste?
And by what leaven, with coldest poison fraught,
Was Zoilus, Frélon or Thersites taught?
A friend of Flora's regions of perfume,
Near pink beholds the baneful hemlock bloom,
'Tis the Creator's will holds sovran sway,
That hidden hand which all things must obey,
Unseen by eyes in doctor's pedant pate:
Their useless prattle we'll not imitate.
  Lourdis, grown curious, sought all to see,
His sight renewed employed instructively.
That night, toward the town he saw incline
An host of cooks, who carried in a line
Such fare as a most dainty feast implies,
Hams, truffles, wood-hens, partridges and pies;
The chased glass flagons of the rarest wine
Into the cooling ice the grooms consign,
That brilliant liquid, juice of ruby glow,

Brought from the blessed cellars of Citeaux.
To postern gate in silence thus then sped
Lourdis, new science buzzing through his head—
Not Latin, but that still more happy code,
Leading us through this scurvy world's sad road—
Of eloquence the flow anon displayed,
By kindest courtesy and prudence rayed;
Regarding all through corner of keen eye,
With deepest craft abounding—courtier sly;
The monk, in fine, of monks was most complete.
'Tis thus in all times we his fellows meet,
Speeding from kitchen to the council-hall,
In peace or war intriguing, troubling all;
Who first in rooms of humble burghers waits,
Then steals into the halls of potentates;
Disturbs the world, and aye on discord bent,
Is sometimes clever, sometimes insolent;
Now greedy wolf, now full of fox's wiles,
Now antic ape, or using serpent's guiles;
Who wonders that the British knaves decreed,
That Britain should be purged of such a breed?
    By unfrequented path our Lourdis sped,
Which, through a wood, to royal quarters led;
Conning this mighty mystery in mind,
He went good brother Bonifoux to find:
Don Bonifoux, just then with thought sedate
Posed most profoundly o'er the page of fate,
He measured links invisible to sight;
Which time and destiny in bonds unite;
Deeds trifling and events supremely great,
The world to come and our material state;
The whole he drew to focus in his mind,
Effect and cause enraptured he defined,
Their order saw, and found a *rendezvous*
Might save an empire or a state subdue.
The Confessor in thought still kept enrolled
How once were seen three lilies all of gold
On alabaster field—the rump of page,
An English page! Nor less his thoughts engage
Those ruined walls, Hermaphrodix the Mage;

But what astounded most his wond'ring brain,
Was to see Lourdis to some sense attain,
From which he prophesied that in the end
To good Saint Denis, Britain's host must bend.
   Lourdis by Bonifoux, in form polite
Presented was to the royal favorite;
Her beauty and the King he compliments,
Then takes his story up and represents
How Talbot's prudence had been lulled to sleep,
That night a *rendezvous* he went to keep,
By postern-gate, and how the chieftain there
Was to be met by Louvet's love-sick fair;
Quoth he: "A stratagem one may pursue;
There follow him, surprise his person too,
As by Dalilah, Samson was of old.
Oh! Agnes most divine, this theme unfold
To mighty Charles." "Ah! reverend Sir," she said,
"Think you this monarch is at all times led
On me love's soft effusions to bestow?"
"I think he damns himself, though naught I know!"
Lourdis replied; "My robe condemns love's sway,
My heart absolves him. Fortunate are they
Who at some epoch shall be damned for thee!"
Quoth Agnes: "Monk, your converse flatters me,
And proves your head with ample wit supplied."
To corner then conducting him aside,
Thus whispered she: "Hast thou amidst our foes,
The youthful Briton seen, who's named Monrose?"
The subtile monk in black replied: "In sooth,
I have beheld him; 'tis a charming youth."
Agnes deep blushing bent to earth a look,
Then grew composed again; his hand she took;
Thus cunning Lourdis, ere the night had fled,
With his great king and master's closeted.
   Lourdis then made a more than mortal speech,
To which good Charles' wits could barely reach;
His sovran council he assembled straight,
His almoners, war's chieftains too, sedate.
Amidst these heroes, her compeers, sat Joan,
With mind for counsel as for combats prone;

While lovely Agnes in a gentle way,
With thread and needle made discreetest play,
From time to time, deliv'ring good advice,
Which good King Charles adopted in a trice.
  'Twas then proposed to seize, with skilful care,
Beneath the ramparts, Talbot and his fair:
So Vulcan and the Sun in Heav'n were taught,
Mars with the golden Aphrodite caught.
This mighty enterprise was swift prepared,
Where head and hand an equal danger shared.
Dunois first started by the longest road,
Made a forced march which well his foresight showed,
An artful scheme that history vaunts at last.
Betwixt the army and the town they passed,
And lo! before the postern-gate deployed,
As Talbot with Dame President enjoyed
Of dawning union the first keen delights,
Flatt'ring himself, that from the couch to fights
Quite hero-like, but one step he should make,
Six regiments in defile the road must take.
The order's giv'n: the city has been ta'en—
But the foregoing eve each soldier's brain
Was petrified with Lourdis' long discourse,
Each gaped, bereft of motion and of force;
Asleep and side by side on plain they laid;
Such the great miracle which Denis played.
  Joan with Dunois and the selected train
Of gallant knights, soon having past the plain,
Already lined, 'neath Orléans' ramparts strong,
Of the besiegers' camp the trenches long.
Mounted on horse of Barbary's famed breed,
In Charles' stable then the only steed,
Joan ambled, grasping in her sturdy hand,
Of Deborah renowned, the Heavenly brand;
While noble broad-sword did her side adorn,
Wherewith poor Holophernes' head was shorn;
And thus equipped, with thoughts devout, the Maid
Beneath her breath to Denis' saint thus prayed:
"Thou who hast deigned to feeble maid like me,
These glorius arms confide at Domremy,

Prove of my frailty support divine;
O! pardon, if some vanity was mine,
When flattered senses heard thy faithless ass,
With freedom hail me as the fairest lass.
Dear Patron! deign to recollection call
That through my means the Britons were to fall,
Thus punishing foul deeds in ardour done,
When they polluted each afflicted nun.
A greater feat presents itself to-day;
Naught can I do, without thy fostering ray,
Endue this arm with force like thine to toil,
At its last gasp, preserve the Gallic soil,
Avenge of Charles the lily's tarnished hue,
With presidential Louvet's honour too;
Ah! let us to this gracious end be led,
And Heaven's mercy ever guard thy head!"
      From height celestial, Holy Denis heard,
And in the camp her donkey felt the word;
'Twas Joan he knew, and clapping pennons too,
Anon with crest erect t'wards her he flew;
On knee craved grace, her pardon to procure,
For his attempts at tenderness impure.
"By demons," he exclaimed, "I was possessed;
I now repent": he wept with grief oppressed;
Conjured her then his willing back to cross,
He could not of her weight sustain the loss,
Nor bear another 'neath the Maid to trot:
Joan well perceived an heavenly beam, I wot,
Restored the flighty donkey as her steed;
Of grace the penitent received the meed;
Then whipped she him, and gave him counsel meet,
To prove, from thenceforth, sober and discreet.
The donkey swore; and fired with courage rare,
Proud of his burdon, bore her through the air.
On Britons swift as lightning flash he starts,
Like forked fire that with the thunder parts;
Joan flying, overwhelmed the country round
With streams of blood, imbuing verdant ground
On every side, of limbs dispersed the wrecks,
While heaped were seen by hundreds, slaughtered necks.

In crescent then the harbinger of night
Widely dispersed its pale and dubious light;
Still stunned, the Britons owned stupendous dread,
To view whence the blows came, each raised his head;
In vain they strove to see Death's dooming blade;
With panic struck, they ran, misled, dismayed,
And rushing on, fell into Dunois' power.
Charles was of kings the happiest in that hour,
His foes rushed on, impending fate to dare:
So scattered partridges, in realms of air,
In clusters fall, destroyed by pointer keen,
And torn by shot; imbrued the heath is seen.
The donkey's brayings loudly roared alarm,
Fierce Joan on high extends her virgin arm;
Pursued, cut, pierced, torn, severed, bruised and rent;
All force opposed to Dunois' prowess bent;
While good King Charles takes an unerring sight,
And shoots all those whom fear had put to flight.
　　Talbot, intoxicated with the charms
Of Louvet, and joys tasted in her arms,
As he lay languishing upon her breast,
Was roused by sudden noise of war's unrest.
Glowing with triumph: "By my soul," cried he,
"There are my troops, Orléans falls to me."
Aloud, he thus applauds his wily pains,
"O love, 'tis thou," he cried, "who cities gains!"
Our knight thus fed by hope, replete with bliss,
Gave to his tender fair a parting kiss,
Sprang from the couch, attired himself and fleet
Repaired the vanquishers of France to meet.
　　Naught but a single squire appeared to view,
Who ever dared bold Talbot's steps pursue:
Deep in his confidence a valiant wight,
And worthy vassal of so brave a knight,
Guarding no less his ward-robe than his lance.
"Come seize your prey, my gallant friends advance!"
Talbot exclaimed, but soon joy disappeared,
Instead of friends, our Joan, with lance upreared,
Bore down on him, on her celestial ass.
He saw two hundred French the portal pass

Great Talbot shuddered, palsied o'er with dread.
"Long live the King!" each Gallic champion said.
"Let's drink; advance, my friends, with me;
On Gascons, Picards; yield to jollity,
No quarter give, of carnage take your fill,
Yonder they are, my friends! shoot, fire and kill!"
Talbot, recovered from the dire control,
Which first held potent empire o'er his soul,
Strove by the gate his freedom to maintain.
So erst all bleeding, on the ravaged plain,
Anchises' son his victor dared engage;
But Talbot fought with even greater rage;
Briton was he, and seconded by squire,
Both would the world attack with courage dire.
Now front to front, now back to back they strove,
And torrents of their victors 'fore them drove;
At length their vigour can no longer live,
An easy victory to the French they give.
Talbot surrendered, though unbeaten still.
Dunois and Joan extolled his gallant skill;
Then both proceed, complacent to reclaim,
For spouse, his Presidential dame again.
Without suspicion he received her well—
Your gentle husbands never aught can tell—
Nor e'er did Louvet learn by what strange chance,
Madame Louvet had saved the realm of France.
Denis applauded from the heavenly height;
Saint George on horse-back shuddered at the sight;
The ass intones his hoarse and braying strain,
Which makes the Britons shake and shake again.
The King, now ranked with conquerors of renown,
With lovely Agnes supped in Orléans town;
Joan, proud and tender, having sent away
That very night to Heav'n her donkey gray,
The vow she erst had made had never broke;
To friend Dunois she kept the word she spoke.
And Lourdis 'midst the faithful cohort strayed.
Bawling out still: "*Ye Britons, she's a Maid!*"

Postscript of the Author

'Tis by these verses, children, of mine ease
I sought old age to soften and appease.
O gift of God! soft love, desire so sweet,
'Tis in your image, happiness we meet:
Illusion's first of pleasures, after all.
Freely I went in my secluded hall,
To sing the flames of Dunois and of Joan;
For jealous furies, they might well atone;
For kingly cruelties and slandrous lies,
Shafts of the fool and follies of the wise;
But who's the fiend who steals from me this page?
My broken lyre drops from my hands in rage.
No fresh exploits await—'tis understood,
Reader! my Joan shall keep her maidenhood,
Until those virgins vowed to God alone,
For all their vows, know how to keep their own.

AMERICAN LITERATURE

Little Women — Louisa May Alcott
The Last of the Mohicans — James Fenimore Cooper
The Red Badge of Courage and *Maggie* — Stephen Crane
Selected Poems — Emily Dickinson
Narrative of the Life and Other Writings — Frederick Douglass
The Scarlet Letter — Nathaniel Hawthorne
The Call of the Wild and *White Fang* – Jack London
Moby-Dick — Herman Melville
Major Tales and Poems — Edgar Allan Poe
The Jungle — Upton Sinclair
Uncle Tom's Cabin — Harriet Beecher Stowe
Walden and *Civil Disobedience* — Henry David Thoreau
Adventures of Huckleberry Finn — Mark Twain
The Complete Adventures of Tom Sawyer — Mark Twain
Ethan Frome and *Summer* — Edith Wharton
Leaves of Grass — Walt Whitman

WORLD LITERATURE

Tales from the 1001 Nights — Sir Richard Burton
Don Quixote — Miguel de Cervantes
The Divine Comedy — Dante Alighieri
Crime and Punishment — Fyodor Dostoevsky
The Count of Monte Cristo — Alexandre Dumas
The Three Musketeers — Alexandre Dumas
Selected Tales — Jacob and Wilhelm Grimm
The Iliad — Homer
The Odyssey — Homer
The Hunchback of Notre-Dame — Victor Hugo
Les Misérables — Victor Hugo
The Metamorphosis and *The Trial* — Franz Kafka
The Phantom of the Opera — Gaston Leroux
The Prince — Niccolò Machiavelli
The Art of War — Sun Tzu
The Death of Ivan Ilych and Other Stories — Leo Tolstoy
Around the World in Eighty Days — Jules Verne
Candide and *The Maid of Orléans* — Voltaire
The Bhagavad Gita — Vyasa

BRITISH LITERATURE

Beowulf — Anonymous
Emma — Jane Austen
Persuasion — Jane Austen
Pride and Prejudice — Jane Austen
Sense and Sensibility — Jane Austen
Peter Pan — J. M. Barrie
Jane Eyre — Charlotte Brontë
Wuthering Heights — Emily Brontë
Alice in Wonderland — Lewis Carroll
The Canterbury Tales — Geoffrey Chaucer
Heart of Darkness and Other Tales — Joseph Conrad
Robinson Crusoe — Daniel Defoe
A Christmas Carol and Other Holiday Tales — Charles Dickens
Great Expectations — Charles Dickens
Oliver Twist — Charles Dickens
A Tale of Two Cities — Charles Dickens
The Waste Land and Other Writings — T. S. Eliot
A Passage to India — E. M. Forster
The Jungle Books — Rudyard Kipling
Paradise Lost and *Paradise Regained* — John Milton
The Sonnets and Other Love Poems — William Shakespeare
Three Romantic Tragedies — William Shakespeare
Frankenstein — Mary Shelley
Dr. Jekyll and Mr. Hyde and Other Strange Tales — Robert Louis Stevenson
Kidnapped — Robert Louis Stevenson
Treasure Island — Robert Louis Stevenson
Dracula — Bram Stoker
Gulliver's Travels — Jonathan Swift
The Time Machine and *The War of the Worlds* — H. G. Wells
The Picture of Dorian Gray — Oscar Wilde

ANTHOLOGIES

Four Centuries of Great Love Poems

BORDERS®
CLASSICS

The text of this book is set in 11 point Goudy Old Style, designed by American printer and typographer Frederic W. Goudy (1865–1947).

The archival-quality, natural paper is composed of recyclable products made from wood grown in sustainable forests; the manufacturing processes conform to the environmental regulations of the country of origin.

The finished volume demonstrates the convergence of Old-World craftsmanship and modern technology that exemplifies books manufactured by Edwards Brothers, Inc. Established in 1893, the family-owned business is a well-respected leader in book manufacturing, recognized the world over for quality and attention to detail.

In addition, Ann Arbor Media Group's editorial and design services provide full-service book publication to business partners.